F

REVENGE AND RETRIBUTION

On a muggy August day in 2002, Alexandra Lind was unexpectedly thrown backwards in time, landing in the year of Our Lord 1658. Catapulted into an unfamiliar and frightening new existence, Alex could do nothing but adapt. After all, while time travelling itself is a most rare occurrence, time travelling with a return ticket is even rarer.

This is the sixth book about Alex, her husband Matthew and their continued adventures in the second half of the seventeenth century.

ANNA BELFRAGE

Revenge & Retribution

SilverWood

Published in 2014 by the author
using SilverWood Books Empowered Publishing®

SilverWood Books
30 Queen Charlotte Street, Bristol, BS1 4HJ
www.silverwoodbooks.co.uk

ISBN 978-1-78132-175-1 (paperback)
ISBN 978-1-78132-176-8 (ebook)

British Library Cataloguing in Publication Data
A CIP catalogue record for this book is available from the British Library

Set in Bembo by SilverWood Books
Printed on responsibly sourced paper

This book is dedicated to Johan – again.
Just like Alex says to Matthew, life without you
would be impossible, like having half of me yanked out.

Chapter 1

Some aspects of human life should be accompanied by grey skies, whining winds and a steady drumming rain – executions, for example. To contaminate a day as spectacular as this bright June day with the sordidness of a hanging seemed irreverent. It was hot and humid, a combination that made linen shifts stick to backs, stays itch against irritated skin, and hair curl haphazardly. Alex Graham wished she'd worn a cap under her hat and scowled in the direction of Kate Jones, impeccable as always. Not that the woman was wearing a cap – or much of a hat – but her heavy, smooth hair remained in its neat bun, no matter the weather.

Alex shifted from foot to foot, regretting she had worn her woollen stockings instead of her single silk pair. If she wiggled her toes, she could actually feel puddles begin to form between them, and she could only imagine how they would smell afterwards. Smell: another drawback to spending a day as warm as this in far too close proximity to all these unwashed bodies. She at least was clean – squeaky clean compared to most of them – and when she sniffed the sleeve of her best summer bodice she could only make out a lingering scent of lavender, overlaid by the salty smell of her own skin. She raised herself on her toes to scan the crowds. What was taking them so long?

Matthew Graham frowned. Two dark brows pulled together over light eyes, the mouth set, and the back stiffened – enough for Alex to follow his gaze across the assembled people to where Stephen Burley was being manhandled towards the scaffold, fighting every step of the way.

"So he dies, right?" Alex slipped a hand into the crook of her husband's elbow. Unfortunately, there were two more Burley brothers, and even if it was three years since she'd laid eye on any of them, she doubted they'd forgotten their grudge against Matthew – or their intention to make him pay with his life for killing the youngest Burley ages ago. She swallowed, shifted on her feet, and tightened her hold on Matthew.

"Aye, but not as he should," Matthew said.

No, Alex sighed, because if it had been Matthew who'd apprehended Stephen, he'd have turned him over to the Iroquois – in her husband's opinion, just retribution for all the homestead burnings, all the pillage, Stephen and his brothers had done dressed up as Indians.

"Vengeance is mine, saith the Lord," Alex murmured. "One of the wiser statements in the Bible, if you ask me." She snapped open her new folding fan and attempted to create a draught around her face to cool her overheated skin.

"Revenge for what they did to my son should be mine." It came out in clipped, angry tones.

Alex didn't reply. In this, she and Matthew were in total agreement. Ian had been shot by the Burleys while fending off an attack on Matthew, and as an unfortunate consequence had fallen off his horse, landing on a rock. His lower vertebrae had been damaged, and Ian would never again move easily through his days. Easily enough, Alex smiled, watching Ian thread his way towards them with Betty by his side. Betty, on the other hand, puffed like a whale, one hand on her protruding belly.

"You should've stayed at home." Alex eyed her daughter-in-law, thinking she looked like a balloon about to burst.

"I didn't want to." Betty's hand tightened on Ian's sleeve. Where Ian went, there went Betty, wife and head nurse rolled into one, and as protective as an aggressive cobra when it came to her husband's dignity.

"As long as you don't give birth on the horse," Alex said.

"Oh, I'm sure I'll have warning enough to get off it first." Betty grinned, making Alex laugh.

"I'm not really sure why I'm here." Alex moved closer to Matthew. She hated hangings. From the first one she had witnessed, hidden in a thicket on a hillside, to the subsequent ones she had been forced to watch, they all made her feel sick – and distinctly aware of how fragile her neck was. She rubbed a hand along the side of her throat and swallowed. Could one swallow when the noose tightened? And, afterwards, while you hung dangling like a side of beef, did you still swallow? Want to swallow?

"You don't have to watch, lass," Matthew said, drawing her close.

"I hope it's quick," she sighed against his shoulder.

It wasn't quick. It was a long, protracted affair, and however much Alex agreed that Stephen had this coming to him, she was still horrified by the slow strangulation, the choking, desperate sounds that emanated from the dying man as he struggled to drag air into his lungs. Much better in her time, at least capital punishment no longer existed in the twenty-first century. Umm, she amended, it didn't back home in Scotland, but weren't they still executing people in the US?

Alex allowed her thoughts to meander freely, her eyes closed to the scene on the gallows where Stephen Burley was still twitching. This was 1684, a century more or less before the United States of America broke free from the mother country. And here, in the Colony of Maryland, Alex Graham, born 1976, stood hiding her face against her husband's coat. Totally impossible, entirely ludicrous, but there you are – sometimes strange things happened, even if dropping three hundred years backwards through time had to qualify as being beyond strange, right?

The people around her cheered and catcalled when the next condemned prisoner was led up to the scaffold. Alex peeked. One more?

"Get me out of here," she said. "I don't want to see this."

Matthew took a firm grip of her hand and made his way out of the throng. He paused in the scarce shade afforded by the meeting house and studied her with a little crease between his brows. "Alright then?"

"Yes." She looked down the narrow main street and back at where Ian and Betty were extricating themselves from the crowd. Ian was limping as he approached them, face drawn with one of those sudden bursts of pain that assailed him. Alex knew better than to voice her concern – at best it would be met with an irritated comment that she should not meddle in matters that weren't her concern. Besides, it was his life, and Betty was capable of giving him whatever help he needed.

"Where's Ruth?" she said instead, standing on her toes to look around. From her vantage point, right at the edge of the small square that housed the meeting house, she could see most of Providence. Four larger streets extended like the spokes of a wheel from the central docks and wharves, situated three hundred yards or so downhill from where she was standing. The streets were lined with narrow houses, most of them of wood, here and there in brick or stone. Only Main Street was cobbled – the others were no more than dirt roads – and its gutters were decorated with the contents of chamber pots, garbage in general, and the odd, tenacious dandelion. To her right, she could make out the recently painted exterior of the Anglican church, home to a growing congregation of non-Puritans – as yet a minority, but capably led and represented by their cheerful reverend, William Norton.

Most of Providence was out and about today; most of them were presently cheering what was happening by the gallows, so the town was unusually deserted.

Alex shielded her eyes, looked in the direction of Minister Allerton's house, close to the western palisade, and repeated her question.

"I left her with the minister and his lasses – he didn't want to come anyway," Ian said.

"Oh." Alex set her mouth. She liked Minister Allerton, finding him a devout and compassionate man with a broadminded approach to much of human life. She liked his daughters, in particular Temperance, who at sixteen was a plump, rosy girl with her father's grey eyes and, Alex supposed, her mother's blond hair. She had never met Mrs Allerton, and now she never would – at least not in this life. No, all in all,

Alex was very fond of Julian Allerton. What she didn't like was how the minister regarded her soon seventeen-year-old daughter Ruth, and she definitely disliked how Ruth gazed at him. Twenty years or so her senior, he was, and in Alex's opinion that was far too much. She wondered if Matthew had noticed, and if his reaction was similar to hers.

She waited until Ian and Betty moved off to talk with a group of younger acquaintances and shared her concerns with him. To her huge irritation, all he did was smile. "She's a pretty lass."

She most certainly was, with dark red, sleek hair and eyes so like her father's, light hazel that in sunshine shifted from celadon green to gold.

"Very," Alex said, "and not yet seventeen. She's barely a year older than his daughter, for God's sake!" Nor were things made simpler by the fact that their Daniel and Temperance were betrothed.

Matthew sighed. "He looks, Alex. He wouldn't be a man if he didn't look at a pretty wee thing like our Ruth."

"Hmm." Alex gave him a sidelong glance. "Do you?"

"Oh aye," he said, the corner of his mouth twitching. "It's nice at times to rest your eyes on something young and bonny."

"Absolutely, I do it all the time. Now that young man for example…" She bobbed her head at a man – no, a boy – standing some yards away, and looked him up and down. "Very nice arse."

Matthew clearly didn't find that amusing, glaring down at her.

She snorted and sank her nails into his hand. "If you look, Matthew Graham, then so will I."

"I don't, not really."

"Good," she nodded, "then I won't either." She threw a lingering look at the boy. "Probably very boring in bed. You know, stick it in and, wham, it's over. Not at all like you." She dropped her voice and winked.

"Alex! Hush!" Matthew's cheeks went a dull red, but he tightened his hold on her hand.

"Anyway," Alex went on, nodding a greeting to one of the older Providence matrons, "it's not only Julian looking at her, it's Ruth looking at him as well. And not, I might add, because of his handsomeness, seeing as he's rather plain."

"Inner qualities, Alex, inner qualities. You must learn to look beyond the outer shell."

"He's pushing forty. He's more than twice her age!"

"He won't do anything untoward."

"And should he come asking, you'll just say no, right?" At his silence, she stopped. "Right?"

"And if it is she that comes? If it's our Ruth that comes and tells you she's dying with love for that grey-eyed, balding minister of hers?" He looked at her until she dropped her eyes.

"Oh shit, hoisted on my own petard..." She scuffed at the ground and frowned. "Then I'll tell her she has to wait until she's eighteen," Alex said with a sigh.

Their discussion was stopped by the sudden appearance of Minister Allerton himself, complete with youngest daughter Mercy and a trailing Ruth, walking arm in arm with Temperance.

"And Patience?" Alex asked, offering Mercy a boiled sweet.

"Over there," Minister Allerton replied with a vague wave of his hand in the direction of the bakery. He was doing a good job of bringing up his daughters on his own, and Alex liked the fact that he had insisted they stay with him after their mother's premature death and not be sent back to live with their large family back in Boston. "Any day now." He nodded in the direction of the port.

"I sincerely hope so," Alex said. "We want to leave the day after tomorrow." It had been something of a fluke that Stephen's execution had coincided with the expected return home of one of their sons. Still; they'd been here six days now, and so far no Daniel. She shaded her eyes and looked out at sea, scanning for anything that might look like the sloop from Massachusetts, but the silvered waters of the Chesapeake lay flat and empty, the June heat creating a shimmering haze that floated enticingly a few feet off the surface.

"And has Daniel made up his mind?" the minister asked Matthew.

"Aye." All of Matthew expanded with pride. "He's going for ordination."

"Ah." The minister nodded, sending a shrewd look in the direction of Alex, who kept her face neutral. "It pleases you, Alex?"

"It pleases Daniel, and that's what's important, right?" In her very private moments, the ones she kept even from Matthew, she'd admit that she wasn't all too happy about one of her sons becoming a minister in the Puritan church; so easy to become straight-laced and judgmental, to become inflated with an excessive sense of self-importance – in particular in an age and place like this, when God and his ministers ruled most aspects of people's lives.

Alex sighed. They'd been driven to leave Scotland for religious issues, escaping persecution by coming to this small colony that had early on embraced religious tolerance. Over the last few years, this open-mindedness had narrowed down substantially, with increased conflicts between the state's minority Catholics and predominant Protestants, many of whom were Puritans/ Presbyterians, like her husband. Like herself, come to think of it; at least, in the sense that everyone assumed she was of the same beliefs as her husband.

It always made her laugh. Agnostic, hard-nosed Alexandra Lind had no time for God until the day she'd had the misfortune – or not, depending how one saw it – of being on an exact ninety-degree crossroads when a thunderstorm broke out overhead, effectively creating a rift in time. Even now, twenty-six years later, she had to hug herself at the far too vivid recollection of her fall through time. All that noise, all that bright light, and with a thud she'd landed here, in an age very much defined by faith. With the passing years, she had adapted and conformed, and now she would never dream of not saying grace before eating, or of not sending up a quick, genuine prayer to God at least once during her day. Short and to the point mostly, not a lot of waffling about, sometimes rather acerbic, but still…

"…and I hope you'll agree," Minister Allerton was saying, looking at Matthew.

Alex forced herself back into the here and now. Agree to what?

"Aye, why not?" Matthew said.

Ruth beamed at him, curtsied, and rushed off with Temperance in tow.

"Agree to what?" Alex asked in an undertone when they were walking off.

"Betrothal," he teased, making her pinch his arm. "Ruth is to stay with the Allertons for some weeks, and then they will all come up to Graham's Garden for the harvest."

"Bloody tradition that has become," Alex muttered, but with no real heat. The minister more than pulled his weight on the farm for the three or four weeks he was there, and his girls were all willing to help however they could. "I'm not sure I like it that she stays with them, in particular, given our previous discussion."

"Julian is an honourable man," Matthew said.

"And if he isn't?"

Matthew looked down at her. "Then the minister might find himself short of his balls." He leaned towards her with a grin. "Big balls, by the way."

"Matthew!"

They spent the evening with Matthew's sister, Joan, and her lawyer husband, Simon Melville. Matthew and Simon played chess; Alex and Joan spent several hours talking out in the yard, while Joan sucked hungrily at one of the two joints Alex had rolled for her. As she smoked, Joan relaxed, her normally so tense features smoothing into a bland, woozy expression, allowing that full mouth of hers to curve now and then into a smile. They all knew it was a matter of months before Joan died, but as Joan refused to broach the subject, her family played along, with Matthew and Simon pretending not to notice Joan was as high as a kite when they joined their wives in the yard.

It was almost midnight by the time they made it to bed, a narrow contraption in the small room just under the roof at the inn that stood a stone's throw away from the meeting house. It was like entering an oven, the small window giving very little relief, despite Matthew propping it wide open.

"...so Joan is a bit worried, given that the midwife is convinced it's twins this time, but Lucy doesn't look all that peaked in my opinion, and her girl is what? Nearly two?" Lucy Melville, now Jones, reminded Alex of a well-fed, sleek cat. Astonishingly beautiful, permanently silent due to her deafness, Matthew's niece had turned most male heads in Providence a full 360 degrees before she was safely wed to Henry Jones. Now, at soon nineteen, Lucy was like a gigantic, attractive pear, her ninth-month belly sailing before her. "Personally, I'm far more worried about Joan, she's down to looking like a walking skeleton, and—"

A soft snore interrupted her. Matthew was asleep, sprawled diagonally across the rope-frame bed. In sleep, his face smoothed itself out, the mouth curving into its natural generous expression. The grooves on his brow and around his nose, the network of shallow wrinkles at the outer corner of his eyes, they all softened.

His hair lay dark against the white of the pillow, grey and brown intermingled, and to her he was as beautiful now as he had been the first day she saw him. He looked young and vulnerable in the weak light, his right arm thrown high over his head, the other slung across the pillows. One leg was pulled up, and from beneath the hem of his bunched-up shirt, his penis peeked, half-tumescent. Alex moved over to kiss his cheek, filled with an overwhelming tenderness for this man – her man.

Matthew grunted in his sleep, but her hand on his head and yet another kiss made his lips twitch into a smile before he rolled over on his side, mumbling something about being very, very tired.

Alex returned to sit on the stool and studied herself meditatively. Almost fifty-two, she mused, not quite a year older than Joan. Not an entirely bad age, actually. She scratched at a small scab on her thigh, blotted the resulting blood with her fingertip, and proceeded with a detailed inspection of her body.

Very nice feet, she smiled, but then she had always had very nice feet – that and good tits. They were still good, at least according to Matthew who, with a twinkle in his eyes, would tell her that he was a far better judge of them than she was. She cupped them, squinting down at them. Yes, quite okay, as was most of her, except for that permanent pouch on her belly and the very ugly scar on her right biceps, courtesy of a wolf.

She nipped at the excess belly skin and frowned. In her age, she could have had a belly tuck done and gotten rid of this. On the other hand, a twenty-first century Alex wouldn't have lived through ten pregnancies to begin with. And, in her age, there would have been help to be had for whatever it was that was eating Joan alive. It was getting much, much worse, with Joan increasingly wasted each time they saw her. The marijuana no longer helped all that much so, increasingly, Joan spent her days in an opium-fuelled daze in a desperate attempt to find some relief.

Alex uncorked her stone jar and poured a generous puddle of lavender-scented oil into her hands. At least she'd gotten rid of the quack, she thought as she rubbed the oil into her hands and face. Idiot, to suggest a woman as frail as Joan be bled three times a day. No, what Joan needed was surgery and chemotherapy. What she'd get were invigorating tonics and even more opium. Lucky her.

Chapter 2

Lucy Jones inhabited a world of almost silence and had done so since the day of her birth. A silence in which her thoughts stood stark and sharp-edged against a backdrop of constant visual and tactile stimuli. The odd, muted sound would now and then penetrate to her brain, but mostly Lucy heard through her fingers and eyes; she assessed body language and read lips. She moved through rooms full of people that supposed she understood nothing, and all the while she added nugget after nugget of information to the hoard she kept in her brain. Swift and dexterous, she ghosted her way into offices and studies, sifted through opened letters, journals and ledgers. She read deeds and documents; she perused the odd love note and long, boring tracts on God and Church, King and Country.

She knew everything about the people closest to her: her father and his sordid adulterous matter back in Scotland; her mother and her silent battle against constant pain; her mother-in-law's dalliance with the hot-headed glazier recently arrived from England; her husband's infatuation with Barbra, the new house slave. Lucy smiled at Barbra, inspecting her for signs of pregnancy. No, not as yet, but given Henry Jones' repeated absences from the marital bed, it was just a question of time. Well, Barbra would make a good wet nurse, and the half-breed baby could be handed off to another of the slaves to nurse. Barbra shifted nervously under her assessing look, and Lucy broadened her smile. Barbra swallowed and escaped when Lucy waved her away with the breakfast tray.

Lucy stretched luxuriously and got out of bed, one long, narrow hand on her swelling belly. She twirled in front of the three-foot mirror that Henry had bought her as a wedding present, importing it at an exorbitant price from the famous Manufacture Royale des Glaces in Paris. He'd had it framed here, complaining that the heavy gilded frame had cost him almost as much as the looking glass, but Lucy knew that to be a lie – the glass pane had cost four times as much.

She smiled at what she saw: thick hair the colour of copper threaded with gold, strong cheekbones, and a straight nose, neither too long nor too short. Dimples appeared when she smiled, her lower lip was nice and plump, and all of her was covered with velvety skin of that startling white that only redheads ever have. No freckles, except for a smattering over the bridge of her nose, and ironically her ears were overlarge, protruding somewhat from her head.

Lucy adjusted her embroidered linen shift over her breasts, and looked about for the silk nightgown she'd had made some months ago. She stroked the soft dove-blue surface. She liked this new life of hers, and if that included tolerating Henry's little infidelities while she was pregnant, so be it – however difficult she found it. He'd been honest enough to admit that he found her repellent in her bloated state, going on to underline that it was only her he truly loved. Lucy was no fool, in fact rather the reverse, and of late she had intercepted glances between Henry and sweet lithe Barbra that spoke of more than a male itch. No, Lucy decided then and there, Barbra would have to go, however competent a wet nurse she would make.

Lucy drew the bolt on her bedroom door and sat down at the little table she used as her private desk. The drawer was kept locked, and right at the bottom, her hands closed on the wrapped package and drew it out. This was her treasure, her best kept secret – a little thing that should have been destroyed years ago, had she obeyed her father.

Burn it, her father had said, his eyes wild, burn it, lass! And Lucy had hurried to the kitchen with the wrapped item crushed to her chest to do as he said, but had frozen with her hand extended towards the grate. From the thing she'd held came noise, and Lucy's heart had leapt like a startled hart when, for the first time in her life, she truly heard. Not the muted, distant sounds she would occasionally pick up, not the discordant, jarring noises that now and then broke through her veil of silence: no, this was a veritable banquet of sound – screams, songs, the eerie call of gulls, laughter, voices drowning in each other, the lapping sound of waves against the shore – all of it bombarded her reeling brain.

With a shaking hand, she'd uncovered what she held and found herself looking down at a painting, an exquisite little painting of…she didn't truly know. The sea perhaps, or the sky as it looked to the west moments after the sun had dropped out of sight, leaving a band of shimmering greens and blues in its wake. A painting that spoke to her, and Lucy had clutched it to her heart and lied when her father asked if she had burnt it. Yes, she had nodded, and all the while the little magic painting lay hidden under her bodice.

Three years on, the painting lived in her desk. She caressed its sides and placed it on the table. Lucy closed her eyes and listened, drinking in all those sounds she only heard here, sitting at her desk in solitude. People weeping, crying for their lost ones…the high sound of a girl laughing… the darker notes of a man's voice. To Lucy, they were all intoxicating, a bouquet of sensations that left her mildly drunk for the remainder of the morning, an addiction she no longer could do without.

Her father had never explained why she was to burn the picture, saying only that it was evil and dangerous. Dangerous? Lucy scraped a nail over the thick oil paint, tracing the scrawled M in the right-hand corner. Yes, it probably was, but not to her, even if at times her head would throb and her vision cloud if she looked at it for too long. She pursed her mouth, considering why her father, Simon Melville, would have thought it evil. What could this little square of bright colours possibly do? With a sigh, she rewrapped the painting in its square of muslin cloth and returned it to its hiding place.

At times, Lucy admitted that the single largest benefit of her marriage to Henry Jones was his mother. She liked

Kate, admired her even, and, in particular, she enjoyed spending time with a person who so clearly regarded her as an intellectual equal rather than a halfwit.

Kate was sitting at her desk when Lucy entered the parlour and brightened at the sight of her. She patted at the chair beside her. Lucy smiled back, dancing over the dark hardwood floors despite her huge, protruding belly. Twins, just like Henry had been a twin, even if his brother had died some years ago. Lads, she hoped, heirs to the plantation and all the riches Kate was accumulating. Not that she didn't love her little Frances, but male children were what was expected of her – by her husband and her mother-in-law.

"Good night?" Kate enquired with a smile. She set her quill down and moved the open ledgers aside.

Lucy nodded and pulled the ledgers towards her. Together with her mother-in-law, Lucy kept all the accounts, and it was their neat hands that flowed up and down the columns, detailing expenses and incomes.

New slaves, she noted with a slight frown. Again? She tapped at the item with her finger, raising a questioning brow.

"For the tobacco farm," Kate explained. "You know how quickly they wear out."

Lucy made an acquiescing movement and went on with her inspection of the latest entries. Dyed broadcloth? Dark red? Lucy lifted her eyes to where Barbra was minding little Frances. Definitely a new skirt, and definitely dark red... Lucy scowled. Mayhap she should send Barbra off to the tobacco farm, but something in her gut told her Henry wouldn't like that. Sell her off while Henry was away elsewhere? Lucy sneaked a look at Kate and concluded this was not an option. Her mother-in-law might not approve of Henry bedding a slave – in fact, she probably pretended it wasn't happening – but as long as Henry wanted the wench to stay, stay she would. Lucy sighed. No, she would have to think of something else. With an effort, she returned her attention to the ledger.

"That? Oh, that... You weren't supposed to see that," Kate

said. "It's something Henry wishes to surprise you with."

Lucy smiled. A sizeable amount, spent down in St Mary's City with one of the better merchants. She patted herself on her belly and got to her feet, indicating with her hand that she intended to go out.

Providence in June was at times uncomfortably warm. Lucy snapped her fan open, adjusted the brim of her hat to ensure her face remained in shadow, and hurried off in the direction of her parents' house. In sober velvets and immaculate linens, she swept through the town, her hair modestly hidden under an elegant hat. People bowed and curtsied; young Mrs Jones was a valued customer for all that she was considered simple. Poor lass, old women would sigh as they looked her up and down, unaware that she understood every word they uttered: pretty enough but deaf as a door post. Imagine Henry Jones marrying her!

Minister Walker stopped and bowed, his mouth moving with extreme slowness as he enunciated a good day to her. Lucy simpered and curtsied and wondered if Mrs Walker had any idea of where her God-fearing husband spent most of his evenings. Lucy did, slipping in for the odd visit with Mrs Malone, who not only made the town's best beer to serve at her brothel, but who was also beyond doubt its most competent high-fashion seamstress.

Not that Mrs Malone would ever dream of being indiscreet, but chatter away to her girls she did, while deaf Lucy stood silent on a stool, her eyes leaping from mouth to mouth as she added bit after bit to her extensive information bank − like the fact that Minister Walker was a frequent guest, an old dear who drank far too much beer and flirted enthusiastically with the girls, even if he had never succumbed to his carnal itches − except for that time five years in the past.

"Distraught," Mrs Malone said. "The poor man was so disgusted with himself, it made my heart break." Well, that was as it should be. A minister to do such! Lucy had wrinkled her nose, thinking that no man was above sin.

Lucy didn't like it when they discussed her father, a far

too regular visitor to this establishment. Nor was she amused at some of the detailed descriptions of her own husband, roused and half-naked in Madam's own bed.

"Just like his father in his tastes," Mrs Malone had said, and they all laughed, throwing Lucy pitying glances. Lucy had twisted her hands together to stop herself from hitting her. The woman was older than Methuselah – what in God's name could Henry see in her? A lot apparently, but not only in her, as the other girls added anecdotes of their own, starring Henry Jones and his eager member.

"And Frances?" Her mother didn't attempt to hide her disappointment, her narrow shoulders slumping even more than usual. Lucy gave her a concerned look. She loved her mother more than she loved anyone else in the world, and this long, slow dying was unbearable to watch.

Joan patted her hand and gestured for her to sit down on the bench in the backyard, pouring them both some buttermilk. "It's good for you," she said at Lucy's face. "And it's good for the weans."

Lucy rolled her eyes, but drank. Afterwards they both laughed at each other's white moustaches.

Lucy wasn't delighted by the sudden arrival of her aunt and uncle. Ever since Matthew Graham had caught her reading his private correspondence some years ago, something of a chilly truce existed between them. But her mother brightened markedly in the presence of her brother, smiling as he teased her about her latest addition to her hen coop.

"She's a good layer," Joan said. "Every day during spring and summer."

"She's bald!" Matthew laughed. "You have to knit her something to wear, indecent as she is."

"Who has ever heard of a hen in clothes?" Joan protested.

"And who has ever heard of a hen with no feathers?" Matthew said.

"It's only round her rump." Alex bent down to inspect the said hen.

"Aye, immodest little baggage." Matthew nodded at the cock. "Not that he much cares, does he?"

"Maybe that's why, you know, desperate females and all that." Alex undid her hat, and dropped it onto the table, fiddling with her hair.

"Alex!" Joan eyed her new hen and sighed. "Now I won't see her without noting her nudity. The pot," she said, wagging a finger at the hen. "You go into the pot within the week."

Lucy had only half followed this exchange, utilising the opportunity to study Matthew and Alex in detail. Her uncle was a handsome man, albeit that he was well over fifty: all his teeth, thick hair, and a face that was relatively unlined. At some inches over six feet, he was inordinately tall, as were all his sons, in particular Jacob. Lucy smiled. Of all her cousins, it was Jacob that she truly liked, impressed by how he'd gone to London on his own at only sixteen.

Matthew raised an eyebrow at her intense staring, and Lucy ducked her head. Why was it that he made her feel so transparent, as if all the thoughts that darted back and forth inside her brain stood plain to read upon her face for him? That Alex didn't much like her was obvious, nor did Alex make much of an effort to hide her opinion, even if she always accorded Lucy the respect of treating her like an adult. Lucy didn't much like Alex either, and in particular she didn't like it that the woman looked so radiant, her skin an unlined pink, her dark blue eyes clear and glittering. Her hair was, as always, brushed to a shine, strands of grey highlighting a mass of brown and bronze and chestnut. Mayhap there was some truth in all that posturing around the importance of eating raw greens, Lucy mused, grimacing at remembered meals at Graham's Garden that consisted of far too much spinach and beets, and far too little gravy and pie.

Lucy produced the little piece of sharpened coal she always carried with her and doodled while she waited for her uncle and aunt to leave. She drew swirls and whirlwinds, a small patch of something that heaved and sucked. She smiled down at her effort: the little picture, albeit muted now that it was all in grey.

Joan placed a hand on her sleeve, making her jerk upright. Her uncle's face had gone a sickly white, and as to Alex, she was staring at the little drawing with revulsion.

"What is it you're drawing, daughter?" Joan asked, her grey eyes wide.

Lucy tried to cover the scrap of paper with her hand, but Matthew was quicker, snatching it away to study it closely.

"Oh God!" He crumpled it together.

"Joan?" Alex said. "Has she seen one of those?"

Joan nodded. "We were sent one, three years ago."

"Sent one?" Alex wet her lips with her tongue. "By whom?"

"We don't know. It just came, aye? But we burnt it, didn't we?" She met Lucy's eyes. "We burnt it."

Lucy nodded, several times. Of course she'd burnt it.

"Thank the Lord for that!" Matthew slumped in his chair.

"Amen to that," Alex said, looking as if she were about to faint.

Lucy eyed them both with interest. They were frightened, badly frightened, and once again she found herself wondering what the little painting could possibly do. To ask outright was not going to work, she could see that in all of their faces, and seeing as neither her uncle nor aunt showed any indication of leaving, Lucy chose to cut her visit short. She rose, curtsied politely and left, promising her mother she'd be back on the morrow.

"Luke," Matthew muttered when Joan left them to escort her daughter to the door. "It has to be Luke that sent them the picture."

Alex nodded. There was no doubt in her mind: this bore the elegant signature of Luke Graham, Matthew's estranged brother – and she knew for a fact that he'd had one of these horrible paintings in his possession a few years back. Even worse, she knew who'd painted it, hating this reminder of her strange time travelling witch of a mother. She kept a cautious eye on Joan, moving around in the kitchen to find them something to drink.

"How could he do that?" Alex said in an undertone to Matthew. "He knew the painting was dangerous. I told him!" Not that she'd wanted to, but upon realising Luke had one of Mercedes' pictures in his possession, she'd felt compelled to warn him – more for the sake of her son, Jacob, who at the time was in London and spending a lot of time with Luke. She smoothed at her skirts, a sudden itch flying up her legs. She could still remember the fear that had gripped her upon reading Jacob's detailed description of the painting, down to admitting just how ill it made him feel. Alex drew a deep breath. If you looked too long, the painting trapped you. It sucked you in and transported you elsewhere, and… Damn Mercedes! Why, oh why had she chosen to litter the world with these dangerous portals through time? She knew why: Mercedes was trying to paint her way home to fifteenth century Seville, but ironically her little portals did not seem to work on her.

"Simon is Luke's least favourite person in the world bar one. To send it to me wouldn't do him much good as he knew we would recognise it for what it was." Matthew shrugged. "Ah well, it didn't work. That evil piece of magic is safely burnt."

"Thank heavens for that," Alex said before turning to smile at Joan, returning with pitcher and mugs.

Chapter 3

"But with the Duke of York openly papist, God alone knows where all this will end," Simon Melville said, receiving nods of agreement from the assembled men. The recently failed plot against the king and his brother, the duke, had left England heaving with religious conflict – again. Matthew shifted in his chair and caught the eye of Thomas Leslie. The latter smiled weakly. Both of them had fought for the Commonwealth back in the 1640s, and neither of them wished to see the country plunged into the devastating disaster of civil war again.

"There are rumours that the king himself holds papist sympathies," William Hancock said, "and as to his wife, well, we all know she is."

More murmurs. Catherine of Braganza was undoubtedly Catholic, and it was very fortunate from a staunch Protestant view that she had proved incapable of giving Charles II any children. Now it was too late, she being near on forty-six, but who knew what influence she exerted over the king?

"It must be terrible to have your own son plot against you," Matthew said, thinking that Monmouth was an ingrate. Everything he had, the royal bastard owed to his royal father, and then to conspire against him, plan the murder of him no less…

Hancock shrugged. "All that need not concern us, but the situation here is becoming strained as well."

They all nodded. Squabbles between neighbours acquired undertones of religious fervour. Protestants of all colours ranged themselves against the few Catholics that had made it this far north of St Mary's City, and, increasingly, the protests against Catholic Lord Baltimore grew.

"We must rid ourselves of the papists," one man Matthew

didn't recognise said. "Force them to leave lest they stab us in the back."

"They came here for the same reasons we did," Thomas reprimanded, "to live in accordance with their conscience. They've built themselves lives and families just as we have."

"A Test Act, that's what we need," the unknown speaker went on, rudely ignoring Thomas. "Have them swear an oath by which they disavow themselves of all that papist heresy."

"Papist heresy?" Matthew laughed. "It's us that are the heretics, at least to them. After all, the Catholic Church came first."

"For shame, Matthew!" William Hancock looked quite severe.

"Tolerance is a virtue," Matthew said.

William shook his head. "Not always, not when it puts our faith at risk."

Matthew chose not to reply, somewhat relieved Alex wasn't present. His dear wife would by now have been most incensed, berating them all for bigotry while reminding them that they lived in a colony that had passed an Act of Toleration, allowing for all Christian faiths to live side by side.

"What?" Matthew was brusquely returned to the ongoing discussion by Thomas' hand on his back.

"We were saying that at present we need do nothing," Thomas said. "It's not as if we've experienced much violence – at least not from our fellow colonists."

"Ah, are you having problems with the Indians?" William asked.

Thomas pursed his mouth. "At times, but it's mostly theft, no more. No, it's the others that worry me more."

"The others?" The unknown man leaned forward.

"Renegades: bands of white men that have lost much in the previous Indian wars and now compensate themselves as they can." Matthew regarded his hands, fisted them a couple of times. Men like the Burley brothers, men who burnt and killed and ravaged.

"Papists." The new man nodded. "See, I told you."

"Papists?" Matthew said. "I don't know about that, but

it seems to me they're not much concerned with religion anyway."

The meeting broke up shortly after. Thomas and Matthew strolled back to their respective lodgings. The June evening was agreeably warm, and as a consequence business was brisk in the taprooms that abutted the port area.

"Who is he?" Matthew asked as they made their way across the deserted marketplace.

"Lionel?" Thomas made a disgusted sound. "A young hothead, recently come from the home country with the intent of building More's Utopia over here – in glass, no doubt, given his profession."

"Ah. As intolerant as the author, I gather."

"It would seem so," Thomas agreed. "More was a rabid and cruel pursuer of those that held faiths other than his own."

Matthew wouldn't know: he was nowhere as well read as Thomas, and said so, making his friend smile at him.

Ten years older than Matthew, Thomas suffered from hair loss, and had decided to compensate for this with an exuberant wig of glossy black hair, which if anything made him look even older than he was.

Now he lifted the hairpiece off his head and scratched. "Damned heat! Were we like him? In our youth were we as righteous as he is now?" He sounded out of breath, chest heaving slightly after their quick walk up the main street.

Matthew thought about that for some moments.

"Probably." He had per definition hated Papists and Anglicans as a youth, had signed the Solemn League and Covenant that called for the extirpation of popery and prelacy. And then, several years later, he had sworn an Oath of Abjuration of his previous loyalties, officially bowing to the supremacy of King and Church of England. "An oath I took without any intention of upholding it," he said, grimacing somewhat.

"One does as one must, and at the time you couldn't have done otherwise without placing your family at risk."

"I placed them at risk anyway." Riding off to Conventicles, helping Covenanter preachers… Now those

28

memories made Matthew shake his head at that younger self burning with convictions he no longer held.

"That isn't true. You still hold to your beliefs. A society ruled by free men for free men, a church that recognises every man's right to speak directly to God." Thomas patted Matthew on the back. "And some of these things we have here."

"Aye, some we do."

Matthew was somewhat disgruntled when he arrived at the inn to find Alex had already supped, but at least his wife joined him at the table as he ate.

"I saw Constance today," she said.

He picked at the stew on his plate. Bower's Inn was relatively clean, served a good breakfast but a dismal supper, and this was awful.

"Constance? Peter Leslie's wife?"

"Mhm." Alex grabbed a piece of bread. "With a man," she added, waggling her eyebrows.

"Mayhap her father."

"Too young, and no, it wasn't her brother either – not unless she's into incestuous relationships."

"Ah." Matthew wasn't all that interested.

Alex chewed her bread in silence. "If—" She drank some of his cider and took yet another bite.

"If..." Matthew prompted.

"If she were to take a lover, would that be considered adultery? Given that Peter Leslie doesn't want her back, but refuses to divorce her?"

"Of course – she's a married woman."

"Who hasn't had her husband in her bed for what? Four years? She's not even thirty yet!"

"Peter Leslie is doing mankind a favour by keeping her out of the marital market, surely you agree? What that wee baggage did to poor Ailish Leslie..." He shook his head. Peter's daughter-in-law, Ailish, was permanently scarred – badly scarred – after the time Constance threw hot sugar in her face.

"Yes, that was pretty bad, but to leave her permanently

in limbo… It wasn't her idea to marry Peter in the first place, was it? That must have been a pretty dreary initiation in the pleasures of the marital bed, what with her nineteen to his fifty-odd."

"For better and for worse," Matthew said, even if he considered his neighbour had shown severe lack of judgement in wedding the lass. He shoved his wooden platter away with an irritated gesture. "If the boat doesn't come in tomorrow, we leave for home anyway. I can't go on eating pig swill." And he had to get back home – in these uncertain times, all of him itched with an urgent need to ensure his family was safe.

Alex yawned and nodded. "Tomorrow, and then we leave."

The sloop was visible already at dawn, and with Alex's hand safe in the crook of his arm, Matthew stood waiting by the docks, eyes stuck on the tall shape he assumed to be his son. Daniel whooped when he came within hearing distance, using his hat to wave at them, and Alex tugged her hand free from where it lay on Matthew's arm, using it to wave at their son.

"God, he's big," she said with evident pride, near on tripping over her feet as she dragged him towards where the sloop was being moored.

"Aye, he is." The lad had grown yet another inch or two; was now near on as tall as Matthew himself was. Blue eyes, hair so dark it was almost black – his son was a handsome lad and educated to boot. His wee Daniel a minister in the making; it made Matthew's throat constrict with emotion. He dashed at his eyes, smiled at how effusively Alex greeted their son, and finally pressed the lad to his chest.

"Best in your class," he crowed, "well done, lad." He looked him up and down." You even look the part," he said, taking in Daniel's sober clothes.

"So do you," Daniel said, making Matthew laugh.

He wiped at his dark grey sleeves and tapped a finger to the cuffs. "Embroidered," he said, showing Daniel the intricate designs of revolving stars with which Alex had chosen to decorate this his best summer coat.

"A cravat?" Daniel teased, tugging at the flowing linen around Matthew's throat.

"Some things you don't attempt to fight," Matthew said.

"Oh, come off it," Alex snorted from behind him. "You enjoy looking good."

Matthew draped an arm over her shoulders to gather her to him. "And do I? Look good?"

She stood on tiptoe and whispered just what a delectable piece of eye candy he was, and went on to describe exactly what she wanted to do to him – later. Matthew felt his cheeks heat into bright red, a tingling sensation rushing through his privates.

Beside them, Daniel groaned and shook his head. "Da! It's unseemly. What will—" Whatever else their son had intended to say was interrupted by Ian, who came limping towards them with Betty and one of their huge dogs in tow.

"Can you still ride, or will you be riding pillion?" Ian said with a wide smile for his brother.

"I can," Daniel huffed. He bent down to scratch Dandelion behind his ear. "He's growing old," he stated, fondling the huge head.

"So are all of us," Matthew said, "and back home we now have a Delilah and a Daffodil as well."

"Daffodil?" Daniel laughed. "You can't call a dog Daffodil!"

"Try telling your sister that." Alex nodded in the direction of where Ruth was flying down the street towards her favourite brother. Daniel rushed to meet her, swinging her in several wide arcs before setting her back on her feet.

"Oh, Daniel!" Ruth kissed him, her dark red braids tumbling free from cap and hat. "I've missed you so much!" She seemed to dance on the spot, and Daniel danced with her, for a moment becoming a young lad before recalling he was now almost a minister and a certain gravitas was to be expected.

After Ruth came Temperance, light eyes wide with

pleasure at the sight of Daniel. But no wild embraces, no more than a curtsey and a bow.

"Tss," Alex murmured, clearly disappointed by this rather formal reunion. "Do you suppose he's ever kissed her properly?"

Matthew swallowed a surprised gust of laughter and coughed.

"He has," he said once he got his breath back. "And more than that, aye?"

"How do you know?"

"I caught them at it in the hayloft last year, threatened to belt them both if something like that ever happened again."

"But you've never told me!" Alex let her eyes wander over their son and his sweetheart.

"You never asked."

Alex sniffed and eyed him from under lowered brows. "I'll keep that in mind next time I find out something concerning our children, shall I? Unless you ask, why tell?"

Matthew grinned down at her. "You could try, but that tongue of yours is mightily fond of wagging."

Yet another blue look, this one bordering on glacial, but Matthew just laughed and moved over to talk with Minister Allerton.

"Bloody man, more or less accusing me of being a gossip." Alex adjusted her new shawl and turned to find her daughter-in-law frowning.

"Who's that?" Betty said, ducking her head in the direction of a woman who was staring at them – and in particular at Ian, who was staring back, his back stiff as a board. Alex had to squint to make out the woman standing by the fish stalls.

"Fiona!"

"Fiona?" Betty growled in a way that indicated she knew all about this particular woman and liked her not one bit. "What is she doing here?"

"She lives here," Alex said, "down behind the school, at the cobbler's." Well, she assumed she did. She hadn't seen Fiona except for the odd glimpse in almost a decade, and the intervening years had not treated Fiona kindly, at least not from what she could make out from here.

"Her children?" Betty asked, looking at the three boys who were hovering around her.

"I suppose so." Alex shrugged. "She looks awfully worn, doesn't she?"

"That's what you get," Betty said icily. "Some God punishes already in this life, doesn't He?"

Alex threw Fiona a look. Given how thin and old she looked, how threadbare her clothes were, it would seem she had more than paid for seducing Ian when he was a boy, trying to coerce him into marriage by assuring him the child she was carrying was his when all the while she'd known it wasn't.

"She's not had an easy life," Alex said, feeling quite sorry for Fiona.

In response, Betty snorted and walked over to where Ian was standing. She said something to him that made him laugh and shake his head, one arm sliding round her waist. When Alex looked again, Fiona was gone, as were the scruffy boys.

Chapter 4

"And you are surprised?" Matthew blew into her nape, tickling her.

"She was pretty harsh," Alex said, "and Betty generally isn't."

"Except when it comes to Ian. Surely you've noticed how protective she is of him?"

"Protective? She was flamingly jealous!"

"And you wouldn't be?"

"You know I would," she grumbled. She still was, a wave of puce green washing over her whenever she thought of Matthew and his first wife, Ian's mother. "Are you?" she asked, pummelling at her pillow. Occasionally, she wanted to claw Kate Jones' eyes out as well, she reflected, in particular when Matthew was too attentive to her.

"Am I what?"

"Jealous." She could feel him laughing behind her.

"Is it William Hancock that has caught your eye?"

"William?" Alex twisted round to see him. "What would I see in William?"

"I don't know," Matthew said, "but he, I think, is overly fond of you."

"He is? Oh, don't be silly. He looks at me with mild disapproval most of the time."

"I know, aye? I see it in how his eyes follow you around, and how he lets his gaze linger a wee bit too long on your bosom and your arse." It came out in a very dark voice, and Alex smiled.

"So you are jealous."

"Not as such," he replied with a yawn. "Not of him." He sounded very dismissive.

"So who?" she said, now very wide awake.

Matthew groaned and pulled her down to lie against his chest. "Sleep, aye?"

"Who?" she repeated.

"Of John," Matthew admitted sulkily. "I don't like it that I wasn't your first."

Alex rubbed her face against his chest. "Idiot. I was twenty-six when we met."

"Aye, and I still don't like it. I would that no one but me had ever touched you, taken you, loved you."

Alex struggled up to sit, making the whole bed sway.

"I'm glad that you weren't." She smiled at the way his eyes narrowed. "Otherwise, how would I have known just how lucky I was?" She kissed him: a long kiss. "Very lucky," she said, licking her lips.

"Very," he agreed huskily.

The sun had just cleared the eastern forest when they set off next morning: six horses, two loaded mules, and seven people. Thomas Leslie took the lead, with his armed manservant riding just behind him. For practical reasons, Alex was riding pillion behind Matthew, while Daniel rode the roan she'd ridden down. Given the general bustle of departure, it took Matthew some time to realise his wife seemed out of sorts, uncharacteristically quiet and distracted. She didn't join in the banter between Ian and Daniel; she expressed a vague "Hmm?" when Betty asked her something; and to Matthew she didn't say a word – a silent warmth at his back, no more.

"What is it?" he finally asked.

"Bad night." She tightened her hold round his waist.

She'd tell him in her own good time what it was that was preying on her mind, so instead Matthew concentrated on the way his stallion moved beneath him. Aaron was in many ways a throwback to his sire, but where Moses had been a singularly docile horse, Aaron was far more hot-blooded, capable of taking a leap to the side in an attempt to dislodge his rider – or get closer to the mare.

"You've had her already, you wee daftie," Matthew said, slapping Aaron on the neck. "She's with your get."

"Do you think he knows?" Alex sounded very amused.

"What? That he's served her, or that she's with foal?"

"Both, I suppose."

Matthew thought about that for a moment. "I hope for his sake he recalls the serving of her. It's not much more than a dozen times a year for him. But, as to the foal, nay, he doesn't know."

"Oh." Alex fell silent for a while. "Do you think he's alright?" she asked with a hitch to her voice.

"Who?" Matthew did a swift count through his head – all their bairns were, as far as he knew, safe.

"Isaac," she whispered.

"Ah." No wonder she'd been tossing through the night: she'd been dreaming of her lost life, of her people in the hazy future, foremost amongst them her future son – this no doubt brought on by the discussion they'd had some days ago about that accursed little painting. He shifted in the saddle. Thinking about this made him right queasy: his wife a time traveller, her mother a gifted painter that painted portals through time, and wee Isaac seemed to have inherited his grandmother's magical gifts. After all, it was one of Isaac's paintings that Magnus Lind, Alex's father, had used as a time portal all those years ago, appearing one day much the worse for wear in yon thorny thicket back home.

Matthew strangled a nervous laugh. First his wife, then her father. And as to those paintings... Ungodly, such paintings could only be created with the help of potent magic – black magic. Matthew tightened his hold on the reins and uttered a brief prayer to God, begging him to protect them all – and especially his wife – from evil. He coughed a couple of times.

"What do you think?" he said.

"I'm not sure. I never miss him, not truly. Yes, I think of him, wish him well in his life and all that, but he's no hole in my heart. What if I'm a hole in his?"

Matthew reached back to squeeze her thigh. "He was but a lad when you disappeared from his life. Aye, surely there are nights when he dreams of you, moments when you are a vaguely remembered shade, but a hole in his life that you are not. Man is too resilient for that."

She didn't reply, but he felt her relax, and after a few minutes of silence, she changed the subject by asking him what he thought of Lionel Smith, pompous shit that she found him.

It was nearly noon before they stopped for a break – by then Alex had been fidgeting for some time. She more or less fell off the horse and made for the closest screen of shrubs. She hiked up her skirts and crouched. Cocking her head to where her men were busy lighting a fire in the glade, she grinned when Daniel loudly complained about the state of his buttocks, tore off some moss to wipe herself with, and rose.

"Mrs Graham, what an unexpected surprise."

The voice froze Alex to the spot but, with an effort, she turned, only to find herself a scant yard or so from Philip Burley: still with that messy dark hair that fell forward over his face in an endearing manner that contrasted entirely with his ice-cold eyes, still with a certain flair to him, albeit that he was dishevelled and dirty. Alex opened her mouth to yell, but all that came out was a squeak.

"Down to witness the demise of my dear brother?" Philip continued, his voice far too low to carry to her companions. Low, but laden with rage.

"Good riddance," Alex managed to say. She whirled, screaming like a train whistle.

Things happened so fast Alex's vision blurred. The ground came rushing towards her, her face was pressed into the mulch by Philip's tackle. She heard Matthew roar, set her hands to the ground and heaved. Up. Philip grabbed at her skirts, Alex kicked like a mule, and here came Matthew, bounding towards them. Philip scrambled to his feet, and Alex crawled away on hands and knees.

In Matthew's hand flashed a sword. Philip levelled a pistol but had no opportunity to fire it before Matthew brought his blade down, sending the gun to twirl through the air and land in a distant bush.

Men: from all over, men swarmed, and there was Walter Burley fighting his way towards Matthew with an intent look on his face. He was brought up short by Dandelion: over a hundred pounds of enraged dog throwing himself at Walter. A howl, a long howl that ended in a whine. Walter brandished his bloodied knife and cheered, a sound cut abruptly short when Thomas Leslie charged him. A hand grabbed at Alex, she tore herself free and backed away, looking for some kind of weapon, anything to defend herself with. And there was Matthew – everywhere was Matthew: kicking her assailant to the ground, fending off Philip's sword, swinging round to punch Walter, grinding an elbow into yet another man, and all the while he was yelling out commands to his sons and Thomas.

Like a deadly whirlwind was Matthew Graham, and beware anyone coming between him and the man he was screaming at, spittle flying in the air as he advanced, step by step, towards Philip, a Philip who seemed surprisingly taken aback, retreating towards the woods. Matthew lunged, Philip fell back, using a stout branch to defend himself. Again, and Philip took yet another step backwards. Alex intercepted a swift glance between the Burley brothers, and she didn't like the smirk on Philip's face. Matthew charged, Philip turned and fled with a triumphant Matthew at his heels.

"No," Alex croaked.

A dull crack and Matthew staggered, a giant of a man appearing from where he'd been hiding, brandishing a cudgel. Walter Burley whooped, doing a few dance steps.

Alex didn't stop to think. She launched herself at him, toppling him to the ground and landing knees first on his chest. There was a whoosh when the air was expelled from his body, and then he went limp. She picked up Walter's pistol from where he'd dropped it and turned to find her husband locked in a fight with two men while Thomas, his man and her sons were kept at bay by seven.

Philip Burley yelled when Matthew succeeded in sinking his dirk into his right arm. For an instant, it seemed as if Matthew was about to tear himself free from the unknown huge man, but there was Philip, whacking Matthew over the head again. Matthew's knees buckled under him, and Alex fired into the air.

"I'll cut his throat!" she screamed, holding Walter's lolling head by his hair. "I'll do it now!" Her hand was shaking so badly, at first she couldn't get to her knife through the side slit of her skirt, but then her fingers closed on the familiar handle, and she pulled it free.

"Let him go!" Philip Burley glared at her. "Let go of him, you fool of a woman, or I'll gut your husband like a pig."

Matthew tottered, blood running in miniature rivulets over the left side of his face.

"An impasse, it would seem," Alex said, struggling to keep her voice steady. "You let my husband go, and I'll let your brother live. For now." She increased the pressure of her blade on Walter's skin, making him gargle.

Philip sneered and glanced down at his bleeding arm. "You stand no chance, Mrs Graham. We are ten to your six."

"Seven," someone said. A shot rang out, and the large man helping Philip to hold Matthew dropped like a stone to the ground, shot through his back. "And now you are but nine."

Burley's men shifted, trying to find the sharpshooter. Thomas' hand flew out, and one of the men fell to his knees, gripping at the hilt of a knife that stuck out from his thigh. A collective muttering ran through the six men left standing, their eyes sliding towards the relative safety of the woods.

Alex's hand was slick on the handle of her knife and to compensate she tightened her hold on Walter's hair, pulling so hard the man squealed.

Philip scowled: at Matthew, at Alex, and at the woods. With a swift movement, he levelled a pistol at Matthew's head.

"If any more of my men are hurt, I'll kill him," he shouted, scanning the surrounding trees. He jerked his head in the direction of the forest, and his men helped their wounded comrade to stand, closing ranks around him. Ian and Daniel closed in on Philip who was dragging Matthew with him as a shield.

"My brother," he said to Alex. "Release my brother, and I'll release your husband."

Ian raised his musket and aimed it at Walter.

"Do as he says, Mama. And if Da isn't released before the count of three then Walter Burley is no more."

Walter's breath came in loud hisses, his pulse leaping erratically against her hand. At less than ten feet, Ian would never miss.

Daniel aimed his weapon at Philip. "Nor is Philip Burley," he vowed, but the barrel trembled a bit too much.

Alex let go of Walter's hair and stepped back, watching as he lurched to his feet. At least one broken rib, and if she was lucky, maybe two or three. Walter Burley wheezed, wrapping his arms around his midriff.

He lifted strange light eyes to Alex. "You'll pay," he spat through colourless lips.

"You can always try, and next time I'll squash your balls instead." It took a superhuman effort to retain eye contact with those eerie grey eyes, but she did, stiffening her spine with resolve.

"One," Ian counted, "two…" Matthew was pushed to land at Daniel's feet, and Ian swung the muzzle of his musket towards Philip and the band of renegades. "Three," he said and fired, as did Daniel.

"Why did you do that?" Alex couldn't stop her teeth from chattering. One more man lay lifeless on the ground; one of the ruffians was screaming some yards away, clutching at his bleeding gut. Unfortunately, neither Philip nor Walter Burley had been hit.

"I couldn't leave that many standing. I don't want to have my throat cut during the night." Ian scanned the woods, pistol in one hand. Thomas muttered an approval, bending over stiffly to relieve the dead men of their weapons.

Alex gulped at that, meeting his eyes for an instant before going back to what she was doing, her hands examining Matthew, probing the bleeding indentation in his head, his arms, his legs…

Matthew groaned, heaving himself up on all fours.

"Are you alright?" she asked in a low voice.

"Nay," he replied, just as low. "My head."

"You should have killed Philip Burley," Daniel said to Ian, setting down his reloaded musket and busying himself with Matthew's gun.

"Yes," Thomas agreed.

Ian tucked the pistol back in his belt. "Oh, I tried, but yon man has the luck of the devil himself. He threw himself to the side at the last moment and—" Ian stopped talking when Betty stepped out from behind the oak where she'd been hiding. She threw the musket she was holding to the ground and held out her arms beseechingly towards Ian. Bright, reddish-brown hair sprouted in all directions from under her cap, light brown eyes were huge in a face so pale it seemed to Alex each and every one of Betty's freckles stood in glaring contrast to it. Ian limped towards her, reached her and caught her just as she sank to the ground, mouth open in a sobbing wail.

Under Thomas' efficient command, things were quickly brought back under control. One of the mules had careened off into the woods but was recovered; a bullet had ricocheted off a tree before nicking the hide of Betty's placid mare; and all around the clearing lay their intended dinner, foodstuffs thrown hither and thither. Ian was set to take care of the beasts, Alex organised the food, and Matthew was instructed to sit still – very still.

"I killed a man," Betty repeated for the tenth time. "And I shot at another." She stared down at her hands and flexed her fingers.

"And if you hadn't, I would have been dead or worse," Matthew said.

He watched out of the corner of his eye how Thomas' servant and Daniel dug graves for the dead men and the dog. Brave Dandelion, Matthew sighed, launching himself in his defence. He looked over to where Ian was inspecting the horses and the pack mules, and one part of him supposed he should go over to help, but the other part was incapable of movement. His head was one loud throbbing, his right arm bruised and numb, and his legs were shaking with pent-up tension, the back of his knees damp with sweat. He clutched the loaded flintlock that lay across his lap, finding some comfort in the smooth, worn wood of the stock, the cool metal of its barrel.

"They didn't plan it," Ian said a while later.

Matthew just looked at him. "Aye, they did, they ambushed us."

Thomas nodded, studying the little clearing. "I think you're right, Matthew. But it backfired, didn't it?" He gestured at the two shallow graves. "I'll ride back to Providence with our wounded prisoner and inform the elders. Having the Burleys close is like having a rabid wolf among the sheep."

"You do that." Matthew rose, ignoring how his head protested at this sudden movement. "But we must be on our way." He kept on seeing the Burleys descending on his home, and, God, what would they do to his youngest bairns, to Sarah and David, Samuel and wee Adam? What would they do to his grandchildren, to Mark and Jacob, grown men the both of them, but outnumbered if set upon by a band of ruffians?

"They're wounded," Alex said in a reassuring voice. She stuck her hand into his and squeezed. "But you're right. We should be on our way."

Chapter 5

Matthew threw up again, and sat back against the tree trunk.

Alex handed him a damp cloth. "You're concussed. You really shouldn't be moving at all."

"No choice, is there?" Matthew snapped, throwing the rag to the side.

"Yes, there is," Alex said. "I can stay with you and they can ride on."

Betty had to get home, and get home soon, and, just in case, two had to ride with her, one to stay with her and one to ride for help should the baby decide now was a good time to enter the world. To Alex's practised eye, that looked a most probable scenario, and from the way Betty was massaging her belly, it would seem she shared that concern, even if, being Betty, she didn't say anything.

"No." Matthew struggled to stand. If Ian hadn't caught him, he would have fallen, swaying drunkenly on his feet. With a groan, he collapsed back down. "You ride on. I'll stay behind. Alone."

"In your dreams, Mr Graham." Alex knelt beside him.

"It's just a concussion," he tried.

"And you've insisted on riding with it," she said. "The brain's been badly bruised, and it swells. You have to rest."

"Here?" He scanned their surroundings. "Not much of a safe haven."

"It'll have to do," Alex said.

"I can stay with Da," Daniel offered. "You can ride with Ian and Betty."

"I stay." No way did Alex intend to leave Matthew in his present state.

★

43

"Quiet, isn't it?" Alex said once she'd made Matthew comfortable on the ground. He grunted, saying that as far as he could make out there were rustlings, and snapping twigs, and the call of birds.

Alex tilted her head at him. "Quiet enough to hear all that, then." She looked over to where Aaron was grazing, and back at the musket, leaning loaded within easy reach of Matthew. "Do you think there are any bears close by?"

Matthew opened an eye and studied her with irritation. "Bears, mountain cats, wolves…"

"Oh." Alex fingered the scar on her right arm. She turned to ask him something else, but found him fast asleep, dappled in the sunlight that filtered down through the foliage of the plane tree.

She tucked the blanket around him and sat down beside him. From further in the woods came the staccato of a woodpecker. He was right. It wasn't quiet: it was full of birdsong, of the rushing sound of water from somewhere close by, of the soft whooshing of the wind through the tree crowns high above them. Deceptively peaceful, she thought, pulled out her knife, and stuck it in the ground beside her.

Matthew slept on and on, a deep, immobile sleep that worried her. Twice, she woke him to make him drink and eat something, but he complained of nausea when she tried to make him sit up, and the short walk behind a bush to relieve himself left him dizzy.

"It'll be better tomorrow," she said, looking about at the darkening woods.

Matthew shifted closer to where she was sitting and subsided with a soft grunt, his head pillowed in her lap.

"Do you never dream of her?" Matthew asked, throwing Alex entirely from her own musings.

"Dream of who?"

"Your mother."

Alex threaded her fingers through his hair and thought for a long time. "No. It's strange, but I never dream of her. Not once, I think."

"But you think of her."

"It happens." Like now, when Lucy's scribble had woken memories of Mercedes' magic little paintings, squares of bright blues and greens that lured you to come closer and look into their depths, and then *wham!* you were gone.

Matthew didn't say anything. He snuggled closer, and she was glad to feel his warm weight on her, aware of how dark the night stood round them, their little fire a pitiful beacon of light. He slept. She yawned and yawned again. They should bank the fire, not advertise their presence this openly. Later, she thought, she would do it later.

"Not much of a sentry," Matthew said in a dry voice when Alex woke with a start next morning. She heaved herself up to sit from where she'd been curled on the ground.

"I must have just dropped off," she mumbled. She had no idea how long she'd slept, but it had been pitch-dark the last time she'd forced him awake to drink and talk to her. "How are you?" He was very pale, his eyes sunk into dark hollows.

"My arm hurts something terrible, but my head is better, I think." He gingerly shifted it from side to side. "Not very much better."

"So we stay one more day here," Alex decided, overruling his protests with a quick kiss to his forehead.

They were both half asleep when Aaron whinnied, his head turned towards the narrow trail they'd been travelling on yesterday. The musket was already aimed at the bend in the trail when the small party of men appeared, two on horses and one on a mule.

"The Chisholms," Alex said, relieved when she recognised their neighbours, and Matthew lowered the musket to his lap.

The Chisholm brothers didn't relax. If anything, they stiffened further at Matthew's greeting, the younger of them sliding a concerned look at the man on the mule.

"Matthew." Robert Chisholm nodded in greeting. Since old Andrew died two years ago, Robert was the new Chisholm *pater familias*, ruling over a huge, rambling family with a substantial settlement to the east of the Grahams –

a small village by now, with their own mill, a cooper, a farrier, a cluster of small houses, and the three original farms.

Matthew traded with them, milled his grain at their mill, hunted with the men, had served in the militia with them, and would never dream of offering for one of their girls in marriage to one of his sons, seeing as the Chisholms were Catholics.

Major stigma in the present political climate, Alex thought, suspecting this might be why the brothers remained on their horses instead of dismounting to see if they could help.

Robert frowned when Matthew told him about the Burleys, eyeing Alex with some admiration when Matthew recounted how she'd broken Walter Burley's ribs.

"Not that difficult," Alex said, "I just sort of sat on him."

The stranger on the mule laughed, the sound cut short.

"How unfortunate you didn't sit that much harder," Martin, the other Chisholm brother, said. He spat to the side and Alex recalled the Chisholms had personal reasons for hating the Burleys – their sister's homestead had been attacked by them.

"I didn't see you in Providence," Matthew said.

Robert shifted in his saddle. "No, our welcome would have been somewhat dubious at present."

"Aye, and you do best to stay away for the foreseeable future."

"This colony was founded by a Catholic, for Catholics." Martin Chisholm's voice was raw with rage. "And now look what happens. On account of our own stupidity in creating a haven for all Trinitarian confessions, we find ourselves outnumbered and threatened in a place where we shouldn't be."

"No one will harm you up here," Matthew said.

Robert patted at his musket. "No, that they won't, and we're a large enough group to be able to defend our own. But what say you of the recent burnings further south? Of Catholics driven off their land on account of their religion?"

"I say it's wrong." Matthew sighed. "And I've argued the point as well as I can."

"Will it help?" Robert asked.

Matthew shrugged. "That depends – on the king-to-be, mostly, and it would seem you'll live to see a Catholic king on England's throne again."

"*Deo gratias,*" the unknown man mumbled.

Alex had by now found the beer, and the three men dismounted somewhat unwillingly to join them. Because of the wide-brimmed hat he wore, it was impossible to make out the stranger's face. After a few clipped courtesies, he accepted some beer in the mug he produced from his bundle and retreated to sit some distance away, leaning back against the smooth bark of a sugar maple.

Alex's eyes kept on gliding over in his direction, her brain scrambling to grab at the vague memories he woke by the way he moved and sat. She had a pretty good idea what this man was, further reinforced by his dark apparel, his soft, uncalloused hands, and the rosary beads she'd glimpsed hanging round his neck. Well, she wasn't about to tell, and it was probably wise to exert caution while travelling with a Catholic priest.

"…so we'll remain here until tomorrow, and by then we hope I'm well enough to continue our journey home," Matthew finished explaining to Robert.

"Alone?" Robert shook his head. "Is that wise?"

"Ian will send Mark or Jacob to meet us," Matthew said, "and they'll be back home tomorrow by noon."

"Ah." Martin nodded. "And the Burleys?"

"Somewhat worse for wear, I imagine, at least for some days yet." Matthew shifted where he sat, and closed his eyes. "I swear, if I ever lay hands on them—"

"…you turn them over to the law," Alex finished.

"Or not." Martin Chisholm mimed a slashed throat.

When the Chisholms stood to leave, their silent companion took off his hat for a moment, smoothing down thick, dark hair. Alex strangled a gasp when she saw his face. No, it couldn't be. It was totally impossible, and this resemblance was nothing but a quirky coincidence. Still, she couldn't help herself. When the young man swung himself atop his mule, Alex stood up.

"*Vaya con Dios, Padre,*" she said. Go with God, Father.

"*Y tu, hija,*" came the automatic reply. Robert Chisholm blanched as did the stranger, but curiosity won out. "*¿Habla Español, Señora?*" he asked.

"*Si,*" she replied, her tongue thick in her mouth with sounds she hadn't made for very many years. She decided to gamble once again. "*Conocí a su padre, Don Benito Muñoz,*" she said, and now the priest really stared at her. Alex wanted to laugh at his expression, but then to hear a totally unknown woman say she knew his father must have been somewhat disconcerting – in particular if she was right.

"My father?" he said in Spanish. "He died very many years ago—"

"In Barbados."

"*Sí,*" the priest whispered, staring at her as if he'd seen a ghost.

"If you ever want to talk about it, my home is open to you," Alex said switching back to English.

"*Gracias.*" The priest smiled. With a curt nod, he clapped the hat down on his head and rode off behind the Chisholms.

Matthew stared after them and then turned to look at her. She explained.

"Don Benito's son?" he said once she'd finished.

"A spitting image." And just like Don Benito, this young priest was an uncomfortable copy of that future Ángel Muñoz, Isaac's father. "Jesus," she said, hiding her face against her knees.

"What?" Matthew sounded concerned.

"That's what I suppose Isaac looks like, just like that. The same hair, the same eyes, the same mouth…" She straightened up to look at him. "That's what Isaac's father looked like, that fucking bastard Ángel Muñoz."

"Ah, lass." Matthew opened his arms to her, and Alex crawled in as close as she could.

"Silly, isn't it?" she said in as light a tone as she could muster. "To become so upset over something that happened almost thirty years ago."

Matthew stroked her hair. "That vile man abducted

you, held you imprisoned for months. I imagine you don't forget that – ever."

"No." She twisted her fingers into his shirt, playing with the laces. "I only ever told you. No one else knows."

"As it should be," he breathed into her hair. "No secrets between you and me, aye?"

"Do you think he'll come? The priest?"

Matthew snorted. "Aye, of course he will. You waved a right big carrot at him. As you tell it, he never knew his father."

"Seeing as his father was a priest and as such sworn to celibacy, I imagine there was no opportunity to build a strong father-son relationship." She dug her bare toes into the soft moss and frowned. "He was so afflicted by guilt. A good man, a genuinely good man, who had the misfortune of falling in love where he shouldn't, and for that he flagellated himself until the day he died." She wrinkled her nose at the memory of that horrid hair shirt – the garment he had insisted he be buried in. She laughed. "Mrs Parson is going to have a fit. I'm not sure I ever told her Don Benito had a son."

"Aye, it is a mite surprising."

Alex looked at him. "You don't approve, do you?"

"It isn't my business to approve or not, but it would seem to me yon priest was unfaithful to the vows he'd made."

"He was a man. Fallible as all of us are," Alex said severely.

"Oh aye? So if I find myself confronted with a pretty young lass and bed her, you'll forgive on account of me being but a fallible man?"

She sat up. "I'll cut your balls off, and, besides, you already have, haven't you?"

"That was ages ago – and different," Matthew said, sounding defensive.

Yes, of course it was different. He'd have died if bloody Kate Jones hadn't cared for him and healed him and fucked him. Not that it helped much to keep that in mind.

"I suppose it was different for Don Benito too," Alex said, elegantly closing the discussion.

Chapter 6

Just by chance, Lucy Jones found out what the little picture could do. Her heart hammered as she held her little daughter in her arms. Frances was crying, she could feel that, and Lucy checked her arms, her legs, her head – all of her for any visible signs of damage, sagging with relief that she was still here, still whole. She barely dared look at the canvas, and her head rang with voices, music, screams, laughter. She flipped the picture over, and the silence was immediate, allowing her to think.

Frances calmed down, resting back as well as she could against her mother's huge belly. Lucy dangled her silver pendant as a distraction, and Frances' plump hands made a grab for it. Lucy shivered, a breath of ice travelling down her spine to collect along the back of her thighs. One more moment and her baby would have been gone, swallowed into the dazzling light that had poured from the painting. A small bare foot was all that had been left of Frances, and fortunately Lucy had managed to grab it in time, her hand, her arm, being pulled into the painting together with her daughter. Her limb ached after the recent tussle with a magic piece of canvas that had no intention of relinquishing its hold on Frances, twisting itself like a vice around the girl and, in the process, mauling Lucy's arm to the point where she actually opened her mouth to scream out loud. She studied herself, fingering the dark discolouration that ran the whole length of her arm. Strange that she should bruise so badly while Frances was unscathed.

She rewrapped the painting and stuffed it back into her drawer, locking it carefully. Burn it – yes, she should burn it before something like this happened again. Where would she have gone, her little Frances, if she'd let go of the foot and let her fall? Lucy had a vague impression of a churning chute, of whipping branches and screeching trees. Green, green, green, and the light so bright it hurt your eyes.

Destroy it, Lucy told herself, but all the while she knew she wouldn't – the little picture had her in its thrall, and she had no intention of going back to a world devoid of sound.

"What have you done?" Kate looked with horror at Lucy's arm.

Lucy shrugged and mimed falling off her bed.

"Your bed?" Kate shook her head. "No, my dear, that I don't believe."

Lucy insisted that was the case and looked about for her husband.

"He's gone," Kate said in reply to Lucy's questioning eyes. "Matters to attend to in town."

Ah. Lucy frowned. He'd spent the night with Barbra – again. The curvaceous slave girl was becoming something of a liability, a chafing thorn in Lucy's perfect life. She threw a look out of the window, eyes locking on the golden hoops that decorated Barbra's ears. Baubles for the master's slave mistress? No, this little matter had to end. Now.

Some hours later, Lucy detoured through her father's office, planting a light kiss on his balding pate. She leaned over his shoulder and scanned the deed he was drawing up.

"Get away with you." Simon covered the paperwork with his hand. "None of your concern, is it?"

Lucy shrugged. Minister Walker's will didn't much interest her. She smoothed down Simon's few remaining strands of light red hair in an affectionate gesture before hurrying off to find her mother.

"What happened to your arm?" Joan gasped when the bell-shaped sleeve fell back to reveal the mangled skin. Lucy scowled, regretting not having worn a full sleeve bodice over her imported French chemise. But it was too hot, and she was too huge, and she hadn't thought much about her arm as she walked up the slight incline to her parents' house.

No, she'd been reliving time and time again that moment of absolute panic when she turned to see her daughter disappearing. She sighed and sat down on the bench in the yard, flicking at her skirts to chase away one of the hens. From her petticoat pocket she produced paper and coal and scribbled a question, handing the note to Joan.

"No." Joan set her mouth in a stubborn line and swept the note aside.

Lucy frowned at her and shoved the slip of paper at her again.

"I said no, and why would you want to know about it anyway?" She gave Lucy a suspicious look. "You did burn it, didn't you?"

Most certainly, Lucy nodded, of course she had burnt it. She scribbled on the paper and handed it to her mother.

"Aye, it frightens us." Joan's shoulders drooped, causing her neckline to gape open. So thin, Lucy thought, skin and bones no more. "If you look for too long and too deep, you disappear," Joan went on. "You fall through time, and God knows where you end up." She shivered. "It must hurt, don't you think? Leave you all bruised and damaged."

Lucy couldn't help it. She cradled her arm to her chest. Joan's eyes glued themselves to her discoloured skin.

"Dearest Lord! Your bruises! You didn't burn it, did you?" This time Lucy's insistent nods that aye, she had didn't fool her mother. She took hold of Lucy's shoulders and shook her. "You were told to burn it! It's an evil thing, aye?"

Lucy twisted loose. Her hands flew through the air, and Joan collapsed to sit, her eyes darting between Lucy's hands.

"You hear?"

Lucy nodded. She couldn't fully explain, her hands fluttering like bird wings as she tried to convey just what a miracle it was for her to actually hear things. Disjointed things, voices that spoke in strange languages, children that cried and laughed, horses neighing and dogs barking, but still – sounds!

Joan slumped even lower in her chair. She stared down at her thin, knobbly hands for a while before raising her face.

Lucy took a step back at the look on her mother's face, gaunt features pinched tight into a mask of absolute fear.

"You have to destroy it. What if Frances stumbles upon it?"

Lucy dropped her eyes, but not soon enough.

"Ah, sweetest Lord! Our little lass, she could have been gone from us, and we would never have known." Joan closed her eyes, clasped her hands together, and recited a heartfelt prayer that God keep her granddaughter safe from magic and evil.

"Straight home to burn it," Joan said in parting, sinking her grey eyes into Lucy's. "Today," she insisted, her grip hard on Lucy's arms. She looked about for her shawl, her hat. "I'll come with you."

For a moment, Lucy feared she would, but the burst of energy left Joan as soon as it had surfaced and, with a little sigh, she admitted she didn't have the strength to attempt the long walk to the Jones' house. Lucy kissed her mother, promised yet again to burn the painting, and was off, trailed by the black man assigned to accompanying her.

"I'll go and talk to her," Simon said after having listened to Joan's abbreviated version of events. "I'll make sure she burns it."

"Today?"

"Aye, today." He leaned forward to pour himself some more beer. "She's far too canny to risk her daughter again."

"Aye," she whispered, "but there are others."

"Joan!" Simon choked on his beer, spraying both her and the table.

Joan hung her head, lifting one emaciated shoulder high. "She isn't always a good person. And the painting, it has her spelled. I could see it in her eyes as we spoke, that she would very much like to see someone disappear entirely – to see if I was speaking true."

"God in heaven," Simon muttered, ignoring her displeased grimace. He lifted the mug to his mouth with a shaking arm and drank deeply. "She wouldn't do something like that," he said with conviction.

"No?" Joan was not quite as certain. Lucy was a detached young woman, observing her surroundings, and most people in them, with much curiosity but little affection.

At first, Lucy thought her father was here to tell her that at last her poor mother had died, but he was far too composed for that, even if he twisted the hat he held in his hands round and round in a way that showed that something was troubling him.

"The picture?" Simon patted Frances on her dark brown head.

Burnt, Lucy signed, she had burnt it. Immediately she had come home, she added with the help of her coal stub.

"Hmm." Simon studied her narrowly, but Lucy was an expert at masking her thoughts, pasting a mild smile over her features.

"I hope you're telling the truth. It's a wee bit of evil, aye?"

Lucy nodded, even though she didn't agree. To her, the painting breathed desperation, not evil, as if someone had been trying fiercely to find their way back to something. Another time perhaps, a lost lover, a child, a home… The fine hairs along Lucy's nape bristled with disquiet.

It would never have happened if Henry had chosen to spend this night with her. Or if he at least had been polite enough to sit with her for a while and then accompany her to bed, perhaps even holding her hand as she fell asleep.

Instead, Henry rushed into the room, kissed her on both cheeks, patted his restless children through the linen and silk that covered her skin, and complained about being tired and needing to sleep – alone. Or not, she noted when she took a short, cooling walk around the garden with Kate. Both of them could see the soft candlelight that spilled from his windows, and while only Kate could hear them, Lucy saw the shadow of a woman and knew her husband was betraying her with the slave girl – again.

Before she went to sleep that night, Lucy withdrew the painting from its hiding place and placed it on her desk.

The carpet of sounds danced around her, filling the dark, humid night air with birdsong and clanking chains, with the slapping of oars against water, and the howling of wolves. Human voices rose and surged around her. They called, they wept, they sang and whispered. Lucy lay in the dark and listened, her eyes fixed on the low fat moon she could see through the open shutters. No, not evil, but definitely dangerous. Very, very dangerous.

It took him some time to ask, but late next evening, Henry strolled over to where Lucy was sitting and lowered himself to meet her eyes. "Have you seen Barbra?"

Lucy smiled and shook her head. Not since the morning, she thought, not since she'd been swallowed by that small, churning hole through time. Afterwards, she could hear Barbra's voice among all the others, a thin plaintive cry, a plea that someone help her back. Lucy ducked her head to hide the satisfied gleam in her eyes. No one would ever know. It was as if Barbra had never existed, and now she was gone, with her dark red skirts and golden hoops. God alone knew where she had ended up.

Lucy lifted her face to her husband and extended her hand to him, indicating that she had to get up. She took his other hand and placed it on the kicking children inside of her.

Chapter 7

A lot of things had happened during their time away from home: Mark had finished the extension to his cabin; Jacob had taught Tom and Maggie to swim after saving the latter from a premature watery grave in the river; Hannah held up a foot to show them she no longer had a nail on her big toe; David had shot his first deer; and Adam had saved yet another animal from imminent death. But, most importantly, Betty had made it back just in time to give birth to her second son.

"Touch and go," Mark grinned, before turning his attention to his father, his brow creasing with concern. "Are you better, then?"

"Aye," Matthew replied, before swinging himself off Aaron and slapping the big bay across its rump. To his left stood the big house, and as always his chest expanded with pride at the sight of his home, nestled against the slope. A soft weathered grey, it stood two storeys high and consisted of three bedrooms upstairs, and a parlour, a kitchen and two wee rooms downstairs. And every plank, every beam he had set in place himself. Not that he ever intended to admit it to Alex, but the feature he most liked were the windows, all of them with panes of glass so expensive he'd grumbled loudly over every single one of them. Alex had insisted, and he had given in, secretly most pleased to have a home so full of light. Flanking the house were the barn and the stables. There was a line of smaller buildings containing everything from dairy to laundry shed, and in the centre of the resulting enclosed yard stood a huge white oak. Just beyond the barn were Mark's and Ian's cabins, and further down the slope, Matthew could make out the river, a glittering band of silver in the late afternoon sun.

Jacob dismounted and came to stand beside Matthew, giving him a one-armed hug.

"Home, hmm?"

Matthew nodded in agreement. "Home."

He looked towards the foundations of the big house and the corner where together they had buried Jacob's gift to Matthew when he came home from his time in London, a piece of stone brought all the way from Hillview. Matthew smiled as he remembered how serious his son had been when he'd handed him that bit of Scottish granite.

"When you miss it badly, it may help to know you have a piece of it here," Jacob had said. And it did, even if there still were days when Matthew was inundated by a homesickness so sharp it twisted through his bones and left him aching with loss. To see it once more, to stand right at the edge of the moor and see the gorse flare a bright yellow. And the heather... Matthew was aware of Jacob's worried eyes and cleared his throat, banishing his maudlin thoughts to the back of his brain.

"Will you see to the horses?" he said and followed Alex inside.

One of the more obvious advantages of her age was that she no longer had any small children to take care of, Alex reflected, watching Naomi, Mark's wife, lift a squirming Lettie off the floor. Instead you only borrowed them when you felt the urge to hold a little one again, as she was doing now with Betty and Ian's newborn son in her arms.

"Strong genes," she said, smiling down at the little boy. "A Graham all the way."

Little Timothy yawned, small hands fisting themselves as his back went stiff like a board before he slumped back in relaxation against Alex's chest. Matthew extended a finger and ran it up and down the downy head.

"Like his mother, this bright fuzz," he protested.

Alex laughed and replaced the cap she had taken off to study her new grandchild. Behind her, Matthew stood silent.

"What?" she asked, turning so that she could see him.

"I miss it. I wouldn't mind a new bairn of my own."

"Definitely not with me," Alex told him, "and forget about making any with someone else."

"Don't you?" he asked.

Alex handed him the baby and shook her head. "No way. I've done more than my share in that department – look at you, surrounded by seven healthy sons and two daughters. Now it's time for me – and you."

His long mouth curved into an expectant smile at her words, and when he raised his face from the inspection of his grandson, she caught his eye and winked.

Alex left Matthew cooing over the latest addition to their family and went off in search of Mrs Parson, finding her in the kitchen. She stood for a moment in the doorway, regarding the old woman, her best friend in the whole wide world. As always in black, as always with impeccable linen, and as always with ears as sharp as a bat's.

"There you are," she said without turning around. "How's Matthew?"

"Well enough. And Betty?" Alex came over to hug Mrs Parson, and was hugged back.

"It was a difficult birth. The lass isn't built like you, aye? Not as broad over the hips."

"I'm not broad over the hips," Alex protested, trying to study her backside.

"Aye, you are," Mrs Parson snorted, "and you would never fit into those wee breeches you wore the first time I saw you now."

"Of course not! That was twenty-six years ago!" Alex smiled at the memory of her beloved jeans.

"It didn't help that she insisted on accompanying us down to Providence," Alex said, returning to the subject of Betty.

"Nay, but in that she is like you – stubborn like a mule." Mrs Parson pulled out a pie from the baking oven and placed it on the workbench to cool. Pecan pie, Alex concluded after some sniffing, and her stomach growled happily.

"She must be careful," Mrs Parson said. "One more may well kill her."

"Not all that easy, is it?"

"Nay, but that lass has no choice. You must speak to them."

"Me?" Alex squeaked. "Why not you?"

"You're the mother."

"His, not hers," Alex said.

"I don't think Esther Hancock will come with much valuable advice, do you?" Mrs Parson pursed her mouth in a gesture of extreme displeasure. Seventeen times poor Esther had been pregnant. Thirteen children had been born alive, and six had died in infancy.

"No," Alex agreed with a sigh, "probably not."

She met Agnes on her way to Ian's cabin, and rolled her eyes at yet another huge belly. The fact that she didn't have any small children didn't mean that her home wasn't overrun by them. Mark and Naomi had three — Hannah, Tom and Lettie — with a fourth on the way; and Betty and Ian had little Christopher and newborn Timothy as well as Ian's two eldest children, Malcolm, of an age with her own ten-year-old Samuel, and Maggie, a wild and constantly talking four.

"Are you sure it's only one?" she teased Agnes.

"Nay," Agnes groaned, sinking her knuckles into the lower part of her back. "I suspect it may be a litter."

Alex smiled at her serving woman. "We'll soon find out."

Agnes nodded morosely.

"You'll be fine," Alex said. "The best midwife in the whole colony, Mrs Parson is."

"It isn't her that will be hurting." But Agnes smiled all the same, and placed a soft hand on the swell that was her child. "I think it's a lass. I want it to be a lass."

"Really?" Alex was surprised. Most women in this day and age wished for sons — at least as their firstborn.

"Aye," Agnes replied, "a wee lass with John's hair."

Alex suppressed an amused snort. John Mason, their field hand, had golden curls that would have made Shirley Temple jealous and that was about it. A good match, Agnes and John:

hard-working and loyal but with a combined intelligence that, in Alex's opinion, fell well short of Hugin's, Adam's tame raven. Both of them had been transported here, Agnes as a consequence of the religious upheaval in Scotland, John for stealing from his master to feed his ailing mother, and both of them had long contracts to work off as indentured servants. Not Agnes, not anymore, but John had two or three more years to go, and Alex doubted they would ever want to leave – Graham's Garden was their home now, the place in which they had finally found soil fertile enough to put down roots. She made a face at her own weak simile and with a pat on Agnes' arm, hurried on to hold an impromptu lesson in sexual education.

With relief, Alex left Ian's cabin five minutes later. Boy, had that been embarrassing, and even more so due to the way Ian and Betty kept on smiling at each other, indicating to anyone but the truly brain-dead that they were quite capable of handling their sexual dilemmas by themselves.

No sooner had she stepped off the stoop, but she was ambushed by Adam and dragged off to inspect the latest victim to his veterinary ambitions.

Hugin cawed at Alex, bobbing his head a couple of times.

"Hi yourself," Alex replied, running a finger over his black plumage.

"Don't talk to him," Adam said. "I'm angry with him."

"Oh?"

"He ate one of the babies." Adam pointed at the wicker cage in the corner.

Alex peeked down at the possum, receiving a hiss in reply. The pouch bulged impressively, several distinct small shapes moving about restlessly. Hugin flapped over to sit on her shoulder and the female possum growled.

"She doesn't like you," Alex told the bird, receiving an affectionate peck in her hair in return. She turned to her eight-year-old son. "You have to let her out. She looks well enough now." Adam looked at her entreatingly, making Alex exhale loudly. "Adam! This is a wild animal, not a pet.

It's cruel to keep it in a cage. You've sewn up the gash, you've fed her for a number of days, but now she has to make it on her own."

"But she's pretty," he tried.

"Pretty? She looks like a giant, white-faced rat!"

"But—"

"No buts. You set her free tonight, after dark."

After a few minutes spent hugging David and Samuel, moments they rather reluctantly took from their wild game, Alex decided she'd earned herself a nice cup of tea and a slice of Mrs Parson's pie. Besides, she hadn't even told Mrs Parson about Don Benito's son yet.

"A son?" Mrs Parson blinked with exaggerated slowness. "The priest with the hair shirt?" She laughed out loud, showing off her remarkably well preserved teeth. "And now he's here?"

"Officially, I suspect he isn't. Catholic and a Spaniard to boot – it's like walking about with a noose already half drawn round your neck to announce your presence here." Alex sat back on the kitchen bench, cradling the mug of precious tea in her hands. She threw a pleased look at her surroundings. She loved her kitchen, from the well-scrubbed floors to the whitewashed walls. As always, a small cauldron was simmering in a corner of the large hearth, an assortment of pans stood neatly stacked beside the baking oven, and on the workbench stood a pitcher and basin and a couple of clay pots, one of which housed Alex's aloe vera plant. On the huge table that took up most of the floor space, Mrs Parson had placed a jug of white roses, the floral arrangement further complemented by strands of grass and lavender.

"But why would he come here?" Mrs Parson asked.

"Well, I suppose to catch up on all those things a priest tends to do: hear confession, baptise, marry, say last rites…"

"You can't say last rites after the fact," Mrs Parson pointed out. "If he's dead, he's dead." She shifted on her chair, lifted her feet to rest on a small stool.

Alex gave her an irritated look. "Okay, so he blesses the grave or something."

"And do you plan on telling him his father died because of you?"

Alex squirmed. "I don't know what his uncle told him but if not, I suppose I must. And, anyway, it wasn't as if I asked him to jump in to defend me, was it?"

"No," Mrs Parson said, "but if he hadn't—"

"I would have kicked that overblown planter's ass." Alex slid over to make room for Sarah, and gave her youngest daughter a quick squeeze.

Mrs Parson's face crinkled into a wide grin. "Aye, I suspect you would, lass. But not any longer, hmm? Too old, too out of practice."

"Oh, shut up." Alex glowered. "I can still defend myself if I have to. And talk about the kettle calling the pot black. If I'm old, you're positively ancient." Beside her, Sarah giggled, the sound cut short when Mrs Parson told her there'd be no pie if she disrespected her elders.

The comment regarding her general fitness rankled, and Alex decided very late in the afternoon to escape into the woods for a physical evaluation, throwing several very guarded looks in all directions before she got down on the ground.

"Ugh!" Alex collapsed into a heap and glared at her hands. "Bloody fucking hell," she said out loud. "You're getting old and flabby, Alexandra Graham!"

Flabby was perhaps an exaggeration, she thought, rolling over to pinch the folds on her belly. A lot of muscle, all over, but unfortunately not enough for her to do the twenty push-ups she'd challenged herself with. She sighed and sat up. Sometimes she missed that old life of gym classes and energetic instructors that stood inches from your face and bawled at you to push and push harder. Even more, she missed her dojo. She studied her feet reflectively. Once she had killed someone with these – something she supposed her karate colleagues would have been aghast to hear. Now, despite her sporadic efforts to retain her martial arts skills, she barely remembered movements that had once been as natural to her as breathing, and she stood up to try and work her way through some of the more complex katas. Not entirely forgotten, but was it really supposed to feel that way down her back? And, Jesus, she couldn't put the palms flat to the ground anymore.

"What are you doing?"

Alex leaped like a startled deer and landed like a geriatric elephant, turning a burning face in the direction of Mark.

"Umm," she said.

He mimicked some of her sweeping hand movements and eyed her with interest. "You look dangerous when you do that."

"I am dangerous. I used to be able to fell a grown man with one kick – easily."

Mark made an incredulous sound.

"It's true, ask your father." Alex did a series of swift chops and ended with a surprisingly agile kick, forcing Mark to rear back with a small yelp. She decided to ignore half her arse was screeching in protest at this sudden burst of unfamiliar activity. "Not at all as I used to be, but maybe if I make an effort…"

Mark shook his head at her, saying that Da wouldn't like it that his wife stood half-dressed in the woods and kicked at things.

"Tough," Alex said, making up her mind then and there that this was something she would begin to do on a very regular basis.

Chapter 8

All day she'd been longing for him. From the moment he rolled out of bed at dawn, his hair standing round his head, Alex had felt the lack of him, and now, well after noon, she just had to… The air hung heavy with humid heat, and her brisk pace across the ripening fields brought out patches of sweat on her back, below her breasts, and all along the insides of her arms. She took off her hat and tugged at her hair as she went, undoing it so that it hung loose around her shoulders. When she finally reached the outer field where he was working, she stopped just for the pleasure of watching him.

Alex set down the basket with food she'd brought, and shaded her eyes with her hand. Alone and in the heat, he'd taken off his shirt, baring his scarred torso to the air. Floggings, sword cuts, deflected knife blades…life had left a patchwork engraved on his skin that he rarely exposed to the eyes of others. Half-naked, his hair tied back with a leather thong to keep it out of his face, he looked like a savage, his teeth white in his tanned face when he caught sight of her and smiled.

Her toes curled themselves against the inner soles of her sandals, a rush of heat travelling like bushfire through her loins. He undid his breeches and let them drop. His genitals were a surprising dark against the light skin of his thighs and belly. He remained where he was for a couple of heartbeats, no doubt to let her feast her eyes on him, and then he took a purposeful step in her direction followed by another and another.

By the time he reached her, Alex had wriggled out of her stays, her skirts a messy heap at her feet, her bodice thrown discarded to the side. She let him undo the drawstring of her worn chemise, standing perfectly still when he pulled it off her.

As white as milk she was, his wife, her skin soft and well cared for. He sniffed at her, smiling as he caught the strong scents of lemon and lavender. She'd bathed herself for him, and he half closed his eyes to bring forth the image of how she would have looked when she scrubbed herself with that strange and expensive mixture of sugar and lemon juice, using the wrung lemon halves on her elbows.

"You should have waited. We could have gone down to the river together, later."

"I could," she agreed, kneeling down. "But then I wouldn't have smelled as nice as I do right now." Her mouth was soft and warm on him, and Matthew stopped thinking, concentrating only on the sensations that surged through his balls and his cock. "Besides…" She released him with a last kiss. "…it's not as if I can't go with you anyway, is it?"

"Nay, an extra swim won't kill you."

He shook out her skirts and spread them as a blanket on the grass. Her breasts, the silkiness of her inside thigh… He took a very long time exploring her, from her toes all the way to her neck and mouth. He kissed her just below her earlobe, laughing at how the skin on her thighs prickled in response. It always did, and he kissed her there again, hearing her bite back a pleased gasp as a shiver flew up her body. His fingers danced down her sensitive flanks, and she twisted. He slid his fingers through her moist and slippery cleft, and she moaned, her head thrown back.

He was throbbing for her by now, his cock demanding that he take her, and take her hard. So he did, feeling her hold still for an instant like she always did when he entered her, relaxing her insides round the size of him. He was big, she'd once told him, flushed like a wee lass, much bigger than any other man she had ever…and he had liked it that he was, but drowned in jealousy that she should be in a position to compare.

He used his legs to spread her wider, and sank himself all the way to his root, his balls pressed hard against her. Again, and again, and again. For an instant, Matthew was transported back to Scotland and a mossy hollow on the moor, and the woman lying with his cock inside of her was young and short-haired, eyes the colour of gentians in autumn staring up at him. As blue today as they were then, and all of her as welcoming now as she'd been then.

He rolled off to lie beside her, his cock protesting at being so abruptly separated from its cosy nest. More, it grumbled, more out of pride than necessity, before subsiding against Matthew's pubic curls. It perked up at her touch, stretching itself like a lovesick cat when she caressed his balls and member with a gentle, warm hand.

"You wear me out," Matthew protested, twisting his head to look at her.

"No, I don't." She nudged at his cock, already hardening again. "See? You want it too."

"Aye," he said, covering her hand with his and holding it still. "But not at once. You can wait a while, can't you?"

"I can?" she murmured, her eyes very close to his. She kissed him, and she tasted of unripe raspberries and lemon balm. She kissed him again, and he thought he detected the lingering taste of newly churned butter on bread fresh from the oven.

He closed his eyes and smiled. If she wanted it that bad, well then he would but lie here and let her have her way. Ah, oh yes! He laughed out loud and cupped his hands gently round her head, holding her still. Moments later, he opened his eyes to where she reared herself above him and lifted his hands to steady her when she settled herself on top, enveloping a cock that definitely wanted more, very much more.

Matthew waved at a fly that had settled on Alex's white calf and stretched himself for yet another slice of bread. He'd been right: still slightly warm from the oven and with a small stone crock of butter to go with it. And there was beer for him in a stone bottle, eggs, a few slices of ham, several newly harvested carrots that he at first attempted to ignore but finally bit into, and, right at the bottom, a large piece of spice cake, pungent with cinnamon and ginger.

"Mmm," he sighed, flipping over on his back. He stared

up at the sky through the trees and, as always, wondered if it was his imagination or if in fact he could see the world turn, revolving against the cloud-dotted blue.

"Mmm indeed," she agreed, following suit to lie beside him. She twitched her shift down her legs. "I spoke to Betty and Ian yesterday."

"Aye, I heard." Matthew grinned. Ian had mimicked Alex perfectly, and then he'd confessed that during almost a year before they were wed, Betty and he had explored the pleasures of lovemaking without risking bairns. "I don't think they saw you as a good example," he teased. "You gave me nine bairns in what? Sixteen years?"

"A couple too many."

"You think?" Matthew took her hand in his, widening his fingers to allow her to braid hers tight around his. "So which one of them would you be without?"

"None of them, you stupid man! Not now that I have them." She turned towards him. "Besides, I have ten children with you, because Ian is as much mine as if I'd given birth to him."

"Aye," Matthew agreed, "that he is." At times, he found it strange that the child so obviously closest to her heart should be his son by Margaret. He smiled, wondering if she knew she loved Ian the best. And Ian adored her, sharing much more of his inner thoughts with her than he did with him, his father.

"What?" she asked, widening her eyes under his intent gaze.

"Nothing," he said, shifting his eyes to rest on the far-off sky. Somewhere up there in all that blue lived his wee Rachel, a little minx of an angel that was surely adored by all the other exasperated angels. It always made him smile to think of his wild-haired lassie as an angel. In his head, she was engraved at full speed, the undone bands of her cap flying behind her, the smock stained and torn, and at her side ran a pig, complete with little angel wings of its own.

"An angel pig?" Alex laughed when he shared this with her.

"Of course a pig," Matthew replied. "She liked pigs." His wee lass had been fascinated by the cannibalistic sow they'd had in Scotland, spending hours sitting on her heels talking to her.

"You can say that again," Alex said. "Something she has very much in common with her youngest brother."

"Adam? Aye, Adam is fond of the sow."

"And she of him, to the point that she stands on her hind legs and glares at me when she sees me."

Matthew grinned. He was convinced the pig thought Adam was a strange and deformed piglet, but a piglet nonetheless.

He was half asleep in the green shade, curled on his side. The air hummed with insects and heat, he heard the chatter of the birds fighting over their crumbs, and from far away came the strident neighing of a horse.

"I don't think Daniel will be coming back to visit us all that soon," Alex said.

"Nay." Their soon-to-be minister son had outgrown his home, and however much he enjoyed being back with his brothers and sisters, it was clear that after less than a fortnight here, he was already restless, his mind more often than not back in Boston with his friends and studies.

"And Temperance?" she asked.

"I imagine they'll wed soon enough." Matthew yawned. It was nice to sleep here under the soaring maples – if only she'd stop talking.

"He's only eighteen," Alex said.

Matthew decided to not reply. Mayhap if he shut up, she would too. She sighed, fidgeted in the grass, and when he peeked at her, he found her staring at the sky, a severe expression on her face.

"Misogynists," she muttered under her breath.

"Misowhat?" Matthew yawned again.

"A man who dislikes women."

"Who? Me?" He opened his eyes fully in surprise.

"No," she said, going on to explain that, in her opinion, Daniel had spent far too much time in the company of men who didn't care for women outside their traditional roles as mothers and dutiful wives. She saw it in his eyes at times – how short she fell of living up to all the female virtues – and, to her surprise, it hurt to be weighed by him and found lacking.

Matthew snorted derisively. "He's but a lad. It takes a man to appreciate a strong woman." He chuckled and closed his eyes again. "Found lacking, aye? He'll have a hard time with yon Temperance then." Buxom and fair she might be, wee Temperance, but a milksop she was not.

Alex laughed. "Yes, that might be something of a wake-up call."

A rather long nap was interrupted by an excited blue jay, and once Matthew had finished off what little was left in the basket, they took the long way home, hands braided together, hips and thighs brushing against each other. There was no need of words. It was enough just to walk like this, all of him humming with contentment after these last few hours. They should do this more often, he reflected: make a habit of escaping now and then for some precious hours of solitude. He said as much, making Alex smile.

"I'm game whenever you are," she said. "How about tomorrow?"

Over the coming weeks, the opportunity to sneak off for some alone time was severely restricted by their respective workloads. Since first settling here, sixteen years ago, Matthew had cleared a substantial amount of land, and as a consequence, he was out and about for most of the summer days, rising at dawn and returning at twilight. But one hot Sunday in July, Alex put her foot down, saying that unless he accompanied her to the river – just the two of them – she would scream. It made him laugh, but he gladly went with her, grinning when she challenged him to a swimming race. He won, of course. He always did. Afterwards, Alex spent well over half an hour seeing to his back, leaving him glistening with oil and smelling like a herbal garden.

The sun was well past its zenith when they set off for home. They started up the long incline that led from the river to the house and, already at this distance, Alex could see the flurry of movement in their front yard.

"It would seem we have guests," Matthew said.

Alex shaded her eyes and squinted. She smiled when she recognised Thomas Leslie, who had already dismounted to greet his grandchildren. Ever since Mary had died last winter, Thomas had become a frequent visitor, dividing his attention equally between his daughter Naomi and his best friend Matthew. Behind Thomas, she could make out three more people, still astride their horses, and beside her, Matthew muttered something rather unwelcoming.

"What?" she said.

"Jenny," he said, jerking his head in the direction of their visitors.

"Jenny?" The last person Alex expected to see in her front yard was Jenny Leslie, Ian's ex-wife. To be quite honest, it was also one of the people she least wanted to see, along with Jenny's new husband Patrick, but unfortunately here they were, larger than life, accompanied by a flustered Peter Leslie.

"What is she doing here?" Alex muttered to Matthew, and his hand tightened around hers in warning.

They reached the yard just as Peter dismounted.

"Peter, Thomas," Matthew said, nodding very briefly at Jenny before Peter put an insistent hand on his sleeve and pulled him away, his face creased with urgent news.

A couple of very tense minutes ensued. Ian remained standing where he was, glowering with such intensity in the direction of Jenny it was a surprise she didn't burst into flames. Patrick leapt off his horse, landing nimbly on his feet before turning to help Jenny down, and Alex hated him for flaunting his whole undamaged body.

A quick glance at Ian verified what she'd already suspected: his back was killing him today, which was why he remained rooted to the ground, as any attempt to walk would result in a limp, or even worse, a shuffle. Beside Ian stood Malcolm, mouth hanging slightly open at the sight of his mother.

"Ian." Jenny came to stand before him.

"Jenny." Ian's voice was clipped, his hazel eyes clouded with mistrust.

"I thought…" Jenny cleared her throat. "I'm here to visit my father, and so I thought that perhaps I could be allowed to see my children?" She adjusted the deep blue bodice and fiddled with the silver clasp that decorated her cloak.

"You could have sent for them," Ian told her. "You didn't have to come here."

Oh yes, she did, Alex snorted quietly. Little Jenny had to show them all that she was well dressed, that her husband was a successful man down in Charles Towne, and that she, Jenny Leslie, had overcome the stigma of being branded an adulterous wife.

"Malcolm." Jenny smiled down at her son. The boy obviously didn't know what to do, craning his head back to look at his father. Ian placed a hand on his shoulder and shoved him forward. Only then did Malcolm approach his mother, but cautiously, like a man tiptoeing round a sleeping bear.

"Go on, lad," Ian said, and with that Malcolm was in his mother's arms.

"Da?" Maggie tugged at Ian's breeches. "Da, who's the pretty lady?" Her hair had escaped the straitjacket of her braids, hanging in soft curls around a face that regarded Jenny with open admiration.

"Your mother, lass," Ian replied. He looked drawn, shifting his weight from foot to foot. Alex took a step in his direction, stopped when Ian glared at her. This male pride thing was at times incomprehensible. Alex sighed.

"My mam?" Maggie pressed herself close against Ian. "That isn't my mam."

Yes it is, Alex thought to herself, and even more unfortunately Patrick is your father – biologically if not legally. It showed in how Maggie's hair rose in a whorl off her forehead, in how her lower lip jutted out, thick and plump. It should never have been allowed to happen, that romance between their then bond servant and Jenny. But, of course, if it hadn't, then Betty wouldn't have been Ian's wife, and that would have been a grave loss.

"Aye, she is," Malcolm told Maggie. "I told you, how our mam went away – to Carolina."

"Why?" Maggie asked.

"Because." He shrugged aloofly.

"Oh." Maggie nodded, but she made no move to approach Jenny, shrinking back when the unknown woman crouched before her.

"His back is killing him," Alex said to Mark, watching her eldest son's stiff stance.

"Aye, but he can't very well show himself disabled now, can he?" Mark nodded in the direction of Patrick whose whole concentration was directed at the little girl pressed against Ian's leg.

"No, I suppose not. Don't they have children of their own?" she said, irritated by how Patrick ate Maggie with his eyes.

"Aye, they do, a lass, I think. The wee lad died last winter of the ague." Mark sounded very callous. "No, he can't remain standing like that. You'll have to offer them something to drink. Distract them, like."

"Is it okay if I spit in their mugs?" Alex whispered, making Mark laugh. He accompanied her to the kitchen, helped her fill the pitchers with cider and beer.

"Did you?" Mark asked Alex once they'd watched the Leslies ride off.

"Did I what?" Alex turned to face him.

"Spit in their mugs." Mark grinned, making Matthew raise a brow.

"Of course I did." Alex grinned back. "Didn't you?"

"Alex," Matthew sighed, sounding very amused, "you didn't…"

"Maybe I did, and maybe I didn't," she teased.

"I did," Mark said, and son and mother broke out in laughter.

"What did Peter Leslie want?" Alex asked Matthew later that evening. They were seated on the bench in the graveyard, looking down at their home spread out below. In the lingering light of the July evening, it was all blues and purples against the darker backdrop of the forest fringe. All the way to the river, his fields rustled with wheat and barley, man-high in its places where a decade ago it had all been trees.

"Off to drink beer down by the river," Matthew sidestepped, nodding to where their four eldest sons were walking through the twilight, Ian's limp making him easily recognisable.

"I hope they bathe first," Alex said, "all of them."

"Mmm." He smiled at the shadow that flitted behind their sons. Sarah was apparently planning on joining the beer drinking, or at least to eavesdrop on it.

"So what did he say?" Alex insisted.

Matthew looked away and sighed. "The Burleys rode into the Ingram place a couple of days ago and held a musket to John Ingram's head, threatening to blow it away unless Mrs Ingram handed over whatever valuables they had." He noticed with detachment that his hands were trembling and fisted them closed. "They took the eldest lass, and poor John was dragged away behind their horses for a mile or so before they cut him loose."

"Oh God," Alex groaned.

"Oh God, indeed." He didn't tell her that Peter had been sent to warn them by John and his shocked wife. Graham's Garden was next, Philip Burley had laughed, and there was one very pretty girl there, a very pretty girl.

"And the girl?"

"Gone," Matthew said. "Gone to God knows where." He would talk to his sons, and already tomorrow he was going to ride over to the Chisholms and buy a further dog or two.

"They're coming here," Alex breathed, her eyes very dark in the dim light.

"Mayhap," he said, "but they might encounter more resistance than they expect."

Chapter 9

Lucy combed out her long hair with even strokes, gazing at herself in her mirror glass. Two sons...she smiled with pride, a bubbling sense of achievement fizzing from the soles of her feet all the way to the crown of her head. Beautiful lads, just like their father, and strong and lusty the both of them, latching onto the wet nurse's teat with vigour.

She adjusted the tight linen bands around her chest, creasing her brows at the discomfort. Her mother said she should nurse her children herself, but Lucy had no desire to act the cow, permanent damp spots on her clothes. No, Lucy wanted to regain her normal figure and entice her husband back to bed, away from all those other women his eyes strayed to when she was great bellied. Lucy bit her lip. She knew well enough what little one could do to minimize the risk of getting pregnant, and decided to stock up on an assortment of herbs to drink regularly. After all, now there were two male heirs, and so Lucy had fulfilled her obligations – at least for a couple of years.

With a pleased expression, she fingered her new ear bobs, each set with a drop-shaped pearl. One for each boy, Henry had said, dropping a kiss on her cheek. Very nice – much nicer than the golden hoops he'd given Barbra. Distractedly, she wondered where Barbra might be. She hoped she found herself in a darker time, far removed from the bodily comforts of this age.

Without conscious effort, her hand was already groping in her drawer for her precious treasure, and she placed it on the table before her. Lucy leaned forward with caution. Ever since Barbra disappeared, the pull exerted by the painting had increased, the blues and greens cresting like waves before her eyes. Not enough to make her seasick, nor even queasy, but enough to make her sit back and concentrate on the noise instead: drums, the reedy sound of flutes, the vibrating string of a lute… Lucy hummed along, mesmerised by the way the music floated up around her, trickling in through her skin to lodge itself deep in her brain. So many sounds; so many beautiful, enticing sounds.

It was a week or so later that Lucy found out about a new rival to Henry's affections. A whore, albeit, and perhaps not in any way a major threat, but Lucy's face tightened uncomfortably all the same. She was standing on a low stool while Mrs Malone was tweaking the dark green folds into place around her waist, her eyes fixed on the mouth of the slut leaning back against a wall and talking.

"Does she know?" the whore asked her madam with a little smirk. Lucy supposed Mrs Malone must have replied something because the trollop laughed, fanning herself in the heavy summer heat.

"Every night he comes," the young woman grinned, "and every night he stays. Yesterday, he told me he wanted me to be his exclusively." Mrs Malone straightened up at that, turning round to say something to the girl. Something she didn't like to hear – that was evident from her countenance.

"He loves me," the wench said, pouting. "Look!" She stuck her hand into the front of her chemise and pulled out a pendant on a gold chain. A pearl, the perfect match to Lucy's ear bobs. Belatedly, the whore became aware of Lucy's burning eyes and with a mumbled something escaped from the room.

Once home, Lucy went in search of her mother-in-law, bursting with the need to share her anger.

"All men do," Kate sighed, patting Lucy's hand. "They have other urges, carnal needs so much stronger than ours."

Lucy wanted to stamp her foot. She had carnal lusts as well, needs she'd been suppressing for the last five or six months while Henry had been avoiding her bed.

"She is of no importance," Kate said.

Lucy scribbled on the scrap of paper she held in her hand.

"He did?" Kate's mouth set into a straight line. "No, that's not right. I'll speak to him."

When she did, Henry shrugged. He liked Moll: she was easy to please, laughed a lot, and had the most impressive tits.

"So does your wife," Kate said, feeling most awkward discussing Lucy's physical attributes.

"But her I can't bed, can I?" Henry retorted. "Not for some weeks yet."

"And when you can? Will you stop seeing your whore?"

"Probably not. Why should I? Mrs Malone runs an establishment that I frequent anyway, what with her excellent beer and good food."

"You have a young wife – a beautiful, devoted wife who has just given you two sons. It would behove you to treat her with courtesy, not give away presents you bought for her to your bit on the side."

In an exact copy of his defunct father, Henry raised first one, then the other brow. "I shall do as I please, but I will of course be mindful of my sweet wife's feelings." He frowned and tilted his head. "Are you sure you don't know what happened to Barbra?"

Kate shook her head. The last time she'd seen Barbra she'd been carrying a loaded breakfast tray on her way to her mistress. Kate gave her son a helpless look. "As if she'd gone up in smoke."

Henry nodded. "At times—" he began, but then broke off.

"Yes?" Kate leaned towards him.

"I…" He took a big breath and averted his face from her. "She can be somewhat disconcerting at times."

"Lucy?" Kate laughed. "Yes, of course she can. All that silence… But she's a sweet girl at heart, and she loves you."

"Hmm," Henry replied, sounding rather unconvinced.

Lucy had taken to carrying the little painting with her. Not always – never when she visited her mother – but now and then she held it in her petticoat pocket and liked that it was there. The sounds were at times too distracting, making it difficult for her to concentrate on other things, and sometimes days would go by when it remained behind lock and key in her drawer, but more and more, Lucy felt naked unless she carried the painting close.

There were individual voices now, and she listened in fascination as these anonymous people told her their tales. In particular, there was one voice, a dark, rich female voice, that she heard over and over again. This voice had the most to tell, and Lucy had no idea what language was being spoken but she understood it all anyway. A small girl growing up in an ancient city in the south of Spain, a girl whose mother died, who had a sister and a father that she dearly loved and saw burning at the stake.

Lucy covered her ears at this, shaking her head back and forth to stop herself from hearing the detailed description of how these unknown died. But she had to hear more, and it dawned on Lucy that it was this voice that was the creator of her magic square. Mostly, the voice spoke of a man. *Mi amor*, it whispered, and it lightened when it described long gone summer evenings when she and this man…such passion, Lucy thought, and her insides burnt with heat for her own man who still kept his distance, even now that the twins were nearly one month old.

She took her time one lovely July evening, dabbing perfume here and there, rolling up her cream-coloured stockings well above her knee before she gartered them with light blue ribbons. A new embroidered shift, the tight-fitting blue bodice he so liked, a silk petticoat to match and then her new skirts, slashed to show off petticoat and lace. Even her shoes looked new, whitened with chalk by the house slave. Her hair: she dug her fingers into it and twisted her head this way and that while considering what to do with it. Now, in summer, the deep, golden red was highlighted by streaks that were almost white, creating a most flattering effect, and Lucy decided it looked its best tumbling free – after all, they were not expecting guests.

Her stomach was tight with apprehension when she made her way down the stairs, smiling at Henry, who actually gaped. For a fleeting instant, Lucy was certain she had succeeded, that he had understood the message and was as eager as she was to rejoin her in their bed. An instant, then he bowed and said he was compromised elsewhere and had to be off.

Kate came forward to hug her, lips moving rapidly, and for once Lucy had no idea what she was saying, her eyes blurring with tears. She tore herself free, signed something about going outside, and fled the house for the garden. She sat for a long time on the bench that faced the flat expanse of the shallow bay. Somewhere to her far right, down in the port area, her husband was cavorting with his whore instead of being here with his wife. She took hold of her silken petticoat and tore it apart, ducking her head to hide her tears. He would pay for this, she vowed, and so would that smirking Moll.

The second girl was a mistake. She'd never intended for Mrs Malone's niece to see the picture, but before Lucy could react, the girl was gone, evaporated into nothingness. Lucy stuffed the picture into her loose pocket and turned to stare out of the window, her fingers gripping the sill. So quick! The weight against her thigh burnt and throbbed, and for a moment Lucy swayed, overcome by an urge to pull it out and stare at it herself. To drop away – what would it feel like? Lucy shuddered at the thought of never seeing her children again and leaned her forehead against the thick, greenish glass.

A hand closed on her arm, and Lucy near on leaped out of her own skin, startled to see Mrs Malone's face very close to hers.

"Have you seen Eileen?" Mrs Malone said, mouthing each word carefully.

Lucy did her best dim-witted look.

"Eileen!" Mrs Malone repeated, a fine spray of spittle flying from her mouth. She looked most upset, she did. "I saw her enter this room, moments after you."

Here? Lucy shook her head. No, she wrote, she had not

seen anyone, but then she'd been at the window, and so...
Mayhap Eileen had stepped outside for a breath of fresh air?

"I think not. She was to help me with your fitting."

Lucy spread her hands in a helpless gesture. Mrs Malone muttered something Lucy did not catch, shrewd eyes locked on Lucy's face. Quite uncomfortable it was, to be so inspected, and in particular given that Lucy knew that behind Mrs Malone's plump exterior whirred a brain as sharp as Lucy's own.

Moll was sent off to find Eileen, and came back flushed like a newly boiled ham, telling the madam that Eileen was not to be found, not in the house, not in the town.

Mrs Malone turned to frown at Lucy. "Are you sure? Have you not seen her?"

Lucy shook her head repeatedly, but didn't like it one bit when the madam's eyes locked on her neck and cheeks. Lucy rarely blushed, but right now she could feel her skin heating into a deep pink hue.

Henry was somewhat taken aback upon entering the bawdy house that evening. Mrs Malone had retired to her bed, the girls were moping, and only the man in the taproom was his normal, jovial self, saying with a little shrug that apparently the disappearance of Mrs Malone's niece had affected the whole complement of whores badly. Moll came over and dragged him away, recounting the incident in hushed tones as they made their way to one of the private rooms.

"I swear," Moll said, pouring them both some more wine, "she knows – something your wife knows. Poor Madam is most distraught about Eileen and she insists that your wife must be made to tell."

"Tell what?" Henry downed his wine in one long swallow. "She said she hadn't seen her."

"Madam saw Eileen enter the fitting room. That was the last time she was seen. Don't you find that somewhat strange?"

Henry blanched, recalling Barbra had disappeared in a similar, abrupt way. "Maybe Eileen had a fancy man of her own."

Moll shook her head. "If a girl plans to run away, she packs her best clothes. Eileen was in her housedress, and all her clothes and trinkets remain in her room. No, there's something here that isn't entirely right." She came over to sit on his lap, winding her arms round his neck. "She knows about us," she said in a shaky voice. "I can see it in her eyes, and she doesn't like it. It frightens me."

"It does?" Henry laughed. "My wife is no fool. She knows men have lustier appetites than one woman can cater to."

"A witch, Mrs Malone says she might be a witch," she breathed, a wary look in Henry's direction. He didn't reply, but filled up his glass with more wine and raised it with a shaking hand to his lips. A witch, he had married a witch. Fancies, he snorted to himself and emptied his glass.

Henry had drunk somewhat more than he should, and was weaving his way up the stairs to his bed, when the door to Lucy's room crashed open. He winced at the sound, raising a hand to his tender forehead. Light patterned the landing floor, and cast in shadow against all that light stood his wife, wearing something that shimmered transparently. Lord, she was beautiful, and now what was she doing? The neckline…slowly, she undid it and widened it, and her breasts popped out, free and unencumbered, the nipples a soft light pink. She held out her hand, and Henry stumbled towards her, in his befuddled state not truly caring if she might be a witch or not.

Lucy slipped out of bed and went over to use the chamber pot, padding like a gracious cat across the floor. The moon hung huge and white in the night sky, and in bed Henry scrunched up his eyes against the weak light and rolled over on his side, his naked skin covered by a sheen of perspiration.

Lucy opened the window wide to the night air, heavy with the scents of roses and honeysuckle. Well after midnight, and still warm enough that she could stand like this and not feel cold, even in the sea breeze that drifted into the chamber. She stopped by the desk and cocked her head. Yes, there it was: the soft muted sound of her painting. Poor

Eileen. How careless of her to leave the painting in the open as she had done, hoping that it would be Moll that came into the room first.

She studied the shape of her sleeping husband and pulled at her lip. She had smelled Moll on him, she had tasted her on his lips, and, worst of all, she had seen his mouth move as he came, and it hadn't been Lucy he had said. Eileen was a most unfortunate accident, but Moll still had to go.

Chapter 10

After several long discussions, Matthew and Alex had agreed that it was best to keep the fate of the Ingram girl something of a secret – at least from the children. As a consequence, Matthew's new rules, effectively making the woods out of bounds unless either he or one of his elder sons came along, were met with protesting groans, in particular from Sarah, who grew increasingly darker of countenance with each passing day.

"I'll be fine. I have Viggo." Sarah hugged the large grey dog that was her constant shadow.

"Your father says no," Alex said, thereby setting Sarah off again, a loud complaint that made Alex's ears hurt.

Finally, Alex decided there was no option but to explain why. Sarah listened and hitched her shoulders, saying that she could take care of herself, making Alex raise two exasperated brows.

"I can," Sarah insisted, chin jutting stubbornly. Hmm. Alex looked her over. Sarah scowled back, kicking at the ground as she muttered that it was not the same, not at all, to walk the rolling slopes of the forest with someone beside her.

"I know," Alex said. "I hate it too." She was equally constrained, but at least she could work off some of her edgy restlessness in the little clearing beside the graveyard. No one came there, and the huge mock oranges shielded her from the forest while she forced herself through sets of push-ups and crunches, slow concentrated revolving movements and quick combinations of kicks and hand chops. It was all coming back to her, and yesterday she had even managed to break through a thin branch. The outer side of her hand still hurt, but it had definitely been worth it. She regarded her daughter and impulsively took a decision.

"Come." She got to her feet. With a rather unenthusiastic Sarah at her heels, she set off for the graveyard, having first detoured by the house for one of Matthew's old shirts.

Sarah made huge eyes when Alex stopped and began to undress, looking even more confused when Alex pulled a man's shirt over her head and used a length of rope to tighten it round her waist. She folded her skirts and bodice, hung her stays from a branch, and stepped into the centre of the clearing, breathing in deeply.

"When I was a child, my mother decided I had to learn to defend myself," Alex said, smiling at her daughter. Blue-eyed and blonde, with thick hair falling down to her waist, Sarah was a throwback on Alex's Nordic antecedents, reminding her far too often of her father, Magnus – in temper as well, one might add, because Sarah Graham was as opinionated, strong-willed and fiery as Magnus had been.

"Defend yourself? Against what?"

"All sorts, mostly men with evil intents. And it has come in useful once or twice." Two men dead on a hillside, the third fleeing for his life.

"You've had to fight?" Sarah's voice fluted into a soprano.

"Yes." Alex chose not to detail further. "So I thought…" She stretched this way and that under the guarded eyes of her daughter. "…that maybe you should learn as well."

"Me?" Sarah laughed.

"You." Alex smiled back.

Afterwards, Sarah walked back down the slope, bright-eyed and rosy like a peony. For the first time in days, she was smiling, despite insisting that Mama had caused her permanent harm with that last awful exercise. She had watched, amazed, as Alex whirled and kicked, and had applauded when Alex chopped a branch in two, making Alex grin before she admitted that it hurt like hell.

"So, do you want to do this again?" Alex took Sarah's arm to turn them both in the direction of the kitchen plot. Mrs Parson was already there, hovering like a black butterfly over the flowering stands of bee balm and yarrow, her white capped head as neat as always. How on earth that woman managed to always look so clean was something of a mystery, in particular as Alex knew for a fact that Mrs Parson had never, ever taken a full body bath. Or if she had, it had been between midnight and dawn and involved no water carrying at all.

"Aye," Sarah replied to her question. "You do it every day?"

"I try." Alex swept her eyes over the rows and rows of vegetables to weed or harvest, and made a face. "Sometimes there's no time." She nodded in the direction of the closest rows, and Sarah bunched up her skirts, tied the straw bonnet tight around her head, and set to work.

"Beets for dinner today?" Sarah asked a bit later.

"Mmm," Alex replied through the carrot she was eating. "Not only," she assured her daughter at the crestfallen look on her face. "Agnes has some new cheese, and there is ham to go with it – and pudding." She looked over to where David and Samuel were moving the cows from one fenced pasture to the other, and saw Malcolm come moping after them. "He's been a bit sad lately," she said, nodding her head in his direction.

"He walks confused," Mrs Parson put in from behind them, coming down the slope with her basket clutched tightly in both hands as a balance aid. She sat down on the fallen log they used for a bench, her black eyes focused on faraway Malcolm. "It's done him no good to have his mother visit, and now he's all too aware that he, of all the children here, doesn't have his mam with him."

"He misses her," Sarah said.

"I don't think so," Mrs Parson replied, "or at least he didn't, not until she made a reappearance. But now…"

"Now, he compares and finds Betty lacking," Alex sighed. "Twice, I've heard him tell her she isn't his real mother."

"Until she slaps him and tells him that for all purposes she is, he'll continue doing that," Mrs Parson said. "He needs her to show him she cares enough for him to punish him."

"Umm," Alex protested. Had she ever punished Ian? She couldn't recall that she had. But she had tolerated no disobedience either, insisting that he bathe and clean his teeth just as her own children did, overriding any protest by folding her arms over her chest and staring him down.

"Are they staying here?" Sarah asked. "Jenny and her husband, I mean."

"I sincerely hope not!" Alex said, imagining far too frequent run-ins with Jenny – and Patrick. "Besides, Thomas said Patrick has a nice business in Charles Towne, a thriving carpentry shop."

"I suppose she misses her children," Sarah said.

"She should have thought of that before she took another man to bed," Mrs Parson snorted.

"Mama, Mama!" David came leaping up the hill, a thin length of maple brandished as a sword over his head. "Samuel says that d'Artagnan wasn't truly a musketeer, not like the other three."

"He's right," Alex replied with a smile, "at least to begin with. But, over time, he became an officer of the Musketeers, I think." At times, she regretted having told them this story, and even more because her whole family, adults included, often demanded a retelling.

"Ha!" David turned triumphantly to his two younger brothers and his nephew who had tagged him up the hill. "You see? I was right. It's d'Artagnan who's the best musketeer."

"That wasn't what I said," Alex said. "I said Samuel was right."

Samuel gave her a fleeting smile and rushed off in pursuit of the others, calling loudly that if he wasn't to be d'Artagnan then he preferred to be Buckingham, albeit that he was an Englishman and a royalist to boot.

"Royalist?" Alex sank down to sit. "The Three Musketeers was before the Civil War."

"And so it follows that the Duke of Buckingham was indeed a royalist, no? Not that I hold it against him, seeing as he didn't know there was an alternative." Mrs Parson had gotten to her feet and was following the heated swordplay further down the slope with keen interest. "That young David, he would make a right fine soldier. Cuts a dashing figure, no?"

"Not on the books," Alex said. He would be boarding with his aunt and uncle for the coming two years, to study at the recently opened grammar school in Providence with Minister Allerton, and then Matthew thought to apprentice him to the gunsmith in Providence. Alex wasn't too enthused, and neither was David, but when Alex asked him what he really wanted, he just shook his head and looked away.

"Walk?" Matthew said after supper, holding out his hand to Alex.

"Swim," she said, tugging at her bodice.

"Aye, it's a trifle hot," Matthew said.

"Sweltering is the word I'd use." Alex flapped her hands at the clouds of midgets that hung like a trailing veil around their heads.

"Good weather for the wheat. Just a few more days and then we start bringing it in." A good year, he nodded to himself, with cartloads of timber ready to sell, the hay already in, and the crops standing golden in his fields. He sniffed the air and scanned the horizon for any signs of rain. Not a cloud; only this infinite span of clear sky that was now shifting from palest white to the deep violet of a summer night. He held Alex's hand and ran his finger over the single adornment his wife had ever had from him: a dark sapphire in a heavy band of gold – her wedding ring. Not that she needed anything more, but at times he wished he could have given her pearls and bracelets, precious gems to decorate her hair with.

"What?" she asked perceptively.

He opened his mouth to tell her but decided not to. Instead, he would buy her something nice once he had the harvest in and sold. Mayhap he could ask Kate to help him choose something – without Alex ever finding out, of course.

They collected people on their short walk down to the water: Adam skipped up to take his mama's hand, David and Samuel came sprinting after them, Sarah called that she was coming too, and suddenly the whole household was on the move towards the river, the children exuberant and chattering, the adults grumbling about the midges and the heat.

"Next time, we take a huge detour," Alex mumbled to Matthew. She looked at their milling family and rolled her eyes.

"A bloody tribe," she said, making Matthew laugh. "Look at all these people!"

Much later, Alex sat back on her heels and patted Matthew on his reddened rump. "All done."

"Uh." He stretched lazily. His whole back was tingling after her thorough ministrations, blood flowing freely through muscles that tended to stiffen more and more. He rolled over on his side, his eyes heavy as he hung somewhere between sleep and wakefulness. Alex lifted her fingers to her own lips first and then pressed them to his.

"Sleep," she suggested, pulling the sheets and quilts up around him.

"Nhhh," he agreed, but he kept his eyes slightly open, watching Alex as she went about her evening ablutions. She cleaned her teeth as carefully as she always did, rinsed her mouth with peppermint water, and shook out her hair. Matthew smiled at how she scrutinised her face in the wee mirror, fingers massaging her skin. On the small table lay a copy of the Aeneid, and Alex flipped it open to where they'd left off latest.

"Bloody man," she muttered, as she always did when she read how Aeneas left Dido behind to embark on the last leg of his journey to Italy.

"He had no choice," Matthew mumbled. "He had to go; his fate was calling to him."

"Huh," Alex snorted and closed the book before blowing out the candle. "Typical male." She slipped into bed.

"Typical male?" Matthew snuggled up close. "You don't think women have fates to fulfil?"

"We don't have time to," Alex said with certain acidity. "We drown in the day to day."

And yet you were fated to fall into my time, he thought, his hold on her tightening. Fated since you were born to be mine. But he didn't say anything. He just kissed the side of her neck.

*

Somewhere in the early hours before dawn proper, Matthew woke, eyes flying open. The dogs were barking, there was a distant yipping, human voices raised in fear, and what was that smell? Fire! But not anywhere close, he calmed himself, scrabbling for his clothes, not any of the buildings.

Alex sat up and blinked, her hair standing in tufts around her face. And then she was on her feet, racing after him through the door with a shawl thrown over her shift and nothing much else.

"Indians?" she gasped.

Matthew didn't reply, running barefoot towards the burning wheat fields.

He twisted in helpless frustration as he watched his crops go up in smoke. Not all of them, thank heavens, he had other fields further off, but this was at least half of it. Nothing left to set aside, he thought bitterly. But how? Indians had never done something like this before. The night breeze flowed from the river to the house, and he could see where the fire had taken hold at the furthest edge to spread upwards. Here and there, he could make out islands of unharmed wheat standing high against the scorched ground that surrounded them.

His sons were already digging, creating channels of damp earth to contain the fire, keep it away from the pastures and the beasts. Ian had crawled in among the animals to soothe them, and there was John and Sarah and Naomi and even his Alex, all rushing to help with the digging. But he stood rooted to the spot and watched the conflagration sputter out and die.

"Da?" Ian's sharp voice broke through Matthew's paralysis. "Da? Come here, aye?"

Not Indians, Matthew stated a few minutes later, staring down at the dead cow. The poor beast had been disembowelled, the heart skewered with a knife and prominently displayed. No, this bore all the hallmarks of the Burleys, a taunting example of how close as they could get without anyone noticing. Matthew met Ian's eyes over the carcass and nodded imperceptibly. War, this was war, and the Burleys were going to die. It was years since Matthew had felt a rage such as this: a slow, seeping blackness that welled from deep in his gut and spread to layer everything inside of him. Ian stiffened, his hand closing on the handle of his dirk, and Matthew knew that Ian was choking on bitterness. It wouldn't be him riding off beside Matthew to hunt the Burleys down – he no longer could.

"You're needed here," Matthew said.

"I'm of no use." Ian turned away into the forest, limping heavily as he ducked out of sight.

It wasn't until dawn that they found the man. Spread-eagled and very dead, the white man was tied to two saplings, his face towards the rising sun. His shirt was stiff with drying blood. In death, his dull eyes stared at nothing at all, and the ground beneath him was dark with blood and excrement.

"So it was Indians you heard," Mark commented to Matthew as he sliced the thongs that suspended the man in the air.

"Aye, it would seem so," Matthew said. "Interrupting the Burleys before they could do us more mischief or harm."

Alex's hand was suddenly in his, a small lump of cold fear that he tried to rub some warmth into with his thumb. He didn't want to look at her, didn't want to see in her face what he was sure she could see in his. This was Qaachow's work, a silent reminder that his men were close and kept the Grahams safe – at a price, of course.

At times, Matthew wished Alex had never saved the Indian wean, but what was she to do when she found Qaachow's starving son? Leave him to die? In gratitude, Qaachow had pronounced Samuel his foster son, but what had once seemed but a cordial gesture had over the years become something of a threat, with Qaachow making it very clear that he intended to claim on Matthew's promise and take Samuel with him to spend a year amongst the Indians.

Three times over the last few years, Qaachow had come by to visit, and every time his eyes had hung hungrily on Samuel. Matthew scuffed at the ground. Alex tightened her hold on his hand, a silent presence beside him that was begging him to say something reassuring, lie even. But what was there to say? There was nothing he could do. For years, his family and his home had been kept safe by the vigilant presence of Qaachow and his men, and all because Samuel was the Indian leader's foster son.

"We could send him away," Alex said once the morning regained some semblance of normality. "If we send him down with David to Providence, well then, he isn't here, is he?"

Matthew grunted. He doubted they'd get very far from home before they found themselves surrounded by a band of Indians.

"But we must try," Alex said.

Matthew sank his knife into the tabletop and turned towards her with a heavy sigh. "I've promised, Alex. And somehow Qaachow will come for Samuel. I don't think it will help the lad to be abducted by force."

"So we just let him go?" Alex breathed, her eyes very vulnerable.

"Aye, lass. We just let him go and put a brave face on it. An apprenticeship if you like, and then he'll come back to us."

"I don't think I can," Alex said.

"I don't think I can either, but we don't have much choice." He kissed her bowed head and stood up, returning his knife to its customary place in his belt. "It isn't yet. Samuel is only ten. Qaachow said twelve."

In the passageway between the parlour and the kitchen, Samuel sank down to sit huddled on the floor. They didn't want him to go, and yet they would turn him over to the Indians. It made his stomach shrink down to the size of one of Mama's prunes. He was only ten, he reminded himself, not yet twelve, and mayhap he could run away before. His Indian foster father intimidated him. He didn't want to go with him; he wanted to stay here, at home with Mama and Da and his brothers. No choice. His da was hogtied by his promise. He dug his fingers hard into his eyes to stop himself from crying, and counted slowly up to a hundred before getting back to his feet. Not yet, he reminded himself, not yet, and mayhap, if he was lucky, Qaachow would die before.

Chapter 11

It was a horrible job to slaughter one pig, let alone six. Alex used the back of her hand to push a stray lock of hair out of the way, and looked with disgust at her blood-spattered apron.

Two days straight, they'd been at it, with Ian in charge of the actual killing, gutting and draining while she supervised the flaying and the cutting up. Dismemberment, she grimaced, looking down at the bucket full of those parts they wouldn't be using themselves. The dogs had been pacing around in anticipation for hours, and from the pig pen she could hear the sow grunt and scrabble, the quivering snout signalling she expected her share as well.

"They're your babies," Alex said sternly, making Ian laugh. The sow just wagged her little curled tail all the harder. "If we sell all of it, it'll make up some of the shortfall from the wheat."

"Some, but not all. We also have timber to sell, and cheese and honey, but it's still a big loss." Ian stretched this way and that, seemingly not that incapacitated despite the day's heavy work.

Alex closed the door on the smoking shed, and for an instant rested against it. All of her hurt; from her hands to her arms to the lower region of her back, but at least now it was all done. Bristles, skin to be cured into leather, lard, the hams meant for smoking already lying in brine inside the shed, and here came Agnes to carry back the last bucket of clean intestines for the sausage making which Alex had delegated to Mrs Parson. Tonight, when the men came back, there'd be ribs for a late supper, barbecued under the expert eye of Naomi in celebration of Agnes' and John's newborn daughter.

Alex threw a look to where Ian had propped up his loaded musket. Further up the slope, Sarah was sitting with a musket over her knees, and even Alex was armed – rather uselessly, as she seriously doubted she'd be able to hit anything with the cavalry pistol she'd placed some yards away. For the last few weeks, Matthew and three of his sons had scoured the woods, looking for any trace of the Burleys, but it would seem the Indians had done a good job of scaring them away. Thank heavens for that, Alex thought, her eyes sliding over to where Samuel sat very alone, fondling one of the cats.

"Damn those Burley bastards," she said out loud. She didn't want to be constantly on her guard, hated that those accursed brothers should have the power to restrict their lives this way.

"Aye." Ian's face tightened into a black scowl.

Alex rolled her eyes. Ian had major problems accepting the fact that he couldn't take part in the ongoing Burley hunt. "Consider the alternatives," she said. "You could have died, or been confined to your bed."

"Or I could still be whole."

"Yes," she said, cupping his cheek. "Yes, Ian, you're right. But at least you're still here, with us." With me, she meant.

Briefly, he covered her hand with his. There was the slightest of nods and a weak attempt at a smile before he went back to his work.

She straightened up and shoved all thoughts of the Burleys firmly out of her head, just as she had outlawed all those frightening images of a hurt or dying Matthew that popped up every time he rode off, grim-faced and emerald-eyed, his hand on his musket. No, she would concentrate on trivia instead, like the coleslaw she was making for tonight.

She had just covered the earthenware bowl full of shredded cabbage, carrots, onions and her secret dressing when a group of men rode into the yard. For an instant, she was convinced it was the Burleys, but then she saw Ian limp across the yard towards them, empty-handed, and relaxed.

She peered through the thick window glass: the Chisholms – and the priest! In a very bad way, she might add, seeing the slight man loll back against the man riding with him. Mrs Parson was already outside, shooting questions with the speed of a machine gun while her arm waved in the direction of the kitchen. Alex sighed and poured hot water and salt on the table, scrubbing it in preparation for its double duty as operation theatre.

"Oh dear." Alex swallowed, placing a finger on the swollen lower extremity. The priest yelped at her light touch, his skin tight as a drum over something that seemed to be seething inside. It stank: a heavy, putrid scent that made Alex want to gag.

Mrs Parson frowned, her nose almost touching the wound. "When did this happen?"

"A week ago? Ten days?" Martin Chisholm shrugged to show he didn't quite collect. "A scythe."

"Aye, I can see that," Mrs Parson replied. "Lying about, was it?"

"No," Paul, the other Chisholm brother, replied snappishly. "But he's a clumsy man and has clearly never wielded one before."

Mrs Parson straightened up and handed a leather strap to Paul, who coaxed it in between the clenched teeth of the semi-conscious priest before beckoning Alex closer. "You cut."

Alex nodded. Normal repartition of labour these last few years, ever since Mrs Parson's hands had begun to tremble continuously. Betty was already pulping garlic and bee balm into a green mash, the battered kettle was whistling with boiling water, and Mrs Parson rinsed out a bowl, added handfuls of salt, lavender, bee balm and St. John's wort before pouring hissing water over it all. The priest had time to sniff appreciatively before the sterilised knife sank into his leg.

"Worse patient I've ever had," Mrs Parson said once it was over. Alex agreed. The man had bucked like an unbroken horse on the table, and the knife had cut far too deep, much, much too deep. Blood and pus had spurted wildly, and only Martin's quick reactions, throwing himself across the priest to pin him down, had allowed some modicum of control over the situation. Now, the shin was stitched from ankle to halfway up his calf and wrapped in bandages that seeped green from the mash with which they had covered his leg.

"We may need to open it again," Mrs Parson sighed.

"Let's hope that won't be necessary, and, if it is, someone else will have to cut." First the pigs and then this. Alex felt like Sweeney Todd.

Matthew returned home after yet another wasted day spent chasing after the Burleys – everything pointed to the accursed brothers having left the area, and although relieved, it also made Matthew seethe. He needed to find them, kill them, for his family to be safe. He was not overly pleased to find Father Carlos Muñoz installed in the small room just off the parlour, not that he had anything against the man as such – except for the obvious fact that he was a papist priest – but he could see how affected Alex was by his presence, eyes gluing themselves to the heart-shaped face, the soft curls and the long, dark lashes. Her lost son, he realised. In everything, she was imagining it was Isaac sitting before her.

Nor did he like the fact that they conversed in Spanish, effectively excluding him from the discussions. After a whole evening attempting to decipher what was being said, he'd had enough.

"English," he said.

"Sorry," she muttered, "it's just—"

"Aye, I know. You may of course speak Spanish when you're alone, but not otherwise."

"My apologies, Mr Graham," Father Muñoz said. "It was not our intention to be rude."

To Matthew's relief, Alex had very little time to spend at Father Muñoz's bedside, and even less when Minister Allerton rode in two days later, accompanied by his three daughters, Ruth, and two hired menservants.

If nothing else, his wife's attention was at times entirely diverted by the way their eldest daughter behaved around the minister, commenting in a rather dark voice that did he notice how their Ruth shone up in Julian's presence and dimmed when he left?

Aye, of course he did but unlike Alex, he wasn't overly worried about the age gap – after all, it was common that men took a second wife if their first passed, and of course a man would look first for a fertile replacement. Also, it was apparent to him that Julian was as smitten by Ruth as Ruth was smitten by him, but Julian was struggling with this, his eyes flitting often from Ruth to Temperance and back again. No, Matthew decided, should Julian come asking, he would say yes, no matter that Alex would in all probability bury her nails in his back.

"I'll never speak to you again if you do," Alex threatened when he told her this one morning.

"Aye, you will. You know she wants it too." He kicked bedlinen and quilts out of the way, settling himself beside her in the bed.

"It's an infatuation! A young girl mistaking admiration for a man she respects with love."

"Admiration and respect seem to me good, stable foundation stones to build a marriage on," Matthew said with a grin. "It's seemly in a wife that she regard her husband with utmost devotion and respect." He laughed at her angry face and pulled her close. She set her hands to his chest and shoved.

He still loved this game of theirs: a half-aggressive foreplay where she tried to break free, pretending to deny him, while he demanded her submission, reminding her with his body and his hands that she was his wife, and his wife never, ever denied him – anything.

Afterwards, he remained heavy on top of her, very much in place. Her hands were drifting with extreme gentleness over his hair and back, small, strong fingers tracing the contours of his neck, his shoulders, the rounding of his buttocks. With the early morning sun, their bedroom was alive with colour, the small panes of red and green glass that he had bought her some years ago throwing multi-hued light to dapple the well-scrubbed floor, the white linen and their bodies. He kissed a red reflection on her cheek and moved to lie beside her, one leg over hers.

"Daniel might not like it."

Alex snorted. "Of course he won't. Imagine having your baby sister as your mother-in-law! It's probably borderline incestuous."

Alex raised the question a few hours later with the priest, more to distract him from her examination of his leg than out of any genuine interest in his expert opinion.

"No, I don't think so." Father Muñoz creased his brow together in deep thought. "It's perhaps somewhat irregular, but not incestuous."

"Too bad," Alex muttered, making the priest laugh. He stopped laughing rather abruptly when she undid the bandages and pushed hard against the skin on either side of his healing gash. "Does it hurt?"

"Yes," he squeaked.

She pressed a finger into his undamaged shin. "Does that hurt?"

"Yes."

"Sissy," Alex said under her breath. His leg seemed to be healing, but she was worried the damage to muscles and tendons was such that he would never walk with ease again.

He shrugged when she told him this. "I still have a leg, and I don't use it much in my daily work," he said, surprising her into a burst of laughter.

Conversation became somewhat livelier with two men of God in the house – maybe a bit too lively, Alex sighed, when Father Muñoz and Minister Allerton settled down for yet another intense religious debate, the minister seconded by Daniel, the priest fighting his corner alone.

Father Muñoz sat up straighter and looked at Minister Allerton.

"No." He shook his head. "Absolutely not. God allows our actions to speak for us."

"Of course," Minister Allerton said, "if we belong to the chosen few." He gave the young priest a challenging look.

"Hmph!" Father Muñoz drank deeply from his mug of beer. "God is not that fickle. We live on this earth a short while, and it's in many ways a testing ground for eternal life that comes later. God is merciful and forgives us our trespasses on behalf of His Son. He sees us labour and strive to be good, and He is pleased. He sees us fall into a life of evil, and He decides if the stay in purgatory will be long and painful or if we go to hell directly. But it's the quality of our sins and the genuineness of our repentance that ultimately decide our eternal fate."

Too right, Alex agreed, even if she sincerely hoped God was somewhat selective when it came to deathbed repentance. If not, heaven would be chock-full of some rather nasty types.

"Purgatory!" Minister Allerton waved dismissively. "Nowhere in the scriptures is that mentioned. It's nothing but a figment of imagination that allows the dying sinners to hope they may still be saved."

"Not to me," Father Muñoz said, looking quite mulish. "To me, God is more prone to forgive than damn, and as such He has created one last opportunity for the lost soul to gain entry to heaven."

The argument went on and on, the churchmen plunging deeper and deeper into the scriptures and the history of the Christian Church.

"Why be good?" Father Muñoz argued. "Why should we strive to lead exemplary lives if God has already preordained who goes to Heaven?"

"Why be good?" Minister Allerton replied mockingly. "Why strive to lead exemplary lives if all you have to do is beg forgiveness for your sins before you die?"

Most of the adults around the table nodded in agreement.

"Lewd and sinful," Mrs Parson muttered to Alex. "All papists are, more or less. And then, on their deathbed, they recant. Not that it helps the misguided souls, bound for hell as they are. Pity on the wee priest who seems a good enough man – just like his father."

"Hmm," Alex said as neutrally as she could, and then brought the whole discussion to a halt by plonking down the pudding dish in the middle of the table.

The minister was an enthusiastic and hard-working extra pair of hands during the harvest, resulting in him eating like a horse and retiring more or less immediately after supper, so tired those beautiful grey eyes of his were reduced to narrow slits. His daughters and Ruth always left when he did, and mostly Sarah would trail after Ruth, thereby leaving the parlour to Alex, Matthew, Mrs Parson and the priest, who never seemed tired at night – probably on account of his late mornings.

"My father," Father Muñoz spoke haltingly. "*¿Mi padre, cómo era?*"

Alex sat back in her armchair and let her mending sink to her lap.

"A bit of a fop." She grinned, recalling the first time she had met him. "All ribbons and lace and cuffs and high-heeled boots and a most impressive hat!"

Mrs Parson chuckled from where she sat. "An eye-catching gentleman, he was, Don Benito."

"You knew him too?" Father Muñoz sounded very surprised – and eager.

"Oh aye. I had the pleasure of several months in his company," Mrs Parson said. "It was I that found out, no? That added two and two together."

"She spied on him." Alex rolled her eyes. "Probably ogling him on the sly."

Father Muñoz went a vivid red. "He was a priest!"

"We didn't know that. It wasn't something he announced to the world, was it? And he was a bonny man, he was, with right well-turned legs." Mrs Parson smiled and looked at the priest. "You look like him, not that I've seen you in the flesh as I did him, but—"

"He presented himself as a royal envoy," Alex interrupted, "destined to the colonies on behalf of the king."

"The king? Charles that is?" Matthew leaned forward with interest.

Alex nodded. "Yes, and if you ask me, he's a closet Catholic – the king, I mean."

"Oh aye? And you would know how?" Matthew gave her a fond smile, hovering very close to being patronising.

"Call it a gut feeling." His mother was a devout Catholic; his brother had openly converted; he had never allowed persecution of Catholics – Alex ticked off one argument after the other. "Let's just say he definitely isn't Presbyterian – a bit too lax morally." That made Father Muñoz frown.

"It's true," Alex said, "all those mistresses, his poor queen humiliated by an endless procession of royal bastards, and the brother has quite an eye for the girls as well, as we hear it."

"The Duke of York is a most devout man," Father Muñoz said primly. "When I saw him last, he seemed utterly devoted to his young wife, Maria de Modena."

"You've met him?" Alex asked.

"Yes," the priest replied, "twice."

"And does he have the Stuart nose?" Mrs Parson asked.

"The nose?" The priest sounded bewildered.

"Aye." Mrs Parson mimed a gigantic beak.

"Ah." The priest laughed. "I suppose he does. I only saw him but briefly – messengers are rarely dealt with face to face by the royals, even when they come from the Holy See. Besides, what's important is that he has a young Catholic wife – surely there will be issue to ensure a strong Catholic line of kings on the English throne."

Alex scoffed. "It won't happen."

"How would you know?" Father Muñoz frowned.

"I just do. One Catholic king the English may countenance, but a Catholic line – never. Anyway," she said, bringing them back to the original subject, "it was Mrs Parson here who caught on."

"Aye, I saw the hair shirt," Mrs Parson nodded, "and then…" She looked somewhat embarrassed. "I found his vestments, and his rosary beads."

"Oh, just like that?" Father Muñoz said. "Lying about in the open?"

"No," Mrs Parson replied, snapping her mouth closed with an audible click.

"Poor man," Alex said, "living in that horrible hair shirt. His skin was covered in rash, and it itched and itched, making him scratch himself as if he had fleas or something."

Father Muñoz brushed at his sleeves and nodded. "A penance – and rightly so."

"You think?" Alex gave him an irritated look. "And how would you know? Did you live his life?"

"He broke his vows." Father Muñoz sounded priggish.

"He loved," Alex corrected, "and if he hadn't, you wouldn't have existed, would you?"

"And maybe that would have been just as well," Father Muñoz said in a voice so desolate all three of them turned towards him.

Chapter 12

Harvest time was as exhausting as it always was: long days spent in the vegetable patch, evenings in the kitchen preserving what had been harvested from the garden, and on top of that a convalescent patient. As his strength returned, Carlos Muñoz insisted that he should help as well as he could, and so Alex took him along to reap raspberries.

As they worked, she told him about his father, doing her best to describe a man with likes and dislikes, views and opinions. She told him of Don Benito's tendency to sing, no matter that he couldn't hold a tune if his life depended on it, of how hopeless he was at chess, and of how prone he was to vicious headaches.

"Just like me!" Carlos said a couple of times, dark eyes looking at Alex with such hunger that she realised no one had ever spoken about Don Benito before – unless it was to condemn him as a sinner bound for everlasting hell. Mostly, it was Don Benito's innate sweetness she emphasised, how compassionate he was, how his eyes would rest upon them all with warmth and humour.

Haltingly, she told him of the fight that had resulted in his death, and how he had insisted he be buried in his hair shirt, nothing else. "He took a blade meant for me. It was all my fault."

"I am sure he has forgiven you for that," Carlos said with a small smile. "You were his friend."

Alex nodded, her eyes filling with tears. "And he was mine; a good, generous man."

Once they were done with the berries, Alex got to her feet and stretched, bending this way and that in slow, regular movements.

"Backache," she said at his surprised expression.

"Ah." He nodded, and she could swear he was trying to calculate her age.

She suppressed a grin. Father Muñoz had spent the last few minutes throwing her furtive, if admiring glances. For all that he was a priest, he was a typical male, his eyes having a tendency to glue themselves to her chest. She grabbed an empty basket and made her way to the opposite side of the garden, Father Carlos limping along beside her.

"Your father had been sent to spread the word of God among the Indians," Alex said, now picking corncobs.

"The Indians?" Carlos threw a timorous look at the surrounding forest.

"*Sí.* He was to stay among them until he had a congregation of twenty or died, whichever came first. It would probably have been death. He was very frightened. He'd heard all these terrible stories about how the Indians would roast missionaries to death, or make sport of killing them piece by piece."

"Do they?" Carlos asked with a quaver. "*¿Los Indios, matan a los misionarios?*"

"At times, I imagine. After all, to them, hearing about our God must be as heretic as it would be to you to hear of their gods."

"But our God is the single true God!"

"He is?" Alex said. "Can you prove it?"

Over the carrots, Carlos Muñoz told her of how his uncle had begotten sons of his own, and how the unwanted nephew had been turned over to a nearby monastery to raise. He was only six, and already given in vocation to God, with his uncle Raúl promising the monks a sizeable monetary donation once the boy had taken full vows.

"So I did," Carlos said with a shrug.

"And was that what you wanted to do?" she asked, overwhelmed with pity for the orphaned and abandoned little boy she could see in her head.

"No." Carlos looked over to where the Graham men were returning from the fields. "I wanted to be a seafarer, like *Cristobal Colón* and discover new lands and territories."

"So why?" Alex said. "*¿Porqué?* Why did you take your

vows if you weren't sure this was what you wanted to do?"

He twisted his mouth into a wry smile. "I was made to see reason, and now I am well reconciled to the fact." He stared out at the forest and crossed himself. "Maybe I can achieve what my father was sent out to do: to bring the word of God to the heathen."

"Don't be ridiculous! I told you, didn't I? They might kill you."

Carlos shrugged. "I have been charged with a holy mission – just like my father. Besides, if it happens, it happens. And *Tío Raúl* would be very pleased – especially if I were to die." With that he turned away and began harvesting the squash.

"He's spent time in Ireland in preparation for coming here," Julian Allerton told Matthew, watching the slight priest hobble down in their direction.

"Aye, you can hear it in his English," Matthew nodded. "I suppose it makes it easier to meet his congregation. It's not as if the Chisholms have much Latin."

"Enough, I dare say," Julian said. "They can't say Mass or take the sacraments without it."

"Learning by rote is not knowing for real." Matthew had no Latin, and he was intensely jealous of Daniel for having it, and now David would soon as well. As did Jacob, he reminded himself, feeling a swelling pride that his sons should be better educated than he himself was.

"Is he here purely as a priest?" Julian asked.

Matthew had been wondering that himself. After all, Carlos Muñoz was a Spaniard.

"I don't know, but he is a mite young to be entrusted with espionage."

"Too young?" Julian laughed. "Surely it is the young and daring that stick their heads into the hornets' nest."

"He's been sent to bring the comfort of the Holy Church to the Chisholms – and to evaluate the possibility of a concerted effort to bring Catholicism to the Indians," Alex told both

103

of them later that afternoon. "Spreading the True Faith is a major concern for the Spanish crown."

"Oh aye," Matthew agreed, "and just by chance it would halt any Protestant expansion into the wilds."

"Really!" Alex grinned. "How can you think they might be that wily?" She jerked her head to where Carlos was sitting in the shade. "It scares him silly, to ride out among the savages."

"It should," Julian said. "They don't, as a rule, take kindly to missionaries."

"And still he'll go," she sighed. "Even more now that I've told him his father was meant to do it."

"God help him," Julian Allerton uttered with sincerity. He looked over to where Ruth was sitting with the other girls. As if she'd felt his eyes upon her, Ruth raised her face to Julian and flashed him a blinding smile, making him smile in return.

Alex watched this side play in silence and bored her eyes into Julian until he flushed.

"Umm..." he stammered. "Err..." He furrowed his brow for an instant. "Have you heard about the girls in Providence?" Without waiting for their answer, he launched himself into a rather long monologue.

"How do you mean, disappear?" Alex slipped her hand hard into Matthew's. Unexplained disappearances could of course mean a lot of things, but her knees were of the firm conviction that this was bad, really bad.

"There one moment, gone the next," the minister said. "Three – no four – so far. All young women." He shook his head at that and threw another look in the direction of the girls seated beneath the spreading white oak. "First, it was a slave girl at the Jones' place; then it was Eileen, Mrs Malone's little niece, you know?"

Matthew nodded that he did, making Alex give him a very long look.

"And then another girl at Mrs Malone's, a Cornish girl called Moll, and that same day a girl who was sent on an errand by her mother." Julian shook his head. "There is rumour that it may all have something to do with Henry Jones, and, of course, people suddenly recall his father's sordid business."

Alex made a face: Dominic Jones had been a detestable man with a heart the size of a pea – and in the business of abducting people, no matter colour, and selling them like slaves.

"I've told the girls they may not go out alone," Julian finished, "and the elders are considering putting into place some kind of voluntary constabulary."

"How terrible," Alex said. "Poor girls! Stolen away, no doubt."

Matthew tightened his hold on her hand. "Aye, like the Ingram lass."

"The Ingram girl?" Julian leaned forward. "What happened to her?"

"The Burleys," Matthew said, "that's what happened to her."

Alex pressed her leg against his, and she just had to glance at her girls and ensure they were still there, laughing with Temperance and Patience.

Several weeks of hard work took their toll, and, on a Sunday in August, the whole Graham house lay sunk deep in sleep when Alex woke. She dressed, patted Matthew on his back, and slipped out, stopping to grab something in the pantry.

It had rained during the night, a mild summer rain, and now the world lay sparkling under the rising sun. The white oak rustled in the breeze; over by the barn, a stand of hollyhocks dipped and bowed, their flowers dashes of pink against the silvered grey of the wooden walls. The rosebush that grew by the door shivered in a sudden gust of wind, showering the ground below it with scented, white petals. Standing on the door stoop, Alex stretched and caught sight of Jacob, moving at a steady pace in the direction of the river. Her son would probably appreciate her company – as well as his share of the cinnamon bun she carried in her apron pocket – so she hurried after him, unwilling to break the scented peace of the morning by calling out his name.

After a while, she realised he was walking and stopping, walking some more and stopping. She kept her distance, observing his slow progress, and it came to her that what she was seeing him do was what she had watched Matthew do well over fifteen years ago at Hillview. He was saying goodbye – to trees and stones and slopes, to fields and woods – and finally he stood before the river. From the set of his shoulders, Alex suspected he might be weeping, so she took her time walking down the last incline. He turned when he heard her, a rueful smile hovering over his long mouth, sat down on the log, and patted for her to come and sit beside him.

"You're leaving." Alex felt her heart disintegrate into bits and pieces that landed with heavy plonks in her stomach.

Jacob just nodded, keeping his eyes on the shimmering surface of the river. "I'm no longer at home here," he said simply.

"You've outgrown it, just like Daniel has outgrown it."

"No." Jacob shook his head. "That's not it. I love my home, would like nothing more than to stay and build a life here. But how?"

"We could help you perhaps," Alex tried, hearing the eager tone in her voice.

Jacob dropped his eyes to his hands and shook his head again. "I'm an educated man," he said with a faint smile. "A trained apothecary, no less, and I want to use my knowledge, somehow."

Alex blew out her cheeks, raised a hand to brush at his thick, fair hair. For the last few years, he'd worked here and there: a stint in Boston, a town he'd found far too straight-laced; half a year down in Jamestown where he had collected the seeds of several rare plants and sent back to that Master Castain in London; some months at the apothecary in St Mary's City, working with a man who unfortunately had a son to take over after him.

Jacob lobbed a stone to land in the water. "I'm going

106

back to London. Master Castain has offered me a share in his business – and his daughter."

"And do you like her?" Alex asked, forcing herself away from the realisation that this time he would leave for good and she would never see him again.

Jacob shrugged. "Well enough. A kitten with claws is Isabelle Castain, but pretty and rich."

"You can't marry someone because you like her well enough, or because she's rich. You have to love them."

Jacob gave her an irritated look. "Most make do with less," he said in a quiet voice that made Alex want to cry.

"Not you, not my beautiful Jacob. You must find a woman with whom to share your life and heart."

He stared out at the flowing water before them. "Not everyone does, Mama." He put an arm around her and hugged her. "But Isabelle is bonny and wild, and has a tongue on her that makes me at times laugh, at times want to whip her. She makes me laugh a lot, aye?"

"She was twelve last time you saw her – a child, Jacob. You've no idea what kind of woman she is growing into."

"Nay, and nor is it a prerequisite that I wed her." He caught her eyes and smiled. "I don't aspire to what you and Da have, but I'd like to have someone to return home to."

"You should aspire to what we have. Look at your brothers. They've found it."

Jacob tilted his head at her, his eyes a vivid green in the morning sun. "You think? Ian and Betty, aye, perhaps. Mark and Naomi… Oh aye, they like each other, those two, but is it like the heat that burns between you and Da? Nay, I don't think so."

"Of course it is," Alex said, even though she knew she was lying. Naomi and Mark were content, suitably matched and the best of friends, but no, it was nowhere close to what bubbled in the air whenever she rested her eyes on her Matthew.

"Symbiosis, that is you and Da. You can't truly live the one without the other. It would be like taking a fish out of water and leave it to flop on land." Jacob slid off the log to sit on the ground instead, using the trunk as a backrest.

"You make it sound like a disease or a weakness." Alex was shaken by this accurate description.

"I'm jealous, I think," he said softly.

"Oh, Jacob! You're not yet twenty-one, sweetie. I was an ancient twenty-six when I met your father." She slid down to sit beside him, trying to cradle his much longer body against her own.

"And Ruth is not quite seventeen, and she has already found it."

Alex sat up straight. "Ruth? What do you mean by that? She's a child, for God's sake!"

Jacob grinned. "You know what I mean, Mama. You see it too."

"I have no idea what you're talking about," Alex huffed.

"Oh aye, you do. I see how you watch them and you don't look very pleased."

"He's old!" Alex blurted, and Jacob laughed out loud. "Old and rather plain, I might add."

"And yet..."

"And yet..." Alex sighed. "I still think he's far too old."

"Love is blind," Jacob replied, and now his voice was very serious.

"Which is why parents must use common sense at times." She didn't want to talk about Ruth and Julian.

"It isn't only your profession as such, is it?" she asked as they made their way back up towards the house.

Jacob gave her a wary look but didn't reply.

"You miss him, your uncle, don't you?" Alex made an effort to keep her voice neutral.

From all accounts, Luke, Matthew's estranged brother, had been very decent to Jacob, and even if Jacob no longer spoke of Luke with the enthusiasm he'd used when he just got back, Alex was convinced that was more due to the very cool reception his panegyrics got than a fundamental change of his feelings. She knew he corresponded regularly both with Luke and his cousin Charlie, and just as regularly came responding letters in Luke's driven, strong hand.

"Aye," Jacob said with an edge of belligerence. "I'm fond of Uncle Luke."

"Hmm." It would be Luke who saw her grandchildren, Luke to whom Jacob would turn for advice. And she…she wiped at her overflowing eyes.

"Mama." Jacob took her in his arms. "I must, aye?"

"And I'll never see you again," she sobbed, her fists knotting themselves into his shirt.

He held her to his chest. "You know I always carry you with me," he said, sounding as if he was about to cry as well. "You and Da, my brothers and sisters—"

"And that doesn't help one bit." She stepped out of his arms and turned her back on him, struggling to regain an element of composure. This is what life is like here, she reminded herself. One son in Boston, the other in London, and they could both as well be on the moon.

"I must," Jacob whispered behind her, his voice broken.

"I know," she whispered back, crossing her arms over her chest. He touched her shoulder, but she just shook her head and leapt away from him, escaping into the woods.

Matthew came to find her some time later, walking barefoot up to where she was sitting alone in the furthest corner of the herbal garden. He lowered himself to sit beside her. "He isn't leaving yet, not until next spring."

"Eight months in which to make our farewells, and then I'll never see him again." His thick, blond hair, the size of him, the way he always scratched his cheek when he was thinking, how his long mouth curved into a smile…so like his father, and yet uniquely Jacob, a child of sun and air. She inhaled and sat up, rubbing at her red-rimmed eyes. "I'll never meet his wife. I'll have no idea what she sounds like when she laughs or even if she laughs. I'll never be able to see, with my own eyes, if he's happy, yes or no. And his children – to them we'll be storybook figures, not even real." She dug at the damp soil with her bare fingers. "I don't want him to leave."

Matthew blew softly in her face before leaning his unshaven cheek against hers. "I know that, lassie. And you know that he must. He has a life to lead." He licked his thumb and rubbed at a smudge of something on her cheek. "Breakfast? You can make me pancakes, if you want."

Despite herself, she snorted with laughter. "Pancakes," she agreed, and allowed him to help her up on her feet.

Chapter 13

August had been one very hot, long month. Joan lay in only her shift and a shawl in the shade of the backyard tree, and breathed properly for the first time in weeks. Though still humid, the air was no longer heavy with water, and even here, in the enclosed yard, Joan could feel the briskness of the unseasonal wind. A storm, she thought yearningly, a real Old World storm with rain and hail and cold winds that buffeted you from side to side as you struggled up the hill in the direction of the Castle.

She longed for Scottish rain, for the smell of damp soil and drenched fallen leaves. She wanted to see the startling red of rowanberries outlined against the autumn gold of their fronds, to draw in lungfuls of crisp air, and feel her nose and cheeks redden with cold. She sighed, staring up at the flecks of blue she could see through the crown of the tree.

The sudden appearance of Lucy startled her, but with a weak smile she sat up to allow Lucy room to sit. Her daughter looked very well, and this new gown of hers in deep green suited her colouring. Joan did consider it somewhat immodestly cut, showing off too much bosom, even if Lucy had draped a linen shawl to cover herself with. Frances was carried into the garden by a silent black man, and Joan opened her arms to her little granddaughter who prattled happily but unintelligibly, her hands flying in simultaneous sign language.

"And the twins?" Joan asked.

Lucy smiled, using her hands to indicate just how big and strong Jeremy and James were.

Joan laughed. "They're only some months old, so they can't be that big, can they? Not unless they've grown mightily in the week since I saw them last."

Lucy adjusted her hand span somewhat. She got to her feet and bustled into the kitchen, returning with a pitcher of barley water and two porcelain mugs. With a concerned expression, she reached over to take Joan's wrist, strong young fingers closing round bones so frail Joan suspected it would take very little effort for her daughter to pulverise them. Two perfect eyebrows rose into an unvoiced question.

"I'm homesick," Joan said. "I wish I were in Scotland instead."

Lucy brought her brows down in an irritated little frown, exhaled, and after some more minutes of conversation got back onto her feet. She had some errands to run, she explained, and tomorrow was Kate's birthday.

"Ah, yes. I don't think I'll be coming, lass."

Lucy's face fell, but she found a smile for her mother and assured her that was alright, before kissing Joan on her brow in goodbye.

"You be careful," Joan admonished. "I don't want you to disappear as those other lasses have done." Not lately, thank heavens, but four lasses to go up in smoke... Not a trace had been found of them, except for the small lace cap of the youngest girl.

Lucy's face broke up in an amused smile. No, she promised, she wouldn't go up in smoke.

Once Lucy was gone, Joan sank back down on her bench in the shade, thinking of her vibrant, beautiful lass. Not yet nineteen, and already such composure. Mayhap it had to do with being deaf, this having forced Lucy from an early age to become adept at studying and copying behaviour – mostly adult behaviour. She frowned. At times, she got the impression that Lucy was keeping a secret from her, something the lass wanted very much to tell her but chose not to. She pursed her mouth and made a note to ask Simon if he had ensured the painting was destroyed.

"She says so," Simon said in reply to Joan's question. "I have no reason to doubt her."

"She said so once before," Joan replied.

"But she saw her little lass nearly fall through! She loves

Frances too much to risk something like that again."

"Aye, you're right," Joan said, flooded with relief. Of course Lucy would have destroyed it, if nothing else to keep her bairns safe. She ran her tongue over her dry lips and looked at Simon for a long time. "It's all a wee bit strange though."

"Hmm?" Simon looked up from the meat pie he was presently enjoying. "Beer?" he asked, using his knife to point at the pie.

"Aye, beer and broth and a lot of onions to go with the beef."

"Good," he said through a huge bite. "Very good." He sat back and wiped his mouth. "What's strange?"

"All these lasses... The first one was a house slave out at the Jones' – Kate says that the last she saw of her was Barbra entering Lucy's room with a breakfast tray..." Joan let her voice trail away. Too much time, she chided herself, you have far too much time on your hands to concoct all these improbable stories.

Simon was sitting very still, staring at her.

"And then..." Joan cleared her throat. "...then we have wee Eileen. And Mrs Malone swears she saw the lass enter the parlour only minutes after Lucy."

"What is it you're saying, wife?"

"I don't know," Joan whispered. "But it worries me. And you yourself said how Moll was one of Henry's favourites, and one day she was gone as well."

Simon squirmed, making Joan smile. He didn't much like being reminded by her that he spent time at Mrs Malone's. They'd arrived at some sort of armistice lately, whereby Joan turned a blind eye to his regular visits to the whores, and he restricted himself to once, perhaps twice a month, and never stayed away the night. Her eyes met his, and they shared a smile, considering the unorthodox state of affairs. He'd come home and find her waiting, and they would talk an hour or so before repairing to bed where he'd hold her while she slept.

"She wouldn't do something like that," Simon said, returning to the matter at hand.

Joan was unconvinced. "You think?" She hid her face in her hands and sighed. "We should have burnt it ourselves, and God help us if it's her and they catch her."

Simon came round the table to hold her. "She wouldn't, of course she wouldn't." But he promised he would ask her again if she'd burnt that little piece of evil.

On the evening of Kate's birthday, Lucy stood beside her mother-in-law to welcome the guests, curtseying prettily to the elders. She beamed when her father approached them, but was taken aback when he took her to the side and asked her about the painting. Again! Lucy gave him an angry look. Had she not already told him she'd destroyed it? What did he require, she scrawled, a handful of ashes to show him she was speaking the truth? And what about her babies, she added indignantly, did he truly think she'd risk them? Her father mumbled an excuse, looking mortified.

Lucy sniffed and walked back to Kate, and all the while the picture in her petticoat pocket laughed and sang, wept and whispered. Lucy Jones could no more set a taper to it than she could chop off her own arm.

Lucy had no fondness for large social gatherings, her lip-reading skills rendered useless when so many people spoke at the same time. On top of that, she had problems concentrating. Pressed to her thigh, the painting called and whispered, making it difficult for her to hold up her end of the conversation. Not that she needed to. All that was expected of her was to look pleasing, to beam at her husband whenever his eyes strayed in her direction – which they did quite often – and on occasion to share a look with her mother-in-law.

In between these onerous tasks, Lucy could allow her mind to float free, to hear yet another instalment in the story of the Voice. Lately, it had been a lot about the daughter that had plunged through time and whom she, the Voice, would never see again, just as she would never lay eyes on any of her grandchildren, or on her wonderful man, not even after death, she suspected.

After death – was the Voice dead?

The Voice laughed. Death was a relative in respect of time. For a person born in the future to fall back and die in this time, how could they be dead if they had as yet not been born? No, the Voice clarified, some people died – the lucky ones.

Lucy sank her nails into her palms, deeply disturbed by the heavy sadness in this statement. The Voice laughed again, a sound rich in texture, flowing like silk over Lucy's mind. I'm dead, it told her, of course I'm dead. I was born in 1461 and died in 1999 – or was it 1599? Lucy's nails sank even deeper, leaving painful crescents in their wake.

After supper, Kate invited her guests to walk the gardens, throwing the doors wide open to allow the cooling air to enter the house. She strolled down one of the meandering paths with Lionel and the elder Mr Farrell.

The younger Farrell chose to walk with Henry and Lucy, dropping comments about his wife, his horse, and the new girls at Mrs Malone. Lucy had problems following what he was saying in the dark. Only when they paused at the lit lanterns could she read his lips, but it was enough for her to gather that in Farrell's opinion Henry was lucky to have a wife as pretty as she was, going on to add that one of the new girls at Mrs Malone had hair that – truthfully – fell like spun black silk all the way to her nice, tight little arse.

Lucy felt Henry's arm tense with interest at this latest comment but decided that she didn't want to know more, not tonight. Instead, she leaned against him and kissed his throat. He looked down at her and she smiled – a slow, lazy smile. When a few moments later she returned to the house, Henry was at her side. When she took the stairs, he shadowed her, hands on her waist, and when they reached her bedroom door, he pulled the pins out of her hair and kissed her.

Once Henry left next morning, Lucy had hot water brought up and set her herbs to steep. For indigestion, she sighed to the slave girl, miming a stomach ache. It was partly true, she smiled to herself as she drank it down.

She stretched and viewed her half-naked body in her looking glass, liking what she saw. She shook her hair loose and grinned when she recalled Moll's surprised face. *For me?* the stupid girl had said, clearly disturbed to have Lucy this close. And when Lucy had nodded, she'd unwrapped the little package, probably more out of obligation than any real desire to see what was inside. But once she did... *Oh*, she'd said, already drowning in it. Afterwards, Lucy had tucked it away, thrown Moll's hooded cloak over herself, and walked out.

It was unfortunate that the other girl had barged into her just as she was disposing of the cloak. Very, very unfortunate. Lucy flexed her hand. No, that had been wrong, but what was she to do?

Chapter 14

Even now that Ruth was back home, Sarah seemed to spend most of her time either alone or with her, Alex reflected when Sarah appeared in the little clearing looking rather put out. Alex nodded a greeting, puffing as she counted off her push-ups.

Once she was done, Alex rolled over on her back. "Ready to try?"

Sarah nodded, but eyed the branch with trepidation. "Will it hurt?"

"If you think too much about it, yes it will. You have to see your hand going straight through it."

"Hmm." Sarah sounded unconvinced.

"Don't aim for the branch; aim for something beyond it."

They didn't say much as they settled down to do their workout together, two women dressed in shifts and men's shirts, who stretched and bent, kicked and chopped, whirled and turned. Sarah blocked a kick from Alex, and the next second she'd swiped Alex's legs from under her, sending Alex to land on the ground, all air knocked out of her.

"Bloody effing hell," she coughed. "Well done, Sarah."

"Are you alright?" Sarah was kneeling beside her, two parallel lines between her brows.

"I live and breathe." Shit, that hurt! Still, she got back on her feet and smiled reassuringly at Sarah. "If that had been someone intending you harm—"

"...I would've kicked him in his privates while he was down and then I'd turn to run," Sarah filled in.

"Kicked him hard, very, very hard. Although the first option is always to run, okay?"

Sarah rolled her eyes, but nodded all the same. She danced on her toes, using her head to indicate the branch. "Now?"

"Be my guest." Alex clapped loudly when Sarah smashed her hand through the wood.

"You're not spending much time with Ruth," Alex commented later. She sat down in the shade, thinking she deserved a little rest after her recent work-out.

"She isn't spending much time with me. She's either with Daniel or Temperance, and failing that, she discusses scripture with the minister." She made a face. "She goes all cow-eyed whenever the minister is close – and he an old man with almost no hair!"

"Umm," Alex said, thinking that the cow-eyed one was mostly Julian.

Sarah threw herself down on her back and yanked at a long straw of grass, chewing on its stalk. "Daniel never talks to me," she complained.

"He's a bit busy: harvest work and then his sweetheart to catch up with." Alex waggled her brows, making Sarah laugh.

"Will they wed soon?"

"I imagine so, although Daniel must be ordained and have some income first."

"So many years of study," Sarah said, "and for what? To preach sermons that bore his congregation to death?"

Alex grinned. "I think his aspirations are slightly different." She patted her lap in invitation. Sarah scooted closer and pillowed her head on Alex's knees. Her fair hair had come undone from its braids, and Alex spent some minutes smoothing and plaiting all that hair back into place. "Ruth wants to stay with the Allertons in Providence."

"Aye," Sarah said with a sigh.

"If you want…" Alex didn't want it, definitely not, but still she had to offer. She cleared her throat and smiled down at Sarah. "Should you want to, I'm sure we can arrange for you to go as well."

Sarah just shook her head, muttering that she wouldn't be welcome, a third in a cosy two. It hurt, she added, to see herself replaced in her sister's affections.

"Of course you're not." Alex made a mental note to

have a long chat with Ruth about sisterly duties. "It's just that Ruth knows you're always there, and Temperance is still a novelty."

"Always there?" Sarah looked up at her. "No one is always there. I might sicken and die tomorrow, or…" She paused. "You know, like Rebecca Ingram."

"Shush, you shouldn't tempt fate like that." Just the thought of her daughter in the hands of someone like Philip Burley had Alex's throat closing up.

"I know what to do," Sarah said. "Send them flying and kick them in the balls."

"I thought we agreed that the first alternative was always to run."

"That too," Sarah said.

Alex stuck her face up to the sun. Insects buzzed; birds chattered and squabbled; in the distance, a cow lowed; the sound of laughing children came in snatches with the wind; and somewhere to her left, Carlos was singing out of tune. Sarah seemed on the verge of sleep, her breathing slowing, and Alex was considering whether to stretch out for a little nap when a shrill sound sliced through the air. Alex rose, making Sarah grumble loudly when her pillow disappeared.

"What was that?" Alex said, tilting her head in the direction of the river.

"What was what?" Sarah yawned.

"Don't you hear it?"

A carrying keening, and Alex shielded her eyes with her hands, swallowing back a gasp when she recognised the tall Indian who was jogging towards her home.

"Qaachow!" She snatched up her shawl and ran for the house with Sarah running beside her. Alex's head was spinning with thoughts: Qaachow here. Oh God, oh God, why had he come? But she knew, even more so when she saw just how many Indians were filling her yard. Matthew was far away, out with the other men in the fields that lay to the south-east. Not Ian, she recalled with a flare of hope. No, Ian was at home, hurrying into the yard with his musket in hand.

"Go!" Alex wheeled to Sarah. "Fetch your father. Run like the wind! Tell him Qaachow has come."

Sarah nodded and turned to leap away, her skirts bunched high around her legs. Fleet like a deer she was, speeding away among the trees like an arrow, and Alex turned to rush down to the yard.

Alex skidded to a stop, panting heavily. Her hair had come undone. She could feel it stand like startled vipers round her head, but despite her disarray and her unorthodox dress, she pulled herself together to stand very straight and eyeball Qaachow who was waiting in the yard. Samuel, where was Samuel? With the men, she hoped, but then she saw that he wasn't. He was already standing with the Indians.

"Unhand my son," she snapped, striding over to take Samuel by the arm and yank him free. She hugged him to her side and glared at Qaachow who glared back.

"It's time." He pointed at Samuel who shrank away from the piercing look in those dark eyes. "White Bear must learn about his other people. He must grow into a brave with Little Bear." He made a gesture with his hand, and a young boy came to stand beside him, stark naked except for a breech cloth. His hair was the same blue-black it had been when he was a baby, and he peeked at Alex, a timid smile hovering over his mouth.

"You said twelve," Alex said hoarsely.

Qaachow hitched his shoulders. "It's time," he repeated. He said something in a low voice, and his men spread out in a half-circle. Suddenly, there were arrows and muskets aimed at Ian. He said something again, and a group of at least ten Indians slipped away up the lane.

"You promised it like a gift. You take him under threat," Alex said. "I don't want to let my son go with you, and so you show up in force to compel me to give him up."

Qaachow regarded her stonily. "My foster son." He nodded in the direction of Samuel. "He and my son have nursed at the same breast."

"Because I chose to save your boy!" Alex's voice rose in anger and fear. "Am I now to regret that I did? Should

I have left him and your wife to starve?" Qaachow flinched but kept his eyes locked on Samuel.

"You come across the seas," he said bitterly. "You step ashore on our land, and you say it's yours. You kill, you rape, you offer trade with one hand and stab us in the back with the other. My people are no more because of you. The lands that were ours since the Earth was new are trod by the feet of white men. You bring sickness with you, and our people die while you multiply. How many sons have you got, Alex Graham? Seven? I have one – one left alive. But I have buried three and just as many daughters, and they have died because of you."

"Because of me? I saved him!" Alex pointed at Little Bear.

"Your people are our destruction," Qaachow went on, ignoring her interruption. "And now I come to take something back. A son, a healthy, well-grown boy."

"He's mine," Alex groaned.

"And mine," Qaachow replied, not giving an inch. He made as if to grab Samuel. Alex slapped at his hand.

Matthew flew over the wooded ground, his sons at his back. They were almost home when they heard the barking of the dogs. Angry, overexcited barks, and, threaded through them, voices raised in fear and protest. Matthew swung his musket up into his hands and picked up his pace, his heart thundering in his chest. Alex, he could hear her, and there was Ian saying something as well... Something struck him over the head, and he dropped like a felled tree to the ground. His musket. He fumbled for it, but it was lifted out of reach, and hands came up to help him up. Once he was on his feet, they didn't release him, they held him, leading him down his own lane as a prisoner.

"Qaachow." Matthew attempted a nod, but winced.

The tall Indian nodded back, arms crossed over his bare chest. Dark eyes regarded Matthew impassively, and dark hair hung in a braid down his back, decorated with an embroidered length of rawhide and a couple of feathers. Round his waist was wound a braided belt from which hung a tomahawk and a knife, and his feet were encased in moccasins decorated with quills and beads. Qaachow was tense, muscle playing under his coppery skin. He regarded Matthew in silence for some minutes, jaw set, mouth pressed into a thin line.

"I've come for the boy."

"It's too soon," Matthew protested with a woolly tongue.

"No, it's almost too late. Look, he shrinks back in fear from us." He waved his hand at Samuel, who was plastered to Alex's side, but whether out of choice or due to the hold Alex had on him was difficult to tell.

"That might be because he doesn't want to go with you," Matthew said.

"But go with us he will."

"Aye," Matthew said, not knowing how to meet his son's eyes. He straightened up and beckoned for Samuel to come to him. Reluctantly, Alex released her hold on him. Matthew dropped to his knees before his lad and raised his hands to cup a face that was so like his own.

"Son." He choked and cleared his throat. "I once made a promise, aye? I promised that you would go with Qaachow and learn all there is to know about the Indian way of life. And now he wants you to do that."

"But I don't want to," Samuel whispered back, his lower lip wobbling.

"Ah, lad!" Matthew kissed him on his eyes. "You have to, son. If you don't go willingly, they'll take you by force. You see they can, don't you?"

Samuel nodded, one grubby finger tracing the tears that were running down Matthew's cheeks. "So David is right." Samuel's voice could barely be made out, and still Matthew heard every word as clearly as if he had screamed them out loud. "He said you named me Samuel Isaac, because I'm just like Isaac in the Bible: I'm your sacrifice."

"Oh God, no!" Matthew hugged him to him. "No, lad, that you're not. And Qaachow will see you safe. He will return you unharmed but wiser."

"I still don't want to," Samuel whispered in Matthew's ear.

"Aye, I know that," he whispered back. "But sometimes men have to do what they don't want to do. That's the difference between a boy and a man."

The words helped Samuel straighten his spine, and after some minutes, he was able to step out of Matthew's arms and turn to face Qaachow.

"I'll go with you," he said with a quaver. He took a hesitant step towards the man that was to be his father for a year, and the stern face broke up into the slightest of smiles.

Alex made as if to rush at him, her arms open to hug, but Matthew's hand closed on her arm, and with a slight shake of his head he indicated that she should not. This was difficult enough as it was for the lad.

"I'll go with you too." Father Muñoz stepped forward.

Qaachow eyed him sceptically. Why would he want to take a limping man along?

"It's my destiny," Father Muñoz said, and that Qaachow seemed to understand. The wee priest moved over to take his place among the Indians.

Once Samuel was standing among the Indians, Qaachow said something in a low voice, and most of his men melted away, Samuel carried away with them.

Alex moaned a low Samuel, tore herself free from Matthew, and ran after her son. "Samuel!" she cried. "Samuel! I love you, son!"

There was no reply.

Alex turned to Qaachow and stalked towards him. Had she been a mountain cat, her tail would have been whipping with anger. Her eyes regarded the Indian chief with such contempt the tall Indian shuffled on his feet.

"Keep him safe," she growled. "I expect him back unharmed."

"Of course," Qaachow said, "he's my son."

"No," Alex spat at his feet, "he's my son and you've stolen him. I respected you before. I even liked you. Now, I no longer do. Had I found your son or wife tomorrow, I would have walked away and let them die because of what you've done to me today."

123

Qaachow paled and backed away. "He will return a man." Together with his last few men, he stepped into the protective shadows of the forest, with Carlos Muñoz hastening after them.

Matthew moved to take Alex in his arms. She swung for him, landing a punch on his chin that had him reeling back.

"Don't touch me!" she shrieked. "This is your fault, and now my son…" She gulped. He tried yet again to embrace her, and this time she slapped him. "He's gone! Goddamn you, he's gone, and you did nothing. You just stood there!" She shoved him away from her.

"What was I—?"

"Shut up! Leave me alone, you bastard."

"Alex…" He held out his arms to her. "Please, Alex."

"I hate you!" Alex swivelled on her toes, glared at the shocked, assembled household. She backed away, wiping her nose and her eyes on her sleeve. "He's gone, my baby is gone! Why aren't you riding after him? How can you just stand there? Bring him back, goddamn you, bring him back!"

With that she fled, pushing at whoever stood in her way, yelling at one son, at another, and all the while she was weeping, loud sobs that echoed through the balmy air, sounds of such desperation that Matthew had no idea what to do. She didn't want him, that much was clear.

He strode off towards the tool shed, found an axe and made for the trees. His son. Sweet Lord, his Samuel.

"Oh God," he groaned, stuffing a hand in his mouth to stop himself from screaming out loud.

Down by the river, Samuel was told to undress. He was handed a breechcloth, a knife and moccasins just like those Little Bear wore.

"Today, you leave the white man in you behind," Qaachow said. "You will not speak English; you will not wear white men's clothes. You are one of us now, White Bear."

"I don't know your language," Samuel hiccupped.

"You will learn." With a terse nod, Qaachow set his group of men moving, and Samuel had to run to keep up.

At one point, he thought of turning back – he could still see the river, and so he could find his way back home. Mama, he sobbed and wiped his eyes with his arm, my Mama.

A hand grasped his; two friendly, dark eyes met his. "Brother," Little Bear said in English and grinned at him.

Chapter 15

Alex couldn't sleep. She couldn't eat. She couldn't talk. She sat for hours in her bedroom staring blankly at the sky outside, tracking time by the red reflections moving across the floor. She didn't wash, nor did she brush her hair or clean her teeth. At times, she tried to crawl out of the dark hole she'd dug for herself, but the knowledge that Samuel was gone, that they'd given him up voluntarily, sending him off to meet God knew what on his own, had her turning tail and scurrying back to hide some more.

On the third day of this, Mrs Parson entered Alex's bedchamber with a bang. "How much longer?" she barked, startling Alex to sit up straight. "Are you planning on staying in here forever while life goes on outside?"

Alex didn't reply, swinging her feet back and forth.

"Alex Graham!" Mrs Parson shook her hard. "It isn't only you, aye? You have a husband that's hurting, you have two wee lads who don't know what to do!"

Matthew...a dull ache soared through her heart as she thought his name. He must be so angry with her.

"I don't care," Alex said, forcing the words up her throat. "I just want to be left alone." She giggled out loud. "Like Ferdinand the Bull."

Mrs Parson eyed her with exasperation. "I have no idea what you're on about, but you stink, Alex Graham."

"I do?" Alex hitched her shoulders. She couldn't care less.

"And have you not spared a thought to where your husband might be?" Mrs Parson asked.

Alex blinked owlishly. Matthew? Well, he was here, wasn't he? She blinked again. No, he wasn't. In fact, she hadn't seen him since the moment she'd slapped him. Something shifted in her belly – Matthew? "Where?"

"We don't know," Mrs Parson said, and Alex could hear how close the old woman was to tears.

"You don't know?" Alex felt something stirring inside of her.

For the first time in days, she looked at her own reflection and she didn't like what she saw, not one bit. She sniffed and made a face. Mrs Parson was right; she did stink. Things began to drop into place in her head. Samuel was gone, with Qaachow, but he would come back some day, of course he would – Qaachow had promised, hadn't he? But David… Adam…and, oh God, Matthew! He must be twisting with guilt. She had to go to him, now!

"But you must have looked!" His sons would look out for their father, wouldn't they?

"We have," Mrs Parson said, "but we can't find him."

That made Alex's guts begin to revolve. What did they mean: they couldn't find him? Hadn't they seen him go?

Mrs Parson sighed. "It was a mite chaotic."

Alex scrunched up her face, making a huge effort to pull out the memory of the moments just after her Samuel had been taken from her. Someone had been screaming, and detachedly she realised that must have been her. David… he'd been crying, and Mark had stood with his arms around him. And Adam? Hugin, the bird, had flown over to sit on her head, disturbed by her screaming, and Adam's eyes had been very close to hers, but she couldn't remember… Yes, she could. Oh God, she had shoved him away, screaming that her Samuel was gone, and could he just fuck off and leave her alone? A wave of bile washed through her mouth.

"Adam," she groaned. She rose, holding on to the bedpost.

"Aye, Adam." Mrs Parson stopped Alex on her way to the door. "Not like that. You'll frighten your bairns even more. I'll have Sarah come up with water."

Half an hour later, Alex had returned to the world of the living, her brain frantic with worry for Matthew. No one had seen him! Not at the Leslies, not at the Chisholms, and Ian assured her they had checked the decaying cabins up at Forest Spring as well.

"But why?" she asked Mrs Parson.

"Why?" Mrs Parson eyed her disapprovingly. "Maybe because you told him it was his fault? You screamed at him like a fisherwoman, telling him not to touch you."

"Well, it is," Alex said.

Mrs Parson just looked at her.

"It was him that promised," Alex tried again, feeling flayed by those black eyes.

"And you could have said no," Mrs Parson said. "If you had already then this wouldn't have happened."

"I didn't think he'd ever come to claim him," Alex whispered, "and when I finally realised he would, it was too late."

"And don't you think Matthew reasoned the same way?" Mrs Parson shook her head at her. "For him to give up his son to the heathens…unthinkable, no?"

Alex sat down. "Samuel, my little Samuel."

Mrs Parson sat down beside her on the kitchen bench. "He isn't dead, Alex."

"No," Alex said, blinking furiously to stop herself from crying – not that it helped. "But we just gave him up, tossing him away like a defect toy."

"Nay, you didn't. The boy left knowing you love him." She stroked Alex's face. "And he has the wee priest with him, no?"

Alex laughed through her tears. "It will be Samuel having to take care of him."

"And that's not a bad thing. It will take the lad's mind off other things."

"All my children," Alex moaned. "Jacob to go to London, Daniel to Boston, and now Samuel with the Indians—"

Mrs Parson slapped her shoulder, hard. "You're fortunate. You have living children, no? And even if they go abroad, they're still alive. Wee Samuel will live, Alex."

"He'll live," Alex repeated, "yes, he'll live." She kissed Mrs Parson on her wrinkled cheek and then stood up.

"First things first, I have to find Adam and apologise." And then David, and finally Matthew. Where could he be?

Something wild and toothy lived in her stomach, a gurgling monster that told her maybe he was dead. But, no, she took a deep breath, she took another and turned inward, searching for his beat. There, but thready and weak, and Alex's eyes flew open in panic.

"He's hurt!" she gasped.

Mrs Parson took her hands. "Your wee sons first. Then your husband."

"My sons," she repeated, but all she wanted to do was to pick up her skirts and run to find Matthew.

She found Adam down by the pig pen, held him hard and whispered that would he please forgive her, but she hadn't been herself, and she really, really loved him, but he knew that, didn't he?

She placed her hand over his heart. "Here you know that I always love you, even when I go a bit wild and crazy."

Adam hugged her back and told her that the pig seemed to miss Samuel too, although perhaps not as much as he did, or David did.

"I'm sure she does," Alex replied and kissed him once again. "Do you know where David is?"

"Up in the graveyard."

David was far more difficult. His face was pinched with exhaustion, and Alex was washed by a wave of guilt that she should so have dropped into herself, wallowing in her own dark feelings of loss, and leaving her son to cope on his own.

"Why are you sitting here?" she asked, joining him on the bench.

He shrugged and studied his bare feet. In his hands, he held the knife Matthew had given him for his last birthday, every now and then sinking it into the wood of the bench. "Where else? Here I see it all so, when he comes, I'll be the first to see him."

"It will be a while before he comes back."

"If he comes back," David whispered and began to cry.

That was when Alex saw that on the nearest tree someone had carved a large, unsteady Samuel, and she held her eleven-year-old to her chest and shushed and comforted, her fingers running through his dark hair. Twins they could have been, him and Samuel, so alike were they, and, like twins, they had grown up in constant companionship, but now one half of them was gone, leaving David hurting badly.

Alex kneeled down before him. "Honey, I can't promise you he'll come back." She bit her lip so hard it cracked, her mouth filling with the taste of her own blood. "But I believe he will, and until he does, I'll pray every night that God returns him safe and sound." She kissed the sad face before her and coaxed his chin up so that she could see his eyes. This close, they were an amazing mossy green with flecks of deepest brown. "He'll come back. Now," she said, getting back onto her feet, "I have to find your father. Do you have any idea where he is?"

No, David didn't, but he had a very long list of where he wasn't.

"Hmm," Alex said, staring off in the direction of the river. And that is when she knew where he would be. How stupid of her not to realise that immediately! She flew down the slope, half-ran across the yard, swerving to avoid crashing into Minister Allerton when he appeared from behind the privy.

"Alex!"

She ignored him.

"Alex!" Minister Allerton puffed in his effort to catch up with her. She threw him an irritated look. She didn't want company on her walk. She definitely didn't want an audience should she find Matthew where she hoped. Actually, she was irritated already before, with her husband. To have everyone worried out of their mind like that! Her elder sons had ridden like couriers back and forth, searching for their da, and with a shuttered face Ian had voiced the opinion that mayhap Da had... Alex felt her insides tear themselves apart with worry. What if he was hurt? Deep inside of her, she could still feel him – a quickened pulse, not at all his normal, steady beat.

"Has anyone ever told you you have a most transparent face?" Julian said once he drew abreast with her. He held up

130

a hand to stop her from saying anything. "I just want to let you know that I'll help as well as I can. It's difficult to lose a child."

"He isn't dead!"

"No," the minister said, "but lost all the same."

Julian Allerton was still reeling when Alex disappeared into the woods, his hand caressing his reddening cheek. Serve him right, Mark thought, sending the minister a dark look. He had only caught the tail end of the conversation, having been busy in the tool-shed when he heard Mama's voice.

"Now that was a very daft thing to say," Mark commented.

"It's the truth," Minister Allerton said. "The next time they see their son he'll be a heathen savage. These years are crucial."

"I don't think you should say that," Mark suggested with a certain chill. He could still see Mama, a blur of colour moving at speed through the trees.

"No," the minister said, deflating rapidly, "you're right. I should let them keep their hope."

"Aye, they'll need it." With a curt nod, Mark hurried on in the wake of his mother.

She was walking – nay, running – with determination towards the north-west, cutting across fields and ditches, ducking under thickets, and swerving through the trees.

Mark increased his pace. She might need him. He sighed, imagining all kinds of gruesome scenes at her point of destination.

He woke reluctantly, half opening his eyes before closing them again. What was the point? Out of a sense of obligation, Matthew attempted to move the trunk once again, but gave up, falling back to pant with frustration and fear.

His axe lay just out of reach, and yet again he stretched himself towards it, fingertips grazing the smooth handle, no more. He had screamed himself hoarse, but no one had come, and this last night, he had lain half-delirious, trapped against the damp softness of the moss. He was chilled to the bone, and here, in the thicker stands of forest, the sun never fully reached the ground, dancing a few feet up in the air. He was no longer hungry, but, God, he was thirsty! He tore off another chunk of moss with his free hand and sucked at it.

He filled his lungs with air and called out again. "Aleeeeeeex! Aleeeeeex!" He didn't want to die here – not like this, pinned beneath a log due to his own stupidity.

He had been so angry: with Qaachow, with Alex for shouting at him like she did, but mostly with himself. Why hadn't he done like Alex suggested and sent Samuel off? Tried, at least, to save his son from this hasty promise, made so many years ago?

So he had come here, to the clearing that had once housed Qaachow's village. He and Alex had occasionally come here through the years, and this was where Samuel had been made. Mayhap it was all decided already then; the lad was created here, among the ruins of an Indian village.

He licked his chapped lips and swallowed, light-headed with lack of food and water. He shivered, his trapped limbs trembling, and closed his eyes on all the green that surrounded him. Up to the other day, this had been a place he approached with reverence and respect, but the afternoon that Qaachow stole his son, Matthew had taken his axe and come here to desecrate, eradicate.

He had done a good job. The few remaining mounds he had kicked to pieces, he had felled saplings to drag them together in a heavy pile that he had planned to set on fire, and it was as he stood panting and covered with perspiration that he had leaned too hard against one of the old fallen trees. He was only vaguely aware of what had happened. He had slipped, the ground giving way below him, and scrabbled backwards, seeing in slow motion how the heavy pine log shifted and began to roll. It hadn't hurt, and even now he could move both feet, but the log had settled itself across his torso and upper thighs, effectively imprisoning him. Revenge, he assumed, for the destruction he had wreaked.

He was tired and wet, and his mind wandered. Would

they ever find him? And when they did, would his bleached bones lie here? He laughed hollowly at his own morbidity. Alex...he wanted his wife to hold his hand while he slipped away into the afterlife. He closed his eyes and tried to sleep. Maybe he could avoid waking up again to despair and fear, mayhap he could dream. In his dream, she was there, a short-haired lass in strange breeches and a bright red jacket, and she laughed at him, her eyes glittering in the sun. Matthew smiled in his dozing state.

"Djeens," he mumbled out loud.

"I haven't worn them in over twenty years," a voice said somewhere over his head. "I don't think they'd fit."

"You don't have them," he said without opening his eyes. "You burnt them."

"Yes, I did." The voice smiled, and Matthew thought that this was not too bad, to die while talking to his imaginary wife.

A hand closed on his and his eyes opened to see hers, wells of deep blue only inches from his.

"Hi," she said, kissing his ice-cold nose.

"Hi yourself," he replied. A huge tremor flew up his body before he slumped into a faint.

Chapter 16

"I thought you'd died," Alex said later. "A smile, a shiver, and then, boom! Dead to the world."

"It wouldn't have been too bad, to die with you beside me. It was worse when I thought I might die all alone." Matthew's entire body ached, and now that he was back in the safety of his own bed, he could feel the shivers running up his legs, his skin itching and hot with returning circulation.

No major damage, Mrs Parson had concluded. Nothing but a fever and a chest cold. He drank down the wintergreen tea that Alex held to his mouth, and subsided with a pleased sound against the clean pillows. "Why didn't you come looking earlier?"

Alex hitched her shoulders and fingered the tassels of the new quilt. "I didn't miss you. All I could think about was my Samuel."

Merciful Lord, but that hurt! Matthew closed his eyes at the terrifying thought that, had she not roused herself out of her grief, he would still have been lying out in the woods.

"And I was angry with you," she said.

"Aye, I gathered that," Matthew managed to say. He was still trying to assimilate the fact that she hadn't missed him. He had lain there in the forest and cried for her, called for her, wanting only her, while she had blocked him out of her head. It had never happened before, that they had been separated and she not care, and it made him feel orphaned.

Alex snuck him a look from beneath her lashes and moved over to sit beside him in the bed. He shifted away.

"I wasn't myself," she said, "and Samuel, oh God, Matthew! They found his clothes folded down by the river."

He made a strangled sound, and when she extended her hand he took it, braiding his fingers tightly around hers.

"I…my head…I just couldn't take in more. And it was all Samuel, Samuel." Haltingly, she described how these last few days had been for her, how she had walked in a mental fog to shield herself from confronting the fact that their son was gone.

"And you weren't there," she said in a choked voice. "You weren't there to hold me, and I thought maybe you were angry with me because I had yelled at you, blaming you for something that was really my fault. If I hadn't been stupid enough to save Qaachow's son to begin with, if I'd not nursed the boy, none of this would have happened." With that, she began to cry, and he gathered her as close as he possibly could, ignoring the twinges this sent up his legs and back.

Matthew was fast asleep when Mrs Parson opened the door a few hours later, his head a heavy but comforting weight on Alex's chest. The old woman beckoned for Alex to come, whispering that supper was on the table. Alex extricated herself from Matthew and followed her, adjusting her hair and cap as she went.

"He could have died," Alex said in a low voice as she closed the door behind her.

Mrs Parson rolled her eyes at her, saying that people could die all the time, no? In fact, people did die all the time.

"But he didn't," she pointed out. "God didn't want him yet."

Alex mulled that over. "You think God will want him?" She somehow suspected her own assessment of Matthew was very biased.

"Oh aye." Mrs Parson grinned. "I'm not quite that sure about you, though."

"Huh," Alex snorted. "If we're talking Presbyterian heaven, I somehow think hell will be more fun."

"Alex Graham!" Mrs Parson gave her a scandalised look.

"Kidding," Alex muttered.

It wasn't easy. In fact, at times it was near on unbearable, and more or less on a daily basis Matthew caught Alex doing what he was doing – looking for a third lad where now there were only two. But life picked up around them. The last of the harvest work had to be done, and in the day to day, his name was rarely mentioned, not even by mistake. Where before David and Samuel had been inseparable, it was now David and Adam that did everything together, with Malcolm a permanent third.

"He stays," Alex told Matthew, indicating David. "We don't send him down to Providence, not now."

"He must be adequately schooled," Matthew protested, without much heat.

"He's needed here. I won't have two boys yanked away from me in less than a month. Besides, what will it to do poor Adam?"

Matthew sighed but nodded, very relieved that she should insist. It was enough that both Daniel and Ruth were leaving, and next time they saw Daniel, he would be a man of God.

"In Boston," Matthew promised his son. "We'll come to see you at your ordination." He threw yet another stone to land in the river before them.

"Both of you?"

"Of course," Matthew replied, "God willing." He shared a concerned look with his son, and looked over to where Alex once again stood scanning the distant rolling hills, a sinuous band of dark blue and green against the lighter blue of the sky.

"He'll be alright, Da," Daniel said, gripping Matthew's arm.

"You think?" Matthew gnawed at his lip. "I myself think he must be very confused. And will he remember to say his prayers every night, like a good Christian boy? Will he speak of us in English, say our names? If not..." He swallowed. "...if not, how will he ever make it back to us?"

"He will." Daniel sounded so certain Matthew felt the constant lump of ice in his belly thaw somewhat.

Julian Allerton was much more blunt, cornering Matthew out in the stables.

"You must pray for him, and I and the congregation will

pray for him too. But you must prepare yourself, for I fear he is lost."

"Lost? How lost?" Matthew bristled, keeping his back to the minister. He concentrated on the burnished golden hide of Aaron instead, counting brushstrokes in his head.

"Matthew…" Julian sighed and settled himself on a nearby overturned bucket. "He's only ten. The coming years he will spend among savages."

"Not years – a year," Matthew said.

"That's not what Qaachow said." Julian brushed at a stain on his breeches. "He said he'd bring him back a man."

"I promised him my son for a year, no more," Matthew replied through his teeth.

"And what will you do if the year comes and goes, and Samuel isn't back? Ride out into the wilderness to find him?"

Matthew stumbled, an arm flying out to steady himself against the horse that snorted in surprise at this unexpected embrace. "Aye."

"No, you won't. You can't, not with a wife and a family to care for here. And so your son will grow to manhood among others than us, and when you meet him again, he will no longer be a white man. He'll be an Indian. He's lost to you. Samuel Isaac is to all purposes dead, and in his place stands White Bear, but he is no son of yours."

"Get out!" Matthew said, pressing the currying brush to his chest to stop himself from throwing it at Julian. "Just get out, aye?"

Some days later, Matthew settled himself beside Alex and draped an arm over her shoulder, saying in an undertone that it would be nice once they had their home to themselves.

"Yes." Alex nodded, sounding rather distracted. She pursed her mouth. "I'm not sure I like it," she said, eyes lingering on their eldest daughter. "Should she really be staying with them?"

Sitting a couple of feet apart, Julian and Ruth were involved in an intense debate about the book that lay in Ruth's lap, and it was obvious from how their eyes met and held that it wasn't the book that was the main attraction.

Matthew scratched at his chest. He hadn't spoken properly to Julian since that encounter in the stables, and he wasn't sure he wanted to either – not yet. The minister was right. His gut told him so, his heart and mind as well, but it was a truth Matthew couldn't reconcile himself to, nor had any intention of sharing with his wife.

"And does Daniel know, do you think?" Alex went on, nodding to where their son appeared from the woods, flintlock in one hand, Temperance in the other.

"Temperance does," Matthew said. "Those two lasses talk so much it must make their ears bleed, and if so, Daniel knows as well."

"And he doesn't mind?"

Matthew had no idea. "It isn't as if they'll be living close together, is it? He'll be in Boston with Temperance, not here with his sister turned mother-in-law."

"Assuming of course that Ruth and Julian are married," Alex said. "I wonder if they've kissed."

Kissed? Matthew straightened up. The minister kiss his lass? No – he wafted away the thought like one might wave at an irritating fly. Unfortunately, just like a fly, the thought buzzed insistently through his head. Nay, he decided, of course not. Ruth was still a bairn in many ways, and Julian would never abuse her trust. But still…he narrowed his eyes, seeing just how soft Ruth's mouth was, how her eyes gleamed when she gazed into Julian Allerton's face.

"If you think it better, she can board with Simon and Joan. She can still spend time with Temperance and take her lessons with the minister, but at least they won't be sharing the same house."

Minister Allerton had a dragon of a housekeeper, and Matthew had no real doubt that the minister acted with propriety, but it was always better to close the stable door before the horse bolted.

"Good idea." Alex beckoned Ruth over and told her it was their opinion that it was better if Ruth stayed with her aunt and uncle instead – she would surely be welcomed, and

Joan would appreciate the company. Ruth listened stonily, wheeled and stalked away, her thick red braid like a copper snake against the pale green of her bodice.

"Oh dear," Alex murmured.

Matthew chuckled.

Julian got to his feet, seemed uncertain whether he should follow Ruth, thereby making his infatuation obvious, or wait.

"Having Ruth stay with Simon is a wise decision, I think," Matthew said, noting how Julian's eyes hung on Ruth's receding back.

From the way Julian threw eye darts at Matthew over the table, it was apparent Ruth had told him of her parents' decision. After supper, Julian requested a private moment with Matthew, looking somewhat put out when Matthew, as a matter of course, invited Alex to join them. Smart move, Alex thought, winking at her husband as she entered the room carrying a tray.

"Are you implying I would dishonour a girl left in my charge?" Minister Allerton looked quite the part, standing as straight as if someone had rammed a poker up his arse.

"No," Alex said, "but you very much want to, don't you?" She almost laughed at the way his hue changed, his tanned face whitening so quickly she could count the freckles that dotted his nose.

"Mrs Graham!"

The formality of address only made her want to laugh even more. "Where I come from, we call a spade a spade, and unless you're an absolute idiot, a green man from Mars, or blind and deaf, the attraction between you and our daughter is tangible – very tangible."

"A green man from Mars?" Julian sounded intrigued. "Are there green men on Mars?"

"Not as far as I know. It's just an expression." She motioned for Julian to sit on one of the stools and handed him a mug of herbal tea, the rich scents of mint and honey making him sniff appreciatively.

"I would never abuse of Ruth," Julian said, "and I resent that you should feel obliged to remove her from my care."

Matthew bit into a large slice of squash cake and munched. "She might force your hand. Ruth is a canny lass."

"I wouldn't let her," Julian retorted, smoothing at his sparse hair – a rather unfortunate ginger.

"Oh aye?" Matthew stretched out his long legs and crossed them at the ankles. "And a naked lass in your bed wouldn't lead you to temptation?"

Julian choked, coughing loudly.

Matthew blew at his tea and regarded Julian over the rim of his earthenware mug. "We are right, aren't we? You have a fondness for her."

Julian smoothed down his dark coat and thought about it for some minutes.

"Yes, I have a fondness for her. I want to marry her."

"Hmm," Matthew said, "you're a wee bit too old."

"I'm not yet forty!" Julian snapped. "I'll be thirty-six in November."

"And she will be seventeen in December," Alex said, looking him over. He had very nice hands, and seeing him in shirtsleeves on the fields showed off a relatively good physique. Not like her own man, not by a long way, but then Minister Allerton spent his days mostly reading and writing.

Matthew got to his feet and went over to open the door. "Ruth! Come here, aye?"

Ruth appeared so quickly Alex suspected she had been eavesdropping.

"The minister wishes you to wed. Do you want it as well?" Matthew said.

Ruth just nodded, hazel eyes flickering into gold in the candlelight. Matthew met Alex's eyes over their daughter's head and raised an interrogative brow.

"She's too young," Alex said.

"That I am not!" Ruth replied heatedly. "I know what I want, I know what I feel!"

"You're a child, Ruth. Girls your age have crushes and infatuations, and then they grow out of them." In her time, a girl as pretty as Ruth would have been out having a party most weekends, and boys would come and go. Some she'd kiss, some she'd sleep with, and then one day, when she was much, much older than seventeen, she'd meet her future man. Ruth had apparently said something while Alex was lost in space, looking expectantly at her mother.

"Mmm?" Alex asked.

"She said as how you don't know what's best for her," Matthew said, "but she knows that best for her is to wed Julian."

"Fantastic," Alex said, seeing a flare of hope flash through her daughter's eyes. "But not until you're eighteen."

"Mama!" Ruth groaned.

"Eighteen," Matthew repeated in a quiet tone. "And no betrothal as yet."

Next evening, the house was very quiet. Daniel was gone, the Allertons and Ruth were gone, and where Samuel should be sitting yawned a giant, empty hole that all of them were very aware of. The meal was eaten under silence – even the younger children were subdued, Tom and Maggie escaping to sit huddled under the table.

"You could perhaps tell us the story of Ferdinand the Bull?" Mrs Parson said, handing Betty the bread. "You know, no? The bull that wished only to be left alone."

"Ferdinand the Bull? How on earth do you know of him?" Alex looked at her in surprise.

"I know a lot of things. Much, much more than you might think, aye?"

"Given that you've been around since the Flood more or less, that isn't surprising," Alex bit back, and to her own surprise, they were all suddenly laughing. And it felt good to laugh; to sit at her kitchen table surrounded by the sizeable family left to her and laugh, while beside her sat her man, his leg pressed against hers, and on the opposite side sat the woman Alex more and more considered to be her mother. Thank you, she mouthed to Mrs Parson, who just winked before serving herself a slice of bread.

Chapter 17

Abruptly, Henry took to spending the evenings with his friends again. Young Farrell's fault – it was him and all his enticing descriptions of the new whores that titillated Henry's mind. Not that he had reason to go, his member was well-exercised at home, but when Lucy wrote something along those lines to Kate, her mother-in-law shrugged.

"He's a man, Lucy," she said, thereby exonerating him from a list as long as Lucy's arm. "Some men are very vital. Don't let it worry you – as long as he returns to you, and holds to Mrs Malone's, where the whores are fresh and healthy."

Lucy made a disgusted face. Need she worry about disease as well?

"I would think not, Mrs Malone isn't about to risk her reputation by bringing in the pox."

The pox? It killed you! Lucy sat down, signing that it wasn't right. Her husband was well cared for – in every sense – at home.

"Those are his friends," Kate said. "They meet and talk, and sometimes it's only beer and food."

Lucy sniffed ostentatiously, shaking her head.

"You smell them on him?" Kate laughed, but her dark eyes hardened. "His father – God curse him – took a woman to live with." Kate's fingers tightened round the glass she was holding. "A redhead, very pretty and, from what I heard, quite wild." She set down the glass and traced an invisible pattern on the polished rosewood table – a luxury item brought at great cost from Portugal. "There was nothing I could do. I was but his wife."

And, very soon after, she was his widow, but Lucy saw no reason to divulge that she knew all about Kate's part in getting Dominic Jones hanged.

"They even had a son," Kate said.

A son? Lucy had never heard a bastard brother mentioned.

"Henry doesn't know – why should he?" Kate looked out at the black night and gnawed her lip. "I bribed her to leave and never return, and to ensure that she never would, I took some further precautions. As far as I know, she's still in Jamaica somewhere, bonded to a plantation owner."

Lucy just stared, impressed by this novel, ruthless side to her mother-in-law.

Kate made a dismissive gesture. "I took a page out of Dominic's book. It's a good way to make undesired people disappear, to bond them somewhere very far away."

Ah. Lucy recalled that her uncle had been so treated.

"Yes." Kate's mouth softened into a sad little smile. "Matthew Graham was one such. His brother sold him into slavery, and Dominic reaped the profits." Kate cleared her throat. "So, the occasional visit to the bawdy house you have to live with, but if it gets more serious, that's when you have to act."

Oh yes, Lucy agreed, suppressing a grin.

Lucy kicked at the bedclothes in frustration. Well over two weeks since he had bedded her, escaping out after dinner with a hasty farewell to spend the evenings with Farrell and the others. Damn Farrell! And he came back late, slinking in to sleep in the adjacent dressing room instead of joining her in their bed. Because he stank, of course. Even in the mornings, he stank – of cheap perfume and beer and tobacco.

Lucy got out of bed and went to stand by the unshuttered window, crossing her arms over her chest. This was not the way things were supposed to be, not when she was pretty and always smelled nice, not when she had given him three children in as many years. Very rarely did Lucy cry but, as she stood looking out at the dark night, silent tears slipped down her cheeks to trickle into her mouth. She wanted him to be here, with her, but instead he escaped her strangeness, preferring the world of those that could speak and hear to her mute presence.

She rubbed her cheek against the heavy brocade curtains and cried some more. She was a freak – albeit pretty – but a freak nonetheless, and the day would come when even her children would shun her strange company for those that, like them, could hear without the aid of a magic picture.

She sank back down on the bed and dragged a hand across her eyes. Throughout their courtship, Henry had been so attentive, taking the time to read her little notes, making sure he spoke so that she could always see her mouth. But, now, he spoke to his mother over her head, shook his head, and said he had no time when she had things to tell, and then off he went in pursuit of beer and whores. A black-haired one, no doubt, one that taught him all those things he then came back and did with her. No, that was in all probability Mrs Malone herself.

Lucy threw a longing look in the direction of her drawer, but sighed and shook her head. Too dangerous. Mrs Malone was wily *and* suspicious after Eileen and Moll. Lucy curled herself together and pulled the quilts as high around her as she could – not for warmth but for comfort.

Next morning dawned in extraordinary light, and when Lucy went to the window, she gasped. The air was full of sparkling mist; droplets of water hung suspended in the air, glittering like diamonds in the sun. She threw her nightgown over her shift and rushed downstairs, eager to go outside and bathe in all that dewy light.

She undulated in the dispersing September mist, her face turned to the sky, and in the shining air, she looked a goddess come to earth. Henry stood in his window and watched her silent dance, her unbound hair spilling down her back, and wondered why on earth he didn't bed her every night. He knew, of course: she frightened him. The way her eyes devoured him, the silence of her movements, the absolute stillness with which she could sit for hours – it put him in mind of a stalking cat. And then it was the whispered "witch" that now and then echoed in his head. What had happened to them? To Barbra, to Eileen, and to

Moll? One moment there, the next no more… Henry shook himself like a dog. Watching his wife in the dewy garden, her face open to the light, Henry smiled at himself. She was deaf, he reminded himself, and all the rest were but fancies.

He made an effort, and she bloomed. He smiled, and she beamed. He sat down to listen and was handed page after page of rambling thoughts. He held out his hand, and she came dancing, and at night he loved her, discovering just how warm and passionate she could be. She fell asleep in his arms and woke to his touch, and Henry was entranced by his beautiful, voracious wife.

For a brief interlude, all was perfect in Lucy's world – some weeks in which she hoped that this was the way things would continue forever. But then Henry was called away to St Mary's City and the meeting of the Colony's representatives, and with him went young Farrell. When he returned, it was no longer quite as magic, with Henry once again disappearing to spend evenings – even nights – with his friends. And Lucy's world shrank back down, to hasty notes and quick caresses, and bitterly she knew that never would she hold him like she wanted to. Not only was she deaf, she was a woman too.

Chapter 18

"He did what?" Robert Chisholm gawked. "Our priest?" He frowned, muttering that after a long, heavy month of work, he had looked forward to celebrating Mass, and there was a new baby to christen, and Liam and Roisin to properly wed and...

"I told you," Matthew said. "The wee man stood up and said he would go with the Indians."

"But he was hurt!" Robert scrubbed a hand through his hair. "And why would he do such a thing anyway?"

"I think his intent is to bring the word of God to the heathen." Alex served the men cider and sat down beside Matthew.

"You should have stopped him," Martin Chisholm said. "He won't survive long out there in the wild." It could have been funny, if things weren't as painful as they were, the way he went a bright red. "Being a priest, I mean," he qualified.

"We had our attention elsewhere," Matthew said.

"Yes, I suppose you would. I'm most sorry for your loss," Robert mumbled.

"He isn't dead!" Alex exploded, lifting herself off the bench in one fluid movement. "He'll come back, okay?" She banged the door behind her and barged off in the direction of...she didn't know, slowing her pace as dejection flowed back into her body.

Matthew followed her exit with a slight crease between his brows. Days would pass in which she acted entirely normal, and then there'd be these moments when life drained out of her, leaving her a husk. He smiled wryly to himself. It was the same for him, but he was better at submerging himself in the tasks at hand, channelling the emotions that coursed through him into something else. He returned his attention to the Chisholms, listening with interest – and relief – when Martin told him the Burley brothers and their gang had retreated into Virginia, chased all the way there by Chisholm and Leslie men.

"Not as many as they used to be," Martin said with quiet satisfaction, running a hand down his rifled flintlock.

"You shot one?" Matthew asked, surprised.

"Oh yes." Martin leaned forward and caught Matthew's eye. "It doesn't make sense for them to keep on returning here. We're all too well protected. Unless, of course, they are hoping to avenge themselves for perceived wrongs."

Matthew's body hair crept up to stand at attention.

Martin nodded seriously. "Tread with care, Matthew, you and your wife both."

"I still can't grasp it," Robert said later, looking down at the little bundle of possessions in his hand. "He never said anything about going out into the wilds to christen Indians."

"Partly he did it for our son, I think," Matthew said.

"That was a most Christian thing to do," Robert said.

"It was a foolish thing to do. He was unwell, still limping badly. I don't think he finds it easy to keep up with an Indian band." Matthew stared off in the general direction of the west. Somewhere out there was his son, and he hoped that he was well and safe. He had very little hope for the wee priest. "Let's pray he knows to keep his mouth shut, at least to begin with. They don't much take to missionaries, do they?"

"No," Robert said, "I've never met one who came back."

"Mama?" Ian placed a hand on Alex's shoulder and squeezed. "Why are you staring at that tree?"

"I'm staring at the name on it," Alex corrected, moving over to allow him to sit beside her.

"Ah," Ian nodded. "David?" he asked, studying the unevenly written Samuel.

"Yes." Alex slid lower on the bench, her eyes searching for her sons.

"They're down by the water with Jacob," Ian told her.

"Weekly bath." As if on cue, a high whooping sound carried through the September air, and Alex smiled.

"Jacob." She shook her head. "I bet you he's horseplaying with them instead of making sure they're actually using the soap."

"Hmm," Ian replied vaguely, looking as if such behaviour was something he sympathised with.

"Will someone make sure Samuel keeps himself clean?" Alex said.

"They're a clean people, and I suppose Thistledown will make sure he washes regularly."

"And will he come back?" The question she hadn't dared to ask either herself or Matthew, she burdened Ian with. He gave her a lopsided little smile. She rested her head against his shoulder. They had sat here so often, she and him, talking about life and death, his bitterness when his back was damaged, his love for both his wives, and always had they been honest with one another. She hoped he would be now as well.

"I don't know, and if he does, he'll be very changed."

Alex nodded, gouging at the ground with the toe of her shoe. "Will he know me?"

"Aye," Ian replied with conviction. "He will know you the instant he lays eyes on you – just as I'd recognise Mam immediately, should she appear here."

Given that Margaret was dead, Alex sincerely hoped that wouldn't happen. A small note of happiness hummed inside of her. At least he'd recognise her, know her for who she was: his mother. The rest they could take from there.

In this much improved mood, Alex decided to drop in for a chat with Betty. She might have been distracted lately, for obvious reasons, but not so distracted as to not notice that Malcolm was giving Betty a hard time, growing increasingly rude – as long as his father was nowhere close.

Betty gave Alex Timothy to hold and laced herself back up. "I don't like it," she said.

"No, I can understand that." Alex stopped Christopher from helping himself to yet another bun.

Betty made a face. "I thought they were going back to Charles Towne as quickly as possible, and now Ian says they'll be here over the winter."

"Mmm." Alex nodded. Peter Leslie had been struck with apoplexy, and Jenny insisted that she and her family stay, at least until they could ascertain whether he was on his way to recovery or not. Most dutiful, Alex supposed, and how convenient that Malcolm and Maggie lived but a short hour's ride from Jenny's father. "Just because she's there doesn't mean Ian needs to let her see them more often."

"Malcolm wants to," Betty sighed, "and what Malcolm wants, Maggie wants."

"But Ian decides."

Betty smoothed back her riotous hair, struggling to bring that mass of coppery curls into some sort of order. Malcolm wheedled and begged, she said, nagging insistently that he should be allowed to see his real mother, and Maggie... Just yesterday, the girl she had always cared for as her own had shoved her away, shrieking that she wanted her real mother, not Mam. It had forced Betty to step outside so as to hide her tears.

"And what does Ian say?" Alex asked. Idiot of a man! He should have put a stop to this ages ago.

"He doesn't know what to do. If he refuses them to see her, Malcolm shrinks into himself. If he lets them see her, they become more and more unbearable."

"Time to put your foot down, honey." Alex stroked her daughter-in-law over her arm.

"So what do I do?" Betty asked, her eyes huge. Remarkable eyes, Alex always thought, like carnelians.

Alex scrunched her brows together. "I'll handle it, okay?"

It took her two minutes to find Malcolm. He was sitting outside the stables, polishing an assorted collection of harnesses and bridles. He was looking quite grumpy, and when Alex came over, he took the opportunity to complain, saying that it wasn't fair that he had to do all this alone.

"Tell your grandfather that," Alex said, suppressing a small smile when Malcolm sighed, boyish shoulders slumping in defeat. "I thought you liked Betty." Alex sat down beside him.

The boy shrugged. "Aye, but she isn't my mother."

"No?" Alex regarded him in silence. Malcolm squirmed under her eyes. "Who sewed your shirt?"

"Mam – I mean Betty."

"Mmm. And your breeches? Your stockings?"

"Betty." It came out sullenly.

"And when you were ill last winter, who was it that took care of you?"

"Betty."

"Mam, you mean."

"Betty. My real mam—"

"Your real mam left, Malcolm. She left your father. She left you and Maggie."

"She didn't want to! She wanted us with her, but Da took us and—"

"And what?" Alex bored her eyes into the boy.

"He made her leave. On account of Betty."

"That's a huge lie." Alex stood up and looked about for a suitable escort. Not Ian, because he would throw a major fit, nor Matthew for the same reason. She saw Jacob come out of the privy and waved him over, telling him she urgently needed to go to the Leslie place, and would he be kind enough to ride with her?

"Right," Alex said, sitting down to face Jenny with Malcolm beside her. "I want you to tell Malcolm exactly why you left Graham's Garden."

"I already have," Jenny said.

"Well then, you can tell it all again." Alex smiled dangerously. "And I'll correct you when your memory fails, shall I?"

Jenny glared at her, at Jacob who was lounging against the wall.

"Start the summer before Maggie was born," Alex prompted.

Jenny threw her a hateful look, said that she had no reason to repeat herself, and stood, for all the world as if she intended to leave.

Think again. Alex clamped down on Jenny's wrist. "Tell him. Otherwise, I will – in detail."

There was a flash of defiance in Jenny's eyes. She yanked at her wrist, but Alex had no intention of letting go, staring her former daughter-in-law firmly in the eye.

"So, you or I?" she said.

Defeated, Jenny looked at her son and hung her head. "I fell in love with Patrick."

Malcolm nodded, saying that he knew that, they were married now.

"Before, while I was still married to your father." She raised her eyes to his. "I didn't intend it to happen."

"No," Alex interjected, "love has a tendency to just happen. But you chose to act on it."

"Act on it?" Malcolm looked confused.

"She bedded with him," Alex explained for his benefit, and a wave of bright red flew up Jenny's face. "Well, you did, didn't you?"

Jenny nodded.

"You did?" Malcolm stared at his mother. "But why? Didn't you love Da?"

"He had Betty," Jenny flashed.

"No, no, Jenny, that isn't right. Tell your son the truth," Alex said. "Betty was living with us at the time, Malcolm, but your father never touched her in any way until after he divorced your mother. Isn't that right, Jenny?"

Jenny's mouth compressed into a thin line. "Yes," she mumbled.

Malcolm sat very still, eyes hanging off his mother.

"You said—" Malcolm licked his lips.

"I was ashamed," Jenny said in a low voice. "I didn't want you to think less of me. And I didn't want to leave you, I swear I never did."

"That, for what it's worth, I can assure you is true," Alex said. "Your mother loves you very much, of course she does. But so does Betty, and you've been treating her very badly lately, haven't you?"

Malcolm nodded mutely.

Alex stood up and with a quick smile suggested that Jacob follow her and leave Jenny and Malcolm alone for a while.

Jacob led the way to the kitchen, no doubt attracted by the promising smell of biscuits. Most of the Leslie family were there, seated round the table. The door was propped open, the sunlight revealing a floor that could have done with a good scrubbing – as could several of the children milling about.

"How's Peter?" Alex asked once they were settled in the kitchen.

"Not well," Ailish said from where she stood in a corner, placed so that the light fell on her undamaged cheek, leaving the ugly, puckering burn scar that covered the other half of her face in the shadow. "It was a fearful thing to witness," she went on, receiving a confirming grunt from Thomas. "One moment he walks tall and straight across the yard, the next he lies flat on his back on the ground. He hit his head badly coming down."

"Very much blood," Nathan filled in, "but Father never lost consciousness. I'm not sure whether that is a good or bad thing." He sighed, and Ailish drifted over to give her husband a comforting squeeze on the shoulder.

"And now?" Jacob helped himself to yet another hot biscuit.

"He sits in a chair or lies in his bed, incapable of moving his right side," Ailish said. "Tears flow constantly from his eye, drool runs from his mouth, and he can eat but soups and mash, poor man."

"Can he talk?" Alex asked.

"He understands everything, and he attempts to talk, but the paralysis makes it difficult to understand him." Thomas scratched at his short grey hair and shook his head. "He finds it difficult to let others see him like this."

"I can imagine." Alex stretched across the table to clasp Thomas' hand. Poor Peter: he wasn't that old, just a few years over sixty.

"Our main worry is Constance," Thomas said as he accompanied them back to their horses.

"Constance? Why would that be a worry?" The woman hadn't been anywhere close to here in four years or so.

"She's his wife. And how is he to fend himself if she decides she wants to sit close and take care of him and their sons?" Thomas made a sound conveying just how ridiculous the thought of Constance caring for anyone was, and brushed a few crumbs off his dark grey coat.

"Nathan can tell her to eff off," Alex suggested.

"Eff off?" Thomas said.

"Umm, you know, not bother you," Alex said, seeing her son grin at her over Thomas' head.

"It is not quite as simple, Alex." Thomas smiled crookedly. "All these years he has refused her divorce, and so he hasn't regulated the legalities as he should have done."

"What? He doesn't have a will?"

"Of course he has a will," Thomas said, "but he also has a wife that has certain rights."

"Oh." Well, Alex assumed that was as it should be – Constance had come well-dowered and must as a consequence have a good jointure. "He isn't dead, so you can draft whatever documents he needs now."

"And how will he sign them?" Thomas asked her.

"He doesn't have to. You can bring a lawyer and one of the ministers up here, and he can talk to them, verify the documents in their presence. Witnesses, like."

"Hmm," Thomas replied, and a small smile touched his lips. "Yes, that could be done, I suppose."

It was the first time Ian had been truly angry with her, his eyes so cold it turned her stomach.

"I won't have you meddling in my business," he barked, "and it's I, not you, that decides what truths my children must be told."

"Oh, really? And what were you actually doing to sort it all?" Alex snapped back, helping Malcolm down before dismounting.

"I was planning to talk to the lad myself," Ian replied, drawing his son towards him.

153

"Wonderful. When? You were letting him get away with being rude to your wife, his Mam, day after day."

Malcolm twisted at her words, eyeing Ian warily.

Ian flushed. "I was going to handle it, but I wasn't planning on involving my ex-wife."

"Tough." Alex stood with her hands on her hips, glaring at him. "Me, personally, I think the truth comes better from the horse's mouth."

"It wasn't your call! This is my son, not yours! I don't recall asking you to meddle."

"Meddle? I wasn't meddling, you idiot! I was trying to help Betty, who, in case you haven't noticed, has been having a rough time with both Malcolm and Maggie lately."

"I have noticed, and next time my son speaks out of line to her, he'll feel the strap." Ian griped Malcolm hard to him and stared belligerently at Alex.

"Great! Fantastic way of addressing the problem – so proactive."

"You don't tell me what to do! You're not my—" He bit off so abruptly, Alex snorted with involuntary laughter.

"I'm not what, Ian?" she asked with deceptive mildness. "Go on," she went on at his continued silence. "Tell your son."

Malcolm craned back his head to look at his father.

"You're not my mother," Ian whispered.

Alex closed the distance between them so quickly Ian backed away, his son a shield between them. She was swimming with hurt, but kept her voice low and composed.

"Oh yes, I am, Ian Graham. In everything that counts, I'm your mother, and you know that, don't you? And if it weren't because I have better things to do, I'd lay you over my knees and belt you for saying what you just did."

"Mama," Ian said, but Alex was already ploughing away from them, running in the direction of the house.

"Is it true?" Malcolm stared after his grandmother. "Is Granny not your mother?"

"You heard her. In everything that counts, she is." Ian looked down at his son and ruffled his hair. "But no, she isn't my birth mother." He leaned back against the sun-warmed stable wall, his eyes on Alex until she stepped inside. "She didn't have to love me, and yet she always has and made me know it." He smiled down at his son. "And I love her. More than anyone else in the world bar my wife and my bairns."

"More than your da?" Malcolm asked.

"Aye," Ian breathed, "even more than Da."

They made it up, of course. Just before supper, Ian came to find her and offered her a rosebud. Wordlessly, she opened her arms to hug him close, this her beloved son, thinking that the ways of the heart were totally inexplicable.

"I'm too old to be belted," he murmured.

"You think? Don't tempt me, Ian Graham."

Chapter 19

"I'm not sure I like it when you read from Leviticus," Alex told Matthew once he had finished the customary Sunday evening reading. "It's very harsh." All those callous instructions to kill – for adultery, for homosexuality...

"Those are the laws," Matthew replied.

"Very primitive laws. It's never quite as black and white in real life, is it?"

"Are you saying adultery can be condoned?" Matthew asked her, following her up the stairs.

"Sometimes. If, for example, a young girl is married off to a man she doesn't much care for, and then falls in love elsewhere."

"No." Matthew shook his head. "It's wrong. Adultery is a grave sin."

"Strangely enough, mostly when it's the woman who commits it. All those men who visit whores, aren't they in principle adulterers?" She set the pitcher of hot water down on her little table and began unbuttoning her bodice.

"Aye," Matthew agreed, looking somewhat uncomfortable.

"And so, if we're to follow God's law, then they should be put to death – them and the whores, of course." Alex slid a look at him. "I don't see that happening much, and if it did, Minister Walker would be one of the first to go up in flames."

"Alex! How do you know—?" He snapped his mouth shut, flushing at his indirect admittance of Minister Walker's more sinful side.

"Know what? That he frequents Mrs Malone quite often – as does dear, distinguished Mr Farrell?" She laughed. "You've told me, remember? Men are awful gossips." But no one would dream of telling Mrs Walker, and in Alex's opinion, the fact that Minister Walker occasionally roamed the fleshpots probably led to him being more humble and understanding in his ministry.

"It isn't as if he is a regular," Matthew said. "Aye, he goes often for the beer, to flirt with the lasses, no more. I don't think he does more than grope and kiss – mayhap but once or twice in all these years."

"Still, according to good old Moses, he should be put to death." Alex slashed her finger across her throat.

"It's on account of the bairns." Matthew stretched out on his side on the bed while she undressed and did her evening things.

"The bairns?" Alex met his eyes in the looking glass. She'd been round to kiss her children goodnight, all three of them, seeing as Jacob told her he didn't want her to come and tuck him in, and Ruth was in Providence. Adam and David shared a bed that resembled a battlefield, even now that they had one quilt each, while Sarah lay very alone in her and Ruth's room. A hollowness came over Alex every time she went into the boys' room. There still hung Samuel's extra pair of breeches. There still stood the horses Matthew had carved him for his birthdays – ten of them – but there no longer lay a boy to kiss and cuddle.

She picked up her brush and began to work her way through her hair, hiding her eyes from Matthew. Two months and counting, and every time it rained, every time the autumn winds came flying from the north to make the window glass shiver in its frames, she thought of her Samuel, out there without her. She thought about him much, much more than that, and now she ended every evening with her own little ritual, ignoring Matthew's worried eyes on her back. First, she prayed silently to God that he take care of her lost son; then she lit a lantern and placed it in the window to burn like a beacon throughout the night – in case he should by some miracle come stumbling home.

Matthew watched her rise from the stool and make her way to the window. When she clasped her hands, so did he, silently joining his prayer to hers.

May You care for him and keep him safe, oh Lord; may You help him remember we love him and miss him; may You guide him home, to us, lest we die of broken hearts. But, most of all, dear Lord, comfort him when he weeps, as he must surely do.

Matthew drew in an unsteady breath, held it for a couple of heartbeats before releasing it.

By the window, Alex had lit the lantern, placing it right in the centre of the sill. She seemed to freeze, arms locked hard over her chest, back curving. Matthew rolled out of bed and padded over the room towards her. She was holding her breath, upper teeth sunk into her lower lip.

"Alex? Come to bed, lass."

She didn't respond, nose touching the windowpane, and Matthew gripped her by the shoulders, giving her a gentle shake. She exhaled and leaned back against his chest, her eyes still on the dark outside.

"How do you mean, the children?" she asked in a voice that clearly showed the strain of attempting to sound normal.

"The bairns? What bairns?"

"You said how it was all on account of the children."

"Oh." Matthew rested his chin on the top of her head and enveloped her in his arms. He had to think back a bit to recall what they had been talking about before she so evidently sank into thoughts of Samuel, dragging him with her. "Adultery is a worse sin for the woman on account of the children."

"Because the man never knows." She nodded. "Still, very hypocritical if you ask me," she said, her voice resuming its normal timbre.

"Hypocritical?" His hands cupped her breasts. "How hypocritical?"

"To turn a blind eye to male infidelity while punishing female indiscretion. Mind you, I would definitely punish male infidelities."

Matthew laughed against her hair. "You think I don't know? You'd claw my eyes out."

"Your eyes? Why on earth would I go for your eyes?" She turned in his arms, one hand delicately cupping his naked genitalia beneath his shirt. "I like your eyes," she murmured. "So very much do I like your eyes."

"Oh aye?" He kissed her upturned face, her eyes, her nose, the corner of her mouth, and the mouth itself – a soft kiss, close-lipped and warm. "And you don't like him, down there?" he whispered as she pushed him down to sit on the bed. In reply, she bent her head and kissed him back before he pulled her down on top of him.

It still amazed him: he knew this woman inside out; there wasn't an inch on her body he hadn't touched, kissed at one time or the other. He had held her breasts millions of times in his hands, had taken her in a multitude of ways and places, and yet there were times when it was all startling and new, her reactions a gratifying surprise, from the gurgling laughter when he tickled her with his hair to how she bucked below him, eyes burning into his. Tonight, her hunger for him was whetted by grief and loss, making her more demanding, rougher and louder. He replied in kind, rolling her over to pin her to the mattress with his longer, stronger body, driving into her with increasing force. He closed his eyes when her nails sank a bit too hard into his skin, leaving tracks of stinging pain along his back and flanks.

"Ah!" he exclaimed, half in anger, half in arousal when she bit him, far too hard. "Merciful heaven!" he breathed to the night at large, dipped his head to kiss her, bite her as she had just bitten him. She urged him on with heels and hands, her head whipped back and forth over the pillows, her eyes rolled back, her throat was bared to him, a wordless surrender to his strength and vitality. Afterwards, they lay silent and sweaty, legs still twisted together, his wet mouth pressed to her throat, his hand held hard by hers.

"I love you," he whispered.

"I know." She raised his hand to her mouth, kissed his inner wrist. "And I love you."

"Of course you do." He smiled into her hair. "Who wouldn't, after that performance?"

"Braggart," she muttered, and Matthew drew her closer and laughed.

★

Laundry days were days best spent far away from the house, as Alex's mood tended to deteriorate as the day progressed, no doubt due to a combination of weariness and bodily aches. Today was no exception, with Matthew taking his sons with him to repair the fencing along one side of the meadow while the women assembled in the yard, none of them looking all that enthused. The linen had been set to soak already last night, Mark had piled wood within easy reach of the laundry shed, and when Mrs Parson appeared from the kitchen carrying the lye, Matthew raised his axe in a little wave and set off.

Four hours later, Betty came to find them, still more wet than dry, still with the clout tied tight round her hair, and her fingers reddened with lye.

"Naomi," she gasped, "the babe."

Mark dropped the fence pole he was holding and broke into a run, Jacob at his heels.

"How?" Matthew was already moving towards the house with Betty and Ian in tow. Betty shook her head, inhaled a couple of times.

"It just…" She looked away.

"She shouldn't have helped with the laundry," Matthew said.

Betty hitched her shoulders, saying that Alex had kept Naomi well away from the heavy lifting.

Once back home, Matthew was met by Mrs Parson who, with a heavy voice, told him it was too late. The wean was dead, and a small, shrivelled thing it was. "They're in there," she said, nodding in the direction of Mark's cabin. "Alex is with them."

The cabin was dark and stuffy. It smelled of blood and urine, and Mark was kneeling by the bed, his wife held to his heart.

"I'm sorry." Naomi was red-eyed from weeping. "I'm so very, very sorry." She began to cry again, this time with her head hidden against Mark's shoulder.

"It's alright," Mark soothed. "It wasn't your fault."

"Yes, it is," Naomi whispered, gripping at his shirt. "You see, at first I didn't want it, not so soon after Lettie." She snivelled and pressed herself even closer. "I was scared, and just then, at the beginning, I hoped it wouldn't be... But now I wanted him, God, I swear I did!" She burrowed even deeper against his chest.

Alex placed a hand on Naomi's head. "That's bullshit, okay? You miscarried – through no fault of your own."

Naomi cried all the harder, repeating that this was God's punishment.

Mark lifted her face to see her eyes. "It's alright. We'll have more bairns when you're ready for it. And surely you don't think God would end this little life for your convenience?"

"No," Naomi sobbed after a while. She clung to Mark, and Mark clung back.

"Leave them be," Matthew murmured in Alex's ear. "They are better off alone." Without a word, she followed him out of the little house.

A few hours later, Matthew entered the stables.

"If you curry him much longer, he won't have any hide left." His voice made Mark start awake from whatever dream he had been playing in his head. "I'm sorry for your loss, lad."

"Aye." Mark nodded, rubbing the horse behind its ears. "I didn't even know the wean, and still I miss him."

"Of course you do. He's a promise unfulfilled."

"Did he...do you suppose...did it hurt him, the dying, and he all alone?"

"Nay, lad, I think not. As deaths go, it must be right comfortable, there in your mother's womb, surrounded by her sounds and warmth."

"And do you think he was scared that he was dying?"

"I don't know," Matthew said, "but I've seen many men die, and it has always seemed to me that if the dying was easy then there was no fear." And very rarely did that happen – most of the deaths he'd seen as a young soldier had been frantic fights to stay alive.

Mark's shoulders relaxed somewhat at his words and, with a last pat on the horse's neck, he stepped out of the stall. "But now he is with God," he said.

"Assuredly," Matthew agreed, "a wee soul called home." He embraced his son and reflected that Alex was right: it was so much easier to comfort a small child than a grown one.

"This is turning into a rather depressing week," Alex said in an undertone to Matthew a couple of days later.

"Aye."

Peter Leslie had suffered yet another seizure, and this time he was laid flat on his back, incapable of any kind of speech. And as a buzzard at a kill, Constance Leslie had ridden into the yard of Leslie's Crossing only hours after, demanding she be given access to her beloved husband and her sons.

"Nathan refused," Thomas now said, shaking his head at yet another helping of one of Alex's strange vegetable concoctions. "But she came with her lawyer cousin, as well as with the new minister – you know, the rather big man, Gregor something."

"Minister Macpherson," Alex supplied, sounding as if she had her mouth full of worms.

Matthew slid her a look. She was not much taken with this new minister, a feeling that was obviously reciprocated. Plus she insisted he reminded her of Richard Campbell, for all that he was twice the size of that scrawny toad of a minister. Matthew had hummed and hawed when she'd pointed this out, uncomfortable with remembering that long ago summer when he'd brought Richard Campbell home, only to have his marriage more or less collapse as a consequence.

"Yes, that's him." Thomas regarded Matthew in silence. "I can't say I warm much to the man, for all that he is most devout."

"He's got a broomstick up his arse," Alex muttered, "and I guess it leaves him full of splinters and constipated to boot."

Thomas grinned. Matthew did as well, winking at his

friend before turning a serious face to his wife. "You shouldn't speak of your betters with disrespect."

"Betters? How is he my better? Bloody narrow-minded man, if you ask me! All that sermon we sat through, with him going on and on about how women must at all times be held in check, lest their natural sinfulness take them over! I bet he doesn't get laid all that often!" Belatedly, she registered that Matthew was grinning, and with a small snort she shifted to sit closer to Thomas, which in turn made Thomas smile.

"So, now what?" Alex asked, returning to the original subject.

"Well…" Thomas fidgeted back and forth, muttering something about it being mightily cold to sleep outdoors.

"Uh-uh, no way," Alex said, standing up.

"But what are we to do? And it's only for a few days."

"No way do I open my house to that minister!" Alex snapped.

Matthew caught her eyes and raised his brows, stifling a little smile at how she flushed at this silent reminder that such decisions were his, not hers, to take. Not that he had any intention of disagreeing with her on this particular issue, but still.

"Not to him, to Constance," Thomas said.

"Oh, Jesus," Alex sighed, glaring at Matthew as if this was his fault.

Matthew made a helpless gesture. What were they to do, given the circumstances? "We will offer them a roof over their head and board," he said, "but let's hope they don't expect a warm welcome."

Chapter 20

"This is just too much!" Alex shook her head. "Thomas could at least have mentioned that Constance brings Fiona with her as her maid." This was going to be cosy: Ian and Fiona at close quarters with Betty hovering like the jealous demon from hell.

"It isn't certain that he knew," Mrs Parson said. "He didn't know her very well, did he? And she has changed, no?"

"Immensely, and I'm talking in less than six months." Alex pursed her mouth and studied Fiona, who was standing in the yard, surveying what had once been her home. The worn, gaunt woman she'd seen down by the fish stalls in Providence was still gaunt, still worn, but much better dressed, her hair pinned up beneath a sedate cap.

Ian came to a halt at the sight of Fiona.

"What's she doing here?" he asked, sounding as if he'd much rather share a bed with a rattlesnake than having Fiona within a stone's throw.

"I don't know," Matthew replied, "but my astute observations lead me to suspect she is here as Constance Leslie's maid – or chaperone." He nodded in the direction of the third rider, a man on a flamboyant skewbald in chestnut and white with beautiful feathers on its fetlocks.

"Chaperone?" Ian shaded his eyes against the low November sun. "Is that not her lawyer?"

"Not only, according to your mama," Matthew replied. "To quote her, she says that last time she saw them together, in Providence, Constance was doing some in-depth probing of that man's tonsils."

"Hmm." Ian nodded. "Tonsils?"

"I don't know – something in your throat."

"Ah."

The intervening years had not in any way improved Constance's disposition. No sooner was she off her horse than she began to complain.

"I still don't understand," she said to the man beside her. "Not at all do I understand why we were sent off to stay here, rather than in the comforts of Leslie's Crossing." She looked with undisguised contempt at the Graham home.

"Oh, by all means, be my guest and ride out into the woods or something. Maybe you could run into a bear." Alex nodded to Fiona, swept her eyes over Constance, and regarded the stranger. "And you are...?" she finally prompted, interrupting the man's minute examination of her home.

He went the colour of a beet and swept off his hat before bowing in her direction. "Jefferson," he introduced himself, "Thomas Jefferson." Alex almost choked, before reminding herself that Jefferson was as yet not born. "From Virginia," he added with certain pride.

"Well, aren't you the lucky one," Alex said.

"I'm here to support my cousin in any way I can," he went on, smiling down at Constance who, to Alex's surprise, smiled back quite sweetly, ducking her head in a way that made all those carefully contrived ringlets dance around her lace-edged cap.

"Constance, Mr Jefferson." Matthew shook hands and bowed, was as curt as Alex had been in his nod to Fiona, and with a movement of his arm invited them inside.

Constance stood in the doorway and surveyed the parlour, eyes flying from the few armchairs, the game table with the chess set, the desk, the shelves above it, the two pewter candlesticks, the cushions, the knitted throws and the rug before smiling condescendingly. She strolled over the floor, stopped for a moment to run her finger over one of Matthew's more exotic efforts, a vine that clambered up one of the chairs' legs to explode in wooden blossom along the backrest, and came to a halt by the bookshelf. One thin white hand caressed the wooden lion that served as a book rest.

"Are these all the books you have?" She laughed, waving a hand at the thirty-odd volumes that stood shelved.

Alex chose not to answer, but was presently entertaining herself by picturing Constance wallowing in the privy pit.

Constance perused the titles, one well-manicured digit travelling down the battered spines, and then went to peer at the single drawing that decorated the wall.

Mr Jefferson joined her, studying Alex's depiction of her children with some admiration. "This is very good." He smiled at Alex, earning himself a black look from Constance.

"Oh aye, Mama is a right good limner," Mark said. "Has a full set of wee sketches upstairs."

"Really?" Mr Jefferson sounded interested. "Of what?"

"My children, mostly," Alex said, avoiding Mark's amused eyes. In truth, most of her sketches were of Matthew.

"We prefer oils," Constance sniffed. "Portraits done by real painters."

"Ah," Alex said, before leading the way to the downstairs bedroom she'd put aside for Constance's use.

"Here?" Constance looked about with a displeased expression. "Why, it's smaller than the room my slave girl sleeps in back home." She took off her cap, smoothed at her dark hair before pinning the nominal scrap of lace back into place.

"Well then, go back there," Alex suggested. Over the last few minutes, Constance had spewed barbed comments about everything. What? No instruments? No settle? No upholstered armchairs? Why, it was all very simple, wasn't it, but then, out here in the woods… If Matthew hadn't taken hold of Alex's hand and held it firmly in his own, she would have raked her nails over the prim expression on Constance's face.

Constance ignored Alex and went to sit on the bed. "Very narrow."

"I'm sure you'll fit," Alex replied.

"Fit, of course I'll fit!" Constance snapped.

"And Fiona is rather thin, so that shouldn't be a problem."

"Fiona?" Constance shook her head. "No, Fiona will sleep elsewhere."

"No, she won't," Alex told her. "But it's up to you to fight it out between yourselves if she should sleep on the floor or in the bed."

If Mr Jefferson was unhappy with his assigned sleeping nook in the parlour, he was intelligent enough to keep it to himself, attempting to compensate for Constance's stinging remarks by his own appreciative murmurings.

"It's a bit difficult for her, what with her husband and her sons." Mr Jefferson looked a bit hangdog, dark eyes darting in the direction of Constance, now busy haranguing Fiona. "She's such a warm person, so easily upset by the plight of others, and to see Mr Leslie like that…" He let his voice drift to a stop.

"She hides it well," Matthew said.

"Timid," Thomas Jefferson sighed, and Alex had to convert a guffaw into a cough. Sometimes men were really, really stupid.

After a long, endless afternoon, punctured by shrill demands for this or that, the household sat down to supper. Agnes placed rye bread on the table, set down a pitcher of ale, and helped Alex serve the soup. Constance sniffed, stirred and tasted, grimacing as she shoved away the plate.

"I'm not partial to peas, and all these herbs…" She shook her head, throwing Alex a sly look. "Well, one never knows what they might be."

"Thyme," Alex said, using her ladle to stir the thick pea soup that smelled not only of thyme but also of mustard and salted pork.

"Hmm." Constance muttered a comment to Mr Jefferson.

Once the soup bowls had been cleared away, Constance sat up expectantly, only to slump theatrically a few moments later.

"No main course?"

What did she expect? Silver platters laden with pheasants and swans?

"That was the main course," Alex said.

"Then I'd better have some," Constance said with ill grace. "I can't risk to starve."

"Too late," Alex snapped. "We're moving on to dessert."

Constance perked up. She had quite the sweet tooth, she admitted with a low laugh. In fact, her father at times cautioned her against eating too much as it might make her unnecessarily sweet.

Alex made a face. Was the woman inane or did she just enjoy being an enervating little bitch? She put the pudding dish on the table, seeing her family shine up at her cheesecake – the Swedish kind, with curd and almonds and eggs.

"Swedish?" Constance nibbled carefully. She served herself twice, heaping her plate with far more than her fair share, but when she stretched herself for a third, Alex whipped away the dish.

"Everyone hasn't had their seconds yet," she said, making Constance blush at the implied criticism.

Constance looked around the table and back at Alex. "You don't need yours. In fact, it might do you well to abstain."

"What?" Alex planted her hands on the table, half rising to stare at Constance.

"You're fat," Constance elucidated, shoving away from the table.

Matthew very slowly sat back, wiped his mouth, and locked eyes with Constance. "Who do you think you are, Constance Leslie, to sit at my table and insult my wife?"

Constance glared at him, her pointed chin jutting. "I was just pointing out the truth: your wife could do with shedding a pound or two."

"Constance!" Mr Jefferson hissed, squirming on his seat.

"What did your mother do to you? Dip you in a vat of vinegar and leave you to soak?" Mrs Parson said.

"She did no such thing! I was raised properly!" Constance's face set into a scowl.

"But they missed out the part about respect to your elders and politeness in general, did they?" Mrs Parson said. "And they forgot, didn't they, to teach you not to hurt people on purpose, no?"

Constance went a bright red, leaping to her feet. "It was an accident!"

"Accident, my arse," Alex said. "You just happened to cross the kitchen, dig out the ladle, fill the ladle with boiling sugar and fling it at Ailish. Happens all the time."

"Constance?" Mr Jefferson got to his feet as well. "What is this they're talking about?"

"You misconstrue!" Constance shrieked. "And that Ailish: who did she think she was?"

"Misconstrue?" Mark echoed. "What is there to misunderstand? You could have blinded her."

"Constance?" Mr Jefferson repeated.

"She didn't tell you?" Mrs Parson chuckled. "How she was thrown out of the Leslie home on account of her throwing hot sugar in her daughter-in-law's face?"

"Be quiet!" Constance yelled. "Be quiet, you old crone! I know all about you and her..." She swung to point at Alex. "...the two of you, making strange decoctions and salves." She wheeled on her toes and rushed from the room, leaving a stunned silence behind.

Mr Jefferson hovered between door and table, not quite sure what to do.

"You gather, I hope, that we're not overly thrilled to have Constance here," Matthew said.

Mr Jefferson nodded unhappily.

"We're only doing it as a favour to Thomas and Peter Leslie," Matthew continued, "and, rest assured, Mr Jefferson, that if Constance doesn't improve her behaviour, you will be sleeping in the stable with the beasts. And I'll not have her insinuating things about my wife or Mrs Parson, so you'd best reprimand her in private."

Jefferson nodded several times, assuring Matthew that of course he would, and Constance had not really meant it how it came out.

"Huh," Alex put in, rather shaken by Constance's veiled accusation of witchery.

"She's very upset at present." Mr Jefferson looked apologetic. "And you are well acquainted, I presume, with

Peter Leslie's refusal to allow her access to her sons. What mother wouldn't suffer from being separated from her babies, and Constance is a most tender-hearted woman – deep inside."

"Deep enough that no one ever sees it," Alex said. "As I recall, she gave the babies over in the keeping of their wet nurse, and that was that."

"But of course! A well-bred woman doesn't nurse her own. Surely you are of similar thoughts, Mrs Graham, and—" He came to a stop, eyes flying to Betty who had Timothy in her arms.

"A good mother nurses her own," Alex said. "It ensures a healthy child."

"But..." Mr Jefferson cleared his throat. "I must find Constance," he mumbled and left the kitchen.

Fiona got to her feet. "I should go as well, help her with her undressing and all that."

Alex raised her brows. "She must be old enough to manage that on her own, so why does she need a maid?"

"For the lads," Fiona said, "on the way back."

"Oh." That was news to Alex. She assumed Peter's intent was for the boys to stay with Nathan and Ailish, and grimaced at what she perceived could be a huge legal battle.

She raised the subject once she and Matthew were alone in the parlour, receiving an amused look in return.

"Nay, it won't be much of an issue. Guardianship of the lads rests with their closest male relative, and that is Nathan. Or Thomas." Matthew closed the book he had been reading, marking his place with a piece of ribbon.

"So, if you were to die while our youngest boys still are underage, it would be Ian, not me, who'd be their guardian?"

Matthew nodded. "But I don't intend for that to happen."

"I dare say Peter wasn't planning on having a stroke either."

"I'm nearly ten years younger. And," he added with a twinkle, "I'm far, far healthier."

"Yes, I suppose you are," she said, eyeing him critically. Except for the heavy colds he always got in winter, he was remarkably healthy, and his daily work kept him lean and fit, with only the slightest of softness around his middle. He could still run almost as fast as his sons, still wield an axe or drive the plough into the stony ground, still hit a raccoon from well over 200 yards, and in bed... She concentrated on the shirt she was mending, turning the cuffs to get some more wear out of it. Once she was done, she folded it away and stood.

"Is she right?" she asked, walking over to sit in his lap.

"Is who right?" He stuck his nose in between her breasts and exhaled, tickling her.

"Constance. Am I too fat?"

Matthew kept his nose where it was for some time, arms pleasantly tight round her. "I love you just as you are."

"I sincerely hope you'd love me even if I was the size of a gorilla. That wasn't what I asked, was it?" She leaned back to see his face. "Am I?"

Matthew just shook his head. "You're just as I want you to be. Round and bonny, but not fat, definitely not."

"Hmm," Alex replied, somewhat mollified – even if she decided then and there that she was going on a diet.

Chapter 21

Lucy nearly fell down dead the day she found her mother-in-law holding her little picture. How careless of her! She flew across the room and snatched it out of Kate's hands, all of her shaking with fear. She didn't even try to explain; she just whirled and bounded up the stairs, wondering how on earth the picture had made it all the way downstairs. In her pocket – she sagged with relief. Yes, it had been in the petticoat pocket and mistakenly been carried down for laundry.

Lucy had expected Kate to subject her to a barrage of questions regarding her odd behaviour and was dumbfounded when her mother-in-law instead came up to discuss an evening event, complete with music and dancing. Dancing? Lucy enjoyed dancing and was good at it, the soles of her feet quick at picking up on the deep bass vibrations of certain instruments. A new dress? No, Lucy assured Kate with a smile, she had dresses enough, and the new green one...

"A new one," Kate insisted. "I think perhaps in rich red with a pale yellow petticoat to match."

Henry was doubtful about the whole thing, but knew his mother well enough to not even attempt a discussion, promising that he would invite some of his friends.

"I want it to be mostly young people," Kate said. "An opportunity for Lucy to be with people her own age, and I've already arranged for music so that there can be dancing." She sighed, placed a hand on his arm. "I fear she's lonely, and even if she attempts to occupy herself with this and that – she's even dabbling in paints, I think – time must pass dreadfully slowly for one who cannot talk or hear."

"Paints?" Henry had never seen Lucy as much as raise a brush.

"Not very good," Kate said. "A little nondescript thing, mostly in blues and greens."

"Ah." Henry shrugged.

"So, we're in agreement? You invite your friends, and I will arrange for music and dancing."

"Dancing? Is that entirely wise?" Henry frowned at her. The new minister was a solemn man, much given to promoting the narrowness of the dutiful Christian's path, and even if Henry had a roomy conscience, he had no intention of riling the ministers.

"Oh, come!" Kate scoffed. "It will be a most proper affair. I shall invite both Reverend Norton and the new minister, if you like."

Henry shook his head. "Minister Macpherson is not the most expansive of men, and as I hear it he isn't in town, but why not include Minister Walker and his wife?"

They both grinned.

The only one who was not dragged along in the general enthusiasm over the upcoming party was Lucy. She had quickly concluded that Kate was doing this for her sake, creating a stage for her misfit daughter-in-law to shine, and she was in two minds about all this.

Yes, she very much looked forward to glowing in her new gown, whipped together at impressive speed by Mrs Malone and a bevy of assistants. No, she didn't want to be paraded like the village idiot before the condescending eyes of what counted as Providence's high society. Besides, she had other concerns. Where before it had been enough to spend a solitary half-hour with the painting, increasingly she found herself losing track of time to find the morning gone, sunk into all those stories that the painting whispered and dripped into her head.

Twice, she had considered destroying it, and once she had even brought it close to her lit candle, but the voices, the sounds... Cold sweat broke out along her spine at the thought of once again immuring herself in silence, and she just couldn't do it. The Voice had become like a close friend, a person whose secrets had been handed over into her cupped hands to hold and cherish.

Kate rarely did anything half-heartedly. The household groaned with all the preparations for the upcoming event, and Lucy took to escaping the house, either by visiting her mother or by taking Frances walking along the shoreline. Frances was an easy child: give her some sticks and some water and she'd keep herself happily entertained, while Lucy sat beside her, free to let her mind wander. Frances tugged at her skirts, and Lucy looked down at her from where she'd been staring out at the sea, mentally hearing the water crash against the rocks.

"Mama," Frances mouthed and patted her leg. "Look, Papa."

Henry? Lucy followed the pudgy little finger to see it was indeed her husband and his boon companion, Edward Farrell. She took her daughter by the hand and strolled towards them. Her cloak stood wild around her in the rising wind, and even with one hand clapped to hold her cap in place, she could feel her hair beginning to escape its braid to whip around her face.

She saw them laughing, an admiring flash flying through Edward's eyes, and she stopped, waiting for them, quite aware of how appealing she must look against the backdrop of the swiftly moving clouds. She squinted to better see them, focusing on their mouths. At a distance of only a dozen yards, she could easily make out the lip movements, and smiled at Edwards's frank comment on how the wind had moulded her clothes to her bosom. It was unfortunate that he kept his face turned in her direction and that the rising wind forced him to enunciate with far more precision than he normally would use; otherwise, she would never have caught his follow-up.

"It must be difficult for you," Edward Farrell commiserated, "to live with a woman as strange and simple as she is."

In vain, she waited for Henry to say something cutting in her defence. Instead, he just nodded, clasped his hands behind his back, and continued towards her.

Some things a wife must never do, Lucy thought bitterly much, much later. She must never taunt her husband, never flaunt his authority, and never, ever refuse him access to her bed. She winced as she stretched one limb at a time, making sure all of her was still there before getting out of bed to pad across the room to where she had her chamber pot. It hurt to crouch, and she wondered what her back and buttocks looked like, but decided she didn't want to know.

It had all begun by chance: Henry placing a hand on her lower back to draw her close, capturing her eye before telling her that he would be up shortly to spend the night in her bed – as if it were a boon she must be grateful for. Something had flared in her. She had scribbled a note and pressed it into his hand before striding off.

She hadn't expected him to be so quick, nor had she thought her little note would so aggravate him. All she had written was that his strange and simple wife had no wish to see him in her bed that night, hoping to cause him shame, not anger. She had expected a chagrined apology, not a hand that closed on her arm and threw her into her room. And she had no idea where her own anger had come from, but where he had hurt her, she had hurt him back, sending him stumbling with an open-handed slap that caught him straight across the mouth.

She straightened up and looked over to where her bed was in total disarray, one pillow torn in two, the top mattress halfway on its way to the floor. On the floor lay her clothes, torn from her, and there, in a corner, was his coat, the sleeve barely hanging on. He had punished her for hitting him, and she had hit him again. At one point, they'd stood panting like animals, both of them half-naked. And then…Lucy ran a tongue over her teeth, used her fingers to inspect her face. A bit puffy on one side, that was all. At least he had bruises of his own, and next time… Yes, next time. She waited until the new maid had finished making up the bed and smiled as she placed her little picture openly on the pillows.

When Henry came down for breakfast, she was already

there, smiling serenely at him. The bruise across her cheekbone was expertly concealed, her hair fell in soft waves round her face, and very much on purpose she sat back, allowing the silk nightgown to gape open over her breasts. She saw his nostrils widen, eyes glazing somewhat as they locked on her chest. He stood and with a jerk of his head suggested they repair upstairs. Slowly, she smiled and slowly she stood, placing her hand in his.

She nearly hurled the painting against the wall in her frustration. He had looked at it, shrugged and pulled her down onto the bed, and when she struggled, it had only excited him further, and now she was even more bruised than before and just as dishevelled. She drew her knees up close and used a finger to prod at the picture. Maybe the magic was gone, she thought with a mingled sense of relief and disappointment. Not entirely, it wasn't, because it still whispered and sang. But Kate had not seemed much perturbed, and as for Henry, he had held it this way and that, said that perhaps she needed to become better at defining the horizon. Not everyone was susceptible to the tide of time, she concluded. Maybe only women?

She left it out in the open the following few days, and Henry looked at it at times, not at all at others. No, because Henry had found a new wife beneath the silent, well-groomed demeanour, a woman who snarled and fought back, giving as good as she got. My lioness, he'd laugh, promising that he'd tame her this time too, and she would increase her efforts to fight free, aroused by the violence and the intensity. It was hard and rough, she had splinters in her knees, a constantly sore posterior, while he had bite marks up the inside of his legs that made it difficult to walk.

They sleepwalked through their days, and then came the night, and in the hours when the world lay bleached of colour, he rose above her and demanded more. Every time Lucy fought him, and every time it ended as he wanted it, with her widening her thighs, her skin flaming from her last punishment.

★

Kate's evening event was a great success. The dancing had gone on well into the small hours, and when the guests finally left, Kate sank down to sit in her favourite armchair.

"Oh dear," she groaned. "I fear this evening will carry quite the price on the morrow."

"Evening?" Henry laughed. "Night, Mother. At one point, I was convinced they would all stay for breakfast." He smiled over to where Lucy sat with closed eyes, her foot tapping in a remembered rhythm. "She enjoyed it."

"She seemed to," Kate said and yawned. "She was beyond doubt the prettiest wife here."

"Yes, very fetching, and a competent dancer as well."

"I wonder how she does that," Kate mused.

Henry scratched at his hair. "She can feel the vibrations of the tabor, and as that sets the beat, she can easily follow." He stood and stretched, dropped a kiss on his mother's head, and went over to where his wife was sitting.

"Bed?" he mouthed, holding out his arm. She swayed onto her feet, somewhat woozy from having drunk a bit too much, and slipped her arm under his. As they were leaving the room, Henry's eyes caught on the polished lute that lay atop the virginals.

"Emily Farrell forgot her lute," he said to Kate. "I dare say that means we'll see her early tomorrow as she comes to reclaim it. Edward has confided he suspects she is fonder of her instrument than she is of his." Henry laughed at his own double entendre and then hastened Lucy up the stairs for yet another marital bout in the wide bed.

Lucy woke late, and beside her Henry lay snoring. Lucy smiled. This new game of theirs had an appetizing edge to it, almost so that she had forgiven him that first time. Almost. But she was glad he hadn't disappeared into nothingness, she thought, sneaking a look at him. She stretched. Not a patch on her where he hadn't somehow left his mark over the last few weeks.

The door opened. Lucy threw a sheet over her husband's nudity, gestured for the maid to come in, and sat back against the pillows, fiddling with the long ties of her shift. He woke when the tray was set down and they shared the food in silence – well, she was always quiet – and then Henry rolled out of bed with a grunt and looked about for shirt and breeches.

"Business," he said as he left the room.

Business indeed. Lucy smirked at his back. It was Kate, not Henry, who ran the Jones estate, with Henry doing what his mother needed done. He didn't seem to mind much, trusting his mother's judgement implicitly, and why shouldn't he? Since his father's death, Kate had more than tripled its worth through a series of astute investments and, as she admitted to Lucy, sheer luck.

After waiting while the breakfast tray was cleared away, Lucy sat down for her daily communion with her patch of blue and green. Strange – where before she could sit and stare at it for hours with no discomfort whatsoever, the last few days she had experienced a sensation of sudden tilts and whirls, exhilarating at times, exceedingly disconcerting at others.

Today, the painting shared with her the million sounds that live within the sea: the song of whales and mermaids; the rush of currents through the endless forests of seaweed; the clatter of a pelican's beak; the dull plop of a jellyfish landing on a rock.

Only by chance did she happen to look up in time to see Emily Farrell come up the garden path with little Nicholas in tow, and in her haste she left the painting on her desk and hurried down the stairs to greet them.

Lucy neither liked nor disliked Emily, but she was fascinated by her hands: very narrow and very white. Emily used them to underline whatever she was saying, and to Lucy it was like watching the mating dance of a pair of graceful birds. Everything Emily had close she touched, light fingers caressing tabletops, embroidered cushions, the ornate silver candlesticks – even the frames around Kate's paintings. And when she picked up her lute, her hands splayed themselves wide over its rounded back, sensually running over the dark wood. Up and down her hands went, sinuously her left hand flew up the neck to where the peg box reared back, and Emily smiled, content in that her beloved instrument was whole.

If it hadn't been for those hands, it wouldn't have happened. Hypnotised by them, Lucy's attention wandered. When Lucy saw Emily look about for her son, it was too late. The boy was already standing at the open door to her bedroom, and with a falling heart, Lucy recalled that the painting was still on her desk. With a strangled moan, she made for the stairs, with Emily at her heels. The boy entered her room, the door swinging shut behind him, and Lucy flew the last few yards. She wrenched the door open and froze. Emily pushed by her and threw herself at her disappearing son.

Chapter 22

"A moose?" Matthew laughed. "We'd have our work cut out for us getting that back home."

"But we'd only need the one beast," Mark said, "and Offa always said they made good eating."

"We have to find one first, and so far, we haven't." Ian was moving gingerly, face pale and drawn, and Matthew pursed his lips, wishing he had insisted Ian ride while they walked.

"For beasts the size of a large horse, they're quite canny," Jacob put in. "Difficult to find."

"Which is why we have the dogs," Matthew said, "although so far they haven't been much use, have they?"

"These aren't hunting dogs," Mark snorted. "These are mostly mastiff. Now, Robert has a lurcher bitch that he's planning on mating with that otterhound of his, and—" Whatever else Mark was going to say, he swallowed back at his father's raised hand. Delilah was standing stock-still, every quivering muscle in her body indicating something was not as it should, and by her side, Viggo had adopted a protective stance, floppy ears laid back tight against his head, teeth already bared.

"What?" Mark whispered.

"Over there," Jacob replied in an undertone, and then the slope before them was full of men on horses.

Matthew couldn't help it. His first reaction was to turn and flee, blood chilling rapidly into slush when he recognised the lead rider. How many of them were there? Seven, no eight, and by now Philip Burley had seen them, sneering as he clapped his heels to his horse, charging towards Matthew.

A stillness came over Matthew. The horse came thundering towards him, and it seemed to him he registered every clod the hooves dislodged, every steaming exhalation from the distended nostrils. His musket lay snug against his shoulder, and he wasn't even aware of having raised it, all of his concentration on the approaching horse and the man that sat astride it. He squeezed his finger round the trigger, waited. Sixty yards, forty yards, and still Matthew held back, because this was a shot he had no intention of missing, and as Burley was wearing a breastplate, Matthew aimed at his head.

Beside him, Ian crowed and fired his musket, hitting Burley's gelding squarely in the chest. Damn! So close, and now his son's itching finger had ruined this golden opportunity to once and for all rid this world of one of God's bigger failures. The large roan toppled to the ground, flinging its rider over its neck. With a bloodcurdling cry, Matthew leapt towards him, and on the ground, Philip screamed.

He landed atop Burley. In his hand was his knife, tantalisingly close to Burley's dirty neck, and any second now, Matthew would slit it. The handle slipped in his hand. Burley tried to rise, and Matthew brought his knee down on Burley's chest, wincing when it connected with the cuirass. So intent was Matthew on his prize, that he didn't see the other man bearing down on him, nor did he hear his sons' warning cries. Something slammed into him. A dull jolt ran from his shoulder and down into his arm, and the knife fell unhanded to the ground.

Philip tried to wrest himself free. Matthew was vaguely aware of a weight on his back, round his neck, but he wasn't about to let go, not now, and he drove his fist into Burley's face once, twice. His knife – where was the goddamn dirk? There! He tried to reach it, but the man on his back clapped him over the ear, and Matthew's head was forced back, a blade at his neck. He gagged. Not like this! He wasn't meant to die like this! Ian was screaming something, there was a loud thwack, and the man on Matthew's back was gone, with Ian raising the stock of his musket to deal the outlaw yet another blow.

Matthew turned to finish Burley off, teeth bared in a snarl. Philip had crawled a few yards further into the forest, and Matthew threw himself towards him. Ian appeared by his side, moving with a speed and agility Matthew hadn't seen in years, and there was Walter, and Ian swung for him, driving him back.

From behind them came a scream, and Matthew froze, recalling that he had other sons here, and, God, was that one of them? His single-minded focus on Philip wavered, eyes darting over the clearing. Mark was on the further side, and there was blood on his hand, up his arm, but he was alive, and back to back with him stood Jacob using his musket as a club. Ian's loud curse had him swivelling back, only to find himself staring at a pistol.

"I'll shoot!" Walter screamed, dragging his dazed brother backwards. "I swear I'll shoot the cripple if you come any closer." The muzzle was now pointing steadily at Ian.

"Cripple? I'll give you for cripple!" Ian launched himself towards the Burleys but Matthew grabbed him by the arm. At such a close range, Walter wouldn't miss.

"Nay, lad. It's not worth your life."

"We can take them, Da!" Ian was almost jumping on the spot.

"Not like this," Matthew said, indicating his useless arm. He called back the dogs, and had no choice but to watch the Burleys disappear into the undergrowth.

"Damn!" Ian crashed his musket into a nearby shrub, raised it to do it again, and froze halfway through the movement, face contorting with pain.

"Sit," Matthew said, helping Ian down onto the ground.

"I can stand," Ian snapped.

"Aye, of course you can," Matthew replied, "but it's a long walk back, and after having incapacitated at least two of them, you might need a wee rest."

"Two?" Ian asked.

"Aye, two."

It took them hours to get back, with Ian having to be carried over the rougher parts, even if he loudly insisted that he could walk – he was no weakling, aye? When their home rose into sight, Ian was set down, and, with gritted teeth, he walked the last part on his own, eyes going a dangerous green when Jacob suggested that he at least lean on him. Doors opened: from the smoking shed came Alex, and there came Betty, flying in the direction of Ian who, by now, was a sickly yellowish white.

"I'm not sure, but they were more than six." Matthew stood aside to allow Jacob and Mark to enter the kitchen first, supporting Ian between them. Moments later, he was seated at the table, the makeshift bandage over his shoulder straining with his movements. He studied his hurting fists in silence, and raised his face to meet Ian's eyes over the table. A huge bruise covered Ian's right cheek, there was a deep gash across his forehead, his knuckles were badly skinned and he could barely move on account of his back. But all the same, Ian glowed.

"But how?" Alex couldn't stop touching Matthew. Since the moment he'd staggered in with their three sons, she hadn't taken her hands off him, in one way or the other. He shrugged her hands off, and with a nod indicated that she do something about Ian's face where the blood had begun to well again from the gash that sliced through his eyebrow to rise in a curving line all the way to his hairline.

"They didn't expect us up there, and nor we them," Mark said through a bruised lip.

"So it wasn't an ambush," Alex said, relief colouring her voice.

"No," Jacob said, "they were coming from the north-east."

Mr Jefferson and Constance stood quiet in a corner and listened while Jacob and Ian took turns telling them what had happened, from the moment they heard Philip laugh to when Walter had dragged his brother off to safety.

"And were they hurt?" Alex applied a poultice to Ian's face.

"Walter no, but Philip – well, he seemed in a bad way." Jacob grinned.

"But not dead," Ian muttered, flinching under Alex's hands.

"Oh, so this hurts, does it?" she said. "More than having your brow sliced open by a knife?"

"Aye," he said, eyeing the needle she had in her hand with trepidation.

"And then what?" Mrs Parson asked, dabbing at Mark's lip.

"I shot one of them," Mark slurred, looking greensick. Matthew extended his good arm to give him a hug.

"They ran off, the Burleys," Ian said. "They just left their men to fend for themselves."

"How nice." Alex put the last stitch in. "Here," she said to Betty, "you take care of the rest."

"What were they to do?" Jacob asked. "Philip was nigh on unconscious, Ian was swinging at anything that moved, and Mark and I had the rest well under control." He shared a smile with his elder brother who smiled back.

"And the others?" Alex looked at Matthew. "What happened to Burleys' men?"

"Two were in a bad way," Matthew said. "One shot in the groin, the other badly bludgeoned around the head. As to the others, no more than the odd cut or so."

"And you let them go? Outlaws on our land?"

"Nothing else to do, Mama." Mark smiled briefly at Naomi who was hovering over him. "They took off, and what with Da's arm and Ian…" He broke off when Ian glared at him.

"They'd be fools to come here," Jacob put in. "I reckon they're making for Virginia as fast as they can."

"Oh." Alex went over to the hearth and poured boiling water into a bowl, adding crushed handfuls of lavender and chamomile. "Take your shirt off," she threw over her back, directing herself at Matthew.

"Who are these Burleys?" Mr Jefferson said. "Are they old Sam Burley's sons?"

Matthew grunted from under his shirt. With Jacob's help, he succeeded in pulling the shirt over his head, uncomfortably aware of how his guests' eyes widened at the sight of his scarred torso.

"I don't know the man in question, but if these are his sons, I can but commiserate. From Virginia, aye? Four brothers, one dead since years, one already hanged, and the others, with God's help, will soon adorn a gibbet of their own."

Very briefly, Matthew described the Burleys' colourful career, and then he almost jumped off the stool when Alex took hold of the bandage and tore it away to bare his shoulder. "Lord in heaven, woman!"

Mrs Parson came over to take a look. "Symmetrical," she said, patting Matthew on his unharmed shoulder. "Last time I treated you for a shoulder wound, it was on this side, you collect?"

"Nay, I don't. Alex dragged me all the way down from the moor, didn't she?"

"A strong lass," Mrs Parson said, "and so protective of you."

"Yes, yes," Alex interrupted, "but that was ages ago, and now we have to do something about this instead."

"Not a wink of sleep," Mrs Parson went on, unperturbed. "All night, she sat with your head in her lap and yon dirk in her hand to defend you."

"This dirk?" Matthew studied the knife his father had given him when he turned fifteen, knowing that it wasn't. No, she'd been brandishing the blade he stole when escaping prison.

"Aye, and she in breeches and short—" Mrs Parson broke off, throwing a look at their guests, both of whom were listening avidly.

"Breeches?" Constance laughed. "Really, Mrs Graham!" She smoothed down her impeccable dark blue skirts, fiddled with the matching full-sleeved bodice, and threw Mr Jefferson a discreet look, forming her small mouth into a seductive pout.

"What had happened?" Mr Jefferson asked, oblivious to Constance's preening.

"Nothing much," Alex replied, "and it was so long ago I barely remember anyway."

"Aye, you do," Matthew said so quietly only she could hear him.

"Of course," she whispered back. "Every moment of that first month with you."

Matthew's jaw ached with the effort of keeping quiet when they were finally done with his shoulder. He took the pewter cup that Ian held out to him, and shared a silent toast with his eldest son, going on to toast the other two as well. He was light-headed from not having eaten since breakfast, and the alcohol created a burning warmth in his belly that spread in comforting waves all through his body. He clasped Ian's hand in his own. "You saved my life, lad."

"That's what you get from playing the hero," Alex said to Ian next morning. He couldn't move, not even to get out of bed to piss, and Betty had come running to fetch help, hiccupping with fright that maybe this time her Ian was bedridden forever.

"Not that I'm not grateful," Alex said, rolling him over on his front.

"Ah!" His breath caught in his throat, and he threw a panicked look in her direction.

"It'll be alright," Alex soothed, helping him down flat. She could see the swelling, a puffy redness at the lower end of his spine. Inflammation in muscles that had been strained well beyond their capacity, but a careful probing along the vertebrae indicated no new damage, even if he hissed at times. She worked out the worst of the tensions, and covered him with cold poultices.

"Some days on your front, and then you'll feel much better," she said to Ian, stroking his dark hair. He mumbled something unintelligible into the linen. "Was it worth it?"

Ian twisted his head to see her. "Aye." His face broke into a huge smile. "It was. I…" He waited until Betty rushed over to stop Christopher from hitting Timothy again, and fumbled for Alex's hand. "I was made a man again," he said, gripping her hard.

"Idiot, you've been a man since the day you saved Matthew from sure death by hanging, back in Scotland, and you were only twelve."

Ian flushed. "Not to myself, not since the accident."

"Idiot," she repeated and kissed his bandaged brow. She sat with his hand in hers until he fell asleep.

"Quite the healer," Constance commented when Alex entered the kitchen an hour or so later.

"Excuse me?"

"Well, you are, what with all those strange concoctions, all those smelly poultices." Constance paused. "You slice your men open, clean their wounds, sew them up…" She tilted her head, and a weak ray of November sunlight struck her in the face, making her squint.

"Things any competent housewife knows how to do," Alex said, looking about for Matthew. "I suppose that's why it so impresses you."

"He's gone outside," Constance informed her, impervious to the jibe. "To help your youngest son with the new puppy."

"Ah." Alex threw a look out of the window. Huge dog. She grinned. Yet another hairy monster that she refused to let inside.

"So many sons," Constance said enviously.

"Yes, very many sons."

"Unfortunate that you've lost one," Constance continued, with very little genuine compassion in her voice.

"Lost one?"

"The little Indian – gone with the heathen."

"He isn't lost." Alex kept her voice calm.

"Oh yes, he is. As lost as my boys are to me."

No, he isn't, you fucking cow, Alex thought. She considered cutting herself a slice of cake, but after Constance's comment the other evening, Alex had been forcing herself to abstain, so she sucked in her stomach and broke off a dried peppermint leaf to chew.

"I'll never get them back," Constance said. "Not even when he dies will I get them back. At most, I will be allowed to see them a couple of times a year."

"They have their home here," Alex replied – and a far better mother than Constance would ever make in Ailish.

"I do love them," Constance said, meeting Alex's eyes. "It wasn't them I threw sugar at."

"What you did to Ailish—"

"Irish cow! Usurping my rightful place, ordering me about as were I one of her serving wenches – and she a bond servant herself!"

"She'd been running the household since Elizabeth died. And, if we're going to be honest, you didn't much want to, did you? At least, not at first. Even more to the point, you had no idea how – you probably still don't."

"That's what you have slaves for. I would've bought some well-trained house slaves and set them to run the place – properly."

Alex shook her head at her. "I don't hold with slaves."

"Oh?" Constance laughed. "Well, I do." She moved over to the door. "Most educated people do, but it's not to be expected of half-illiterate peasants – after all, what would you do with all that spare time?"

"Educated? You?"

"In my home, we have a library." Constance smiled wickedly. "Not a paltry collection of thirty-odd books."

"And in my home, we actually read them and broaden our minds. Seems to be something you've missed out entirely." Alex folded her arms over her chest and stared Constance out of her kitchen.

Two days later, Ian was up and about, albeit somewhat gingerly, and sufficiently recovered to scowl when Matthew rode out yet again with Mark and Jacob in search of the Burleys, leaving him at home.

As she had done the two previous days, Alex spent most of the day worrying, and when the threesome finally came back, well after nightfall, she shooed them all inside for a late supper, listening with half an ear as Matthew recounted just how fruitless their day had been.

"Gone west," Matthew said, "and, from the look of the tracks, four or five horses."

"Let's hope they fall into a swamp somewhere." Alex

placed a plate of fried cabbage on the table.

"They won't be back this side of winter." Matthew speared a slice of salted pork with his knife and stretched for the baked onions.

"Mayhap they'll never come back," Mark said.

Constance made an amused sound. "The Burleys? Stubborn as mountain goats, the lot of them, and they have an axe to grind with you."

"Good friends of yours?" Mark asked, making Constance flush.

"Of course not!" Thomas Jefferson sounded irritated. "But, seeing as they were born close to where we come from—"

"Ah," Mrs Parson nodded. "Blood kin. That explains quite a lot."

Thomas Jefferson glared at her, pulled Constance to her feet and left the room.

"I swear, Matthew, if she doesn't leave soon, I'll throttle the woman!" Alex stabbed the needle through the cloth, wishing it was Constance's arm. They were alone in the kitchen, Mrs Parson having retired early. She could hear Constance and Mr Jefferson conversing in the parlour, but had no inclination to join them, preferring the peace and quiet of her emptied kitchen.

"One or two more days," Matthew said. "I heard the minister comment to Mr Jefferson how there was no hope in budging the Leslies on the lads, but that her portion in the will has been agreed with Nathan."

"Peter is still alive, and his will is being torn apart?"

"Aye, Thomas said how it broke his heart to see his brother still as a corpse while the minister and the lawyer argued with Nathan over his bed."

"Well," Alex said, "he should be there, to express what his opinions are."

"Express his opinions? He blinks: once for aye, twice for nay. But Nathan has been a good lad in this, taking the time to read everything back to his father, and ensuring he agrees to it all. And the one thing Peter wouldn't countenance was his wee sons ending up in Constance's tender care."

"Good for him," Alex muttered. "How long do you think he has?"

"The minister said how it could be days, or years, but he doesn't think it will be long in this case. Two apoplexies in less than a month does not bode well."

"No," Alex said. "I'm going to miss him."

"So will we all." Matthew sighed. "And his brother most of all."

Chapter 23

Lucy saved the picture from Emily Farrell, stuffing it inside her bodice. It wasn't her fault, nor the picture's, she tried to communicate. It was the snotty-nosed boy who was to blame, for entering where he wasn't welcome.

Her brain was reeling with the potential consequences of the last few minutes, and her eyes kept straying to Emily Farrell's mangled hands. Not a whole nail; two fingers looked as if they had been crushed and the left wrist seemed somehow disjointed, hanging at an odd angle. As she watched, she saw bruises springing to the surface of that oh, so white skin, and as to the boy... In difference to little Frances, Nicholas had a spectacular bruise over his right cheek, and he kept on complaining that his shoulder hurt and so did his arm.

Lucy regretted having gotten to her feet. If she had stayed where she was, chances were the boy would simply have disappeared, and then her secret would still have been safe, not flayed wide open as it now was.

She could see Emily was screeching, spittle flying from her mouth, but the articulation was far too bad for her to make out any more but the repeated witch. Witch? Lucy shook her head in denial. She was no witch, had no special gifts. It was the painting, and it wasn't her fault, was it, if people looked too closely at it.

The bedchamber was suddenly full of people, agitated people with arms that waved: Emily's servant, the wet nurse with one of the twins, little Frances with her hysterical nurse, and then Kate appeared at the door and, with a smart clapping of hands, brought things back to normal. Lucy relaxed. Her mother-in-law would know what to do.

Kate listened to Emily's account of events and turned

to Lucy. "Is this true? Did Emily's little boy begin to vanish into your painting?"

Lucy couldn't deny it, so she nodded. Not my painting, she tried to tell Kate. Nothing I have ever done.

"Where is it now?" Kate asked.

Lucy chose not to reply, but Emily pointed an accusing finger in the direction of her chest.

"She took it back. I think she hid it under her clothes." It lay warm and comforting against Lucy's heart, whispering that all would be alright, there was no reason to become unduly upset.

Kate extended her hand. "Give it to me."

Lucy shook her head, backing away.

"Lucy, give it to me. I must see it."

Lucy handed it over, and for some moments, Kate stood looking down at the little thing before shaking her head. "Impossible, this is but an amateurish attempt to capture the sea. Lucy must really improve on her brushwork."

Not me, Lucy screeched inside. It isn't me who's painted it!

Kate beckoned Nicholas forward, but the child hung back, gripping his mother's hand hard.

"Tell me what happened," Kate said.

She straightened up after a couple of minutes.

"The day your arm was so badly bruised," she said to Lucy.

Lucy's eyes flew to Frances, and Kate gasped, rushing over to cradle her granddaughter to her.

"What is it you've done?"

Nothing, Lucy assured her, she had done nothing. Hastily, she scribbled how she had found the painting, no more.

"But you knew what it could do!"

Lucy shook her head. No, she insisted, she hadn't known. Not at first. She snatched at the picture from where Kate had left it, and held it to her chest. It fills my world with sound, she explained to her mother-in-law. With it, I can hear.

"How hear? Hear me now?"

No, not like that. But she heard all the same, sounds from the past and perhaps from the future.

Kate stared at her and ordered everyone out of the room, before following them out.

"Lock the door," she said to one of her slaves.

Lucy was left alone at last, and sank down to sit at her desk.

Joan felt her heart shrink to the size of a gallstone and drop heavy like lead to land well below her middle. Her eyes flew from one face to the other, hoping to see that this was some kind of sick jest, but the three men before her remained solemn and serious.

"Lucy?" she croaked. "My Lucy?"

William Hancock helped her to sit, keeping a supportive hand on her shoulder.

"I'm so sorry, Joan, but yes, it would seem your daughter has been taken over by Satan himself."

"No," Joan protested in a whisper. "She's a good girl, my Lucy. She goes to church regularly. She knows her Bible."

"That doesn't always help," Minister Allerton said.

"What…" Joan wet her lips, wondering where Simon was. "What is it you say she's done?"

"She didn't do anything as such," Minister Allerton said, and Joan closed her eyes in grateful relief. "Not today," he added.

"A child was nearly swallowed by a painting of hers," William explained, patting Joan when she moaned. "The mother pulled him back to safety. We have as yet not questioned her properly, and, to be fair, Lucy seems very distraught, even if she refuses to relinquish the painting."

It speaks to her, Joan almost said, but bit her tongue at the last moment. A comment like that would implicate her as well, and that would do neither Lucy nor herself any good. She stared at the small parlour window, catching a glimpse of her reflection in the thick glass. A witch, verily a witch she looked, thin and stooped with eyes that burnt like grey coals in an otherwise inanimate face. What had Lucy done?

Joan picked at the dark wool of her winter skirts, and hid

her face from the three pairs of eyes that studied her with a mixture of compassion and fear. The lasses that had gone missing during summer... Joan swallowed back a groan and tried to sit up straight to meet the concerned looks. "I'm sure you are wrong. My Lucy is a good lass. She wouldn't do anyone any harm."

William sent a boy to fetch Simon, and a mere half-hour later, he came rushing in, out of breath. Simon was very rarely lost for words, but the bald description of events given him by William left him moving his mouth soundlessly. He staggered across the room to join Joan, gripped her hand hard, and looked at his friend and business partner with entreating blue eyes. "You're jesting."

"No, Brother Simon, I'm not. At present, Lucy is held under lock and key at the Jones' residence, but we'll move her over to safer quarters this evening."

"Safer quarters? How safer quarters?" Joan asked.

"We'll keep her in the cellars of the meeting house," Minister Allerton said. "To leave her where she is now is to risk major upheaval and damage to both property and life." Briefly, he explained that Emily had shouted her story out loud to the people of Providence, and people were already baying for blood – in particular the Farrells and the family of the girl who had disappeared back in early August.

"The girl?" Simon looked very confused. "Why the girl?"

"Had Emily not come in time, her boy would have been lost, invisible to us. That is what happened to little Cynthia as well," William replied. "Just as it did to the little whore and Mrs Malone's niece."

"Conjecture," Simon said. "No proof, none at all. Those lasses might have left voluntarily, or been abducted, or slipped off the wharves to drown! We don't know what has happened to them, do we?" He gave Joan's hand a little squeeze, as if to reassure her that all would be well.

She sighed, recognising the expectant look that settled on his face. Simon Melville was an excellent lawyer, and his daughter would not go defenceless.

"No, we don't, but people leap to conclusions, and in

view of what nearly happened to Nicholas..." Minister Allerton shrugged.

"Besides, there is the matter of the picture as such," Lionel Smith spoke up. He had so far remained silent in the company of his elders.

"The picture?" Simon swallowed noisily. "How so?"

"It must take considerable skill in the dark arts to create something like that," Lionel said.

"Aye," Simon said, "most considerable."

"And if so, then you can but agree that your daughter is indeed a witch," Lionel concluded.

Simon looked up at him with a deep crease between his bushy brows. "You must forgive me, young Lionel, but somewhere in your reasoning you lost me."

"Well, it follows that if she has painted it—"

"But she hasn't," Simon interrupted, "and she has said so."

"She can't very well admit to it," Minister Allerton said.

"She hasn't." Simon got to his feet, his paunch straining against the dark green coat and its pewter buttons.

"No proof," William said, "and Kate seems to think she has."

"I know she hasn't," Simon insisted. "I know. I've seen such paintings before, wee pieces of evil."

"You have?" Minister Allerton eyed him doubtfully. "Where?"

"In the keeping of Alex Graham," Simon said.

"No," Joan whispered, trying to grab at his coat. "No, Simon, don't."

"It's she who brings them with her," Simon went on, directing himself to Lionel. "Go and ask her, ask Alex Graham where those witch things come from!"

"Are you accusing Alex of being a witch?" Minister Allerton said.

Joan closed her eyes. Foolish, foolish man. Now what had he done?

"No," Simon mumbled, "not as such, of course not. But those wee pictures...Lucy didn't paint it, that I know."

★

195

Lucy didn't like it at all when they came to take her away. She struggled and shrieked, throwing wild looks at Kate and Henry, who stood stony-faced and watched. At one point, she imagined she saw Henry start, and hoped he was coming to her aid, but instead he wheeled and left, and Lucy screeched at his betrayal. It was all his fault! If he hadn't gone to others when she was here, waiting for him, longing for him, then none of this would have happened. Kate wrapped her in a cloak and squeezed her shoulders before standing back as Lucy was manhandled out of her home.

Lucy had never been down in the cellars under the meeting house, and balked at the narrow dark stairs. Here? She imagined there would be rats and spiders, and when they shoved her into a small room, she grabbed at the door frame and pushed back, fighting to get out. Another shove sent her flying into the dark, the door was pulled to, and Lucy, who had nothing but her eyes to rely on, was left in absolute darkness. With shaking hands, she inspected her surroundings, and there she found a pallet bed. Lucy sat down on the bed and extracted the painting from its hiding place. Maybe she could lose herself in it as well. She gripped it between her hands but it lay silent in her hold. In the dark, she couldn't make it play for her, and she curled up to cry on the bed.

Next morning, someone brought her a candle, and, from the rapid movements of Minister Allerton's mouth when he came down the stairs, she gleaned that he was angry with her jailers for leaving her so helpless and alone. There was breakfast as well, a heel of bread and a mug of warmed ale, and Lucy recalled she had not eaten since yesterday morning. A lifetime away, a world of clean linen and bright colours with a man in her bed, and in the nursery close at hand, her children. Frances, she mouthed, Jeremy and James.

Once she was alone again, she withdrew her picture, and now it did sing to her, loudly like an angel's choir, softly like the wind as it dragged through the summer trees. But it didn't help. She stowed it away. She wanted to go home, wishing yesterday had never happened.

She must have fallen asleep, waking up with a start when

someone shook her shoulder. Lucy sat up, at first not quite recalling why she was here, or why Minister Allerton and his two companions looked so grave. She had never liked Lionel Smith, not quite understanding what Kate saw in this pompous man, and over the coming hour, she grew to like him even less. He was enjoying this, standing straight and self-righteous before her as he expounded on the gravity of her sins, her depravity and oh, so certain death.

She widened her eyes. Death? For what? An accident that she had never intended to happen? It wasn't her fault the painting had tried to eat the child, was it? But the others, Lionel nodded, and Lucy felt a stirring of fear in her belly. What others? Her handwriting stood clean and strong against the sheet, and she looked from one to the other of her interrogators.

Minister Allerton protested, but Mr Farrell insisted, and Lucy was undressed before them, down to her shift. The painting fell out of its petticoat pocket, and she threw herself after it, but Lionel was swifter, snatching it out of her reach. Look at it, she screamed in her head, look at it and fall. He almost did. At the last minute, Mr Farrell shoved him aside, covering the painting with Lucy's skirts. And then they turned on her, and when she saw what Farrell was holding in his hands, she knew this was going to hurt.

"She has confessed," Minister Allerton told Simon later that afternoon. He was still upset by the spectacle he had been forced to witness, and had insisted someone be brought to help Lucy with her whipped back. But she had confessed. Yes, she had written in a shaking, disjointed hand, yes, she had tricked Barbra and Moll into looking too deep. Not the others, not at all. She had never meant for them to fall, neither Eileen nor Cynthia. But Barbra and Moll…defiantly, she had raised her face to look at them. Whores, she had written, and my husband their whoremaster.

"The Lord have mercy on her soul," Simon said. "The lass has committed perjury. She hasn't done something like that, I tell you. It's the painting that is evil, not her. And she didn't create it, that she didn't."

Chapter 24

Peter Leslie died quietly in the night five weeks after his second stroke. His hand was held by his brother, easing him out of this world and into the next. If there was a next, Alex thought, lifting her face to look at the November skies. The grave was being filled in, and now Peter lay side by side with his first wife, the redoubtable Elizabeth, mother to ten of his children and dead of smallpox before the age of fifty-four. Jenny and Nathan stood close together, the only two of that sizeable brood to be here to say farewell to their father.

Ailish and the children stood to the side of Nathan, and a few steps further back, the grieving widow was held in an iron grip by her cousin. Not that Constance was on the verge of fainting or in any way showed signs of distress, but it would seem Thomas Jefferson was taking no chances that his vitriolic cousin do something to shame herself permanently in the eyes of the minister.

Afterwards, Nathan invited them all inside. In the parlour, tables groaned under massive amounts of food: partridges stewed in wine and allspice, pies, a platter heaped with cabbage and sausages, salted venison, bread, several rounds of cheese for which Leslie's Crossing was justly famous, and in pride of place, a boiled pig's head, decorated with dried fruit.

"Two more nights," Matthew said to Alex in an undertone. "Then they leave."

"Will he marry her, you think?" Alex asked, nodding at where Constance was talking to her cousin.

"Likely, I imagine. Her brother recently died, so the match is a good one."

"And he likes her." Alex couldn't keep the surprise out of her voice.

"Aye," Matthew chuckled. "Mayhap he enjoys having his tonsils probed."

"All men do," Alex said before going over to talk to Thomas who stood alone and forlorn in the large parlour.

"It brings it home." Thomas sighed, thanking Alex for the glass of wine she pressed into his hand.

"Brings what home?"

"That the hourglass is running out. It's only me now. Of the seven Leslie siblings, only I am left alive, and here, at the Crossing, I'm the old man, displaced in the day to day by Nathan and my Adam." He gave her a crooked smile and adjusted his wig. "Time to read and ponder life's mysteries."

"And do you?"

Thomas laughed. "It is that or knit, dear Alex, and I never learnt to knit."

"Your Adam is not yet eighteen, so it isn't as he can cope without your help."

"No," Thomas said, "and my lands are still mine, not his. But soon—"

"You're just depressed by all of this," Alex broke in, patting him on his arm. "This whole last month with Peter, and then Constance like icing on a cake – no wonder you're maudlin! You're only – what – twelve years older than Matthew?"

"Eleven," he corrected.

"See? Not even close to seventy yet. Too early to sink one leg into the grave, Thomas Leslie. And what would Matthew and I do without you?"

She made him laugh with that, and he gave her a warm hug and kissed her on her cheek, all under the disapproving eye of Minister Macpherson. Not that she cared, having found the minister as unlikeable on this occasion as on their two previous meetings. Today, the minister had let drop that his dear friend, Richard Campbell, had sent his regards, hoping that Mrs Graham had developed a more becoming respect for her betters with advancing years and wisdom. As if. Richard Campbell had the intellect of a newt, and looking into Macpherson's piggy eyes, she saw more self-righteousness than intelligence.

*

On the other side of the room, Matthew served himself some more cider, watching Constance sidle up to the minister, an obsequious simper on her face.

"Not seemly," Constance said. "A man dead, and his brother fondling the all too eager neighbour's wife."

"Hmm." The minister nodded.

"Are you casting aspersions on my wife now, wee Constance?" Matthew said. "Can you ever open that mouth of yours without spewing venom or lies?"

Constance went a vivid and unbecoming pink.

"Minister," he went on, "a right good sermon, it was."

The minister smiled complacently, commenting that his sermons were always good, spiced with brimstone and fire, a reminder to all that each soul balanced precariously on the edge of everlasting damnation, and only a chosen few would make it through the narrow stile to heaven.

"Very uplifting," Alex agreed, joining them. "Especially for the mourners."

Matthew pressed his boot-clad foot down hard on her toes. She threw him a warning look from beneath her lashes.

"We must be riding back. The wind is picking up, and there'll be rain or snow before nightfall." Matthew bowed to the minister, waited until Alex curtseyed, and led her towards the door.

"How can you say it was a good sermon? How about talking about green pastures, gambolling lambs, and the comforting presence of angels? You know, paint a picture of a happy and contented Peter, now reunited with his wife, instead of reminding us all that the probability he had gone anywhere else but to hell is microscopic."

"We don't believe in gambolling lambs," Matthew said somewhere between a laugh and a reprimand.

"Well, I do," Alex retorted.

Late next afternoon, the minister rode into Graham's Garden with a dark-clad man beside him that Alex recognised as Kate's secret lover. At present, Lionel was apparently acting

200

on behalf of the Providence elders, his eyes wide with curiosity and something else when they studied Alex. She didn't like the look in those inquisitive eyes, nor the air of suppressed excitement that emanated from the minister. She couldn't help it. She snuck her hand into Matthew's, despite the fact that this made the minister frown.

"It is a grave matter, this is," Minister Macpherson said once they were inside, his eyes travelling the collected Graham household.

"What is?" Matthew asked.

The minister took his time, lowering himself to sit in the proffered armchair, but shaking his head in a refusal when Agnes in a hushed voice asked if he would like some beer.

"We are talking witchcraft," the minister continued, small eyes darting from one to the other.

"Witchcraft?" Alex gave him a blank look. "What? Where?"

"We dinna rightly ken," the minister replied, lapsing into the broad Scots accent he generally kept well suppressed. He coughed. "But we know for sure it's in Providence. It might be here as well." He locked eyes with Alex who just looked back, managing to look unperturbed.

"Here? I don't think so," Matthew said. "This is a God-fearing home, minister."

"Hmm." The minister shared a sly look with Lionel, nodding almost imperceptibly. "Tell them."

Lionel's story left them all shocked.

"Lucy?" Matthew said. "Wee Lucy do that? Nay, I can't believe it!"

"All the same, there is a witness to tell of how that vile piece of magic near swallowed a child, and since then she has confessed that it was her that caused the young women to disappear." Lionel sounded smug.

Alex felt her fingers being crushed to the bone by Matthew's grip. She swallowed and swallowed. A painting, oh my God, one of Mercedes' time squares. But how? And then she recalled the conversation with Joan back in June, how Joan had admitted that they had received a painting from England some years back, and how Lucy had been ordered to burn it. Stupid girl! Young, bright and curious, she must have looked at it and somehow decided not to destroy it.

The minister retook the conversation. "We are not here to only appraise you of these events. No, I'm afraid we are here on a much more serious matter. It has come to our attention that Mrs Graham has dabbled in paintings such as these, and the elders of Providence request your presence at an inquest Wednesday a week from now."

"My wife? What are you on about?" Matthew's voice shook with anger.

"It's your brother-in-law who insists," Lionel cut in. "He says that your wife is well-acquainted with these cursed pictures."

"Simon?" Matthew shook his head. "Simon said that?"

"Acquainted? How acquainted?" Alex was quite impressed by how unperturbed she managed to sound.

"He didn't say," Lionel said. "No more than that you knew what these evil things were all about."

Constance had been watching the proceedings with bright eyes, and now she took a small step forward. "Oh dear," she said with a pursed mouth. She looked Alex up and down with exaggerated caution. "Well, one shouldn't be surprised. Witches beget witches. No wonder you're so fond of all your potions and such."

"I have no idea what you're referring to," Alex snapped, "but I can tell you one thing, and that is that you've just outstayed your dubious welcome. Get out, and get out now!" She raised an arm and pointed at the door. "Now."

"Witches beget witches?" Minister Macpherson looked expectantly at Constance who remained where she was, a small satisfied smile playing over her lips.

"Her father," Constance said.

"My father?" Alex's voice climbed into very painful registers. "What do you mean?"

"He just dropped out of the sky one day," Constance confided in a low voice to the minister.

"He did what?" Ian laughed, and turned to face the minister. "I don't know what the woman is on about, but I can assure you Magnus Lind was not a witch, in any way."

"Fiona said—" Constance began but was interrupted by Ian.

"Fiona was nowhere close, and I don't think she has ever insinuated Magnus was a witch, has she?" He swung round to face Fiona, who shook her head, quailing under that cold, penetrating look.

"Yes, you did," Constance said. "You told me. How one day he was found hanging face down in a huge thorny thicket, and you said how strange it was that he seemed not to have walked here, as neither the Leslies nor the Chisholms had seen him, and how could he have found his way without asking for directions? So, how then had he come here? Had he flown across the sea to perch in that thicket?"

"I never said he was a witch," Fiona said, "and I've never said Mistress Graham is one either."

"So how did he come to be there?" the minister asked with interest.

Ian hitched his shoulders. "I don't rightly know. He babbled about seeing a bear and running for his life, and then stumbling off the hillside to land as he did, but I fear it was a raccoon, aye?"

"A raccoon?" Lionel snorted.

"If you haven't seen one before, and it's not yet daylight and they are halfway up a tree staring at you, they come across as rather strange – in particular, if you're a man in your seventies, exhausted from days of travelling."

The minister's mouth stretched into a brief smile, shaking his head in dismissal of this little aside. "So, Mistress Graham, have you ever dabbled with these paintings?"

"Dabbled?" Alex shook her head. "That I have not. But I may have seen something like it once."

"In which case, it won't be a great matter for you to appear before us in Providence."

"No." If it hadn't been for Matthew's continued grip on her hand, she would have fallen or screamed, but with his fingers round hers, she could still breathe normally.

"Good." The minister heaved himself out of the chair with considerable ease for one so large. "We'll ride down together, three days hence."

Matthew accompanied the minister and Lionel to their horses, and turned back to the house. He was swaying with anger, his guts heaving at Simon's betrayal. What in God's name had he said, in his desperate attempts to clear his daughter? They would deny ever having used the painting, and it wasn't as if Alex had ever tricked someone to fall as Lucy seemed to have done. She had only used it to help her lost son home.

"Out." Matthew's eyes bored into Constance.

"Now?" Constance looked out at the darkening skies.

"Now. I won't have you one more night under my roof, foul-tongued and evil-minded as you are."

"It's about to rain," Thomas Jefferson protested.

"I don't care. And you're welcome to stay, but she isn't."

"Fiona can stay," Alex offered.

Matthew made an indifferent sound, his eyes never leaving Constance who stood twisting her hands round and round. "You have packing to do," he said.

"I must protest," Thomas Jefferson began, "it's not right, to—"

"You heard me!" Matthew's fist crashed down into the table, making all of them jump and him wince as the unhealed wound on his shoulder broke open. "I won't have a woman who accuses my wife of being a witch under my roof."

"But still—" Thomas tried again.

"No." It came out with ice-cold finality. After a minute or so of eyeballing, Thomas gave up and gestured for Constance to go and pack.

"A viper," Mark spat, following her progress out of the kitchen. "Whoever marries her does best to keep that in mind."

★

"How could he do that?" Alex had said that so many times by now, in a range of emotion from incredulity through anger to sadness. "I – no, we – trusted him, and he does this. The paintings have nothing to do with me, nothing at all, and he knows that."

"I don't know." Matthew's hair stood straight up from his repeated scrubbing at it, and his eyes gleamed dull in the deep hollows that surrounded them.

"I don't want to go," Alex whispered. "I'm scared."

"Scared? Of them? Nay, that you need not be, lass."

She shook her head in exasperation. "Not them. After all, I've never done anything wrong. Of the painting." She gave herself a little hug. "I hate the idea of seeing one of those paintings again. It's as if they drag me towards a precipice." Her insides did a slow elevator ride up and down. Just as she panicked whenever thunder rolled too close, or avoided anything resembling a ninety-degree crossroads… she swallowed. She belonged here, was rooted here, but there had been a couple of times when it had all been a bit too close for comfort, time snapping literally at her heels as it attempted to drag her back to that future where she had been born.

"I'll hold you," he promised. "All the time, I'll hold you."

She didn't even try to look comforted by this. They both knew how close a thing it had been last time.

That night, Alex was unable to sleep, and finally she slid out of bed to go and stand by the burning candle in the window. So many years ago since she'd last seen one of Mercedes' paintings…more than twenty. She leaned her head against the cold glass, shivering in the draught.

Seven, Isaac had been at the time, narrow over the shoulders and with those knobbly knees that some boys have and others don't. And so frightened, not fully understanding what had happened to him. Well, who would? What child could comprehend a fall through time? In a hesitant voice, Isaac had explained how he had found one of Mercedes' paintings, and how, in a corner, he'd seen his lost mama, and reaching for her, he'd been sucked into the painted maelstroms.

She traced a long, strong 'I' on the glass.

She would gladly have kept him with them, but he pined for his time. He hated it without his Offa and John, he wanted his Playstation and TV, to go to school and play football with his friends. At night, he cried for the world he'd lost, and finally Alex decided to try and help him back.

By chance, Alex had one of Mercedes' paintings, and on an August afternoon, she, Matthew and Isaac rode out together to see if it could be made to work. It did. Alex shuddered. Oh God, it did. She closed her eyes in an attempt to avoid reliving the horrible tilting feeling, the endless drop through a funnel that screeched and clamoured with captured grief and death. Unsteadily, she straightened up and wrote 'SAAC' behind her previous 'I', encircling the name with a heart.

Chapter 25

"You think Luke sent it," Jacob said next morning.

"No. I know Luke sent it," Alex said.

Jacob gave her an angry look. "You don't know. How can you?"

Alex tapped her stomach. "Gut feeling. If it comes to a crunch, trust your gut more than your head."

"But why?" Jacob sounded desolate.

"Luke has a long memory, and Simon was instrumental in drafting those final documents that humiliated him entirely before Matthew." She stared off for a moment, recalling that long gone summer afternoon when Luke had been forced to renounce Ian – return him to Matthew, his true father – and, on top of that, to pay the princely sum of five hundred pounds to Matthew in compensation for the multiple wrongs done to him. "I suppose he found it amusing, to imagine Simon looking too deep into the painting."

Jacob didn't reply. He had his herbal open, and had, until she came in, been busy entering the properties and qualities of his latest additions, carefully drawing stems and leaves and bell-shaped flowers. Now, he traced the outline of *datura stramonium* with his finger, lost in thought. Rather apt, given their subject, Alex reflected, this plant being as deadly as a nest of vipers.

"I reckoned he'd destroyed it," Jacob said.

"Yeah, that would have been the right thing to do." She gave her son a long look. From the way he was chewing his lip, she suspected Luke had somehow put the painting to the test, with Jacob as a witness.

"And why, if he knew what it was, didn't Simon make sure it was burnt? How could he be so remiss?"

"Or Lucy so disobedient." She hitched her shoulders to show she had no idea, and now it was all too late. Four innocent women gone, and God knew where they had ended up.

"How come you know of these pictures?" Jacob asked.

Alex sighed and shifted in her chair, uncertain how to answer. Mrs Parson knew since decades back as did Simon and Joan, Ian knew of a need, and Mark she'd told as well, but to share all this with more of them... Jacob's eyes never left her, and, just like his father's whenever he was truly intent, the irises were a bright, penetrating green.

"I just do."

He looked very unconvinced.

"I found one like it," Alex said, deciding a half-truth was better than nothing. "In Cumnock, very many years ago. And it was so pretty to look at, but when you held it too close..." She dropped her eyelashes to hide her eyes. "It made me sick to the stomach – very, very sick."

"Aye," he whispered, thereby confirming her previous suspicions regarding Luke's penchant for empirical observation. "I still don't understand. How can you think Uncle Luke would do something so malicious?"

"He is malicious, and when it comes to your father and his brother-in-law, Luke has some very blind spots."

Jacob glared at her. "That isn't true. He has forgiven Da for all that with Margaret and his nose."

"Oh, how high-minded of him." Slicing off Luke's nose had been a bit primitive, she still thought, and Luke had since then lived with a silver cap to replace his severed nose.

Jacob flushed at her tone, saying that he loved his da, but he loved his uncle as well – a lot – and surely it was not only one's fault if brothers fought?

"No," Alex said, "but let's not forget that it was your uncle who was perfidious, not your father. It was your uncle who tried to have your father hanged; it was your uncle who had your father sold into slavery; and it was your uncle who murdered his father, old Malcolm Graham."

"No!" Jacob rose to his feet. "Nay, Mama, that you

must have wrong. Grandfather died in a drowning accident. And wasn't it Da who stole Luke's sweetheart away, abusing his brother's trust?"

"His brother's trust?" Alex snorted. "Your father was like a lamb before a wolf when it came to Margaret. She, despairing of ever seeing Luke again, made sure her nest was well fleeced, and so set out to seduce Matthew. Which she did quite well, I might add."

She choked on jealousy, on anger. Margaret, drop-dead gorgeous with her black silk hair, eyes a lighter shade of blue than her own. She swallowed in an effort to calm down. A sister, born three hundred years before she herself had been born. And neither of them had known –how could they – even if both had seen and noted the startling resemblance. It had only been when Jacob found the little painting in Luke's desk, and when Luke had told him that the painting was a gift to Margaret from her long-lost mother, that Alex had at last understood why she and Margaret were so alike. Yet another impossibility in her life; yet another unwelcome gift from her mother. *A veces no te quiero*, she thought. Sometimes I don't love you, Mercedes. Quite often, actually, and with this new resurfacing painting, it was even truer. A witch, a witch, her mother was a witch! *Yo siempre te quiero*, I always love you, she heard ringing in her head. *Mi hija, te quiero,* long dead Mercedes seemed to whisper.

"Tough," Alex muttered out loud, making Jacob look at her warily. "It doesn't matter much anymore, does it?" Alex got to her feet. "Matthew and Luke live with an ocean between them, and that, I think, is best for both."

Jacob shook his head. "Deep down, they miss each other."

"Maybe, but not enough for either of them to fully forgive the other. And now Luke has permanently painted himself into a corner, hasn't he?"

Jacob jerked at her tone, his chin coming up. "Not to me."

"And if all this harms me?"

"How can it? You've just assured me you know nothing."

Alex didn't reply. She just left the room.

*

209

Sarah had no recollection of the day when her Offa landed in the thicket up by the strawberry dells, nor had she ever before heard a tale as mind-boggling as that of Lucy and the disappearing girls. And somehow it all seemed to implicate Mama, even if she didn't understand how. She had noticed how Mama hung on to Da's hand during the minister's visit, had seen the infinitesimal protective shift in Ian and Mark as they took that casual step closer to where their parents stood. Sarah drew her knees up even closer to her chest and hugged them hard. She wanted Ruth to be here to talk to about all this, not wishing to speak either to Mama or Da. Finally, she sighed and decided to go and find the only person left to her.

"Do you—?" Sarah stole a piece of pie dough and nibbled at it.

"Aye?" Mrs Parson prompted, slapping away Sarah's hand when it came back for more.

"Is Mama not a wee bit strange?" Sarah blurted, her cheeks heating at her own disloyalty.

"Strange?" Mrs Parson laughed. "Aye, that she is, lass. Opinionated and stubborn like yon mule your da bought last year, strange in what she feeds you, and very, very strange when it comes to all that washing."

Sarah heaved herself up to sit on the kitchen table, using one hand to dig into her bodice and adjust her stays.

"But she's no witch," Mrs Parson went on, "and that is what concerns you, no?"

Sarah lifted her shoulders. "I don't believe her to be one, but she is that wee bit odd." She smiled at the image of her mother in shift and shirt, poised on her toes as she led them both through a series of fighting exercises.

"The world is full of odd people," Mrs Parson said, "and you must take into account that your mother is Swedish. Brought up in a frozen, ice-packed country with God knows what monsters roaming their streets."

"But she was badly frightened yesterday."

"Aye, that she was – as she should be. It's a grave matter, and many a woman has ended their life at the stake, innocent of nothing more than a wee bit of healing."

Sarah blinked. What?

Mrs Parson patted her on the thigh. "Not in this case, lass – your da will not allow it, and woe betide the man who tries to wrest his wife from him. Anyway, it's the picture they wish explained. No one has accused your mama of anything."

"Constance did," Sarah breathed.

"Constance? Spiteful baggage! Nay, what she had to say is easily discounted as nonsense. But Alex isn't too happy about riding down to Providence, and I don't think your da will find it easy to forgive Simon Melville for involving your mama in all this sorry business."

"Why did he?" Sarah sniffed appreciatively when Mrs Parson stirred the heavy meat stew that was to go in the pie.

"Desperation, no? His wee lass to hang for witchery – it would drive most men to extremes. I pity them both, poor Joan and Simon."

"And Lucy?" Sarah asked.

Mrs Parson shook her head in a slow but definite no.

"Do you want us to ride with you?" Ian came over to stand just outside Aaron's stall.

"No," Matthew said, "we ride well accompanied."

"And on your way back?"

"I'll hire some men." With a slap on Aaron's neck, he exited the stall and joined Ian by the wall. "I'm not looking forward to this, and as to Alex…"

Ian nodded in agreement. "She's badly frightened."

"Aye, and so am I, son. God help me, so am I."

"Of her being accused a witch?" Ian laughed.

Matthew gave him an irritated look. "Nay, of course not. I know her not to be one, and never has she done anything that can be considered close to witchcraft. It's the painting. I fear it will be terrible for her to see it."

And for him. Twice had he seen such time squares, twice his insides had risen in panicked rebellion, and the last time… Ah, God! He'd nearly lost her there. Damn Simon to everlasting torture for not having destroyed it! And for this, for having called on Alex as a witness of a sort, insisting she was somehow to be blamed for what Lucy might have done. Matthew's knuckles protested in pain when he drove them into the wooden planks.

"I'll ride with you," Ian said, giving him a hug.

"Nay, lad, you don't. You stay and mind our home. And you must promise to keep the candle lit of a night, should wee Samuel stumble home."

"You need me."

"We do, God knows we do, but we'll manage this ourselves" Matthew sucked at his grazed knuckle. "Why, Ian? How could Simon do this? And why didn't Joan stop him?"

Chapter 26

Matthew held Alex by the hand as they crossed the small square in the direction of the meeting house. It was raining, a foggy drizzle that clung like a damp sheen to their clothes and skin, the cobbles under their feet slippery. Just by the door, they ran into Simon and Joan. Matthew steered Alex away from them, but Simon stepped out to block them.

"Matthew." Simon put a hand on his sleeve.

"Don't touch me," Matthew said. "Lay a hand on me again and I'll break every bone in you."

Too right. Alex crawled out of her bubble of fear long enough to throw Simon a scorching look. Simon snatched his hand back as if burnt. "She's my wee lass. I must try."

"And this is my wife, and I'll not let you, or anyone else, harm her."

"We don't mean to harm her," Joan said. "Just explain that magic exists of itself and that Lucy hasn't done anything evil."

Even in her present state of panic, Alex was inundated with pity at the sight of Joan. Frail to the point of transparency, her beloved sister-in-law looked about to collapse. Grey eyes met hers beseechingly, a skeletal hand extended towards her. Alex stretched out her hand, but was arrested halfway through the movement by Matthew, who at present was too angry to register Joan's desperate state.

"She hasn't? Hasn't she enticed the unaware to fall through?" Matthew said.

"So has she," Simon pointed at Alex.

"I don't know what you mean, Mr Melville," Matthew said.

Simon looked stricken. "Matthew," he tried again.

Matthew looked him up and down for a long time. "I once had a friend I trusted with my life and loved like a brother.

I no longer do." With a curt nod, he ushered Alex inside.

Alex was incapable of speech, her tongue glued to the roof of her mouth. She hung on for dear life to Matthew, and even when Minister Walker indicated she step forward, she still held on, forcing Matthew to stand beside her. The room was bare. Apart from the long desk behind which the three ministers and two elders sat, there were a couple of stools and, on a separate small table, a leather bound Bible. No people, except for themselves, the Melvilles, Lucy and Kate, but the single thing Alex truly registered was the small square of colours that stood propped with its back to the ministers and therefore, unfortunately, in full view to her.

It made her ill. Her head filled with sounds of agony and pain, and her knees shook with the effort to keep upright. Her eyes she kept on the floor, on her shoes, on the unseasonal fly that buzzed around Minister Walker's head – anywhere but on the beckoning, seductive little canvas that begged her to come closer and look very deep. From the way Matthew's hand tightened around hers, she knew he was badly affected as well, and that in itself was a comfort.

"Mrs Graham." Minister Walker cleared his throat and peered at her from above his wire-framed spectacles.

"Minister," Alex managed to push out of her mouth, curtseying.

"Do you know why you're here?" the minister continued, waving at the fly that hovered round his head.

"Not really, no." If she kept her head turned to the side, she avoided even peripheral eye contact with the picture, making it easier to function as she should.

"Hmm," Minister Walker said, sharp eyes darting from Alex to the picture and back again. Beside him, Mr Farrell was looking sick, droplets of sweat beading his forehead, and from the way he was sitting, eyes glued to his hands, Alex deduced he was as perturbed by the canvas as she was.

"Does it affect you?" Minister Walker asked, tapping at the picture with a rather dirty finger.

"Yes," Alex whispered. Minister Walker produced an old shawl and dropped it over the painting. A sigh of relief swept through the room. Only Lucy Jones remained unperturbed, eyes staring vacantly straight ahead.

"Mr Melville has come forward to inform us that you have earlier experience of paintings such as these," the minister said. "That you in fact have a certain familiarity with them and the magic they can do."

"Familiarity?" Alex marvelled that her voice should sound as steady as it did. "I'm not sure I understand. Yes, I've seen something similar before, and yes, it made me feel as unwell as this one does." Even covered as it was, the painting called to her, a continuous whisper that urged her to come closer. Alex felt her resolve weakening and took a shuffling step in the direction of the painting, but was brought up short by Matthew's hold on her.

"And what did you do with it?" Minister Allerton asked, leaning forward to catch her eye.

"Destroyed it," Alex said. "I burnt it behind the privy back home, and it screeched when I did."

The men before her looked at her, aghast.

"It screeched?" Mr Farrell licked his lips, eyeing the propped-up canvas with caution.

"That's how I remember it." Alex swayed on her feet, cold sweat running in rivulets between her breasts and down her back. "Matthew," she whimpered, and he gripped her waist and pulled them both a few steps back.

"That isn't true!" Simon stepped forward, avoiding looking in their direction. "She sent a child through it, she did."

"A child!" Minister Walker exclaimed, staring at Alex.

"Aye, a lad. She used the painting to send him back to his time. She says these little squares are windows through time."

"Is this true?" Minister Walker looked at Alex who just shook her head.

"Alex! You know it is," Simon said.

She stared straight through him, hating him for what he was putting her through.

"A lad, you say? What lad?" Matthew interrupted.

"Isaac," Simon clarified.

"Isaac!" Alex moaned. "Oh God, Isaac!" Awful it had

been, a terrible, terrible thing to do, to send her seven-year-old back through time. But what choice had she had, when her son so clearly pined for his other life?

"I don't know what you think you're doing, Mr Melville," Matthew said, staggering when Alex more or less collapsed against him. He turned to face the ministers. "Aye, we had a son called Isaac, and he was gone from us before the age of eight. His stone stands among the other stones in the graveyard back home, and, as you see, the thought of him still makes my wife distraught."

"He didn't die!" Simon insisted. "You sent him back! Through one of those accursed paintings!"

"Were you there to witness this?" Minister Allerton asked.

"No," Simon said, "but—"

Minister Allerton waved him quiet. "Have you ever seen Mrs Graham use a painting such as this?"

"No," Simon repeated in a whisper.

"Ah." Minister Allerton sat back and regarded him thoughtfully before directing himself to his fellow elders. "I must say I don't fully understand the relevance of Mrs Graham's presence. She doesn't stand accused, does she?"

"Nooo…" Minister Walker dragged the vowel out. "No, Brother Julian, she doesn't. Not unless we can prove that she has been dabbling in these dark arts herself, and Mr Melville says she has."

"Mr Melville can prove nothing – you just heard him admitting to never having witnessed Mrs Graham do anything, and you've heard Brother Matthew say how the child lies buried in the old country." Minister Allerton sounded almost bored.

"But we must ascertain beyond doubt, must we not?" Minister Macpherson said. "We can't risk leaving a witch at large."

"A witch?" Matthew growled. "Are you calling my wife a witch?" He leaned forward, glaring at Minister Macpherson who leaned back as far as he could.

"No, no," he said, "I'm just saying it must be further investigated."

"It sounds preposterous," Minister Allerton broke in. "Has anyone ever accused Mrs Graham of any untoward behaviour before?"

"No," Minister Walker said, "no, no one ever has." He turned to where Simon was standing. "You have just accused your sister-in-law of dabbling with magic, of being a witch. Surely you have something you can bring forth to substantiate such a grievous accusation."

Simon looked as if he wanted to sink through the floor, eyes darting from Alex to the minister.

"I've never said Alex is a witch – never! I have just said how she knows about these wee pictures."

"Is it she that paints them?" Minister Macpherson asked.

"No." Simon threw Alex a look. "I don't think so. But she has used them, I swear she has!"

"And I swear she hasn't," Matthew said, "and I will gladly put my sword up to the test, should it be needed."

Simon blanched. "You lie, Matthew, you lie and you know it!"

"No, Mr Melville, it is you that lie, in a pathetic attempt to save your daughter from a punishment she justly deserves. Mayhap if you'd raised her better, this would never have happened," Matthew said, with so much ice in his voice Simon took a step back from him.

Minister Macpherson cleared his throat. "You have no proof then, Mr Melville? You can't prove she's used them, nor can you say it is she that paints them."

"I know she used them. I saw her ride out with the lad and return alone."

"And is there anyone to corroborate this?" Minister Macpherson pushed. Simon turned towards Joan. She was sitting hunched together on the bench, face hidden in her shaking hands.

"No," Simon replied after a couple of beats of silence. "I don't think there is."

Matthew released some of the pressure on Alex's hand.

"Hmm," Minister Walker said, looking Alex up and down. Minister Allerton drummed his fingers against the table, shaking his head from side to side. "Really, Minister Walker, to insinuate a man as upright and devout as Brother Matthew would countenance a witch as a wife... No, it stretches my mind. Besides, Mrs Graham doesn't deny having seen a picture such as this before, does she? And you need only look at her to see how terrified she is of it." He smiled in her direction.

"Precisely," Simon cut in. "And why would she be, unless she knows what it can do? She knows they lead to other times, gentlemen. She fears she might be dragged from this time to another if she comes too close. And how does she know? Because—"

"Lies, Mr Melville, preposterous imaginings!" Matthew broke in, voice cracking with anger.

Simon ignored him, raising his hand to point at Alex. "Because she doesn't belong here, gentlemen. She comes from a future time!"

"Simon," Joan protested hollowly.

No, Alex pleaded silently, *please don't do this Simon. Not to me, not to Matthew.*

"She's a time traveller!" Simon screeched. "She brought them with her, these evil, wee things! It is her fault, aye? My daughter just found one—"

"...and used it," Mr Farrell thundered.

"Exactly," Minister Allerton agreed, causing Simon to deflate as quickly as a pricked balloon.

Minister Walker turned very appraising eyes on Alex. "Is it true, Mrs Graham? Have you indeed fallen through time?" He sounded frightened.

Alex shook her head, attempting an eye roll to show how ridiculous that concept was.

"And yet your brother-in-law says you have," Minister Macpherson said.

Joan struggled to her feet. "He doesn't—"

"He'd say anything at the moment," Matthew cut in. "Disgusting, lying lawyer." He spat in the direction of Simon before looking Minister Walker fully in the eyes. "My wife is a God-fearing woman, a loyal companion and helpmeet.

To insinuate she is something else is a lie – a blatant lie."

"Mrs Melville?" Minister Walker said. "You were about to say something?"

Joan looked at Alex, at her brother. She licked her lips, waving away Simon when he tried to steady her. "Alexandra Lind is not a witch," she said. "I don't know—" She broke off, throwing Simon an agonised look. "I'm not sure why my husband—"

"Joan," Simon groaned, "please, Joan." He held out his hands to her.

Joan backed away. "…why he is speaking such untruths." She turned to look at the ministers. "I dare say he's distraught, mayhap even out of his wits what with Lucy and…" Her voice wobbled. She took a deep breath. "Alex is my most beloved good sister. I have known her for most of our lives, and I will gladly swear on anything – everything – that she has never performed magic. Not in any way, aye?"

For a long time, Minister Walker studied Alex before nodding towards the Bible.

"Will you place your hand on the Holy Writ and swear that you have never practised any type of magic?"

Alex took a step towards the table, bringing her far too close to the painting. Still, she managed to put her trembling hand on the worn leather covers.

"I swear I have never practised magic."

Several things happened at once. Simon uncovered the painting, Matthew threw himself after Alex who was helplessly propelled towards it, and Lucy rose to her feet. She watched with fascination as Alex was dragged towards the painting, and this time the sounds Lucy heard were louder than ever before. Her aunt's face contorted itself in despair, her uncle was gripping his wife around her waist, trying to pull her free, but the painting tugged and tugged, dragging a frantic Alex towards it. *Alejandra*, it roared, and Lucy blinked. The Voice was calling her daughter home, but the daughter didn't want to go. Lucy vacillated for some seconds. Hands closed on her arm.

"For the love of God, daughter, if you can, do something!" Joan pleaded. "Please, Lucy, save her!"

Alex's eyes rolled back into her head. She was no longer here; she couldn't feel her body or the pressure of Matthew's arms around her. All she could see was a whirling, beckoning maelstrom of colour, and, winking in the distance, home. Not the home she wanted, nor the people she truly loved, but home nonetheless, and the whirlwind tightened its grip round her head to the point that she thought it might burst. Something screamed – an extended high-pitched howl that had her brain writhing. Alexandra Ruth scurried away to hide from all of this in the deepest reaches of her mind.

Lucy held the broken picture in her trembling hands. It had screamed in agony when she snapped the frame, and from the expression on the faces around her, they had heard it too. On the floor, Matthew was cradling an unconscious Alex, and Minister Allerton kneeled beside him, with Joan hovering uncertainly behind her brother's back.

I should have burnt it, Lucy thought, I should have done as Da said. Carefully, she fitted the broken pieces of frame together, staring down at the reassembled picture. No more noise, she reflected, no calling voices, nothing. A white spot – she had never really seen it before, hidden in the depths of all that blue. The spot shimmered, it pulsed like a living heart, and light poured out: bright white light that made Lucy laugh out loud at the sheer beauty of it.

She didn't hear the voice calling out behind her – of course she didn't – and in any case, it was too late. Lucy Jones allowed herself to fall into the open gates of time.

Inside her skull, Alex was reeling. Where was she? She saw pinpricks of light that burst into stars; she waded through a thick sludge of freezing darkness; she heard Isaac calling for her – a man's voice, not a child's – she even saw him, in jeans and an unbuttoned shirt with a marten brush in his hands.

Her brain stretched like a narrow tightrope between this

time and that time. Below her gurgled an inky blackness. Isaac...she could hear him, but where was the other man, the man with beautiful eyes and a hand that braided itself so hard around her own? Matthew...yes, she sighed with relief, his name was Matthew. There was his voice, a thin, barely audible sound at first.

"Come back," she heard. "Come back to me."

In her head, Alex slid her bare foot onto the tightrope and began the dangerous walk across the abyss. She could smell him now, the fear that hung like a sour top note over the fragrance that was purely his, of wood smoke and freshly cut peat, of water murmuring over a pebbled bed. She drew in a shaky breath, and he filled her lungs. She groped for his hand and she could feel his pulse, his beat drumming loudly into her. His heart under her ear, her heart under his hand... Alex opened her eyes to stare into the hazel eyes above her face.

"Matthew." She raised a hand to touch him. Tears hung from his eyelashes; they seeped out of the corners of his eyes and ran down his cheeks.

"Oh God," he whispered, crushing her even harder to him. "My beloved heart."

Minister Allerton had kept a cool head throughout the havoc, and after ensuring the trampled canvas was burnt to ashes, he surveyed the scene before him dispassionately.

Simon Melville had sunk down to sit, his face hidden in his hands, and from the way his shoulders were heaving, the minister surmised he was weeping. Well, he would, wouldn't he? His only daughter gone, his brother-in-law forever lost to him. The implacable look that Matthew threw in Simon's direction only confirmed that never would he forgive Simon for putting his wife through these last minutes of sheer terror.

As to Joan Melville, the poor woman was shaking as an aspen leaf, her gaunt features tinged an unhealthy grey. Thankfully, Kate Jones was standing beside her, one arm slipped around Mrs Melville's waist to hold her upright as she gently led her towards a nearby bench. Joan Melville wasn't weeping. She was staring straight ahead, those large, luminous eyes of her blank and unfocused.

Minister Allerton drummed his fingers against his thigh, his eyes stuck on Alex who was still hiding against her husband's chest. Something was not entirely right there. Not that he suspected Alex Graham of practising black arts, but still… He scrolled back through the recent proceedings, and there it was again: a niggling something. The way Matthew's face had shuttered at the word time traveller, and how Alex had hunched when Simon said that, her eyes wide with… surprise? No, not surprise, nor confusion. Julian drummed his fingers against the tabletop. Betrayal, he nodded, that was it. She had looked at Simon with the eyes of someone who finds her deepest secrets betrayed.

Julian attempted a silent laugh. Ridiculous all of it. People weren't swallowed into the maw of time. It was all a flight of fancy – except that Lucy Jones had disintegrated into nothingness, and not a trace remained of her.

Chapter 27

For days afterwards, Alex barely functioned. Julian had offered them to stay with him, explaining sweepingly to his daughters that Mrs Graham had been struck by sudden illness and had to be allowed to rest before they began the long ride back home. Matthew and Alex spent almost all their time in Julian's little attic room. All Alex seemed to do was sleep, but it was a restless sleep, and Matthew sat like a guardian angel by her side, snatching sleep when he could. Repeatedly, he woke her to ensure she wasn't slipping away from him through her dreams, and every time the waking came a little bit easier, even if there was a long frightening moment when she would look at him blankly, blinking when he called her name. It drove shards through his heart, as did those instants when her eyes dulled into an opaque blue, her features whitening with remembered fear.

"If…" Alex let her head fall back and made an appreciative noise when he dragged the brush through her tangled hair.

"If?" Matthew prompted, exchanging the brush for his fingers, sinking them all the way into her multi-coloured hair: brown mostly, but here and there greys and bronzes and from her temple that white tendril that she'd had for years now.

"I'll die," she said. "If I'm ever pulled back, I won't survive." It came out so cracked he could barely hear her. She turned anguished eyes in his direction. "You know, right? You know that should something like that happen, I'll die thinking of you."

"Shush." He placed a finger over her mouth. "You will never leave me."

"If Lucy hadn't snapped the frame, you wouldn't have been able to hold me," Alex said in a weak voice. "It was dragging me towards it, and I would have disappeared, no matter how hard you held on."

"So you must never come close to such again," Matthew replied with a calm he didn't feel. No crossroads, no wee pictures, no thunderstorms… He felt himself bowing with the burden of keeping her safe from the rifts in time.

Alex rolled towards him and nestled against him. "No, I suppose I had better not." She patted at his chest. "Go to see Simon, Matthew. Simon and Joan, they need you." He shook his head, but she didn't see, almost asleep against his shoulder. "What he did to me, to us… How could he? But she'll die soon," she mumbled, "and they've lost their only child."

"I don't know how she can be so willing to forgive," Matthew said to Julian, nursing a generous brandy in his hands. "It was Simon's unsubstantiated accusations that put her so at risk."

Julian Allerton nodded, sipping at his own glass.

"Look at her! Weak as a mewling kitten, she walks dazed through her days, incapable of much more than feeding herself! She doesn't talk much, not even with me, and at night…" Matthew shuddered and downed the rest of his brandy in one gulp. "She dreams, Julian, she weeps and wakes, but isn't awake, and then she dreams again, and it is violent and restless. You should hear her—" He snapped his mouth shut before he said too much.

"But she's right." Julian topped up their pewter cups. "Joan and Simon have need of you. Simon may have acted wrongfully, but they've lost their only child, and Ruth says how Joan has taken to her bed, refusing food. She is not long for this world, and she's your sister, is she not?"

"Aye, she is that." Matthew dragged a hand through his hair and got to his feet, swaying with exhaustion and too much drink. "Ruth is with her, and that's good."

"Ruth is seventeen in two weeks, too young to be left to handle this on her own, and, from what I understand, Simon is so filled with despair he is no help, no help at all."

Matthew sighed profoundly. He had no wish to leave Alex, not even for a minute, but he couldn't very well ignore his sister in her last hours on earth. "I'll go and see her tomorrow."

Upstairs, Alex was struggling to keep afloat on the surface of a dream-filled sleep. She didn't want to sink down into those swirling mists. She tried to remain in a dozing state where she at least knew who and where she was.

She turned on the bed, feeling the rope bottom give. That brought her up to the reassuring surface again. Yes, this was Matthew's time, and the bed stood in Julian's house, and someone had to tighten the rope frame because the middle was sagging. She tried to blink herself awake, but she was too tired after endless nights of vivid, frightening dreams. She sank into the black of her subconscious.

Isaac was there, and he smiled at her, beckoning her to come close, to return to them. No, she didn't want to, and Isaac's eyes stared reproachfully at her, inches from her own. She got the distinct impression she was lying in a bed, and people were hovering around her, eyes on things that beeped and thumped, monitoring her every thought.

Leave him, Isaac whispered, *come back to me, to me, Mama. Am I not owed for all these years?*

Alex twisted in anguish, and all around her the future life took horrifying shape: TVs that hung flat and embedded on the walls, computers that were called tablets and were run by touch, electrical light that poured from fixtures in the roof.

It's just a dream, Isaac went on. *None of that life you think you've led is true. A dream, Mama, that has encapsulated you for years while we've sat waiting at your side.*

No, Alex moaned, no, it isn't a dream! Not my Matthew, not my sons and daughters.

A dream, Isaac repeated, his dark eyes suddenly cold and hard. *A dream, your life is a dream*, he whispered, laughing gratingly.

"No!" Alex shrieked out loud, was awake for a moment

with her heart in her mouth and then was dragged inexorably back under.

"Alex?" Hands holding, shaking gently, lips that brushed her forehead. "Alex, my heart."

A dream, a dream, nothing but a dream. He doesn't exist, this man of yours. Isaac giggled maliciously.

But he did. Alex struggled back into the light, and the man holding her was solid under her hands, his concerned eyes a gold-flecked green in the light of the candle he had lit.

"Matthew?"

"Aye, Matthew, that's me, lass."

Alex struggled to sit, her sweat-drenched shift sticking to her skin. Matthew handed her a mug of cider, helping her to hold it steady. She blinked, trying to clear her mind of the fragmented images of Isaac. Jesus, I'm going insane, she thought. She drained the mug and with trembling hands began to undo the laces of her chemise.

"Let me," Matthew said. He got her out of the sopping garment, and found a towel to pat her dry with, sitting with her shivering, naked body on his lap. She curled into him, her arms tight around his neck, and he ran his warm hands up and down her bare skin, crooning her name in a hoarse, breaking voice.

"I'm not sure," she groaned. "Are you for real? Or are you the dream?"

"I'm no dream," he whispered back, "nor am I a ghost. I'm here, now, and so are you. It's the others that don't exist, Alex. It is them that are the dream."

"A nightmare," she said against his chest, "not a dream, never a dream. A black hole of loneliness. An absolute freezing emptiness."

"Ah, lass." Matthew kissed the top of her head and gathered her to him. Alex needed him even closer, pulling at his shirt, his breeches in a frenzied attempt to get at his skin, his warmth. Yes, oh yes, he was real, and Alex sighed when he laid her back naked against the pillows.

Her skin sizzled under his hands. A long, strong finger followed the curve of her hip, and she imagined she could see the blisters popping up in its wake as searing heat flew like a shadow behind his digit. Beneath her skin, blood called to blood, and when his fingers manacled her wrist, she was entirely taken over by his beat. Strong it flowed into her, demanding it drove her pulse before it, and Alex no longer knew where she ended and he began.

The candle on the chest gasped, shrinking down to a weak blue glow before it flared back into life, this time a long, dancing flame that backlit them against the wainscoting that adorned the walls. At a remove, she could feel the stubble on his unshaven cheek against the tender skin of her thighs, her belly. He dragged his face across her, and she arched herself against him, because he was hers and she was his and she was very much alive. The soft warmth of his lips; his hot breath in her ear, down her neck, on her chest; his hands with those long, dexterous fingers... Her breasts in his grip, and when he slid down to kiss her, she sank her fingers into his hair and called his name.

"Matthew," she said to the night air. "My Matthew." Of course she would die if she were dragged back in time – how could she survive with half of her yanked out? And he, she saw in his eyes, he would dwindle and die as well. Bit by bit, the fire in him would falter and go out, and he would float away like top soil in a drought.

He cupped her buttocks and lifted her closer to his mouth, and she no longer thought, she simply was, awash with colours and sensations that flowed from her curled toes to the tip of her ears.

"Oh God," she groaned, and her hands gripped at his head, his hair. "Ah!" she said, and Matthew's muffled laughter ran like a vibration up her spine.

He raised himself up, used his knees to widen her thighs, and leaned forward to kiss her as he thrust himself into her. "Mine," he said into her ear. "Only and forever mine."

She clenched herself around him in response, her legs coming up to hold him in place. He kissed her again, and she tasted herself on his lips and the skin round his mouth. She clung to him, refusing to release him. Glued from hip to chest bone they lay, scarcely moving, and in the wavering candlelight, his eyes were black as they stared down at her. She made a demanding movement with her hips. With tantalising slowness, he moved, and she groaned out loud.

"I burn," she said hoarsely. "All of me is burning." And she was, consumed alive by a fire that he expertly stoked and throttled, fed, banked and finally let go, riding her until she cried his name out loud and sank her teeth into his shoulder.

They lay face to face, knees against knees, and noses almost touching. Matthew smoothed back the hair that lay stuck to her damp cheek and tugged gently at her bared ear.

"Alright then?"

Alex nodded. God, she was tired – in a way she hadn't been since well before the incidents down at the meeting house. For the first time in days, her brain was free of any images but those of him, the pictures and people of a long gone future receding grumbling to slither down her brainstem and pop into non-existence.

"Hold me," she whispered, and he rolled her over to fit against him. His hand came round to cup her breast, and Alex relaxed in his warmth. She yawned, wide enough to crack her jaws, and with a little grunt closed her eyes.

"I love you," she said through yet another yawn. She covered his hand with her own, one finger on his wrist to feel his reassuring pulse.

"I adore you," he replied.

Alex didn't hear. She was already drifting into sleep. But she knew all the same.

Chapter 28

It was a long final act to a death that had been three, four years in the making. Matthew brushed back Joan's hair from her brow, adjusted her cap, and kissed a face so without flesh it was already a skull.

"You must eat," he chided, lifting a bowl of soup in her direction.

"To what purpose?" she replied dully. "What is there for me to live for?" She shifted restlessly in her bed.

Matthew took her hand in his and sat in silence, running a thumb back and forth over skin that was already loosened from the bone, the muscle beneath vanishing at a horrifying pace.

"I don't mind to die," she said, breaking the quiet, turning so that she could see him. "I do mind the dying, though. So slow, Matthew, so very, very slow."

He nodded, thinking that her heart was too strong, protesting that it had years of wear left, and her lungs continued to draw in air, oxygenating blood that ran through a body so lightweight he suspected he could lift her with one arm. As fragile as a dandelion gone to seed – one strong gust of air, and the white puff head disintegrated to spread itself in the wind. Matthew groaned, cradling her as gently as he could to his chest, and ironically it was her comforting him, not the other way around.

"Shush, aye?" Joan tugged at his hair. "You know I don't mind, not really. For years, I've waited to stand before my Maker and hope His grace extends to me."

"It should. You're a good person, devout and strong in faith."

Joan sighed against his shoulder and he helped her to lie back against the pillows.

"Some days, I don't care one way or the other. All I want is for this to be over." Joan fiddled with the coverlet, peeked at him. "He shouldn't have done what he did."

"No," Matthew said, and something in his tone must have alerted her to the fact that broaching the subject of wee Simon's betrayal was far too premature. He clenched his jaws, overwhelmed by a rush of rage – and grief, for the friendship he had lost.

"How is she?" Joan asked a while later.

"Better, I think. Tired, aye? She hasn't slept well for almost a week, but last night she did, and this morning when I left her, she was still sleeping." Supervised by Julian, who had offered to sit and read in a corner of their room while Matthew hurried off to see his sister. That made him frown, but he trusted Julian, and Alex had been sleeping dreamlessly when he left.

"She was nearly dragged back." Joan met his eyes. "We had no idea. I swear, Simon wouldn't have put Alex at risk, not knowingly."

"But he did. The painting aside, he insinuated she was conversant with magic. And that is a hard suspicion to lay to rest once it has been woken – even more difficult after he screamed to the world that she's a time traveller."

It hadn't helped that she had been so affected by the painting, but Julian and Minister Walker had overruled Minister Macpherson's opinion that this in itself was a sign, and Mr Farrell had declared that he was so seasick, so unbalanced by the little canvas, that if Alex Graham was a witch then he must surely be one as well.

"I'm so sorry," Joan whispered.

Matthew just nodded. His Alex was safe for now, and he'd ensure she attended service a number of times before they rode back home.

"Will she…?" Joan swallowed. "Do you think she'll come to see me?"

Matthew stroked her face. "Alex never holds grudges so aye, I think she will."

"I would like that, very much would I like to see her."

"I'm sorry about Lucy," Matthew said as he was leaving.

"Nay, you're not. You think she was justly punished."

"She wasn't punished, but aye, I think it was just she should be swallowed as those she tricked were."

Joan's dark grey eyes looked at him for a long time. "She was all I had," she said in a voice cut to shreds with pain. "God help me, but something I did very wrong." She turned her head into the pillow, waving at him to leave.

Alex was having something of a strained morning, waking to find Julian by her bed, light eyes alight with enthusiasm as he explained just how they would go about dousing the rumours of witchery that Simon's insinuations had woken.

"And I assume that being raised a Protestant, you're familiar with the concept," Julian said. "After all, regular catechising is part of that Church as well."

"I'm a woman fully grown," Alex said through gritted teeth. "I have no intention of having my faith tested by a panel of black-clad men who consider themselves my betters."

"They are your betters, and it will serve its purpose. To once and for all squash these slanderous accusations about your general character."

Alex gave him a look so full of dislike Julian reared back. "Just because a man carries the title of minister it doesn't automatically make him my better. In this particular case, I have no intention of being goaded by that toad Minister Macpherson."

"But why does this concern you so? You're well versed in the Bible and catechism. You lead a life in accordance with the laws laid down in scripture—"

"Oh, come off it! You know as well as I do that when I get carried away, I throw myself into arguments that a narrow-minded person easily can construe as evidence of heresy."

"But not of witchery, and that's the issue at stake here." He gave her a reassuring smile. "I'll be there, and you'll do very well."

"I'm coming too," Matthew insisted once he'd been

appraised of Julian's little plan. His face shifted into a nasty red at Julian's shake of the head.

"She does this alone. Your presence will be taken as an admission on her part that she doesn't wish to face this."

"Of course she doesn't want to!" Matthew yelled at Julian. "Would you want to see yourself so humiliated, and all on account of the groundless accusations of a whoring lawyer?"

"Your brother-in-law," Julian reminded him.

"Not for long – and then I'll never as much as bid him good day."

"Forgiveness is a Christian virtue," Julian told him – rather primly, in Alex's opinion.

"What will they ask me?" Alex asked Matthew as he accompanied her to the meeting house later that same day. "It's not as if I know the whole bloody Bible by heart, is it?"

"It will help if you don't refer to the Holy Writ as the 'bloody Bible'," he said drily. "They'll ask you from the catechism, and you know most of it."

"Unfortunately, I don't always agree with it."

"That you must keep to yourself. Concentrate on the questions and on replying to them, not on voicing your opinions as to how Lot treated his daughters, or how unfair some of the laws are to women."

"Hmm." Alex wiped her hand surreptitiously against her skirts.

All in all, it wasn't too bad, Alex thought afterwards, curtseying to one after another of the ministers. Despite being barraged by questions from Minister Macpherson, she had acquitted herself well enough to earn herself a wink from Minister Walker.

There had been a long, uncomfortable part where she had been submitted to very many questions regarding the paintings, and how she had come upon that first one, and why it was that she'd seen fit to burn it – was it perhaps because she had seen it at work? Alex had repeated she had not, and kept to a censored version of the truth: the painting she had bought in Cumnock, entranced by its suggestive beauty, but once she had studied it closely, she had become convinced that somehow it wasn't right.

"It made all of me heave," she said. "It forced my eyes to lock themselves on a distant point, and all along my body, I broke out in sweat. I only broke away from it by reciting the Lord's Prayer," she lied, "and so I knew it had to be evil."

Minister Walker almost patted her on the head at that point. But this time, Minister Macpherson insisted, it had seemed as if the painting was calling out to her, bidding her to obey – a master calling its creature to heel.

"It was awful," Alex said. "I couldn't hear myself think, and no matter how hard I tried, I couldn't find a point on which to concentrate. But I fought it, didn't I? You saw, didn't you, how I struggled against it." Well yes, even Minister Macpherson had seen that, and all of them could testify to the look of absolute terror on her face.

"And what of your brother-in-law's accusation that you're a…err…time traveller?" Minister Macpherson asked just at the end.

Alex had expected this to come up, had practised for hours before the little looking glass in the attic room, and now she turned a calm face in the minister's direction. "Simon is a desperate man: his daughter accused of sorcery, his wife on her deathbed. Excuses must be made, the poor man is drowning, and so…" She hitched her shoulders and smiled sadly.

"It's a strange accusation to make," Minister Walker said, eyes very sharp.

"Very," Alex agreed. "I've never even heard of such – I'm not even sure what it means. Do you think it possible: to travel through time?"

Minister Walker's bushy, grey brows pulled together, giving the man a surprisingly ferocious look. "One never knows. Sorcery is a great – but powerful – evil."

"Amen to that." Alex didn't have to pretend she trembled, a shiver running up her spine as she relived her recent tussle with the painting. So close, so goddamn close. She knotted her hands and took a couple of steadying breaths. "I don't know why Simon said what he did, but I can only repeat that I have never done anything wrong. I am no witch, no time traveller." She raised her face, met their eyes one by one.

"So there is no truth in this?" Minister Macpherson pushed.

"No," she said.

"Prove it," he said.

"Prove it? How can I prove it?" She looked entreatingly at Minister Walker. "This is unbearable. I stand accused and am asked to prove my innocence. Where is the proof that I am guilty?"

"This is a serious matter, daughter," Minister Walker said, "and your brother-in-law was most adamant, was he not?"

"Lies, even Joan said as much, didn't she? But if you feel it necessary, let's go and ask her. We go thirty years back, she and I."

"No, no," Minister Walker said, "that won't be necessary. Poor Mrs Melville has enough to handle as it is."

"Yes, I would think she does," Alex said.

Julian rose to his feet. "Mrs Graham insists she is innocent. Apart from Mr Melville's somewhat emotional outburst, we have not found one shred of evidence proving differently. She came here today voluntarily, and she has twice sworn on the Holy Writ that she is no witch. What would you have us do? Should we duck her and see if she floats?"

Alex nearly choked. What?

"Maybe we should," Minister Macpherson said, a rather eager look in his eyes.

"Don't be ridiculous!" Minister Walker glared at him. "To do so would be to make public an accusation we have nothing to substantiate with. Besides, what would it do to Mrs Graham's reputation? And what do you think Matthew Graham would do? He'd have our guts for doing such!"

"We are within our rights," Minister Macpherson sniffed.

"No, we're not," Mr Farrell put in. "No one has ever levied such accusations towards Mrs Graham before. One man's word — and the word of a desperate man at that — is not enough." Not that Alex was overly fond of Mr Farrell, self-important slaver that he was, but then and there she'd gladly have kissed him.

"We vote," Minister Macpherson insisted. Alex's knees dipped, but she succeeded in remaining on her feet.

"Vote? Very well. I say nay." Minister Walker sat back.

"Nay," said Mr Farrell.

"Nay," said Julian.

"Nay? How nay? You proposed it," Minister Macpherson blustered.

"I did not. I was merely making the point that there was no evidence."

Huh, Alex felt prone to agree with Minister Macpherson. Besides, she didn't quite like the assessing look in Julian's eyes when he regarded her, as if he were, in fact, not entirely convinced of her innocence. Fancies, she decided. Julian smiled at her. Definitely fancies. Alex's shoulders sagged with relief.

Matthew was waiting for her by the meeting house door, and after bowing at the departing ministers, tucked her hand into the crook of his arm and walked off in the direction of the sea.

"Where are we going?"

"No particular place." He smiled down at her. "But a walk would do you some good, and today is a fine day for it."

She looked about and agreed that it was. A chilly December sun gilded the Chesapeake, the winter bare trees stood in stark outline against a sky that was so clear it could have been made of glass, and the storms of the last few days had subsided, leaving fresh salty air in their wake.

"I want to go home." Not quite three weeks to Christmas, and they had already been away twelve days. Their family must be worried that something had happened to them.

"I can't leave, not now," Matthew told her.

"So this is it, then?"

Matthew broke off a drying head of yarrow and nodded morosely. "She wants you to come," he said, halfway between a question and a demand.

"I will, first thing tomorrow. And Simon?"

"I won't talk of him," Matthew replied frostily.

"To me you will." Alex looked about for a stone she could sit on and perched herself on it, tucking her billowing skirts under her thighs. "He's the closest thing you have to a brother, a lifelong friend, a man who knows you almost as well as you know yourself. People like that don't grow on trees."

"He betrayed us. When he was cornered, he threw you to the wolves in the hope of deflecting attention from that daughter of his." Matthew spat into the drying grass and came to sit beside her, his back to her side.

"He wasn't thinking clearly, and Ruth says how devastated he is by all of this. His whole life is on the verge of collapsing. His daughter gone and branded a witch, his wife about to die at any moment, and you, his best friend, lost to him because of one irrational, rash act."

Matthew just shook his head, obdurate.

Alex exhaled and got to her feet. "Before you throw it all away, why not reflect a bit on all you've shared and done together. Why not recall all those times when he's been there for you, and perhaps this great wrong is eclipsed by all the good turns he's done you. Like when he saved your life in Cumnock – several times, actually – or when he rode like the wind with you from Edinburgh to give you a badly needed alibi. All those months when he took care of Hillview and Mark, allowing me to go off in search of you, the way he helped you win Ian back from Luke. And all of that you're going to throw to the wind, just like that?" Alex bent down and kissed him on his cheek, noting that he needed to shave.

In the low afternoon sun, she saw just how tired he was, and her heart went out to him. "He's your friend." She placed firm fingers on his lips when he attempted to interrupt. "Your friend. And he needs you now, as he has never done before. Is this the time to leave him out in the cold?"

Matthew averted his face. "I'm too angry. I fear that if I see him, I'll hurt him – badly."

"And you care enough for him not to want to do that." She smiled, smoothing back his hair and reaching into her petticoat pocket for something to tie it back with.

"Aye," he admitted grudgingly.

Alex patted his shoulder. "Go and see him – for your sake, if nothing else."

Matthew found Simon making his way down Main Street, head bowed. When Simon saw him, he froze mid-step. Hands fluttered up to smooth at his wispy hair, he tugged at cravat and waistcoat, and stretched his lips into a wary smile. Matthew remained where he was, making an effort to keep his hands relaxed and open along his sides. Simon took a couple of hesitant steps, ending up well within reach of Matthew's fists, should he be so inclined. A deep breath, yet another, and Simon closed his eyes, jutting out his chin as if giving Matthew permission to wallop him one.

"If I was planning on beating you senseless, I would wait until after dark," Matthew said. "Just a question of settling down to wait until you made your way down to Mrs Malone's."

Simon's eyes flew open, his face mottling into patchy red. "I go there to eat."

"Oh aye? And is that why you return home in the wee hours so drunk you can barely piss without wetting yourself?"

"No, I drink to forget what lies waiting at home. It doesn't work very well, mind you."

They fell into step with each other, Matthew with his hands clasped behind his back, Simon mimicking his stance.

"She's hurting badly," Matthew said to break the silence.

"Aye, but that has been a fixture in her life for years. You don't know how it is to live with someone so afflicted, no matter how bravely she bears it. For her sake, I'm glad that she is close to finally passing on, but as to myself…" Simon choked, digging into first one, then another ornate coat pocket for a handkerchief. "I don't know what to do once she isn't here beside me," he admitted in a voice trembling with despair. "It will be a right lonely place, this world, without my Joan."

"As it would be for me, without Alex," Matthew said, unable to avoid the accusing edge to his tone.

"Ah, Lord!" Simon swung towards him, and in his face, Matthew saw his naked shame at what he'd done. "I... Oh God, Matthew! When I saw you struggling to keep her here with you, I wanted to rush and help you, but didn't dare to, and I swear I didn't know it would be that bad for her. It wasn't my intent, I swear."

"But you stood there and accused her of witchery."

"Nay, I never did that," Simon said. "If you collect, I said very clearly that I didn't think she was a witch."

"You called her a time traveller! Before that group of men, you disclosed the one secret you should never have mentioned – not if you love Alex and me both."

"I know what I have done – I have just been to see Minister Walker, taking it all back – and there's no excuse but that of a desperate father confronted with the horrifying fact that his daughter was called a witch, a concubine of Satan. And, even worse, the father knew that some of it was the truth, but couldn't let his child go up in flames without attempting to save her."

"And so you threw Alex into the fire," Matthew concluded.

"Aye, so I did. I thought, nay, I hoped, that if Alex could tell of how these pictures existed independent of their creator then they might see Lucy for what she was: a child entranced by power and magic, not truly a witch. I didn't think further than that." He bowed his shoulders together in misery. "Lucy wasn't always a good person, but she didn't intend for the child to be dragged away."

"Nay, I don't think so either. But the whore and the slave girl – well, those she intentionally tricked."

"Her husband favoured them, and she was jealous." Simon sighed. He put a tentative hand on Matthew's sleeve. "Will you forgive me, brother of my heart?"

Through narrowed eyes, Matthew looked down at him. "I'll try. I can't give you more than that, not now."

Simon nodded, kicking at the ground in a gesture that

threw Matthew back thirty years in time, to when he and Simon went everywhere together.

"It will have to do. At least you haven't broken every bone in my body as you threatened you would," he added in a lighter tone, and in his eyes a glimmer of the old Simon shone through.

"Don't tempt me," Matthew snapped.

Alex was very pleased with her little peace brokering effort, and decided to reward herself by splurging on some precious spices and tea, spending an agreeable hour in the apothecary's and exiting with several small packages, including a vial of poppy syrup and some camphor. To her relief, no one seemed to have heard of the recent events in the meeting house – well, beyond the staggering fact that Lucy Jones had gone up in thin air.

"Alex! Wait!" Alex recognised the voice and stood waiting for Kate, who hurried towards her, accompanied by a small man in an oversized coat she introduced as her chief clerk. The man was dismissed, and Kate beamed at Alex and suggested they walk down to the warehouses – she'd just received a shipment of indigo from Jamaica.

Alex was ambivalent. She liked Kate – despite the fact that every time she saw her she was reminded of Matthew's infidelity all those years ago – but was taken aback by how chirpy Kate was, given the circumstances. A facade, no more, she realised once they were on their way, Kate's voice stripped of all gaiety as she expressed just how sorry she was for Alex's recent ordeal, dismissing Simon's accusations as ridiculous and incredible.

"You a time traveller?" she snorted. "How could he possibly think anyone would believe something that ludicrous?" She went on to talk about Lucy, and to Alex's surprise, Kate seemed to be on the verge of tears, describing in terse sentences just how much she'd loved her daughter-in-law. Well, Alex reflected, she supposed it was nice that someone missed Lucy. She sure didn't.

The warehouse stood to the left of the main dock, a tall,

sturdy wooden building painted in red, and with doors that creaked when Kate pulled them open. After the brilliance of the December afternoon, the space was enclosed and dark, and although Kate seemed not at all disturbed, walking briskly towards the ladder leading upwards, Alex hung back, imagining all kinds of creatures living and breathing in the dark.

"Alex?" Kate's voice floated down from somewhere high above. Sun filtered in through several small apertures set just under the roof, casting narrow beams of light on the upper floors.

"I'm coming." Alex set down her basket by the door and made for the ladder. Something rustled. Not a rat, too big for that.

"Hello?" she said. A shadow detached itself from the wall. A man.

"Oh, don't mind him," Kate called. "It's just Smith."

"Smith?" Alex had her hand on the ladder.

"An itinerant – but literate. He's helping us with the inventory."

"Ah." Alex set her foot on the lowest rung.

A hand closed on her, yanked her with force backwards, another hand clamping down over her mouth. "Mrs Graham, I believe."

Bloody, fucking hell! Alex would know that voice anywhere, had nightmares in which it figured, and now it was breathing into her ear, tinged with amusement. She groped behind her, found something that wasn't cloth and pulled – hard.

"Aaaah!" Burley wailed, and Alex was free, running for the open door. He caught up, wheezing heavily, and Alex was washed with relief as she recalled Philip had been badly hurt in the recent altercation with Matthew. Not hurt enough, though, because he took a leap ahead, blocking off her way of escape.

"Why the hurry?" he gasped.

"Things to do, places to be," she replied, sidling away from him.

"I think not. I think this, Mrs Graham, is when your luck runs out."

It took a huge effort not to squeal and run. Instead, she took yet another step away from him – unfortunately, that also meant stepping away from the door.

He grinned, hair as dishevelled as always falling over his face. With a scraggly beard, with a limp and with one hand pressed to his side, he still managed to scare the heck out of her. Where was Kate? For an instant, she raised her eyes to the wooden ceiling. Philip grinned again, took hold of the ladder, and tipped it to the floor.

"I dare say she's hiding. Mrs Jones strikes me as a woman who much prefers her countenance unmarked, and I…" He produced a knife. "…well, I'll not take kindly to being interrupted."

Alex attempted a sigh. "Persistent, aren't you? It would be a much better world if you just rolled over and died."

Philip Burley chuckled, a most disconcerting sound. "I've said it before, I'll say it again: it takes a lot to frighten you, Mrs Graham."

"You think?" she hiccuped.

"I do. Now, of course, you're so frightened you don't quite know what to do." The blade sliced through the air, as if he were practising his coming moves. Alex shook her head, taking several quick steps backwards. "And you should be," he said and charged.

Fear gives you wings. Like a trapped swallow in a barn, Alex darted back and forth, with Philip always keeping himself between her and the door. But he was tiring fast, having to stop to draw breath on several occasions, and Alex felt a glimmer of hope, edging determinedly towards the dusky skies she could see through the half-open door. She swallowed, bunched her skirts, and rushed for safety. He pounced. Like a rugby player in flight, he flew through the air towards her, blade held aloft, and Alex was thrown to the ground, squashed flat under his weight. He laughed, one hand closing over her windpipe.

"Oh dear, oh dear. And so the invincible Mrs Graham is brought to ground." He was shoving at her skirts with his free hand, knife held in his mouth, but the pressure on her throat was such that she couldn't do much to stop him. He raised his hips, seemed to be tugging at his breeches, and then his full weight was back, and he was horribly, horribly close.

He laughed. "Will it please Matthew Graham, do you think, to know his beloved wife died well served?"

Black spots rose before her eyes: there was no air, no strength to defend herself with. He laughed, grunting as he manoeuvred himself in position between her legs. She attempted a slap, she set her heels to the ground and tried to shift away, and his fingers dug into her throat, squeezing so hard that she had to give up, lie like a broken rag doll below him. She could feel him half-engorged against her thigh, and any moment now she would die. She could see it in his eyes, in the brandished knife.

There was a whacking sound. Philip's mouth fell open in an 'o' before he slumped, pinning her to the ground with his unconscious weight.

"I'm so sorry...I... Sweetest Lord! Almost too late... I had to jump, and... Alex, are you alright? Here." Kate rolled Philip to the side and helped Alex up. She spat at Philip, but her hands were trembling as badly as Alex's own, and for a moment they hugged, clutching at each other.

"Thanks," Alex said, surprised she could sound so normal when her heart had taken up residence somewhere in the environs of her collarbones.

"It was the least I could do. I should have recognised him." Once again, Kate spat.

Together, they tied him up as well as they could, using Alex's shawl and Philip's belt. Kate pulled the door closed, pushed the bolt in place, and set off at high speed up the main street.

"We have to find the watchmen," she threw over her shoulder to where Alex was following much more slowly. "And this time he'll hang."

Just like that, Alex's legs gave way, and she sat on her knees in the street and cried. He would die. Finally, this nightmare would be over, and never again would he touch her or talk to her. She smoothed at her skirts, pressing her thighs closed. Oh God, if Kate hadn't hit him when she did… Someone was talking to her, a hand came down on her arm, and she screamed, slapping it away.

"Alex?" Kate's face hovered before her. "It's alright, sweeting, I'm right here."

"I…" she stuttered.

"Shush, dear," Kate said. "Come, let's get you back on your feet, shall we?"

Alex somehow got off her knees. "The watchmen – find them."

Philip Burley didn't hang. When the watchmen reached the warehouse, they found it empty, a torn shawl left on the floor as a parting gift. The resulting hue and cry was fruitless. Nowhere was there a trace of Philip Burley, not under his own name or that of Smith.

Very late in the evening, a young boy came forward, blubbering that he hadn't had much choice, and that the man had threatened to kill him if he didn't row him over to one of the sloops.

"Shit," was all Alex could think of saying when Matthew brought her the news.

"On his way to Charles Towne," Matthew said, stretching over the table for some more bread. He glanced at Alex and used his free hand to caress her face. He hadn't stopped touching her in one way or the other since hearing of her ordeal, and she couldn't get close enough to him, requiring his proximity, his warmth to reassure herself things had ended well – this time as well.

"Or Jamestown," Julian said.

"Aye. No great difference, is it? The important thing is that he's no longer here." Matthew scowled. "So close!"

"Let's hope he falls overboard," Alex said.

"Too easy," Matthew muttered, "far too easy, aye?"

Alex shoved away her plate. Would this never end?

Chapter 29

The appearance of Ruth just after dawn next morning woke the entire Allerton residence. Untidily dressed, her hair still in its night braid, Ruth rushed to her father. "You have to come, Da. She's dying and Uncle Simon..." She burst into tears.

Matthew was already pulling on his clothes, making for the door, Alex at his heels. Too late, Alex moaned, she should have gone to see her yesterday, and now she'd left it too late to say goodbye to her friend. They ran through the empty, silent streets, and at Joan's house, Matthew took the stairs in twos- no, threes – in his haste to get to her side. Alex rushed after, nearly falling over her skirts.

Joan was still alive. By her bed sat Simon, a Simon Alex had never seen before, pale and shivery. At their entrance, he stood up to allow them room, and Alex squeezed herself into the narrow space closest to the wall, settling herself on Joan's right-hand side. Joan smiled weakly at her, raising her hand a couple of inches before letting it fall back onto the bed.

"You came," Joan breathed.

"I did," Alex said, "and I would never have forgiven you if you hadn't waited for me."

Joan actually laughed, a breathless sound that was cut short by a strange, racking cough.

"And what would you have done?" she said.

"Oh, I don't know. Probably asked Rachel and her angel pig to make your life in heaven somewhat overexciting."

"Angel pig?" Joan closed her eyes, drew a couple of shallow breaths. "You have the most remarkable notions, Alex."

"Actually, the pig is Matthew's notion, not mine. He says how Rachel would be very unhappy without at least one pig, and so, of course, God makes sure she has one."

Joan's mouth relaxed into a genuine smile. "Aye, God would." Her fingers sank into Alex's arm. "I didn't think I'd be frightened, but I am, very frightened."

"Hush." Alex caressed her sister-in-law's face. "I'm here, right? We're all here. Look, Simon, Matthew and me. We'll help you over."

"Help me over to what? Likely to hell."

"Listen, you," Alex said ferociously. "If God doesn't whisk you up immediately into heaven, He has a major fight on His hands, okay? You tell Him from me that if He somehow overlooked you while handing out the winning tickets, then He better find one quick or I will twist His divine balls until He squeals."

Joan's eyes snapped open. "Alex!" she exclaimed, and then she died.

"She's dead," Simon said, and for the first time in all the years Alex had known him, his voice was flat and monotone. In his hands, he turned one of Joan's lace caps round and round, not daring to look at his wife who was already shrinking into a corpse on the bed.

Of course God exists, Alex reflected as she closed Joan's eyes, found a strip of linen to tie her jaw closed, and arranged her hair to lie neat and tidy around her head. He exists and so does the immortal soul – otherwise, how would it be so immediately obvious when someone passed away? I meant it, she added severely to God, so You better make her welcome. She likes honeyed mulled ale, and if You can find her a raspberry pie that will make her very happy. She deserves it. You and I both know she didn't have much of a life down here, did she? And with that she turned to hug Simon close.

"You're a remarkable woman," Julian said to Alex some days later. He nodded in the direction of where Matthew was sitting. "Does he know how fortunate he is?"

"Ask him," she suggested, escaping to supervise Ruth's packing.

Matthew listened with some amusement – and quite some

pride – as Julian extolled Alex's multiple Christian virtues, chief among them her compassion and capacity to forgive.

"He accused her falsely, and still she concerns herself with his wellbeing, supporting him now that his wife is gone. A marvellous woman, most remarkable."

"Aye, she is," Matthew said, "and on top of that, opinionated and stubborn and—"

Julian laughed, shaking his head. "That too. I was somewhat concerned that she should launch herself into a discussion regarding God's grace and predestination the other day. Even worse, I worried that she might state that God in all probability is a papist."

"Well," Matthew said, "none of us know, do we? We can but lead our lives as well as we can and hope it will be enough at the Day of Reckoning."

"Matthew Graham! Do I hear you voicing doubts about our faith?"

"Not as such, no. But I do agree with Alex in that God surely is just, no matter what else He might be, and so He won't pay particular heed to if we're Papists or Protestants or Quakers or such. He'll look to our faith and our actions rather than to a predestined order of things."

"That's heresy," Julian said.

"To us as Presbyterians, aye. To Protestants and Catholics, no. And who is to know? Only God knows, and He isn't telling, is He?" Matthew cocked his head. "Does this disqualify me as your future father-in-law?" he teased, grinning at the expression that crossed Julian's face.

"Err…" Julian coughed. "…umm, well, no I suppose. I must take it upon myself to bring you and your wife safely back into the folds of our beliefs."

Matthew laughed out loud. "You may find that quite the struggle. Not with me, but with Alex, remarkable woman that she is." He shook his head to show Julian just how futile his efforts would be.

The discussion was interrupted by the remarkable woman herself, who came in to inform her husband their daughter was finally packing.

"She could stay here," Julian said, his casual tone belied by the gleam in his eyes.

"Oh, I'm sure she could, but she isn't. Not this time." Alex leaned towards him with a small frown on her face. "Not yet seventeen, and nothing – I repeat, nothing – untoward will happen between you before she turns eighteen."

He flushed. "Nothing has happened."

"Oh yes, it has. You've kissed her, haven't you?" Only this morning, Matthew had seen them, a stolen embrace in the kitchen, and, from the way his daughter melted herself into Julian's arms, he knew it was a matter of weeks at most before something else happened, which was why, of course, Ruth was coming home with them, despite her voluble protests.

"Umm..." Julian said, ducking his head to avoid their eyes.

"And you liked it," Alex stated rather unnecessarily in Matthew's opinion – what man wouldn't? "Well, Julian dear, so does she, and unfortunately, in some aspects she is far too like me: what we like, we want more of." She shared a quick look with Matthew, her eyes dark and promising.

"I would never dishonour her," Julian said stiffly.

"Aye, we know. But she would, and you wouldn't stand a chance in hell."

"Hmm." Julian fussed with his clothes, hand lingering on his starched collar – no doubt to remind them of his impeccable morals, given that he was a minister. "Will I be allowed to take farewell of her?"

"Aye," Matthew said, "and we will even accord you some moments of privacy. Moments, mind."

Simon had decided to sell his little house, having been offered to rent a room with the Hancocks. "They have a room to let, and I don't need much more. Besides, I can't stay there, not in a home so full of Joan. I can't enter the kitchen without expecting to see her there, and our bedroom... No, I can't stay there."

"It may be a bit premature," Alex said. "Maybe you

should wait and see." Esther Hancock kept a nice home, but both Esther and William were very devout – far from Simon's rather relaxed attitude to religion. Fortunately, Betty had not inherited their excessive religiousness, maybe as a consequence of far too many hours spent on her knees as a child.

"Wait and see for what? Do you truly think I'll marry again? Nay, Alex, any bedding I'll be doing will be such as I pay for."

"You don't know," Alex insisted, saddened by the bleakness in his voice.

"Aye, I do." Simon sank down to sit like a collapsed soufflé. "I don't think I could make the effort required to live in marriage – not again. All that hard-won intimacy; those years when you must explain out loud what Joan knew without me saying it." In his hand, he was holding a length of ribbon, a pale dove-grey that Alex recognised as being Joan's. "I will hold myself to Joan. My heart, my soul, she owns forever." He roused himself and stood, tucking the ribbon inside his shirt. "But I won't promise to be celibate – she knows I can't hold it anyway."

"And why change your habits after her death?" Alex said with a certain sting. "Now that she can't be hurt by your constant presence at Mrs Malone's."

Simon gave a low laugh. "We found our way back to each other, and it wasn't constant, at most twice a month. And Joan understood and forgave."

"I never would."

Simon smiled down at her and held out his hand to help her up. "Aye, you would. You love him."

Alex made a doubtful sound, making Simon laugh out loud and comment that it was clear as day that she and Matthew were as besotted with each other now as they'd been when first they married.

On the day of their departure, frost roses decorated the windowpanes of the little attic window, and the floorboards creaked with cold.

"It's snowing!" Ruth sounded hopeful.

"So it is." Matthew nodded. "Best dress warmly," he added and went back to his porridge.

"Mayhap we should wait," Ruth said.

"Wait? For what?" Matthew added a dollop of butter and honey to his steaming bowl and sniffed. Very nice.

Ruth gave him an exasperated look and stomped off. Matthew winked at his wife and went on with his breakfast.

An hour later, they were well on their way, Providence a half-mile or so behind them.

"It's going to be cold," Alex said from where she was sitting before Matthew on Aaron.

"Aye," he agreed, pulling his thick winter cloak closer. Lined with wool fleece, it hung heavy round them both. "Keeps people inside." Given that he knew Philip Burley was nowhere close, he'd dispensed with hiring extra men, but all the same, the whirling snow came as something of a relief. He beckoned Ruth closer and nodded when he saw she held the loaded musket over her thighs.

"If we ride well into the night, we can be home by late tomorrow evening," he said. "Just a short break to allow the horses to rest and get their wind back." Home. It felt like an eternity since they had left, even if it was no more than three weeks.

"In time for Christmas," Alex said. Matthew studied the bulging saddlebags and shook his head. He didn't hold with excessive gift giving, but Alex had insisted they buy something for each and every one – practical things, mostly. In his pouch he carried his New Year's gift to her, and he snuck his hand down to ensure it was still there. Not at all practical, he smiled, but he hoped she would like it all the same.

Chapter 30

It was a relief to be back home, to allow oneself to fall back into routines and everyday life. Sarah was overjoyed to see Ruth – at least for the first few days – and then the house was once again filled with the noise of their continuous bickering and arguing, interspersed with loud bursts of laughter and long conversations where the fair and the red head leaned very close together.

Adam monopolised Alex from the moment she was back, tagging after her like a constantly talking shadow with his black and white dog, now ceremoniously baptised Lovell, at his heels.

"Why Lovell?" Alex crouched down to scratch the puppy.

"You know: '*The rat, the cat and Lovell our dog ruled all England under a hog*'."

"Ah," Alex said. "Want to help me with the turnips?"

No, Adam most certainly didn't, and, with a little relieved wave, Alex set off in the direction of the root cellar. Adam was endearing company – for an hour or so. Almost two days listening to his detailed description of his beloved animals was a bit too much, for all that Hugin starred in a number of amusing anecdotes.

On her way back up from her inspection of her winter vegetables, Mark caught up with her and from the look in his eyes, she knew he was bursting to tell her a secret, but instead he took her by the elbow and guided her to his cabin. Not a particularly difficult secret to guess, she grinned, watching Mark kiss his wife tenderly. "You look well." Alex sat down beside Naomi. As always, Naomi had her lap full of mending, and now she held up a torn, light green smock and sighed.

"That child… I swear, Lettie should have been born a lad!" But her mouth curved into a wide smile, and the way her hand drifted down to her stomach confirmed Alex's little hunch.

"She reminds me of our Rachel," Alex said, looking at the dark-haired toddler, who was suspiciously quiet in her corner.

"Mark says so as well, and given some of the stories he tells of his sister, I quake already."

"Yes, it was a bit terrifying at times. Like when she decided she could fly and jumped from the hayloft, or when she convinced Jacob that children were just like fishes – if you stuck your head under the water and breathed, you'd learn how to swim." Alex laughed softly. She could still recall the sheer fright when Mark came running up the path from the eddy pool back in Hillview, screaming that Jacob was dead.

She turned her attention to Lettie. "Lettie Graham. Don't you even dare, child, you hear!" With surprising speed, she had her granddaughter under one arm, her free hand rooting in the little mouth. "Spit it out! Shit, bloody hell! Don't bite me, you little hellion, or I'll bite you back!" Lettie coughed. She coughed again and threw up, a cascade of half-digested porridge and several pieces of coal. Alex held the dripping, stinking child at arm's length and smiled at her son. "Yours, I think?" she said, handing him the girl. Mark grimaced but took her outside, throwing black looks at the two grinning women.

"And still you want another." Alex rolled her eyes.

"Says the woman who has nine – no, ten – children of her own," Naomi said with a chuckle.

To be home was also to be made painfully aware of the one who was missing. She lived Samuel's absence in a way she'd never lived anyone's absence before. Rachel, well, she'd died, and there was nothing to be done, and Jacob had chosen to run off to sea. But Samuel…at times, the guilt threatened to strangle her. Why hadn't she done something?

Rushed for the Indian boy and forced a trade, or… Like a constant thorn in her heart it was, and every morning there was that infinitesimal moment of time when she thought things were as they always had been, before she remembered that somewhere out in the forest Samuel wandered far from home. Did he miss her? Sometimes, she imagined she could hear him crying, and once she was so convinced he was actually there, she climbed up to the hayloft to look for him.

It was difficult to talk to Matthew about it, partly because she blamed him – and blamed him a lot – for that promise made so long ago; partly because every now and then she would see him stop whatever he was doing, head cocked in the direction of the western forests. If she had problems with guilt, Matthew was drowning in it, and she was reluctant to add more stones to a burden that was already threatening to crush him. And should Samuel not return… Alex slammed the hatch on that treacherous thought.

"He may not want to," Mrs Parson said when Alex broached the issue with her. "Mayhap the lad takes to Indian ways, no?"

Alex gave her a dark look. "He's my son."

"Aye, and he would still be your son, even if he chose to live out there, no?" Mrs Parson waved a hand in the direction of the north-west.

"He's coming home." Alex banged the door hard in her wake.

The day before Christmas, Alex saw David walk off in the direction of the river, and wrapping herself in a cloak, she hurried after him. David had been very silent since they had returned home, or maybe it was because she had been away that she noticed just how often he snuck away to be alone, and almost always to the graveyard or the river.

The snowfall of a week back had melted away, but two nights of freezing cold covered the ground and trees with hoar frost, and David's footprints stood black against the glittering surface. Not that she needed to track him: he was still visible where he walked dejectedly in front of her, scuffing at the ground. His wooden sword dragged behind him, and Alex wept inside, realising just how much this d'Artagnan was missing Buckingham – royalist or not. David walked all the way down to the water's edge, pausing by the flat rock where Samuel had left his folded clothes.

Alex wrapped her arm round his shoulders. He leaned his weight against her. "I don't think he's coming today."

"Nay," David sighed. "I don't think so either. But I hoped, on account of it being Christmas soon."

"Indians don't hold with Christmas, honey. I don't think Samuel will be celebrating the birth of Our Lord this year."

"Aye, he will." David tilted his head back to meet her eyes. "In here, he will." He clapped his chest with his hand.

"You think?" Alex felt strangely heartened by David's conviction.

"He says our names every night," David whispered. "Slowly, slowly, he says them – all of them. And then he prays as you've taught us."

"I'm not sure," Alex said. "He's not yet eleven. It's easy to forget when you're that young."

"Not Samuel, not my brother."

They sat down together on the fallen log, and David rested his head against her.

"Will he ever forgive us?" Alex asked, regretting the words the moment she uttered them out loud. Not a question to ask a child, she reprimanded herself severely.

"Forgive you?" David sat up straight. "And what were you to do? Fight the Indians when they came in force?"

"We could have done something."

"It wouldn't have helped." David hugged her. "Samuel knows it."

They lapsed into a comfortable silence, watching as the sun transformed the frosted trees into prisms of magical colour. It was very quiet, the migrating birds long gone, and the remaining sparrows and thrushes keeping low to the ground, or at least going about their business without expending energy on making noise. A crow cawed, it cawed again, and then it was all absolute stillness.

David shifted closer to her. The frost on the log had melted under her, dampening her skirts, but she was reluctant to move, and so, apparently, was he. There was a far-off rustling, and the crow called again. The shrubs on the other side of the river parted; a group of men stepped out on the further shore.

"Indians!" David breathed.

"Samuel," Alex groaned simultaneously, and now she was on her feet, because he was there, her son, standing only fifty feet from her, side by side with Qaachow. Oh God, my boy, he's brought my boy home, she thought, and her arms went out in an embracing gesture. Samuel took a tentative step in her direction, but Qaachow said something to him, and he ducked his head and stepped back into the forest.

"No!" Alex was already wading through the shallows, ignoring the iciness of the water. "No! Goddamn you, Qaachow! Give me my boy back!" Her eyes burnt into the Indian chief, but he didn't reply, gesturing to his men to deposit the sorry bundle they were carrying by the water's edge. Alex slipped, and had to swim furiously against the ice-cold current.

"Mama!" David was shrieking in fear behind her, but Alex didn't care. She was going after her boy; she had to fetch him home. She slipped again, and the waters closed over her head. Jesus! It was cold!

She resurfaced, spitting like a drowning cat. Samuel was rushing towards the water, and before he could be stopped, he had thrown himself in, buckskins and all, to come to her aid.

"Samuel! Oh God, Samuel! Get back, son." Alex had her head over the water, wiping at her hair with an arm that was unbearably heavy. Her fingers, she couldn't feel her fingers. But her eyes locked into Samuel's, and she smiled. Down she went again, her mouth filling with water. A weak kick, and her head broke the surface.

"I love you, Samuel," she gargled, before being tugged under by the current, and once again she heard David's frantic 'Mama' from somewhere behind her. But she was almost there, only yards separated her from her son, and then there were arms around Samuel and he was being carried away.

"Mama!" he screamed. "Mama!"

Alex sank, her legs useless in the cold. Other hands took hold of her, and she was half carried, half dragged to lie panting and shivering on the shore. By her nose were a pair of moccasins, and, following them up, she found the legs, the torso and then, finally, the face of Qaachow.

"My son," she croaked. "I want my son back. You've had him long enough, and I die, you hear. Every day without him, I die!"

"A year," Qaachow reminded her, backing away.

"Curse you, Qaachow!" Alex managed to get up on her knees. "May your seed fail; may your children and grandchildren wither and die; may your people fall into sickness and suffer iniquity and pain. All of this until my son is returned to me."

Qaachow looked completely taken aback, staring at her with something like fear in his eyes. She rose, tried to wipe her face free of the tendrils of hair that were plastered across it. From the forest came Samuel's voice, calling for her, for his brothers, his da. Out of the corner of her eye, she could see the other shore where Matthew was standing surrounded by their sons, Jacob already stripping off his clothes.

"I love you, Samuel!" she bellowed. "I love you, son, you hear?"

"Mama!" he yelled back, and then there was the distinctive sound of a slap. Alex stumbled towards the sound, but was rudely shoved to land on the ground. Before she had managed to get back on her feet, the Indians were gone.

"Mama?" Jacob materialised by her side. "We have to get you across and inside." Alex was shivering so hard she could barely walk, but followed him, dazed and obedient, to the water's edge.

"They left something," she mumbled through a mouth too stiff to talk properly with.

"Aye," Jacob answered. "Mark and John are taking care of it." Alex inhaled loudly when she re-entered the water.

This cold? The current curled itself round her legs, but she managed to keep her footing a good way out, and Jacob was there to help her. Somehow, she was back on their side where Matthew swept her into a cloak and led her back home, David tagging after.

"I saw him," she said. "Our boy, Matthew. I saw him, and he was tall and strong." And then she burst into tears.

Chapter 31

It was very late in the day before Alex woke. Matthew had insisted on a hot bath in the laundry shed, and after that he'd bundled her off to bed where he had plied her with a potent mixture of brandy and hot milk, sweetened with honey. When she still shivered, he'd undressed and crawled into bed with her, holding her until she was asleep. But he wasn't there when she woke, and at first Alex couldn't quite understand what she was doing in bed on a winter afternoon. She stretched, and as she did, she recalled the happenings of the morning, sitting up so quickly the blood flowed out of her head in protest, leaving her weak-kneed and dizzy.

She dressed, pulled on an extra pair of stockings to warm her ice-cold feet, and went in search of her family. It was Christmas Eve, and she had tons of things to do before tomorrow. The saffron buns she had baked yesterday, the ham was also done, but the pies and the fowl, the trout she was curing, and the bread…!

Someone was taking care of that at least, she sniffed as she came down the stairs. From the parlour came a steady hum of male voices, while from the kitchen came sounds that indicated all the Graham women were there. Her stomach growled, and Alex decided sustenance was her first priority.

"Better?" Mrs Parson bustled towards her, dragging her to sit as close as possible to the kitchen hearth.

"I haven't exactly been ill."

"Nay, you just nearly drowned," Mrs Parson said. "A normal wee thing, no?"

"I didn't nearly drown," Alex said. "I'm a very good swimmer."

"David said how you were well under, and then the Indians pulled you out."

"I would have made it across on my own," Alex said with far more conviction than she felt.

Mrs Parson snorted, obviously not believing her. She served Alex a bowl of hot chicken soup, complete with leeks and carrots, and sat down opposite her. "Did you see him, then?"

Alex nodded, her eyes swimming with tears. "At least he knew who I was."

"Of course he did," Mrs Parson said, smiling at her. "And now he knows you for a daftie as well, no?"

"A daftie?" Alex's voice squeaked with indignation.

"Aye. Throw yourself in the river like that!"

"You could have died," Betty remonstrated, setting Timothy down in Alex's lap.

"I just had to. He was so close." She bent her face to Timothy's bright corkscrews.

"At least he knows for certain just how much you love him and miss him," Naomi said in a soft voice, "and that must be a great comfort to him."

"You think?" Alex gave her a grateful look.

"If my mother had done something like that…" Naomi came over from where she was making pie, and holding her flour-covered hands aloft pecked Alex on the cheek. "I would have been so proud of her."

Alex stayed in the kitchen, comfortable in the warmth and the industrious activity. She helped Ruth with the four chickens, setting them to simmer in a heavy broth, complete with wine, prunes, winter apples and finely diced salted pork. Alex made approving noises at Sarah's squash soup, and had her fingers rapped when she tried to steal a piece of honey cake from under Mrs Parson's nose. By the hearth, Agnes was minding the rice porridge, a staple of Graham Christmas Eves.

"Swedish tradition," Alex said as she always did, ignoring the amused look that flew between her daughters. "You boil the rice slowly in milk and cinnamon, and then you make sure you set a dish outside the door for the little folk."

"The little folk?" Mrs Parson laughed. "I've told you, no? The little folk live in the Old World, not here."

"How would you know? Spoken to any recently?"

"No, on account of them being there, not here," Mrs Parson replied with irrefutable logic.

"Hmph," Alex said, "you never know, do you?" She brought out mustard seeds, her mortar and pestle, sent Hannah to the well for some cold water, and set herself to make tomorrow's mustard. Her eyes watered with the released fumes, and she squished them shut, working by feel alone. Once it was of the right texture, she sprinkled some salt and a measure of vinegar over it, mixing it carefully before covering the dish with a cheesecloth.

"Have you seen the priest then?" Mrs Parson asked, supervising Betty with a narrow eye as she sliced up the smoked lamb's leg.

"The priest?" Alex gave her a confused look.

"Aye, wee Carlos."

"Carlos?"

"It was him the Indians brought back, no?"

"They did?" Vaguely, Alex remembered a black bundle, dropped to lie immobile on the pebbled shore.

"Mmm." Mrs Parson's hand trembled. "You will have to cut his leg off."

"What?" Alex croaked.

"You heard." Mrs Parson beckoned for Alex to follow and led the way to one of the smaller downstairs rooms.

"I've never done something like this," Alex said, after looking in on the feverish priest. Even from the door, she could make out the stench, and when Mrs Parson informed her that was how gangrene smelled, she just nodded, having no idea.

"It's the bone that's the difficult part," Mrs Parson said.

"Yes, I sort of got that. But how do we do something like that and keep him alive?" An axe? No, that wouldn't do, would it? A saw? Yes, a saw, and, shit, what an awful sound that would make.

"If we don't, he dies anyway," Mrs Parson said.

"Not much of a comfort," Alex told her.

"You couldn't save his father when he took a blade for you, but maybe you can save the son by using a blade on him, no?"

Alex gave her a black look. "And when do we have to do this?"

"As soon as possible – tonight."

Alex sighed and dragged her hands up and down her skirts. "He has to make a conscious choice. I'm not cutting him without his permission."

"Hi." Alex smiled down at Carlos. It was very late, and most of the family had gone to bed. Left awake were Alex, Matthew, Mark, Jacob and Mrs Parson. Jacob was presently scrubbing down the kitchen table while Mrs Parson had gone to find aprons and clean head clouts for them all.

"*Hola,*" Carlos replied weakly. He looked about in amazement and relaxed against the pillows. "It's true then," he said through cracked lips. "They brought me back."

"Yes, left you like a tidy little Christmas present down by the river." The wrong present, unfortunately.

"You're disappointed." Carlos groped for her hand.

"Yes. I'm sorry Carlos, but I want my son, *mi hijo*, not you."

"*Te juro.* I swear, if I could have traded places with him, I would."

"*Ya lo sé.* I know, but it doesn't much help." She patted his hand and extricated her fingers from his hold.

"He begged that he be allowed to come home for a few days," Carlos said, "but Qaachow refused. And, in punishment, the boy was forced to come with them, all the way back home only to have to turn away."

"Punishment for what?" Alex asked, her heart crumbling inside.

"In punishment for asking. The boy is forbidden to think of you."

Oh God! Alex swallowed, and had she had Qaachow in front of her, she would have torn his limbs off, one by one.

"And does it work?" Matthew's voice was a pitiful, reedy thing.

"No," the priest answered. "It just leads the boy to hide his thoughts." He closed his eyes, breathing rapidly through his mouth. "My leg."

"Yes," Alex answered, "it's rotting away."

Carlos opened his eyes to stare at her in consternation. "Gangrene?"

Alex inclined her head in affirmation.

"*Dios mío,*" Carlos whispered.

"Mrs Parson says we have to amputate," Matthew said, "but Alex won't allow it unless you give us permission."

"And if we don't?" Carlos asked.

"Then you die," Matthew said. "It has to be soon."

"Now? *¿Ahora?*"

"Yes, now." Alex nodded.

The little priest reflected in silence for some minutes. "Do it, but I cannot promise I'll be brave. I'm bad at handling physical pain." Something stirred in his eyes, so dark as to resemble liquid pools of pitch. "Very bad."

They tied Carlos down. Jacob tightened a tourniquet above his knee, and nodded for Alex to start. Mrs Parson had alcohol and boiled water at hand, and there was a small, flattened iron in the hearth. In Alex's sweating hand, she held a sterilised knife, while Jacob held Matthew's precious hacksaw, just as thoroughly disinfected. With a brief prayer, Alex uncovered Carlos' calf.

The putrid stench filled the room. Alex's previous incision had been gouged and opened repeatedly, there were pockets of pus up and down the old scar, and down towards the foot, the rot lay open to the eyes: a yellowish green, stinking so badly Alex had to breathe through her mouth as she bent to inspect it.

"What?" she asked Mrs Parson, indicating the line of gashes and cuts.

"Mayhap he fell foul of his hosts," she said. "Do it. The man should not be kept waiting."

"Easy for you to say." Alex swallowed. Just below the

knee, Mrs Parson had decided, four or five inches from the uppermost part of the infection. Alex wiped her hand once more, steadied her grip on the knife and cut, slicing perpendicularly towards the bone.

Carlos shrieked through the leather strap, his eyes wild.

"The arteries," Alex said, blocking out her patient's desperate sounds. "There is one hell of a big artery down the leg somewhere."

"Three," Jacob said, leaning forward. "Down the thigh to just below the back of the knee where it splits into three."

"And what do I do with those?" Alex asked, watching the spurting blood with concern.

"Ligature," Jacob said, "or cauterise."

"Great," Alex muttered. She resolutely lifted the small iron and poked it at where the most blood seemed to be coming from. Poor Carlos shrieked again, and the room filled with the stench of faeces and urine. At least the blood stilled, and, with Jacob to guide her, Alex found the other branches of the artery and closed them off.

Carlos had fainted, thank heavens, and when it came to the saw, Jacob offered to do it instead. He was quick, and, even if the patient at one point woke with bulging eyes, it was over far faster than Alex could have hoped for. Mrs Parson poured basin after basin of water over the open wound, and upended the whole bottle of alcohol, at which point Carlos woke, screamed out loud, and fainted again. After that, it was merely a question of stitching it all together, the perpendicular cuts laid tight against each other. More hot water, more alcohol, and they were done, Mrs Parson taking over with the bandages.

Alex moved over to sit in a corner. Bloody hell, she thought, staring down at her by now madly shaking hands, I've cut a man's leg off. Very slowly, she leaned to the side and threw up.

"I don't blame you," Matthew said some time later, drawing her to sit in his lap. "This isn't a Christmas I much wish to relive."

"No." Alex yawned. It was past midnight, and in the

clear sky, a white winter moon rose, throwing its pale light over the ground.

"So cold," she said. "Samuel must have been so cold when he came out of the water. And now…" In the distance, a wolf howled, and then another one joined in.

"…now he is surely abed." Matthew kissed her throat, wrapping a stray lock of her hair round his finger. "You nearly drowned," he said in a matter-of-fact voice.

"I did. But I wasn't really noticing."

"I won't have you risking your life like that." He tightened his hold on her.

"I had to, he was there, and I had to go to him."

"You could have died." Matthew cleared his throat. "What then, Alex? How would I go on without you?"

"One day at the time, I suppose," she answered, nestling in against him.

"Not a life, Alex. Living hell, aye?"

In response, she kissed his cheek. "And if it had been you, seeing Samuel on the other side, would you not have thrown yourself into the river too?"

"Aye, I would. I nearly did, except that there were bows and arrows levelled at me."

"There were?" Alex hadn't even noticed.

"The difference being that I am the stronger swimmer," Matthew said.

Alex hitched her shoulders. At the time, she hadn't really cared about herself. All she had cared about was Samuel, so tantalisingly close.

"Promise?" he whispered into her hair.

"Promise what?" She rose, going to stand behind him instead, her hands kneading at his shoulders.

"Will you swear to me you'll never do something that foolhardy again?" He grabbed at her hands, craning his head back until he caught her eyes.

"You know I can't. It's nothing I set out to do. It just happens." She kissed his forehead, smoothed at his wrinkled brow. "Let's go to bed. Let me hold you in my arms and rock you to sleep, okay?"

★

Samuel was curled up as close as he could get to Little Bear, burrowed deep beneath the pelts that covered them both. He wasn't asleep, reliving in his head over and over again how Mama had come crashing through the water for him. It warmed his heart to have seen her, to have heard her call for him with such desperation. It wasn't only him that missed her; it was her missing him as well.

He mouthed his way through his family, from Da to wee Timothy, and just as silently he recited the Lord's Prayer. Like he did every night, he fumbled for the length of twine he carried like a necklace round his neck. He added another knot, and with his fingers he counted them off, one for every day he had been here. One hundred and nine days... That left only two hundred and fifty six. Only... Samuel scrunched his eyes together hard in an effort not to cry. It was unmanly to weep, Qaachow had told him. And he hadn't, not one little yelp, not one single tear had he shed as Qaachow punished him for throwing himself in the river. Instead, he had thought of Mama, how her eyes fixed on him as she swam through the frigid waters of the river.

"My name is Samuel Isaac Graham," he said in a low voice. "I was born on the 27th of May in Our Lord's year 1674, and I am nearly eleven years old." Not White Bear, no, that wasn't him. He was Da's son, and his name was Samuel.

Chapter 32

"How do you feel?" Alex asked, sitting down on a stool by Carlos' bed.

"Awful." After some days of feverish sleep, he'd been woken by a beam of clear sunlight, lucid, thirsty, and with a bladder that threatened to burst. It had been a shock to throw back the bedclothes and find he was one leg short, and he had looked with desperation in the direction of the chamber pot. How on earth was a man to piss with only one leg? The fair Graham son had been there to help him, slipping a bedpan under him while averting his eyes, but that was just a short-term solution, and Carlos had spent two hours trying to solve this new conundrum.

"A peg leg or a crutch," Alex said, once he had overcome his reluctance to share his problem with her. "Until then, you sit while you pee." She was inspecting his leg, using careful hands to touch the raw stump. She covered the skin with shredded onions, garlic and bee balm before rebandaging him.

"Like a joint of lamb," he jested.

"Don't worry, you don't fit in my baking oven." She sat back with a slight grunt.

"I still can't believe I'm here," Carlos said after some minutes of silence. He groped for the rosary beads that hung around his neck. He drifted into sleep, and he was back with the savages, limping to keep up that first day, a shocked and silent Samuel running a few steps ahead, his hand held by the Indian boy. He woke with a start, and swimming before him was Alex. He thought this must be a dream, because his leg no longer hurt.

"A dream?" Alex wiped his fevered face.

Carlos shrugged as well as he could. "Better a dream than reality – at least the life that I am living."

"You're pretty good at wallowing," Alex said with some asperity. "Here you are, albeit without a leg, but alive and lying in a clean bed among friends. Is that not quite a good life?" His face heated at the unspoken accusation: he was here while her son, a child, was out there.

"Tell me everything about these last months. Tell me about Samuel."

Matthew entered the room as she said that and, leaning back against the wall, nodded for him to start. Two sets of avid eyes on his face made Carlos swallow. Finally, he sighed and with his rosary beads gripped hard between his fingers, began to talk.

"I don't think he fully understood at first. There was an element of adventure to it all, in particular for a young boy. He was given a knife, his hair was tied back, and at night he slept back to back with his new Indian brother. Little Bear is a sweet boy, and so eager to meet and get to know this unknown brother of his. Some months younger than Samuel, near on a head shorter, but lean and sinewy and surprisingly strong. And he was happy with this new brother, prattling on and on in his language, pointing out everything to Samuel as we went."

"Does he speak English?" Alex interrupted.

"Not so that you'd know," Carlos replied. "A few words, no more."

"But then how do they talk?" Matthew had settled himself on the floor, long legs stretched out before him.

"Your son is forbidden to speak English, and even Qaachow only talks to him in their own language, ignoring him if he asks something of him in English." He smiled crookedly. "It worked. In less than a month, Samuel was speaking brokenly in their language." Nor was the boy allowed to mention his family. He had a father and a mother now, Qaachow and Thistledown, and he had a brother and a tribe. In general, the Indians were reluctant to punish their children with force, and in his time at the Indian village, Carlos had only seen a child beaten twice – both times Samuel, and both times for the same reason: for insisting that he was a Graham.

"Dear Lord," Matthew whispered.

"Qaachow aims to make him forget. The boy is watched carefully, and any mention of you, any word of English carries an immediate retribution. White Bear – Samuel – accompanies his Indian father and brother everywhere; his days are filled from morning to evening with Indian things and Indian rites. He must not speak of God, or Jesus Christ. He must think himself an Indian first, because that is what he is destined to become: a brave among the remnant Susquehannock – now adopted by the Iroquois."

"No!" Alex was on her feet. "No, he isn't. He's coming back in a year." She threw a pleading look in the direction of Matthew. "He is, isn't he?"

"Aye, of course he is, lass." But Carlos could see the large man didn't believe what he was saying, and from the way Alex's face fell together, she could see it too.

Carlos hastened on with his story. "He's struggling, working hard to retain his identity, and the few times we have spoken have been of you, of his Christian faith." He looked away. The Indians might hesitate to punish children with violence, but not men. He squeezed the bridge of his nose hard, took several steadying breaths.

"And you weren't allowed to speak to him of such, were you?" Matthew said. "Is that why…your leg?"

Carlos just nodded. And he had squealed like a pig, which made them laugh and do it again.

"I know he says your names every night, and I have urged him to say the Lord's Prayer at least once every day." He hitched his shoulders. That was what he had been able to do for the boy. "Otherwise, he's well cared for, his foster mother ensures he's fed and clothed, that he keeps himself clean, and that he has somewhere to sleep. I think she loves him, and I also think she is ashamed. I can see it in the way she looks at White Bear."

"Samuel," Alex corrected him.

"Samuel," Carlos acquiesced.

"And how did you fare?" Matthew asked. "With your missionary intent."

267

Carlos blinked. What did Matthew Graham care about the expansion of the Catholic Church? And then he realised his host was attempting to change the subject, and a quick look at Alex made him realise why. The woman had her hand pressed to her mouth, blue eyes bright with unshed tears.

"Oh, that." Carlos silently said a decade, his eyes on the whitewashed ceiling above him. "They mostly laughed, and then one of their elders sat beside me one evening and described in great detail what had happened to the last missionary to their people – may God rest his soul." Out of the corner of his eye, he could see Alex relax now that they had left the topic of Samuel, sinking down to sit beside her husband. He wiggled his feet – yes, his feet, because he could still feel the limb that was no longer there – wondering why the Indians had brought him back instead of leaving him to die of his infected wounds.

"And will you go back out there?" Alex asked. "Return to try and spread the Gospel?"

For an instant, Carlos thought she might be taunting him, but realised that she wasn't. She was genuinely curious. He sat up, patting at where his foot should have been. "It would be impossible, I think." All of him sang with relief. He had tried; he had lost a limb in his endeavours. He could go back to other things, and yet be met with respect.

Someone called for Alex, and she was on her feet in an instant. "I'll be back to check on you in a couple of hours," she said as she left.

Matthew stood, massaging his lower back. "He isn't planning on returning him within the year, is he?"

"No," Carlos said, "I think not. He intends for Samuel to become a man with his own son, three years or so from now." He jumped when Matthew smashed his fist into the wall.

"Oath breaker," he spat. "May your balls shrivel on you." He looked down at the priest. "You won't tell his mother. She doesn't need to know – not yet."

"I won't," Carlos promised, although it was his private opinion this was an unnecessary protective measure – Alex already suspected as much. "And maybe he'll change his mind."

"Qaachow doesn't change his mind – not unless someone makes him." At the door, a thought seemed to strike Matthew, and he turned to Carlos. "How far from here is the village, do you reckon?"

"Two days? I'm not sure."

"And you wouldn't find your way back, I suppose?"

"No, I don't think I could." Carlos felt entirely useless when the big man closed the door behind him.

"Talk about a futile gesture," Alex said to Matthew when he found her in the smoking shed, inventorying the damage. "God! I hate those damn raccoons," she continued, studying the neat little paw marks that showed exactly how the canny little creatures had gotten in. From the roof came the sharp sound of a hammer driving nails in place, and Mark was reinforcing the undermined corner, rolling stone after stone into place. "And my best ham as well, bloody gourmets."

"Gourmets? Don't you mean gourmands?"

"No, I know the difference, okay? And these raccoons are gourmets, going for the high quality stuff only." She glared in the general direction of where she suspected the bandits lived and wagged a finger. "You just wait. I'm going to set Lovell and Daffodil on you." She handed down ham after ham for Matthew to check for bite marks or paw prints, double-checked, and returned them to the rafter hooks. "Don't you agree?" she demanded at length.

"That the raccoons are gourmets?" Matthew sounded confused.

"No," Alex said with exaggerated patience. "That it was a bloody futile gesture. For Carlos to go with the Indians."

"Aye, in retrospect, but it took a lot of courage at the time."

"Hmph," Alex snorted. She got off the stool she had been balancing on and regarded the reordered shed. She glanced at her husband. She very badly wanted to ask him if he truly believed Samuel would be home come autumn, but she wasn't sure she wanted to hear his reply, so she didn't.

★

It was late afternoon before Alex found the time to check on her convalescent. The fever was back, but Mrs Parson was not unduly concerned. The poor man was weakened after his recent experiences, and a mild fever was only to be expected.

Carlos slept, sprawled on his back. His dark hair lay in damp feathers against his white brow, and the long lashes shadowed a heart-shaped face that would have been far too feminine if it hadn't been for the strong brows and sharp nose. Just like Isaac, Alex shuddered; this man is an identical twin to my future son. How the hell do you know? her mind sneered. A safe enough bet, Alex countered, because the priest was a throwback – throwforward? – on bloody Ángel. She rested her head against the wall behind her and closed her eyes. These last few days… Christmas had gotten lost in it.

She woke when Carlos shook her. Alex sat up abruptly, making her head swim.

"Are you alright?" Carlos asked.

Alex managed a smile. "Too tired, too much upheaval these last few days."

"Yes." Carlos reclined back against his pillows. "I imagine it must have been."

"Here." Alex gave him the cup of willow bark tea she had come in with. "It will help with the headache."

"How do you know I have a headache?"

"I see it in how you tilt your head and squish your eyes together – just like Isaac does."

"Isaac?"

"Did, I mean," Alex corrected herself. "Isaac is gone since very many years." Without a further word, she left.

On New Year's Eve, Matthew came to find her and placed an object in her hands.

"For me?" Alex held the small package in her hand.

"I thought…" He cleared his throat. "I haven't given you much through the years, have I?"

"Yes, you have, I have a whole collection of your

wooden miniatures." In her chest, in their bedroom, safely tucked away they lay: carvings mostly of her, but every now and then of one of their children or a rose, or a horse… One for every birthday, for every Christmas, for every important event in their lives.

"Aye well." Matthew looked very embarrassed. "Not quite the same thing. I wanted you to have something you can carry with you, like."

"Oh." Alex turned the wrapped little square round and round.

"Won't you open it?" Matthew asked, kneeling down beside her.

"I…" She felt ridiculous admitting this, but this was the first time she could remember ever having received a wrapped present in this time, and just to hold it, unopened, made her recall long ago birthdays and Christmases. "I just want to savour it a bit," she said, but her fingers were already working on the knot.

Her finger shook as she ran it over the little locket. In gold, he told her proudly, and look, on the lid he'd had their initials engraved, while inside… He opened it, to show her a miniature braid, his and her hair wound together.

"Thank you." She held out the pale blue ribbon from which it hung. "Will you put it on?"

Chapter 33

"For a first-time surgeon, I must say I did a pretty good job," Alex commented to Mrs Parson, before they straightened up from their detailed study of Carlos' leg.

"Aye. Nice and neat around the edges... It won't chafe much once we get him fitted with a peg"

"A peg?" Carlos sat up.

"Better than living your whole life on crutches," Mrs Parson said. "Makes it easier to piss, no?"

"Makes it easier to do a whole lot of things. Stand, for example." Alex wiped her hands on her apron.

Carlos placed a careful hand on his stump. "Which is a good thing if I can. With the exception of confession, most of my priestly works calls for me to stand."

"Or kneel," Mrs Parson reminded him, "and that won't be easy for you, getting down and up again."

"Let's cross that bridge when we get there, shall we?" Alex helped Carlos off the table.

She handed him his crutches, opened the door, and waited while he stumped off to enjoy the surprisingly warm February sunshine and the company of Sarah. For some reason, Sarah had developed a protective fondness for Carlos, and these days she was mostly to be found in deep conversation with the priest, Ruth more or less forgotten.

"I don't like it," Matthew said. "That wee priest is enticing my lass away from our faith."

"Don't be silly, Carlos wouldn't do something like that. And it isn't as if Sarah has expressed all that much interest in religion recently, is it?"

"She once wanted to become a nun," Matthew reminded her.

"That was years ago, when she was a child! No, Sarah is

using Carlos to hone her man-baiting skills."

"Man-baiting?" If possible, Matthew's face grew even darker. "I won't have my lasses grow into cock-teases!"

"Not like that. More to see how far she can get with simpers and dimples and the odd widened eye." Alex threw an oblique look in his direction. "Generally quite far." She batted her eyelids at him.

"Hmph," Matthew replied, but the left-hand corner of his mouth twitched.

Just in case, Matthew found the time to talk to his youngest daughter, suggesting they take a walk through the budding woods. Sarah was clearly delighted to be spending time only with him, and even more so when he handed her his new rifled flintlock to carry, on the off chance that they see something to kill.

"Not much chance, mind you," Matthew said. "The winter has been hard on the wildlife."

He watched as his daughter loaded and wadded, ramming the shot forcefully into the muzzle.

"Fifteen seconds," he said approvingly. "Well done, lass."

Sarah went a becoming pink at his praise, and just like that, he was transported back to Scotland very many years ago. Her mother used to go that pleasing colour, he collected with a private smile, and the lass standing before him was very much like her mama, with the exception of her hair – straight and fair where Alex's was curly and dark.

"So, do you like the wee priest then?" he asked, before whistling Viggo back to heel.

"Like him? Aye, well enough. Mostly, I feel sorry for him – but he does that very well himself." She grinned – a flash of white teeth that made him smile back. "I don't mean to sound uncharitable," she went on, "but he's back here, with us. And Samuel…" She hesitated, threw him a blue look.

Where Alex on occasion would raise the subject of Samuel with their bairns, he was incapable of doing so, his windpipe, lungs and stomach shrinking just at the mention of his son. He cleared his throat, formed his mouth round his lost lad's name. "Samuel…" he prompted.

"He's out there, alone and without us. I don't think he'd be whining overmuch about a leg!"

Matthew smiled sadly. How easy to dismiss the loss of a limb as peripheral when you stood strong and healthy like she did. He suspected Samuel would mind very much should he find himself so diminished, his future life permanently curtailed, but chose not to say so.

"Is that what you speak of? His leg?"

"No." Sarah looked away, long fair lashes shielding her eyes.

"Not his leg then, so what? His beliefs?" Matthew narrowed his eyes at her.

"At times," Sarah said, with a little shrug.

Just like her mother, his daughter was a bad liar, and from the way her eyes flitted from side to side, her hands tightening round the musket, he concluded they spoke more than occasionally about the papist priest's beliefs. Besides, he'd heard her himself, a few days back, telling the younger bairns of St Lucia and St Catherine, of visions from God and martyrdom. No, he didn't like this, and for a lass as impressionable as his Sarah, these stories of strong devout women who gave up everything – at times even their lives – for the sake of their faith must be like downing a quart or two of heady wine.

"Mostly we talk about Samuel," Sarah said, bringing him tumbling back from his excursion into issues of faith to the truly important matter in his present life.

"And what has he told you?" He sounded pathetically eager – he could hear it himself.

Sarah hitched her shoulders. She knew how Samuel was dressed; that he carried a wee tomahawk at his belt; that at times he and the other lads were led out to stay alone in the night. Very often Samuel, Carlos had said, describing how he was given a meagre supply of food and water before being taken away to commune alone with the spirits of the night.

"No fire?" Matthew asked in a strangled voice.

"Nay, I don't think so. He said how once Samuel was left alone for three nights running." In punishment, Carlos had said. The boy had once again insisted he wasn't an Indian.

Matthew hid his feelings at what she was telling him, deciding he was going to have a long talk with the priest once they got back, hungry for ever insignificant aspects of his lost lad's life, even if hearing some of it might rip his guts apart.

"A rite of passage, he called it," Sarah said, turning to look him in the face. "What does that mean, Da?"

"It's a step on the way to becoming a man," Matthew answered. An Indian man, he gulped. Oh God, what had he done, giving his son in the keeping of the heathen?

If one daughter was fluttering like a curious moth around the dangerous flame of papist beliefs, the other was busy with her own spiritual advancement, spending hours each day on her Conversion Narrative. Alex was a bit doubtful to all this praying and meditating, and was not at all happy when she realised Ruth got up well before dawn to read through the Bible text set for her daily study. By Julian, no less, in a document that Ruth kept folded in the Bible he had given her.

"It isn't uncommon," Matthew said when she discussed this with him. "And appropriate, in someone in love with a minister."

"And do you think she's doing this out of genuine devoutness or just to impress Julian?"

"To impress him, of course." Matthew nabbed the last piece of cake and stuffed it whole into his mouth, chewing industriously. "But I dare say some of that reading will rub off."

"As long as she doesn't go all fanatical on me," Alex grumbled, using her finger to chase the last of the crumbs.

They were sitting alone in the kitchen, the space weakly lit by the glowing embers in the hearth and the thick tallow candle on the table. The whole house slept around them, and if Alex closed her eyes, she imagined she could hear the rhythmic breathing of the wooden structure. She was very aware of Matthew's eyes on her, and from below her eyelashes, she looked back at him.

He was beautiful in the light cast from the candle, his features highlighted by light and shadow. Here and there, his hair still glinted a deep chestnut, and on the table, his hands lay open against the worn wood. She felt a foot slide up her leg, and across the table, his eyes met hers.

She stood, raised her skirts and undid her garter ribbon, peeling off the thick knitted stocking in a way that would have made Marilyn Monroe jealous. Matthew nodded at her other leg, watching with the intent gaze of a hawk as she slid her hands up, pulled at the bright red ribbon, and slowly bared her skin. He beckoned her over to where he was sitting, shoving back his chair to allow her to squeeze herself between him and the table.

His hands moved up her thighs, caressed her naked hips and buttocks, all the while with his head resting against her belly. She stroked his head, ran her fingers through his hair, traced the outline of his ears. He laid her back over the table, her skirts were at her waist, and his mouth was at her cleft. His tongue, his lips, his warm, warm breath, and all of her was wet.

He slid her down to the table's edge to meet him, and there were some eternally long seconds when he fiddled with her skirts, using them to wad her up an inch or two. Perfect fit. Ah yes, a perfect fit, and she lifted her legs to rest against his shoulders, liked how his hands hardened on her, how he flexed himself against her.

"Mine," he said, leaning his weight against her raised legs in a way that made it impossible for her to move – all she could do was take what he chose to give her. "My wife, my woman, mine."

"Yours," she whispered back, "entirely yours." He laughed, a soft sound of unadulterated joy that she should recognise herself for what she was, and pressed forward, pinning her to the table with his weight, his member. His hips moved, Alex moaned and threw her head back. Again, and he was in so deep it made her sigh and clench in response.

He took his time, moving leisurely in and out, and Alex could do nothing to hurry him on, could do nothing but savour him, the size and warmth of him, the strength of him.

He helped her to sit afterwards, kissing her brow.

"Bath?" he suggested.

"Now?" It was pitch-black outside.

"Now." He nodded, taking her hand.

She slid off the table and smiled. "Now, then."

They walked barefoot over the cold ground to the laundry shed, and it was freezing inside to begin with until Matthew had gotten the fire going and set the water in the cauldron to boil. Not that Alex cared, wrapped as she was in his thick winter cloak, nothing else. They sat close together and talked as they waited, their clothes a tangled heap by the door, lanterns throwing flaring light against the walls. The boiling water hissed when it hit the cold sides of the oversized wooden bath, and the small space filled with damp, misty heat.

"Come here, you." Matthew held out his hand. He washed her, she washed him; he lathered her head, she did the same to him. He gripped at her wet, soapy body, and she slipped away like a giant trout, laughing at him. He did it again, and again she slid out of his grasp, teasing him with her eyes. He got a firm grip on her foot and towed her, spluttering and laughing, towards him, guided her to straddle him, and held himself absolutely still as she did the moving, as she set the pace.

"It doesn't change, ever, does it?" Matthew's heavy, contented voice floated up from where he lay on his front while Alex massaged her way up his back.

"Change? Of course it changes, you stupid man." She found a particular sore spot and ground her knuckles into it, making Matthew jerk like a hooked fish.

"Ooooh!" he protested. "That's bone."

"Wimp," Alex told him affectionately.

"How does it change then?" he asked, relaxing when she went back to her circular movements.

"It gets better." She tickled him on the underside of

his scrotum, visible between his legs, and laughed at the reaction. "For example, I didn't know you liked that quite as much as you do."

"I didn't know I liked it either until you did it," he answered.

She covered him with his cloak and slid in beside him, worming her way in under his arm until she was as close as she could get. "Will they be shocked, do you think, if they find us here, stark naked and fast asleep in the morning?"

"In all probability." Matthew yawned. "Not Mrs Parson, but the rest of them, aye." He opened one eye to look at her. "But it's my home, and I don't plan on moving, do you?"

"No," she said, "I'm fine right here."

Chapter 34

Carlos was proud as a peacock the day he walked all the way to the river and back on his peg leg without overbalancing once. And he was more than impressed when, a couple of weeks later, he negotiated the steep slope to the graveyard all on his own, there to sit on Alex's favourite bench, gazing out over the Graham lands. A beautiful spot, he mused, taking in the sprawling rosebush, the two headstones, and the relatively new stone tablet commemorating Mark's premature son. Yes, a restful place in which to lie waiting for the Resurrection, while your body slowly turned to earth.

"*Ave Maria, gratia plena*," he murmured, rubbing the first bead of his second decade. He voided his head of anything but his prayers, rocking from side to side. Only when he opened his eyes again did he notice he had company, smiling cautiously at Matthew.

"You must be longing to leave," Mathew said.

Carlos hitched his shoulders. "I've been made very welcome here." He scratched at his peg. He often did that, and every time it was a surprise not to feel his own skin beneath his nails. "And well mended." Almost five months since his amputation, an ordeal he recalled very little of, *gracias a Dios*.

"Aye, as well as can be. The Chisholms sent word – they'll be coming for you today or tomorrow. Several baptisms to conduct, I gather."

"Goes hand in hand." Carlos smiled. "I wed them last summer."

"From the age of the weans, it seems the grooms and brides had carnal knowledge of each other well before you wed them. One of them is nigh on six months."

"*Errare humanum est*," Carlos murmured tongue-in-cheek. He wasn't blind, nor was he a complete innocent. It

279

had been obvious that quite a few of the brides were long gone in their pregnancies, but that was to be expected when priests were difficult to find.

Together, they strolled back down, skirting the kitchen garden where Alex was on her knees planting, with her youngest sons and daughters helping. She was singing what sounded like a hymn, in a language Carlos had never heard before.

"Swedish," Matthew said, after having cocked his head to listen. "All about giving thanks to the Lord for the return of sun and warmth to the world."

"Ah," Carlos gave Matthew an impressed look, "you speak Swedish?"

"Nay, but this particular hymn she sings every year around this time." Matthew smiled in the direction of his wife. "And you can't much fault the sentiment."

"No," Carlos agreed, "on a day such as this." He stopped to better see the neat farm buildings laid out before him. Built in larch, the main house, the large barn and the stables had acquired a grey silvered sheen, contrasting with the darker wooden shingles on the roof. Unadorned and plain, except for the windows, the house was of pleasing proportions, seemingly rooted to the ground beneath it. In the centre of the yard stood the huge white oak with its bench, unfurling leaves that blushed shyly pink in the sunlight.

All in all, a beautiful place, but still Carlos longed to be gone – not only from here, but from this whole accursed continent. He ached for the sun-drenched cities of southern Spain, but doubted he would ever see them again. No, he sighed, at best he would be sent to Lima or Cartagena de las Indias; at worst into the interiors of the jungle-infested Vice kingdom of Peru. Unless, of course, he chose to leave the Holy Church, but then, what was he to do? Besides, once a priest, always a priest.

Carlos' dark musings were interrupted by the sounds of hooves coming down the long lane. At his side, Matthew shielded his eyes with his hand, uttered a soft curse, and increased his pace.

★

"Thomas? Are you alright?" Matthew stared up at his swaying friend who nodded, even if his hands were shaking badly. His youngest daughter Judith was the colour of bleached linen, her fingers clenched so tightly round the reins she seemed incapable of letting go. Matthew moved over to help her, lowering his voice into a reassuring crooning as he helped her down to stand on legs so unsteady he had to wrap an arm around her waist to support her.

"We were on our way here, and had it not been for Martin and Paul here, God knows how things would have ended." Thomas tipped his head in the direction of the Chisholm brothers who nodded back.

"What happened?" Alex asked, breathless from her run down the hill.

"They ambushed us a half-mile or so from here. Six or seven men, I think, and they were all around us, lewdly commenting on my daughter." Thomas stumbled towards Judith, arms pressing her tight to him while she hid her capped head against his chest. "They had their hands on her," Thomas went on in a hoarse voice, "and me they held at bay by holding a musket to my head. Jesus, had not the Chisholms come upon us—"

"Who?" Matthew asked, although he already knew. He could see it in Thomas' eyes, in the set expression of Martin's face.

Thomas squeezed his daughter even closer. "The Burleys, and God knows what they'd have done to my girl – we never found the Ingram girl, did we?"

"Curse them!" Matthew strode towards the stables. "We ride out after them, now!"

"Now?" Thomas said, "I'm not sure—"

"Now!"

"Now," Martin said, "all of us. And, this time, we put an end to it. This time, we hunt those vermin down and kill them."

"Amen to that!" Robert clapped his brother on his back.

"Hear, hear!" Mark said, eyes alight with excitement.

★

The yard was a hive of activity: loud male voices, horses that danced with excitement, dogs barking, and there was Matthew already astride Aaron.

Alex was not quite sure what was happening to her: no matter how hard she tried to breathe, no oxygen seemed to be finding its way down to her lungs. Her eyes stuck on Matthew, but he was halfway up the lane, followed by sons and neighbours, and Alex was quite convinced that, at any moment now, she'd die, because something was blocking her throat, and she had no idea what to do to dislodge it.

Someone whacked her back.

"Breathe." Mrs Parson whacked her again.

Alex tried.

Mrs Parson took hold of her hands, sank black eyes into Alex's. Her eyelashes were grey, Alex noted, grey and short.

"Lass," Mrs Parson said, "Alex, love, look at me."

So she did, and when Mrs Parson inhaled so did she, when Mrs Parson exhaled she followed suit, and slowly, her pulse stopped thundering in her head. With a little sound, she fell into Mrs Parson's arms, and for all that Mrs Parson was old and several inches shorter, she stood solid like a rock and let Alex cry into her collar.

"A panic attack," she diagnosed herself a half-hour or so later. They were sitting under the oak, holding hands.

"A what?" Mrs Parson said.

"I was frightened. No, I *am* frightened." Alex chewed her lip, reliving in far too much detail the last time she'd had the misfortune to be eye to eye with Philip Burley. And now he was here, mere miles from their home. She swallowed and swallowed; she coughed and swallowed some more, all under Mrs Parson's concerned eyes.

"It would take a right fool not to be scared of them," Mrs Parson said.

Alex nodded, hating it that her eyes were filling with tears again. Here – they were here, and Philip Burley would never rest until Matthew was dead, and then he'd… Oh God, he'd come here.

Mrs Parson gave her hand a little shake. "We've bested them before, no?"

Alex tried to smile.

"This time we'll best them for good," Mrs Parson said. "It's time to rid the world of yon misbegotten brothers once and for all."

Yet again, Alex tried to smile.

"For good," Mrs Parson repeated.

"For good," Alex parroted, but for the coming hours she remained where she was, eyes glued to the lane, until she saw her man and his companions come trotting down towards her.

"No luck?" An unnecessary question as she could see in their body language that this had been a long day's ride for nothing.

"Nay." Matthew dropped off his horse. "They're like ghosts: no sooner do we pick up their trail but they vanish." He took off his hat and scrubbed at his hair. "I sorely miss Qaachow's sentries," he muttered.

"His sentries? You think they're no longer there?"

"Why would they be?" Matthew spat to the side. "His precious foster son is no longer here, is he?" He sounded bitter – and scared.

It was early evening by the time the Chisholms were ready to leave, this time with Carlos. Alex packed together his few belongings, thinking that it was strange how attached she'd grown to her pet priest. She sighed, dragging her hand over her eyes. This was turning into an emotionally exhausting day, all in all.

"Remember to wash your stump every day," she said.

"*Sí.*" Carlos smiled.

"And to wipe the peg cup clean as well."

"*Sí,*" he repeated, still smiling.

"And you must oil the skin at least once a week, okay?"

"*Sí, Mamá,*" he answered, but now his smile wavered.

"*Vaya con Dios, Padre.*" She gave him a hug.

"*Y contigo, hija, siempre contigo.*" He took a step back and clasped her hand. "I'll pray for Samuel. Every day, until he's home with you."

"And how will you know when he is?" Alex smiled through her tears.

"God will whisper it in my ear."

"Will he?" she asked. "Come back?"

"*Sí*," he answered, wiping her cheeks with his bell-shaped sleeve. He hobbled over to his mule, bowed to Matthew, and sat up. The last Alex saw of him was when he whipped his broad-brimmed hat off his head and waved it in the air.

"God," Alex said to Mrs Parson. "I really, really hate farewells."

"Most people do, no? But that's how life is, lass. You meet people, you grow to like them, you see them travel on."

"Not in my time," Alex sighed. "In my time you can at least talk to each other, no matter how far apart you are."

"Oh aye? Even when you're dead?"

"No." Alex gave her an exasperated look. "Of course we don't communicate across the grave." She sat down at the table and pulled the pie tin towards her, picking at the remains. "Would you want to?"

Mrs Parson turned very bright eyes on her. "Would I want to see my lasses and my man again? What kind of a daft question is that?"

"Sorry," Alex mumbled. This was the big out of bounds subject with Mrs Parson, and even now, more than thirty years since she lost her entire family over the span of a year, she rarely spoke about her girls.

"I still haven't forgiven God," Mrs Parson said. "I don't know what I did wrong to have all of them die away from me. My man, my lasses…even the wee cat."

"The cat?" Alex stared at her.

"Aye," Mrs Parson said, "the cat. Ginger it was, like my man. It was he that gave her to me."

"Oh. Do you ever think of Mr Parson?"

Mrs Parson fiddled with her wedding band, the single tangible reminder of her second husband.

"Aye, but it isn't him I hope to meet in the afterlife." She shrank together on her stool and for an instant Alex saw just how old she was, feeling her gut tightening at the thought of Mrs Parson dying.

"Not yet, I hope."

Mrs Parson looked at her for a long time. "Nay, not yet."

But there was someone who was about to leave, and Alex waited and waited for Jacob to come and tell her that now, today, he had decided he would leave. Finally, she couldn't stand it anymore, and went to find him where she knew he'd be: in the herbs garden. My green fingers, she thought proudly, or rather Magnus' green fingers. Her father, grandfather, great-grandfather and onwards – all had been botanists, and Jacob had inherited that gene, sitting cross-legged in the shade with a frond of fern in his hand.

"*Noli me tangere*," he said when Alex was within hearing distance. "Offa taught me that. Look, you touch it and it closes up. Don't touch me, it means."

"Old news, son. Who do you think he showed that before you were around?"

Jacob laughed, placing the fern carefully between two blank pages in his herbal before closing his eyes and sticking his nose up to the sun. Alex felt her breath hitch in her throat with pride. Her son, tall and well built, with hair the colour of the sun, and eyes that slanted catlike in a face that was otherwise so like his father's. And soon he'd be gone, to Master Castain and Luke and all the other friends he'd made in London. He seemed to have heard what she was thinking, because he opened an eye to look at her.

"I have a lass there," he blurted.

"You what?" Alex was sure she had misheard.

"She'll be four soon, named Rachel by her mother." He explained how he had received a letter last year, where Helen had told him her daughter was his, not her husband's.

"Helen? Who's this Helen?"

"A woman."

"Thanks a lot. I could have worked that out myself."

285

Alex sat down beside him, smoothing his hair back off his brow. "So who is she?"

Jacob smiled and shook his head. "A woman I liked a lot and bedded for a while, my first friend in London. She says the lass looks very much like me, and I...I want to see her, aye? Be there should she need it."

Alex frowned. "I thought you said Helen has a husband."

"Aye, she does, but he's well over fifty, and unwell to boot. A nice enough man, I reckon, and Helen is fond of him, saying how he cherishes her and the child both." He sat up, resting his elbows on his knees. "I won't come between them, but I'd like to meet my daughter."

"So when will you leave?" Alex asked as neutrally as she could.

Jacob gave her a very serious look. "Not until Samuel is back, Mama. Not until the Burleys have been wiped out."

"Oh, son!" Alex kneeled and took his face between her hands. "Don't be silly, Jacob. You can't put your life on hold! We've known for months that you're leaving."

"I won't leave until my wee brother is back – and you need me for now. Da has need of all of us against the Burleys."

"Yes," Alex said, "yes, I suppose we do. But we'll manage, Jacob, somehow we will."

"I stay," he said, "for now."

Chapter 35

Sarah flopped down beside Ruth.

"Must you always be reading?" she grumbled. "Can't we do something together, you and I?" She shifted further into the shade of the tree, glowering at the brightness of the May day.

"What?" Ruth asked with a sigh, putting the book down. "We're not allowed to leave the main yard. We must ask one of our brothers to go with us if we wish to take a walk." She shook her red braids with irritation. "I wish I was in Providence instead. This is such a dull, wee place. There at least there is conversation and—" She interrupted herself abruptly. "I don't mean to say we don't talk," she apologised, but Sarah was already stalking away. "Sarah, come back! It's too hot for me to go chasing after you."

Sarah just lengthened her stride, with Viggo, as always, padding after her. She tried to work off her black mood by doing some of Mama's exercises, but that only left her feeling even more hot and irritated. Still, she did a few swipes with her hands, pretending she was killing one of the Burleys. This was all their fault. It was because of those misbegotten bastards that she was no longer allowed to roam as she wished.

Da was constantly angry. Mama pretended things were like always, but there was a strained set to her mouth whenever she watched the menfolk ride off, and every evening, when they came back, Mama would somehow soften, as if she'd been holding her breath all the while they'd been gone.

If Da was angry, Ian was even worse, no doubt on account of his back. She'd heard him and Da the other day, a loud argument behind the stables where Da was telling Ian he should rest, while Ian had yelled that he was a man too, and if Da could do double duty, well then, so could he.

So, each afternoon, Ian would strap himself into the special corset Mama and Mrs Parson had designed for him and sit up on his horse, and no matter that he returned ashen-faced every night, next day he insisted on going along as well. Sarah gnawed her lip. She knew Betty worried, as did Mama, but she was mostly jealous. At least Ian was doing something, not cooped up here at home.

She made a face in the direction of Jacob, for the day doing sentry duty with David, and flung herself down in the grass. Longingly, she looked at the cool, green forests. It was so unfair. Her brothers were allowed to go about, albeit in twos, but she, just for being a lass, she wasn't allowed out of sight. Not even with a musket, Da had said, nor did it help that she pointed out that she always had Viggo with her.

She lay down in the long grass and frowned. No conversation, she had said, stuck-up little baggage. Sarah was going to show her just how little conversation was to be had here, at Graham's Garden. No, she wasn't going to talk to Ruth ever again – or at least not for the rest of the day. Reinvigorated by this decision, Sarah went off to find Mama and perhaps wheedle a walk out of her.

"No." Mama just looked at her. "What is it you don't understand, honey? Your father has told you that until the Burleys are apprehended, we all stay close to home. Think of what nearly happened to Judith."

"But that may take months," Sarah groaned, "or even years."

"No, it won't," Mama said. "Not now that it's us and the Leslies and the Chisholms working together."

"The forests are vast," Sarah snorted. "They could be less than a hundred yards from here, and you wouldn't see them."

"Which is where the dogs come in," Mama said, nervously scanning the wooded fringes.

"Anyhow," Sarah continued, "it's not as if I'm defenceless, is it?" She did a quick chopping movement through the air.

"Stop that!" Mama grabbed her hard by the arm. "How can you possibly think that would help against six, seven grown men? No, Sarah, should you ever see them, run."

"I can shoot," Sarah sulked, "and Viggo here will defend me, and—"

"…you will stay at home as your father has ordered you to. Right?"

"Right," Sarah acquiesced sullenly.

The men came in for dinner some hours after noon, bone tired after yet another long day out in the fields. First eight hours on the farm, then a further five or six hours scouring the woods for the Burleys – no wonder they all looked half dead. Sarah helped serve them, stared straight through Ruth whenever her sister tried to talk to her, and sat down beside Da.

After dinner, she slouched off to spend more time on her own, as far away as possible from Ruth. Listlessly, she grabbed one of Mama's baskets and decided she might as well take a stroll round the buildings and see if she could find any nettle shoots. Mama would like that, and Ruth hated nettle soup, which was an added benefit.

Viggo bounded round her, and when they ducked out of sight behind the barn, he rushed off in the direction of the forest, looking back at her with pleading eyes and wagging tail.

"No, come here, Viggo." The dog lowered his head and trotted back, tail hanging straight down."I know," she sighed, "but we can ask Jacob later if he'll take us for a walk." She sat down on a rock and placed the empty basket beside her. Too late for nettles, she grumbled, of course it was. In May, they were already tall and stringy, and instead Mama would probably make asparagus soup, which Sarah detested and Ruth loved. Sarah scratched at her throat and waved at the flies.

"Too hot, too many flies, and nothing to do," she told the dog, who seemed to agree, panting heavily.

She stood, and the dog flew to his feet, once again setting off in the direction of the woods. Sarah hesitated.

She wasn't supposed to but if she stayed close, keeping her home in sight... Yes, that's what she'd do – she'd walk a short distance into the forest, close enough to be able to run back should she need to. Enough to get out of the sun, and maybe the lupines were out and she'd bring back an armful for Mama. In a much better mood, she picked up the basket and whistling for the dog, stepped into the welcoming shade.

The lupines were out, and Sarah filled her basket with the heavy flower heads. Mostly pinks and reds, and she knew Mama liked the blue the best. There! A patch of blue, just a few yards further in.

Viggo growled, a low menacing sound that had Sarah dropping to a crouch. With a thudding heart, she looked around, trying to discover what the dog had seen. He growled again. There was a whirring sound, and Viggo dropped to the ground, an arrow sticking through his chest. Sarah rushed towards him, the shrubs beyond him parted, and there were men everywhere. Sarah turned and fled.

They laughed when they brought her down, squashing her against the ground. She tried to get back up, she kicked at something, and she was free, running like a hare towards what she thought was home. Again, they tackled her, and again, they laughed. She was rolled over and two faces smirked down at her, faces with cold, light-grey eyes.

I should have fought, Sarah managed to think. Now it was too late, oh God, it was too late! Still, she tried, heaving angrily, and she scrambled back up and picked up her skirts. She flew, swift as a doe, but then her chin hit the ground, and there were hands under her skirts, horrible hands that uncovered her to the air. Sarah tried to scream, but something hit her in the head, and she was hefted up on her knees, standing like an animal as the first man took her from behind.

She was flipped over on her back, hiccupping with pain, with fear. She begged them to let her go, please let her go, and one of them smiled down at her, and she thought that perhaps they would do as she asked them, because he was smiling.

"Open your legs, girl." He fiddled with his breeches.

Sarah closed her eyes and shook her head. She gasped at the pain when he grabbed hold of her hair and yanked her head up, those bleached cold eyes only inches from hers. "I said, open them."

No, she wasn't going to. She clamped her legs hard together. She tried to curl herself into a ball.

He hit her hard across the face. "Bare yourself," the man said. "Do it, or I'll slice you open with my knife."

Crying, she did as he said, uncovering her privates and inching her legs apart.

He let her go, laughing at his brother as he kneeled between her thighs. "See, easily tamed."

Sarah raked her nails across his cheek. Jesus! The responding blow left her half-unconscious. Hands uncovered her breast, fingers pinched her nipples, and the second man took her.

"My turn, brother," the first man said, and she saw that he was rubbing himself in preparation.

"Nooo," she moaned, but they didn't care; of course, they didn't care. Sarah was turned this way and that, now and then trying to scream only to have a dirty, strong hand clapped over her mouth, and there he was again, the first man, and, oh God, wouldn't this stop?

She was aware of an argument and tried to open one swollen eye, but closed it just as quickly. Five more! Dear Lord, let me die, and die quickly, she prayed. Please don't let me live through this. But God had other things to do, and Sarah was forced to her knees and told to open her mouth.

"She serves you with her mouth only," Philip Burley said to his men. "The rest is only for my brother and me."

Sarah snapped her mouth shut, making the other Burley brother laugh.

"It seems she is as yet untamed," Walter told his brother. Almost gently, he placed a hand on Sarah's head. "Our little whore, hmm?" He bent his head to her ear and described very precisely what they would do to her unless she did as she was told, and when he was done Sarah was trembling from head to foot. She closed her eyes and opened her mouth.

★

When Matthew and his sons rode in, they were met by a frantic Alex who had looked everywhere, absolutely everywhere for their daughter.

"And the dog?" Matthew asked, trying to calm her down.

"Not here, not there, not anywhere… Oh God, Matthew, what has happened to her?"

"Mayhap she's hurt herself," Mark suggested. "Twisted her ankle or the like, and in the dark it makes sense to stay where she is."

"Or she's been bitten by a rattlesnake and is dying as we speak," Alex said, twisting her hands round and round each other. Or even worse. Matthew's mouth dried up at the thought.

"She has the dog with her," he said. "He'll not let her come to harm."

They found Viggo, still alive, some three hundred yards away from the barn. They found the basket, upended but still filled with lupines, and Alex wept, kicking at it.

"Why didn't she stay in the yard as we told her to?" she said through her sobs. "Why?"

"I don't know." Dear Lord; his little lass, as wilful as always, but what would this act of disobedience cost her? The dark came in, making it impossible to see anything more. But Matthew had seen enough, seen the marks of scuffles on the ground, and, inside of him, a scream was building.

They returned home with the injured dog, and after a hasty meal, Matthew and his sons donned cloaks and weapons, lit lanterns, and called their three remaining dogs to heel.

"I'm going with you," Alex told him.

"No," he replied.

"Yes, I am. Either I go with you or I go alone, but I'm going out looking as well."

"Alex," Matthew moaned, "don't you think I have enough to fear for?"

"And do you think I can stand it here, without her, without you?" She wasn't backing down, he could see that, and with a sigh he turned away.

"You may not like what we find."

"And she might need her mother when we find her," Alex said.

"Here." Matthew handed Alex his dirk. "You can't go unarmed." Alex nodded and settled the knife in the waistline of her skirt. He smoothed back her hair and managed to kiss her brow.

"We'll find her," he promised. But how? He wept inside, oh Lord, what have they done to her?

"Of course we will," she said.

It was dark. At a once remove, Sarah noted that there was no moon, only the weak light of summer sky stars that winked high above. She could barely move, and the rope they had tied around her wrists to pull her arms over her head was entirely unnecessary as she wouldn't dare to try and run. Not again, not after what Philip had done to her.

She wished she could somehow smooth her skirts down over her destruction. Her thighs were sticky with blood and semen, and no matter how she swallowed, she could not get rid of the foul taste in her mouth. Philip snored heavily beside her, but on her other side, Walter raised his head and leered.

"No more," she begged, and her legs twisted themselves closed, but when his hand closed around her ankle, she did as he wanted. He kneeled between her legs and she closed her eyes.

"Open your eyes," he said, so she did.

"Smile," he said, and she made an effort to stretch her lips wide. He was busy with her chemise, uncovering her breasts so that he could paw at them, strong fingers closing on her sore skin. She stifled an instinctive gasp when he entered her. God! He was so much bigger than his brother, and he knew it, savouring the way she tried to put a distance between them. It no longer hurt that much, at least not as much as that first time. The man shuddered and voided himself deep inside of her, remaining where he was a while longer.

"We'll get a good price for you. Well-trained and tamed, we'll sell you to one of the whorehouses further south, and all you'll do for the rest of your life is lie on your back and take man after man into your cunt. Tomorrow, we'll let the other men have you so that you can practise properly," he said, wiping himself on her skirts.

"No," she whispered.

He just laughed.

"Please," she pleaded, "I'm only sixteen."

"Becky Ingram was only thirteen, and a right competent little whore when we sold her down in Jamestown, nor was she fool enough to whine."

Sarah moaned.

"Hold your noise." Walter Burley casually slapped her face. She lay mute and uncovered, sandwiched uncomfortably between her two abusers, and she didn't even dare to cry.

Chapter 36

Sarah was stiff with cold when she woke next morning, and for a moment she couldn't recollect where she was or why – until Philip Burley spread her legs apart and took her, saying there was no reason to waste a good morning cock-stand, was there? She sobbed, she couldn't help it, but God it hurt! And when Philip was done, Walter wanted his share, and seeing as she was so sore... He indicated he wanted her on her knees.

Sarah screamed, she shrieked in outrage and pain, and Walter laughed, saying what a tight little arse she had.

"Sweetest Lord," Sarah cried. "Jesus, forgive me my sins, please let me die, please, please, please." The slap shut her up, and she curled into herself, thinking that she no longer cared if she lived or died. But that wasn't true. Deep inside her, something was rearing its head: a toothy, black thing that demanded she live – live and make them pay. Slowly, she clenched her hand, bringing it up to rest between her sore and manhandled breasts.

"Sarah!" Alex almost fell off the horse. "That was Sarah!" She was riding with Jacob and Matthew, while Mark and Ian had gone to fetch help from the Chisholms and Leslies.

"Aye," Matthew agreed unsteadily. He called his dog back, and dismounted. "They're close enough that we can't come riding or they'll hear us." He looped the reins around a branch and indicated to Alex and Jacob to do the same.

"You have the dirk?" he asked Alex, taking her hand in his. She nodded, her mouth so dry with fear she couldn't utter a sound. Matthew inspected his cavalry pistol, Jacob handed Matthew the loaded flintlock, loaded both the snaphance pistols, tucked one into his own belt and gave Alex the other.

"Aim for the belly," Jacob said, before gripping his own musket and nodding to his da that he was ready to go.

They split up, with Alex following Matthew, while Jacob moved through the undergrowth some fifty-odd yards in parallel with them. Alex quelled an urge to laugh hysterically, and at one point nearly fell, her legs shaking with nerves. Her hands were slick with sweat, and she tried to move as soundlessly as possible behind Matthew, the gap between them growing yard by yard.

"Aim for the belly," she muttered, "the belly, Alex." Her arm trembled with agitation, and she was glad for the comforting warmth of Daffodil, pressed against her legs.

She heard the murmurs of voices before she saw them, and then the clearing widened, a stretch of long grass, a large, solitary chestnut, some shrubs, and at the far end, a group of people sitting in the shade. Alex's eyes zoomed in immediately on the single important item in the bucolic picture before her: her daughter.

Sitting under a sapling with her legs drawn up, she looked unharmed, and Alex relaxed – until Sarah raised her head and showed the world a puffy, discoloured face with bruises and swellings. She heard Matthew hiss something vicious, and on her far left she saw Jacob stop, coiled like a lethal cat. At most, they stood where they were for ten seconds. To Alex, it seemed like eternal years, an endless period of time with her eyes glued to her battered daughter. She was wondering what to do next when Jacob charged, roaring with anger.

"No!" Matthew exclaimed, throwing his arm wide in a futile attempt to stop his son.

"No!" Alex screamed, but Jacob was already out in the open, his long legs leaping across the ground at an impressive speed. His long hair stood like a golden mane around his head; he bellowed and screamed, in one hand a pistol, in the other his musket. Like a Viking, Alex managed to think, a berserk Norseman.

The men under the tree were on their feet. A puff, a bullet whizzing through air, but Jacob was moving too fast, ducking this way and that, and all the time he yelled, a wordless sound that had the horses neighing and moving restlessly.

For a tenth of a second, Jacob came to a stop. Up went his pistol, down went one of the Burley men, and Jacob roared. Yet another stop, the musket was levied and fired, and one more man hit the ground. Alex cheered, thinking – no, hoping – that maybe things would turn out alright.

Matthew burst out of cover. Alex followed. Jacob was only yards from the men. A musket – no, three muskets, all of them aimed at Jacob. Her son was still yelling, his discharged musket held like a club. Something slammed into his chest. His whole body jerked, spine bending to absorb the shock. In slow motion he fell. His arms flew out, his head jerked backwards before tipping heavily forward to topple with the rest of him towards the ground. Alex heard somebody screaming and realised it was her, or was it Matthew? Her husband's voice rose in a cracked howl, Daffodil began to bark, and all Alex could see was her son, lying face down in the grass. Someone laughed. Matthew aimed his musket at Philip Burley while Alex raised her gun at the gut of the closest man, tripping in her haste to get to her son.

It shouldn't be this quiet, Alex thought. How come she couldn't hear anything, and what was she supposed to do now? She blinked, thinking that at any moment Jacob would get to his knees and shake his head, but he lay so still, so very still, and what was that seeping through the back of his shirt? Faintly, she heard Sarah, turning clumsily towards the sound. Her daughter was screaming, crying Jacob's name out loud, fighting and spitting like a wild cat when Philip yanked her as a shield between Matthew and himself. Alex was unaware of intentionally pulling the trigger, but suddenly the man before her had a flower of red across his chest, and he looked so surprised, staring at her with an open mouth as he fell. Just like that, the volume switch was flicked back on, and Alex found herself drowning in screams and raised voices, the far-off neighing of horses and, most of all, the sound of her man's voice.

★

Swiftly, Matthew had assessed the situation. There was no way he could rescue Sarah on his own, not against four armed men. Unless… Dear Lord, give him the strength to do this.

"Don't harm her, let her go!" He swung his musket to aim at Walter Burley instead, freezing the man in his movements.

"And why would we do that?" Philip sneered, pressing the blade of his knife hard enough that a line of blood appeared across Sarah's windpipe.

"Let her go, and I'll go with you," Matthew said, ignoring the gasped exclamation from Alex. Walter Burley laughed and said something in a low voice to Philip who laughed back and closed a hand over Sarah's left breast.

"She's been well ridden, Graham, thoroughly ploughed and planted with Burley seed. A nice little ride. Biddable, if you know what I mean."

"Let her go," Matthew repeated, avoiding looking at his daughter. "Take me instead."

Philip Burley stood very still, eyes darting from Matthew to Alex, to the dog. Matthew cocked his weapon, and Walter paled. Aye, him at least he would kill. A short, terse conference between the brothers, the knife at Sarah's throat was lowered, and she was pushed to land a couple of yards in front of Philip.

Philip Burley raised his pistol, aiming at Sarah's uncovered back, and nodded. "Come on then," he said, and Matthew had no idea where he was to find the courage to do this.

Alex had stood mute throughout this exchange. She stumbled towards her husband. Stop him, a voice screamed inside her. Stop him, don't let him do this, they'll kill him! She tried to catch his eyes, but all he did was hand her his pistol, still managing to keep his musket levelled at Walter.

"No," Alex groaned, "no." She stepped up close to Matthew and took his hand, clasping it hard. I love you, she said silently. God, how I love you!

He gripped her back and for a moment his fingers circled

298

her wrist, his pulse flowing as seamlessly as always into her. And then he let her go, taking that first step towards the Burleys, still with his musket held high.

"No," he said when Daffodil made as if to follow him, and for an instant his bright hazel eyes met hers, a lifetime encapsulated in one last look.

Alex felt her heart being yanked out of her body with every step he took away from her. How could this be happening, and why the fuck couldn't the little minx do as she was told? If she had stayed at home instead of sneaking off into the forest, Alex wouldn't be watching her man advance towards certain death. A sound halfway between a howl and a whimper escaped her lips, and there was Sarah stumbling towards her, but all Alex could see was her Matthew, and she had no idea what to do when Walter Burley raised his gun, except to dumbly raise her pistol at his brother.

"No, little brother," Philip said. "I think not." He shared a look with his brother and slow smiles spread across their wolfish faces.

Matthew had come to a stop and at Philip's curt command he lowered the musket, throwing it far into the bushes on the side. He stood still as Philip came over to him with a rope, allowed himself to be tied up.

"What? No glib comments today, Mrs Graham?" Philip jeered. "No witty repartee?"

Alex bared her teeth – that was all she could do.

Philip laughed, called for horses. Once again, he shared a look with Walter, and once again they smiled.

"Want to come along?" Philip asked, making as if to come for Alex. Sarah had somehow retrieved Jacob's musket, and when Philip approached, she swung it at him, shrieking like a flayed cat. Philip laughed and shrugged.

"We'll deal with you later." He swept Alex a mocking bow and returned to his waiting men.

Alex raised a shaking hand to her hair, tried to catch Matthew's eyes, but he wouldn't look in her direction, and then Philip was on his horse, and she saw to her horror that there was a halter round Matthew's neck, and she understood that they would make him run while they rode. He's too old, she groaned inside, far too old – fifty-five and beautiful and strong, but too old for this. She wanted to call out that she loved him, had loved him since long before she was born, would love him well after her death, but there was no air in her lungs, and so she just stood and watched as the Burleys rode off, dragging Matthew in their wake.

The silence was back: a bubble that enveloped her and protected her, assuring her none of this was real. But she only had to twist her head to see her fallen son, and there the branches still swayed from where the Burleys had ridden off, with Matthew their captive. Don't look at her, she cautioned herself, not now. Don't look at her and let her see what you're thinking! It isn't her fault, Alex, of course it isn't... Yes it is! Damn her for being disobedient! She kept her face averted from Sarah, stumbling instead to her boy.

She couldn't stand. Her legs gave way, and she was crawling towards him. She rolled him over, and still she hoped that his eyes would fly open at her touch, but there was no life in the slack face, and his beautiful eyes were turning the colour of slate. But his hair still wafted in the breeze, and when she bent her head to him, she could smell him: the drifting scents of soap and herbs, of his sweat and of sun-warmed skin. She cradled him to her chest, she rocked him, she crooned his name. She told him how much she loved him, and all the things she wanted – no, needed – to say to Matthew spilled out of her mouth, and she didn't really know who it was she was holding, whose heavy head lolled against her breast.

Dead. Her son was dead, and soon her man would be as well. It surged through her, a deep visceral hatred that jolted like electricity through her veins. She threw her head back and screamed. "Jacob Alexander Graham! My son, You hear? My beautiful son, and You let them take him!" There was no reply. Of course not, she thought bitterly. There never is, is there?

She sank together like a deflated balloon, shielding his

face from the sun, kissing his brow, his cooling cheek and the long, curving mouth. Why, oh why hadn't she forced him to leave? Why had she not insisted that he go and live the life he planned to live, so far from her but at least alive?

"I'm so sorry," Alex sobbed, "so sorry that you didn't get to meet your daughter." Daughter... She lifted her head. There was a girl close by that needed her, flesh of her flesh, blood of her blood, but she was so angry with her, no matter how innocent she was, now that Jacob was dead and Matthew... She swayed to her feet, stumbling in the direction he had disappeared.

"Matthew," she whispered, and wished she could die on the spot.

"Mama?" Sarah's choked voice slashed through Alex. Her daughter, the girl they made aboard the ship from Scotland to Maryland. Matthew would never forgive her if she didn't take care of his lass – their lass, their beautiful daughter. Alex opened her arms, and a shaking, shivering Sarah was in them, a crying, snot-faced Sarah that wept and cursed, that spoke in long unintelligible sentences, and Alex didn't want to hear. Thank heavens, she couldn't understand it all.

It was good to hold her, to feel her warm and alive, and standing with Sarah in her arms, her recriminations shrivelled. Her little girl, alone with those vile men...

At length, Sarah quieted, raising her face to look at Alex. Damaged she might be, and bleeding and bruised, but her eyes blazed blue in their hollows. "Are you just going to let them take him?" She stepped out of Alex's arms, moving carefully, as if every movement hurt.

"And what can I do?" Alex sank down to the ground. Matthew, thudded through her head, Matthew, Matthew, Matthew.

"We go after them. We go after them and make them pay." Sarah scowled and straightened up.

"It's too late, he's already gone." But maybe... Alex had heard no shot, and the glance that had flown between the Burley brothers spoke of anticipation – not of killing, but of hurting. She looked at her daughter, a silent determination growing in her gut.

"We go after them," Alex said, having no idea how they would ever find them, and then she saw Daffodil, snout still raised in the direction his master had disappeared.

Less than ten minutes later, they set off. Behind them in the glade, Jacob had been dragged to lie in the shadow, lovingly wrapped in a blanket. A lock of thick blond hair escaped his temporary shroud, lifting in the wind, and Alex just had to go back, smooth it down, kiss his face one more time before pulling the thin grey wool to cover him.

Alex and Sarah each carried a musket, and Daffodil stood by Sarah's side, as large and yellow as his long dead grandsire, Narcissus.

"Are you sure?" Alex swept Sarah's hair back. "Can you do this?"

Sarah's eyes filled with tears and a tremor rippled through her. "I have to." Her hands whitened on the worn stock of her father's musket. "I must." She swallowed.

Alex examined her piercingly. "Yes, I suppose you do." With a nod towards the point where the Burleys had disappeared, she began to move. "So do I," she added, throwing one last look at the blanketed shape of her beautiful, sun-kissed son.

It was hot, and it was full of flies, and why on earth had they decided to do without the horses?

"They'll hear a horse, and in this it's just as fast to walk," Sarah said. "The trees grow so close together, and the shrubs and thickets make it difficult going for a horse."

"And for a human," Alex muttered, concentrating on her discomfort rather than on the image of Matthew being dragged through this. Daffodil moved back and forth before them, his tail wagging like a steady metronome as he followed the scent of his master. Sarah looked a sight. From where she walked behind her, Alex had the time to study her, see the telltale stains of blood and other things on her grey shirts. But the girl walked steadily, light on her feet, even if one eye was swollen almost shut, her lower lip bitten through and her ears…

"What…?" Alex stopped her. "What did they do to your ears?"

Sarah's hands flew up to cover them, an ugly red mottling her face.

"Sarah?" Alex cupped her face. "Sweetheart?"

"They used them to hold me still," Sarah groaned, and her eyes shimmered with tears. "When I… I tried to…" On her knees, she whispered, her mouth serving one bulging crotch after the other, and she was choking; she couldn't breathe through her nose, so she'd tried to pull free. Walter Burley had shoved the man in front of her aside, gripped her ears and twisted them until she gasped. "Like that," he had said, grinning, and the other men had laughed, and all of them had done the same.

Alex listened in horror and dragged her daughter into a long, wordless hug.

"They'll pay," she vowed, and the despair that lay like molten lead in her stomach glowed an angry red.

Chapter 37

He was dead. From the first step he took towards Philip Burley, Matthew knew he was dead. It was just a matter of time and place. He had supposed they would shoot him on the spot, and had at first felt a soaring relief at the unexpected reprieve, but now, stumbling after them with a noose that tightened round his neck, he was no longer so sure if this was a reprieve.

An hour later, the Burleys drew their horses to a halt. Matthew sank down in a crouch, panting heavily. He heard one of the brothers laugh, but kept his face hidden in his tied arms, grateful for his broad-brimmed hat in the glaring sun. Someone jerked at the halter, sending him sprawling on his back. Another jerk, and Matthew had to scramble to get back on his feet.

"Tie him to one of the trees," Philip said, and Matthew was pulled to stand while the rope around his neck was thrown across a branch above him.

"We could hang him," Walter suggested, biting into a piece of bread.

"We could." Philip dragged a hand through his shock of dark hair. He sauntered over and tightened the rope, obliging Matthew to raise himself on the balls of his feet. "Not yet, I think." He drove his fist into Matthew's face. Matthew staggered, the noose tightened, and he could hear himself fighting for breath, loud dragging sounds until he got his bound hands up to loosen the rope, standing now on tiptoe.

The men settled down to breakfast, reclining in the shade while Matthew stood uncomfortably beneath his tree. His head swam with thoughts and images: Jacob crumpling to the ground, Alex's hissed, pleading 'no' behind him, the way her fingers had tightened like a vice around his own in that last silent farewell. His Alex, and now he would never hold her again. Sarah…what had they done to her, and how was she to be healed? Alex would know, he comforted himself. Alex would safeguard all of their bairns and see them into adulthood. Not Jacob. He suppressed a sob. No weeping, he told himself. If you begin to weep, you won't be able to stop. Alex, he moaned deep inside, my woman, my heart.

"Alex," he whispered, and then he pushed her away. All of them he pushed away, locking them down behind mental doors. Here stood Matthew Graham, no longer husband or father, only a man that knew he was to die, and desperately wanted to live.

It was easier not to think of everything he was about to lose when he was being hurt, he concluded some time later, lying in a groaning heap at Philip's feet. He could barely breathe, the punch to his stomach having knocked all air out of him, and when he had fallen into the rope, he had actually thought that now he would die, surprised that it should hurt so much when the rough hemp burnt into his skin. But now he was on the ground, and he was being heaved back up to stand and wait for the next punch. This time, he fought back, raising his tied hands high and driving them hard into Philip's face. Blood spurted, and Burley cursed with pain, causing Matthew momentary satisfaction before a fist slammed into his back, felling him once again to the ground.

That is when true hell began for Matthew. Philip was kneeling before him, forcing his head up to meet his light eyes, and in them Matthew saw a promise that made him quail.

"You'll pay for this." Philip touched his bleeding, broken nose.

Matthew's fists were hoisted high above him, his shirt was torn off his back, and Philip picked up a whip and advanced on him, a small smile on his face.

"There are many ways to hurt a man." Philip Burley

walked slowly around Matthew. "Don't you agree?"

"I'm not in a position to disagree," Matthew retorted with a bravado he didn't at all feel.

"No, I would say that you most certainly aren't." Philip dragged the whip over Matthew's chest, grinning at his instinctive recoil. He raised his hand and brought the leather down across Matthew's face. Matthew gasped when his lip burst apart like a ripe plum, dribbling blood down his chin.

Philip stood staring at his back for some moments and let the whip tickle its way down the bared spine. "Flogged before?"

Matthew didn't reply, concentrating on keeping himself as still as possible. The whip flew, repeatedly it flew, and Matthew hung helpless, twirling in his ropes as Philip raised weal after weal, returning to slash some of them open with a second blow.

"Does it hurt?" Philip inquired.

"Uhh." Blood was running in slow rivulets down Matthew's back to collect along the lining of his breeches, it was dripping off his face, and his wrists were ringed with bracelets of blood where the rope cut into the skin.

Philip laughed softly. "It has only begun, Graham. Inch by inch of your body, we'll cover in pain – for Will, for Stephen, for having us outlawed."

"And still I won't regret it," Matthew slurred.

"Oh, I think you will," Philip said in a voice that made Matthew quake.

A hand took hold of his belt buckle, and his breeches were taken off him, as were his stockings and boots. Matthew kicked wildly, and Walter punched him in the stomach.

"You won't need such where you're going. Indian slaves go naked." Walter circled him, trailing a suggestive hand over the bared buttocks.

Matthew cursed at him, telling him to get his hands off him, or else...

"Or what?" Walter taunted. "Your daughter has a very nice little cunt," he said in a voice as unemotional as if he were commenting on the weather. "A bit tight at first, but my brother and I have opened her well. Did you know she's as fair between the legs as she is on her head?"

Matthew didn't want to hear this.

"Obedient too," Walter went on. "Don't you agree, Philip?"

"Not to begin with, but she quickly learnt to spread her legs when we told her to. Spread them and bare herself."

Matthew groaned with frustrated anger. "Scum!" he spat through his swelling lip.

Philip ignored him, flicking the tip of the whip at Matthew's balls. "So many ways to hurt, Graham."

The bloodied leather left a trail behind it down Matthew's inner thigh. Matthew was beginning to tremble: long, uncontrollable tremors that began in his cramping calves and rippled up his bloodied back.

"I should have taken them with us," Philip said to Walter, "the wife and daughter. That way he could have watched."

Matthew's eyes narrowed with hate. "You won't touch them!"

"And how do you aim to stop us? Once we've sold you, we'll just go back. That daughter of yours…and your wife isn't bad-looking for all that she's old." Walter weighed Matthew's balls, laughing when Matthew shrank from his invasive touch.

"No!" Matthew gasped when Walter tightened his hand round his cock. "No, damn you! You won't touch Alex, you hear? Never will you touch Alex!"

"Maybe we will, maybe we won't," Walter said, and there was a gleam to his eyes, his tongue slipping out to wet his lips. "But you, on the other hand…"

What? No! A hand twisted into his balls, and he couldn't move, couldn't even breathe.

"Yes," Walter said, "you we'll have — even if mostly I prefer my men young — very young."

The sudden release of the rope sent Matthew sprawling to the ground, and there were hands on him, forcing him up on his knees. He fought like a maddened bull, he roared, kicked and tried to tear himself free, but a man pushed his face into the ground, another lifted his arse into the air and then... He screamed into the grass, shrieked in agony and shame.

"Your turn," Philip said to Walter. This time, Matthew didn't even try.

It was over. Matthew slid down to lie on his front.

"Dominic Jones once told me how he made you crawl in the dust for him." Philip's voice was very close. "He said how you had once told him that, yes, you were a slave, not a man, a slave. Do you remember?"

Matthew attempted to nod.

"And now you're a slave once more, and not only a slave but a catamite."

Matthew shook his head: no, he wasn't a slave, no, not at all. He heard the Burley brothers laugh in chorus, a toe prodded him in the side, and they moved away. He lay very still. In his mouth was the taste of blood, in the air hung the scent of his blood, and when he looked at his hand, it was smeared with blood. But worst of all was the wet seeping from his anus, the damp running down between his legs.

"Oh God, oh God, oh God..." Alex's teeth were chattering with the effort of not throwing up after witnessing this total humiliation of her man. "I must...he needs me..." She began to stand up from where they were hidden behind a copse of maple saplings.

"No!" Sarah hissed, clamping down on Alex. "They are too many. The moment they see us they'll kill him, and us they'll—" She whimpered, hands clutching at Alex. "Oh Lord, they'll—"

"They're hurting him!" Alex gasped, trying to prise off her fingers. "I must help him!"

"You can't help him!" Sarah whispered, her breath hot in Alex's ear. "Not yet, Mama." She was crying, her cheeks wet with tears, her breathing loud and irregular. Alex wrapped her arms around Sarah and rocked her, not quite sure if it was her comforting Sarah, or if it was Sarah's warm presence that was comforting her.

"They raped him," Alex moaned once Sarah had calmed down.

"That he will survive," Sarah said in a flat voice.

Alex looked at her for a long time.

"Yes." She took her daughter's hand in her own. "That he will."

Alex clapped a hand over her mouth to stop herself from uttering a sound when the Burleys moved back to where Matthew was lying curled on the ground.

"Don't look," Sarah suggested.

"I have to, that's the least I can do." And so she watched him being forced to his knees, saw him reel with slaps and punches, heard his muted yelps. She hated to see his nudity so displayed before men who were looking him over as if he were an animal. Philip laughed, calling Matthew a slave, and Matthew shook his head. That made Philip laugh again. He beckoned Walter forward, said something in a low voice, and Walter nodded, hurrying over to the fire. Minutes passed, and then Walter came back, brandishing what Alex thought to be a long stick – until Matthew shrieked in pain when the red-hot branding iron was pressed against his bare buttock, filling the woods with the stench of burning flesh.

Alex retched. Sarah was trembling, her arm tight around Daffodil's neck, and in the glade before them, Matthew crawled on the ground while the Burleys laughed and laughed.

He was back on his feet, the halter tight around his neck, his hands tied in front of him. He was shaking with shock and pain, and it was almost impossible to move, but move he did. His whole body screeched in protest, begging him to lie down, to rest. But he couldn't do that, because then they'd... What more could they do, he tried, and his guts shrivelled as he realised just how much more was left for them to do. Branded like a beast! And, dearest Lord, his arse...no, best not think about his arse. Just keep on moving, run or they will hurt you.

His mouth filled with the metallic taste of his own blood, his heart thundered with effort, and still they rode on, jeering when he fell, laughing when he gasped as his naked skin was dragged through thickets and rocks. All of him was bleeding, and in the heavy heat he was plagued by a cloud of gnats, attracted by the scent of his blood, of the filth that streaked his legs. Once again, he fell, and they rode on, dragging him like a carcass behind them until he somehow struggled back on his feet. He didn't think of anything but putting one foot before the other, of running as well as he could with the rope that chafed at his throat. Somewhere in his subconscious a little glimmer of hope lived. He was still alive, and he had other sons to follow his tracks. So he stumbled and fell on purpose, he crashed into bushes and shrubs, leaving a blazing trail behind him.

They made camp for the night in a small, rock-strewn clearing. Matthew collapsed into a heap, his tongue thick in a mouth so parched there was nothing to swallow. One of the men set down a bucket before him, and he drank, gulping loudly. A jerk on the rope, and he was pulled back, tied to a tree, and he concentrated on breathing. Air in, air out, air in, air out...

It took an eternity for his pulse to drop back to normal. In the dusk, he attempted to study the damage done to him. His back he couldn't see, but his burn mark was a swollen, tender red, charred around the edges. His legs and feet were bruised, there were thorns in his soles that he carefully worked out and his whole face was one massive contusion, but other than that... He almost laughed. Aye, apart from being half-skinned, raped, burnt and beaten to a pulp, he was alright.

He shivered with cold, all of him trembled with delayed shock, and around him insects hovered, a constant buzzing blanket. He managed to loosen the noose, tried to rest against the tree but couldn't on account of his back, falling forward to cradle his head in his arms instead. He dozed, and there was Alex, smiling at him in their parlour, and the firelight struck sparks off her hair making her look very young. She laughed at something he said, and he stretched in expectation when she stood to go to him. Just as she bent to kiss him, he woke, his skin aflame and the rope halter a circle of fire around his neck.

It was as dark as it ever got in May, the forest around him alive with sounds. He flexed his fingers, wincing at the pain that flew through them when he forced blood into them. He splayed them, imagining Alex slipping her fingers into his to braid them tight together. In his muddled state, he was suddenly convinced he saw her, there, on the other side of the glade, and a roaring pride surged through him that his woman would do such for him: follow him and his captors into the wilderness. But then he blinked and the apparition was gone, and here he was, tied like a dog with a collar round his neck.

He glanced over to where the campfire was dwindling down to a dull glow. If he could only get the noose off his neck then he could run. He heard a rustle in the bushes close by, and for a moment he was lit within by the flaring hope that it might be his sons, but the rustling subsided and he groaned in disappointment. But the noose... It took several minutes of working at the slipknot before he succeeded in loosening it sufficiently to pull the noose over his head. He got to his feet, his eyes locked on the sleeping shapes. A step, one more step, and then he hurtled off, but he had forgotten about the sentry, and a hand grabbed at him and brought him to a halt.

The sentry grunted when Matthew elbowed him in the gut. There were but a few yards between him and the forest when a blow to the back of his knees felled him to the ground. He was dragged back, Walter was screaming him in the ear, and here came Philip with a torch in one hand and his knife in the other.

"Hold this," Philip said to one of his men, handing him the torch.

Matthew backed away from him, ignoring the searing pain in his buttock when he dragged it across the ground. Merciful Christ! He was going to be hurt again.

"Running away?" Philip bent down to look him in the eyes. "You know what happens to slaves that run away?"

Matthew shook his head. No, he didn't, but he wasn't a slave, was he?

"They are punished," Philip hissed.

"Shoot me," Matthew begged. "Just finish this, aye?"

"Shoot you? Now why would I do that? This is far more fun." Philip's hand closed on Matthew's ankle. He nodded at his brother who stuffed a gag in Matthew's mouth. Matthew kicked madly, he squirmed and rolled, straining against all the hands that were holding him down. Someone sat on him. The knife sank into his foot. Matthew bucked, he shrieked through his gag, his fingers clawed uselessly at the air. Philip held up a bloodied item, dangling it before Matthew's eyes. A toe?

"You won't run again," Philip said, wiping his knife on the grass. "At least not tonight."

Matthew was so overcome by this new source of pain that he barely noted when he was tied back up. He whimpered, tried to get at his foot, but his hands were tied behind his back this time, and the noose was pulled so tight any movement would throttle him. It was a struggle to fill his lungs; his pulse was racing from his severed toe to his heart and back again. He wanted to die.

Alex was too tired, too shocked, by the events of this long day to do more than register that Matthew had been badly hurt – yet again. That effectively killed Plan A, which had been to cut him loose and make a run for it. As there were no Plans B, C or otherwise, she had no idea what to do, sitting with Sarah only yards away from where Matthew drew long, wheezing breaths. After what seemed an eternity, the sentry moved off to guard the further perimeter of the camp, and Alex slunk like a cat towards her husband.

At first he didn't react to her voice, her touch, keeping eyes firmly closed. But when she kissed his cheek, he opened one tear-encrusted eye, and a ghost of a smile flickered over his face.

"Alex." It came out a hoarse croak – far too loud in the stillness of the night – and she gestured for him to be quiet, loosened the noose, and held a water skin to his mouth.

Sarah hissed from behind the tree, and Alex froze, sinking down with the blanket around her to resemble a lump in the ground, no more. Feet passed by uncomfortably close, there was the sound of someone urinating, and the familiar sound of Daffodil's deep growl. Damn! She heard the man mutter, and without stopping to think, she threw herself towards the sound, Matthew's sharp dirk in her hand.

There was another noise, a wet, gargling sound, and the man collapsed against her, sliding towards the ground. So much blood! Sarah whispered a curt quiet to the dog. Alex crouched beside the dead man, wiping her slick hands on his breeches, her skirt. Someone was stirring down by the fire: a shape sat up, looked about and lay back down again. Alex let out her pent-up breath in a long exhalation. She was back by Matthew's side, a quick caress to his head, a promise that she'd be back for him, and then she scuttled off behind the tree where Sarah sat crouched with her face hidden against the flank of the dog.

"What do we do?" Sarah said. Dawn was coming, the dark already shifting into greys, and soon the men down by the fire would discern the boots of the killed sentry should they look this way.

"We hide him." Alex moved towards the body. There was blood everywhere, an arterial spraying that had drenched not only the man's shirt and coat but also the bushes around him. "God, how messy," she whispered, her knees weakening at the enormity of having slashed her husband's dirk through a stranger's windpipe.

"Better than to shoot him," Sarah murmured, and Alex giggled hysterically, muffling the sound in her shawl. They inched him further into the trees, and once they were out of sight, they lifted the man and carried him deeper into the woods.

"Here," Alex said, indicating a deep crevice between

some rocks. "May the snakes eat you," she added, and now it was Sarah giggling hysterically.

"Snakes don't eat men."

"Too bad." Alex grasped Sarah's ice-cold hand in her own as they made their way back to the Burley camp, their dog and waiting muskets.

When Philip Burley shook his brother awake, Alex hunched deeper into her hiding place. Sarah was sitting well to the right of her, and now, when it was too late, Alex regretted not having done as Sarah suggested: sneak up on the bastards and kill them in their sleep. Except that Alex was a lousy shot, and Philip was anything but a deep sleeper, starting awake the two times they had tried to approach the fire. The last few hours he'd woken every other minute to sit up and scan his surroundings.

"Where's Sammy?" Philip said.

"Down there." Walter yawned, waving his hand in the direction they had come. Nope, he wasn't.

Alex shifted on her feet.

"Find him," Philip ordered. Walter grumbled, but did as he was told, ambling off towards where Sarah was hiding.

Alex glanced over to where Matthew was lying like a trussed chicken. He was shivering, and, in the returning light, it was all Alex could do not to weep at the sight of him. All of him was covered in bruises or welts, blood and filth streaked his skin, and, as to his foot, it looked as if it had been run through her meat grinder. But he was alive, and soon...

Her wishful thoughts were interrupted by a squawk. By the fire, Philip froze. To her right, Alex heard Walter laugh, and something cold settled in her stomach when she saw him drag Sarah into the open. This wasn't part of the plan.

"It would seem she couldn't get enough," Walter said.

Sarah whirled. She did it again, and Walter flew through the air, landing in a welter of limbs. Philip was on his feet, yelling as he ran to help his brother. The kick to Walter's abdomen made him scream. The second kick hit him squarely in the balls, and Alex was sure she heard something tear – serve him right, raping bastard. Walter howled, hands cupped round his genitals. Sarah swivelled on her toe and brought her foot down hard in Walter's face. He flopped like a fish and lay still.

"I'll kill you!" Philip yelled.

No, you won't! Alex rose from her hiding place, musket aimed at Philip. He came to a halt. Daffodil chose this moment to growl, and Philip took a couple of steps backwards.

"Shoot! Shoot him, Mama!"

Alex very much wanted to, but couldn't quite remember how, her finger incapable of closing around the trigger. Philip ran like a hare.

"Now!" Sarah yelled, groping in the bushes for her musket. Too late.

Philip sank down beside Matthew and rammed his pistol against Matthew's head. "I'll blow his brains out," he threatened.

Alex had no doubt he meant it, and so Sarah stood with her musket aimed at Philip while Alex aimed at the remaining outlaw. At Sarah's command, the dog lumbered over to watch over a feebly twitching Walter.

"An impasse, I believe," Philip sneered. He cocked the gun. Sarah followed suit. The early morning was silent: no birdsong, no animal sounds, only the uneven breathing of four men and two women, and the heavy panting of a dog.

An ear-splitting war cry sliced through the air. Half-naked men strode into the clearing, and, from where he sat beside Matthew, Philip threw back his head and laughed.

"Iroquois!" he said triumphantly. "And now I have three slaves to sell."

Chapter 38

Matthew was only vaguely aware of the events unfolding before him. He was burning with fever, and the severe physical strains of the previous day made it almost impossible to move – should he have been able to.

His split lip had dried and cracked overnight, and something seemed to be very wrong with his foot. He had only fragmented recollections of yesterday, and as to the events of the night, he was no longer sure if they had been real or merely a dream. He had to piss, badly he had to piss, but he had no intention of reducing himself to wetting his own resting place, and so he tried to wave the urgent need away by thinking of other things: like why Walter Burley was lying like a dead frog on the ground several yards away, and why there was a muzzle uncomfortably close to his ear.

He felt Philip relax, more in that the muzzle no longer ground into his head, but pointed to the ground. He heard him laugh and call out something in a tongue he assumed to be an Indian language. The rocky hollow was swarming with people, men in breech cloths and moccasins, their faces painted into anonymous grimness. Too late, his sons would come too late, and now it wasn't only him, but Alex and Sarah as well, both of them being herded forward by the Indians behind them. Someone helped him to stand, and when he swayed, hands held him steady. He was pathetically grateful of the support because his foot was throbbing with pain.

He tried to concentrate on what was being said, but the language was unfamiliar to him, and so instead he tried to locate his wife again. There, sitting on the ground with her head hidden in her hands, her shoulders shaking, and he stumbled towards her, only to be brought up short by Philip's pistol in his gut.

"Stay," Philip said.

"The girl is beddable," he said, switching to English. "And the woman has some years of work in her. The man is strong but must be treated firmly. Maybe you should geld him – that tends to quieten them down." He grinned at Matthew. "I can do it," he offered, tucking his pistol back into his belt.

"I'm sure you can," the man obviously in charge among the Indians replied, and with a start, Matthew recognised Qaachow's voice. "But we do our own gelding."

Walter was being helped to stand by two of the Indians, and Philip sneered at Matthew. "A slave, Graham. And not only you, but your wife and daughter as well."

"They are my kin," Qaachow said.

Philip's mouth fell open. "Your kin?"

In response, Qaachow snapped a command in his own language, and a young lad stepped forward into the sun. Matthew squinted at the Indian lad: dark hair, with hazel eyes that glinted a disconcerting green in the early morning sun. He blinked. Samuel? His Samuel?

Philip swallowed and backed away, fumbling for his pistol. Two Indians grabbed hold of his arms, making Burley yell and try to yank himself free.

"Their son – and mine," Qaachow introduced with a little smile.

Philip increased his efforts to pull free. Matthew stared at his lad – nay, Qaachow's lad – and received a smile in return. Qaachow barked orders. Samuel flew off in the direction of Alex, and Matthew was lowered to sit, the ropes cut away from him, and a blanket brought to cover his nudity.

"I am so sorry we were not here to stop them." Qaachow placed a hand on Matthew's shoulder. "And I am sorry that your son is dead."

In the events of the last twenty-four hours, Matthew had forgotten his dead son, but now grief rose hot and hard through his chest, up his throat, and he covered his face with his hands.

"Jacob," he whispered, and he saw him running towards Sarah before the impact of the musket ball propelled him backwards for a couple of paces. Matthew would never forget the expression on Jacob's face, or how his body folded into itself to land in a cloud of dust.

"We found him yesterday afternoon, him and your other sons. I sent them home with their brother, and promised to find you and see you safely home." Qaachow sat down beside Matthew and put a light arm round his lacerated frame. "I am here for you, white brother."

Matthew nodded, not trusting himself to speak. "Piss," he finally said. "I have to piss."

Alex was wishing for a Valium – no, make that a whole bottle of Valium – something that would pad her in cotton wool and allow her to process the last days of horror piece by piece. Her world was unravelling, and she had no energy left, none at all. She sat sunk into herself, clenching and unclenching her bloodied right hand – the hand of a killer. Sarah was trying to tell her something, but Alex waved her away.

She had to get back on her feet. Somehow, she had to find the strength to make it over to her shivering, naked man, but the effort required was impossible even to contemplate. So close, and now they would be carried off with the Indians. It was all too much, and having the boy throw himself into her arms brought her dangerously close to breaking point.

Samuel? Here? She began to laugh, and then she was crying, loud, harsh sobs that began in her belly, tore their way up her throat to be expelled in barks.

"It's alright," Samuel said. "You're safe now."

Safe? Alex raised her head to where Matthew was being helped to sit, a blanket swept around him. Samuel hugged her, and she blinked at him. Her son, he was here, her lost boy was back, and Alex crushed him so hard he yelped in protest.

"You've grown," she said, running a hand over his lanky arms. "I think you're taller than David."

"You think? I think not. He's taller, older."

She frowned. It sounded strange, his English, as if he were making an effort to produce the sounds required. Still,

318

that was quickly sorted; a matter of days, no more, now that he was home. With half an ear, she listened while Samuel explained that he and his tribe had been north-west of the great river for the last few months, some sort of Iroquois get-together, which was why they hadn't been at hand to protect the Grahams. Frankly, she couldn't care less, not now, but she registered every 'my tribe', 'my people' with a sinking feeling in her gut.

"How I've missed you," she said, interrupting him mid-flow. She just had to touch him again, making him squirm. She took his hand instead, and it was lean and strong and very brown. "I'm so glad you're home." Out of the corner of her eye, she kept an eye on Matthew, her heart nearly leaping out of her mouth when, for some seconds, he disappeared behind a bush, supported by an Indian.

"Home? No, Mama, I'm not coming home. My fath… Qaachow will not allow it. Not yet." He glanced at the tall Indian, eyes lightening when Qaachow smiled at him. He stood, like an adoring hound at the sight of his master.

"You're our son, not his!" Alex said with more of an edge than she'd intended to.

Samuel's tanned face acquired a red hue. "It is not that many more moons, is it?" He looked at her shyly. "One hundred and twenty-one days left, Mama."

"You count them?" Her eyes darted over to Matthew, returned to her son.

"Every night," he said, and something dark flitted over his face, his eyes leaping to Qaachow, to his Indian brother.

Alex looked at her son, at Qaachow, back at her son. Shit, bloody, bloody fucking hell. Alex was too exhausted to rouse herself much beyond this, even if for an instant she nailed her eyes to Qaachow's back. Instead, she hugged Samuel hard.

"Mama!" He struggled out of her hold and sat back on his heels. "Thistledown has a new son, a brother for me and Little Bear."

"Oh," Alex replied, her insides contorting with jealousy at the pride in his voice.

319

"But she's frightened."

"She is? Is the boy ill?" Alex felt a stab of compassion for Thistledown.

"No." Samuel plucked at a stand of grass, avoiding her eyes. "You cursed my Indian father, his seed and the seed of his seed, and my mother fears for her baby boy." He gave her an entreating look, not even noticing his slip of tongue. "I don't want my wee brother to come to harm, Mama, nor Little Bear. Won't you lift the curse?"

Sarah stood forgotten in the centre of the clearing. Mama was with Samuel, Da was impossible for her to approach. All that he'd lived through, every single mark on him was because of her. If only she'd stayed in the yard, if, if... She snuck a look down at herself, mortified to see so many signs of her ordeal. The neckline of her shift gaped open from where Walter had torn it apart, and she fisted her hand round the tear in an effort to cover her chest, exposed beyond the limits of propriety.

She ducked her head when Qaachow came towards her, glad of the way her undone, messy hair fell in a protective curtain over her battered face. She had no idea what she looked like, but she could feel the bruises, her torn and tender mouth, the throbbing swelling around her left eye. Qaachow stopped before her and with a question in his eyes raised fingers to her hair. She nodded, and closed her eyes when he gently combed the hair back and braided it.

"It is not your shame." He draped a blanket round her and handed her a knife. "You have the right," he said, tilting his head in the direction of the captive Burley brothers.

Sarah weighed the weapon in her palm, finding the balance point between blade and grip so that it hung quivering across her forefinger. "And if I don't?"

"Then we will. And it will be slow and painful, very painful."

"I don't want them to die." Sarah wet her lips. "I want them to live. I want their souls torn from them, their manhood destroyed, I want them to scream for help – as I did – but have their cries go unheard. I want them to live a long time afterwards, and know themselves to be hollowed husks – as hollow as I am."

"If that is what you want, that is what you get," Qaachow said, retaking the knife. "Your brother will bear witness to their agony."

"My brother?" Sarah turned to look at Samuel who was still sitting by her mother. "But he's a boy!"

"White Bear is old enough to watch." Qaachow inclined his head and moved away.

Out of the corner of her eye, Alex had seen Qaachow approach her daughter, had watched him braid her hair, wrap her in a blanket. Now, the Indian turned her way, and Samuel scrambled to his feet at Qaachow's approach. Qaachow said something, and Samuel nodded, giving Alex an awkward hug before setting off in the direction of Matthew.

She could feel Qaachow's eyes on her, but she couldn't summon the energy necessary to be polite, so she kept her eyes on the ground, tried to pretend he wasn't standing right beside her.

"Do you still hate me?" he said.

"How can I?" Alex muttered. "You just saved us." She swivelled her head to look at Matthew who was sitting with Samuel kneeling before him, and she wept inside at the destruction wreaked on him.

"Look what they've done," she moaned. "My beautiful man."

Qaachow helped her to stand. "He will live."

She gave him a long look. "And so will your sons. I hear you have two now."

"Three," he said, eyes resting on Samuel.

"Oh no, he's mine," she told him, hating the way his mouth softened into a little smile. "Make sure you bring my boy back whole." She gave him a stiff bow and set off towards her man.

★

321

Matthew rested his forehead against his wife's and closed his eyes. He very much wanted to put his arms around her, but there was no strength left in them, and so he let them hang by his side. He had a burning need to tell her all that had been done to him, but shame froze the words into hard, ice-cold pellets that clogged his mouth and windpipe. Her fingertips were on his face, walking over the whip slash, the bruised nose and eye, the swollen lip. Very gently, she placed her cool, soft lips against his cracked, bloodied ones. And Matthew knew he was safe and crumpled unconscious into her arms.

It was a terrible homecoming. Matthew lay delirious on the primitive sled behind one of the horses, Sarah had retreated into absolute silence, and with every step down the long lane, Alex knew she was coming closer and closer to confronting the reality of her dead son.

It didn't much help when the whole family came out in silence to greet them. Alex wanted only to disappear, to drag a quilt over her head and sleep until she could wake up to a reality where none of the last days had happened, to a world where Jacob was still alive, Sarah undamaged, and her Matthew healthy and whole. She stifled a sob, she swallowed and swallowed. Don't cry, not now. Later, yes; now, no. Instead, she stood as straight as she could and bid the Indians a courteous farewell, told her sons to get their father inside, and turned Sarah over to Ruth.

"Make sure she has a long hot bath." Alex pushed a mute and unwilling Sarah towards a reluctant and horrified Ruth.

"I'll do it," Betty said, stepping between the girls. "Come here, Sarah. I'll help you."

"Mama," Sarah whispered, "please, Mama." Her hand knotted itself into Alex's skirts, the gesture of a very small child.

"You take care of the lass, Alex," Mrs Parson said. "We'll take care of Matthew, aye?"

No, she wanted to say, bloody hell, no! But what was she to do? She leaned over the sled and kissed Matthew's uncovered nape.

"I don't want to leave you," she admitted to his ear.

"You have to," his breathless reply floated up. "I'll be here when you are done."

"Promise?"

He actually smiled, a slow smile while in the corner of his eye a tear glinted.

"Aye, lass, I promise. I don't think I'll be moving much the coming days."

Sarah flinched and shrank away when Alex undressed her. The shawl, the torn and dirty skirts, her stained stays, the chemise that stank of sweat and semen and blood…each protective layer was stripped off her, revealing dried blood, flowering bruises shifting from near black to sickly yellow.

"I don't know where the bodice is," Sarah said.

"Who cares? I'm going to burn it all anyway." Alex put a tentative hand to Sarah's swollen face. "How on earth could you walk all day yesterday?"

Sarah shrugged. "It was Da. Jacob was dead, and then Da…" She drew in a ragged breath. "It was my fault. Jacob died because of me."

"Jacob died because he was a valiant fool."

"But if I hadn't disobeyed you…" It came out as a gulping sob. "…and now Jacob's dead, and you will all hate me for it."

"No, honey. We'll lay the blame where it belongs: on the Burleys." She almost meant it; not quite, not yet, but as she helped her daughter into the bath, washed her and lathered her hair, the remaining anger dissipated, replaced by a ferocious protectiveness towards her damaged, cringing girl.

She helped Sarah stand and patted her dry, ignoring the instinctive flinching. She motioned for her daughter to lie down, and oiled all of her with lavender oil, attempting to caress the pain and humiliation away. Halfway through, Sarah began to cry, but Alex pretended not to notice. By the time she was done, Sarah was no longer crying – she was fast asleep. Alex sat beside her for a very long time before wrapping her in a quilt and calling for Mark to carry his sister inside.

★

"He'll keep," Mrs Parson said, clasping Alex's hand. "He sleeps like a babe. But you, lass, you look dead on your feet." She led Alex over to the table, more or less forced her to sit.

Alex looked down at the heaped plate before her. She didn't think she was hungry, but once she began to eat, her stomach screamed for more. Well over two days since she'd eaten, and the stew was hot and spicy, the bread was newly made, and when Mark poured her a full measure of whisky, she didn't try to protest. She just threw it down with the rest.

"Tell us," Mark said, "all of it."

"I don't think I can," Alex replied, not wanting to relive the worst parts. Nor did she have any intention of ever telling them everything, as much for their sake as for Matthew's.

"You have to." Ian came over to sit close enough to take her fisted hand and straighten it out to rest in his.

"Matthew," she said. "I have to go to Matthew."

Ian wouldn't let go. "He's safe, Mama."

Alex sighed, concentrating on chasing an escaped piece of onion across her emptied plate. "Jacob," she breathed. "Oh God, my Jacob."

Slightly drunk, and very comforted by the last few hours spent with her eldest sons and Mrs Parson, Alex finally stumbled to her room some time before midnight.

Matthew was fast asleep, not as much as twitching when she stroked his cheek. The room was hot and stuffy, and she went over to open the window to the night, leaning out to draw in the scents of early summer. A nighthawk flew by, its piercing call cutting through the silence, and against the lighter sky towards the river, Alex saw a bat flit by in high-speed acrobatic circles. Behind her came the reassuring sound of Matthew breathing, and on her way here she had tiptoed in to where Sarah and Ruth lay fast asleep. Safe, all of them were safe. Even Samuel was safe, somewhere out in the rustling green of the forest. All except her Jacob, who would never see his twenty-second birthday.

Despite having promised herself she wouldn't, Alex

leaned her head against the window frame and wept, standing at the open window for a very long time.

Matthew woke with a start when she got in beside him, and she wasn't sure quite how to touch him, but he solved that by pillowing his head on her chest.

"Hold me," he whispered. "Hold me and heal me." And she did, as well as she could, stroking the only undamaged part of him she could reach – his head – telling him over and over again that somehow they'd make it through. Of course they'd make it through.

He couldn't sleep. It was a long way to dawn, and he stared out into the dark, his head leaping from one half-baked thought to the other. He was hot with fever; every nerve in him ached, humming loudly that he was alive. Beside him, Alex lay sunk into a sleep so deep it bordered on stupor. He needed her urgently, but didn't want to wake her, so instead he put a hand on her thigh, caressing the softness of her skin. It helped to feel her under his hand, and he shifted close enough to sniff her hair. Sun and dust, sweat and blood... Blood? Had she been hurt as well? But no, she was whole and unscathed under his touch. His foot throbbed, his back was beginning to flare again, and his buttock was raw with pain. His arse... He muffled a sob in the pillow.

She rolled towards him, disorientated and half asleep, but her hands were on his shirt, under the hem, soft, gentle fingers stroking and cupping. She lay back, her legs widened for him, and he shoved her shift out of the way, ignoring how his skin shrieked in protest at his movements. She enveloped him in her warmth, and he was safe. She lay asleep but acquiescing, and he rocked them back and forth, not wanting this joining to end. In his feverish state, he wasn't sure this was happening, and he considered that maybe he should try and roll off, but he didn't want to. He wanted his cock inside of her, buried in her welcoming darkness, testifying to the fact that he hadn't died at the hands of the Burleys. Her hand drifted up to his head, and she pulled him down to lie on top of her.

"Sleep," she whispered hoarsely.

Chapter 39

Matthew was feverish for days, lying like a beached whale on their bed with his whipped back bare to the air. Any movement made him wince, all of him a mass of welts and bruises, and on top of that, there was his foot. Philip Burley had amputated the fourth toe jaggedly, and the remaining stump was a swollen, infected area that had to be drained of pus repeatedly.

In his half-conscious state, Matthew was not at all cooperative, at times kicking wildly to free his foot of the barnacle-like appendage in the form of Mrs Parson, shrieking out loud when the wound was opened with a sterilised knife.

"I don't think I can do that again," Alex said on the seventh day, using a trembling hand to smooth back his sweat-drenched hair from his face.

"You'll have to, but it wasn't that bad today." Mrs Parson dropped the bloodied rag she'd just used on Matthew's foot into a bowl.

"You think?" Alex broke open the aloe vera leaf she had brought with her and scooped out the gel to anoint the blistered burn on his buttocks. Instinctively, he tensed, pressing together the cheeks so tightly they whitened around the edges. Mrs Parson's mouth pursed and she gave Matthew a long, considering look.

"It's me," Alex murmured. "It's Alex, love."

"Alex," he repeated in a grating voice. "My bonny, bonny lass."

Mrs Parson grinned and patted Alex on her shoulder. "He's getting better, no?"

Not much better, and very slowly at that, sinking into deep black moods that spilled over on all of them. He threw a tantrum when he understood that they'd buried Jacob without him, screaming at Alex that how could she take it upon herself to see his son – his son, you hear? – off into the afterlife without him present? "A father should be there to bury his son!"

"He'd been dead five days! What was I to do? Wait until you were well enough to bury a rotted corpse into the ground?" She backed away from him, breath coming in shallow, uneven gasps. Don't cry, no crying – later perhaps, but not now. "A mother shouldn't have to bury her child," she said, and fled the room.

"I'm sorry," she heard him say.

On top of all this, there was Sarah, who retreated into brooding silences and escaped them all as much as she could. At mealtimes, she would sit to the side, eat without raising her eyes from the table, and then flee, mumbling something about having to see to Viggo. In fact, she spent most of her time with the convalescing dog, eyes blank as she stroked him repeatedly over his back, his head. Alex was torn in two by the needs of her bright-haired, mute daughter and those of her husband as he struggled with nightmares that kept both of them awake most nights. It was even worse when she tried to touch him.

After that strange asexual coupling the night they'd come home, he was like a coiled spring, and if she placed a hand on him unannounced, he sprang away, shaking his head in an apologetic gesture while murmuring something about hurting all over. She left him alone as much as she could, and when she noticed how stiff he lay in their bed when she crawled in beside him, she stood up and pulled her pillows and quilts over to the floor rug.

"I'm sorry," he whispered.

She didn't reply, staring wide-eyed into the night.

After a fortnight, Alex decided he had to start moving, bad foot or not, and for the coming week, she hectored and encouraged, always hovering around him to help him should he stumble.

"I can walk on my own," Matthew snapped, shaking off her supporting hand. They were in the yard, having spent the last hour walking back and forth to the stables.

"Of course you can," Alex bit back, tired of his irascibility, of his black moods and uncharacteristic self-centredness.

God knows she tried. She comforted and encouraged, she changed bandages and oiled and soothed as best as she could, she made him special treats in the hope that he would eat, she sat beside him when he woke at night, she took the stairs in bounds if she'd been away from him too long. And when he rejected her, when he closed her out, she escaped to work herself to exhaustion in the kitchen garden, staying out until well after dusk to make sure he was asleep before she came up the stairs. Except that he wasn't, his eyelids fluttering when he kept them closed to avoid having to talk to her.

At times, she wanted to bend down and scream him in the ear, anything to jolt him out of his present behaviour. But she didn't. She made allowances for him, she assured herself that soon he'd be like he used to be, and then she was brought up short by the terrifying thought that how could he possibly revert to being the man he was before those two days in May?

She twisted and tossed through her nights, lonely and unable to sleep, and not once had he asked how things were with her. All she did was give and give and give. Until now, when something snapped inside her. She glowered at her husband and left him standing halfway across the yard as she stalked away.

"Alex," Matthew called after her. "I'm sorry."

In reply, she waved her middle finger in the air. He wanted to apologise, he could bloody well come after her.

She sat on the narrow bench in the graveyard and watched his slow, painful progress up the steep slope. Often he had to stop, raising his foot in the air to take weight off the non-existent toe, and every time he did, Alex sat on her hands to not rush down to help him. He was white to the point of looking green when he finally made it all the way up, stopping to breathe heavily for some minutes before limping his way towards where she was sitting.

"I haven't been up here since you buried him," he said in a voice heavy with grief.

Alex didn't reply, but shifted to allow him room to sit. She came here every morning, often just as the sun cleared the trees on the eastern fringe, to sit and talk for a while with her son. There was as yet no stone to mark the grave as Matthew had insisted he was to do that himself, but Ian had set a wooden cross in place for now. Small offerings of flowers lay scattered around it, disturbingly bright against the dark of the turned soil. Now, three weeks after they'd buried him, a soft sheen of green was sprouting through the earth. Give it one month more and it would all be thick, vibrant grass.

"Do you think it hurt?" That question had been thudding in her head since she'd seen Jacob fall. Matthew sighed, a sound laden with sadness, and tried to take her hand. She pulled it away.

"Aye," he breathed.

Alex nodded. Of course it hurt to have a musket ball claw its way through your chest at close-range.

"Did he know? That he was dying?" she asked, keeping her eyes on her lap.

"Aye, but he didn't have time to fear it."

"That's good, isn't it?"

"As deaths go, it wasn't bad." Matthew groped for her hand again, and this time she let him take it.

"Too soon," Alex whispered.

"Too soon," Matthew echoed, and put an arm around her shoulders.

The dam that had been building for weeks inside her began to crack. Tears slid down her cheeks, an agonising, silent weeping that made her throat and chest ache from the inside out. They didn't talk. He didn't do more than hold her, one large hand caressing her hair as she cried for her son, for her hurting daughter and her damaged man – but mostly, she cried for him, for her golden boy that was dead, lying in his far too early grave only feet away from her.

The tears stilled, the racking sobs subsided. Alex snivelled and sat up, averting her face from him as she adjusted her hair and used her sleeve to blot her puffy eyes.

"I'm not sleeping on the floor anymore," Alex said as she got off the bench. She didn't attempt to help him, but stood waiting, just in case. With a grunt of concentration, Matthew stood.

"No," he agreed with an unsteady voice.

"Good." She moved away from him, leaving him to come down as best he could.

"Alex?" His voice brought her to a halt. "I…I may need help. Will you walk with me?"

Alex smiled to herself, but smoothed both face and voice into calm neutrality before replying that of course she would.

Alex disappeared in the direction of the river after supper. She came back an hour or so later, barefoot and with her dark hair still damp against the back of her clean chemise – her best, Matthew noted, and in his stomach something clenched.

She waved at him where he sat beneath the oak with Ian, Betty and their bairns, and he raised his hand to her, making her face break up into a brilliant smile. He closed his eyes. He was going to have to tell her, and he had no idea how. He was so scared of her touch, that somehow she would know what had been done to him and think less of him.

They hadn't spoken of that terrible day once since they got back, not because she hadn't tried to, but because he had refused, saying that it was enough that she saw the damage on him. His back, his maimed foot, the brand that stood a deep and puckered red against the whiteness of his skin… Surely she didn't expect him to speak of it as well?

"You should," Alex had said. "Some things have to be talked about to properly heal." There had been an insinuation in her voice that he hadn't fully understood.

"I don't want to," he'd told her in reply.

Ian smiled at Matthew, leaned over, and lifted a sleeping Timothy out of Matthew's arms.

"Go." Ian nodded to where Alex had just walked into the house. Matthew looked at him, fisted his hands a couple of times before he stood up, straightened his back, and limped off across the yard.

Matthew made his way up the stairs and into their bedchamber. The room smelled of lavender and sun. She had changed linens and opened the window wide to let in some of the cooling evening air. In the setting sun, the stained glass panes threw reflections of red and green to dance in her looking glass, and from there they shot like beams across the room. He hesitated by the door, and she turned to face him, dragging her brush through her hair. She held it out to him, and for a long time all there was were the sounds of his strokes and her shallow breathing. He plaited her hair when he was done. It smelled of rosemary and camomile, and something he at first couldn't identify but then recognised as almond oil.

"My turn." She took the brush from him and pushed him down to sit before the looking glass. She took her time over his shoulder-length hair – more grey than brown these days, but thick and wavy as it always had been. Once she was done, she used a piece of ribbon to tie it back off his face, rested her hands on his shoulders, and met his eyes in the mirror.

He had to tell her. Her hands were sliding inside his shirt, and he yearned for her touch and yet he feared it. She had undone the fastenings, opening the shirt wide over his hair-covered chest. The shirt slid off to lie like a draped cloth round his hips, and now her hands were running over his healing back.

He trembled under her fingers, swallowed audibly, and cleared his throat. "Alex...I...I haven't told you all."

"Shhh," she whispered in his ear. "You don't have to tell me anything." And in her eyes he saw that she knew, and it was like being impaled on a stake and left to die in slow, dragging agony. She had seen it!

She kissed his cheek. "Never in my life have I felt so utterly useless as when I saw what they did to you. I swear, had I been able to, I would have killed them all then and there." Her hands tightened on his shoulders. "But I couldn't, and so the least I could do was watch."

He didn't know what to say. He just stared at her, uncertain as to how her admission made him feel. "I wanted to die. At that moment, I wished they'd killed me instead."

Alex nodded. "A total wipeout of your inner self. Like a chrysalis you burst, but unlike a chrysalis there's no butterfly inside. It's all an empty black void."

"Aye," he said, thinking that he couldn't have described it better himself. "And afterwards you're no longer what you were before."

"No, something is quenched forever." She met his eyes. "Unless someone helps you find the butterfly that was lost."

Matthew could barely breathe when she helped him to stand. When she knelt before him, he wasn't sure if he would survive the bittersweet rush of sensations that rushed through his loins, leaving him so light-headed he had to steady himself against the wall. She rose and walked backwards to the bed before him, and there she sat down.

"Maybe I can help you," she whispered, and he heard the hope in her voice.

Clumsily, he lowered himself to his knees before her. "I come to you with my need, I come with my desires, and you won't turn me away. Ever."

"Ever," she promised, and guided him home.

Much later, she lay where she belonged: safe in his arms.

"Did Sarah see it as well?" Matthew asked.

"Yes, she came down like a bear trap around me to stop me from charging out of our hiding place then and there, and thank heavens she did." Alex raised herself up on her elbow and looked down at him. "She's late, and with every day she's retreating further and further into herself."

"Late?" At first he didn't understand, and when he did, he looked at her in horror. "You mean…"

"I'm still hoping, and Mrs Parson says that sometimes

the herbs take time to work – but that sometimes they don't. She doesn't dare to increase the dosage because it might lead to haemorrhage."

"Merciful Father." Matthew stared unseeing at the ceiling. Well ploughed and planted, Philip Burley had jeered, and now his lass… No, God wouldn't do something like that, not to a young lass just sixteen.

"That reaction won't exactly help her, will it?"

"How do you expect me to react?" Matthew snarled, shifting away from her in bed. "Should I toast the health of a Burley bastard?"

"If – and it's still an if – but if she's with child, she can't go around hating it. Part of it is her."

He gave her a penetrating look. He knew just how much she'd hated Isaac when he grew in her, how she wished that this child, fathered by a man she had come to hate, would somehow shrivel and die.

"We have to help her with this because if we don't, I fear she might do something really stupid."

Matthew pinched his nose and nodded weakly. A son's life, a daughter's maidenhead, his own humiliation, and now, apparently, a living reminder of it all. He rolled over on his side and collected Alex to lie, as she should, safe in the curve of his body, his arm draped across her waist.

"One day at a time," he murmured into her hair. Please God, let there be no child, he prayed. Lord, look down on my lass, and spare her this last indignity.

Chapter 40

Sarah was sitting on the bench, staring at absolutely nothing, when Da stopped before her and with a crooked smile asked her if she wished to walk with him to the river and back.

"I can't walk well enough to take you hunting yet," he said.

Sarah got to her feet. She hadn't spoken to Da properly since they got back near on a month ago, watching from afar as he struggled to regain control of his maimed foot. The burn rash around his throat had faded, but she knew from overhearing Mama and Mrs Parson that parts of his back, and in particular the burn on his buttock, were far from healed.

"Are you feeling better then?" he asked her. To her surprise, he took her hand in his, something he hadn't done since she was a small lass. It was very comforting to have his big, calloused hand folded around hers, and to her consternation her eyes filled with tears.

"I don't rightly know." No, she wasn't alright. Sixteen days and more overdue, and even if she tried to tell herself it was all fancies, she knew that she was with child, and the knowledge thudded like death knells in her head every waking moment of her days.

"Doesn't it help? To know that they are dead?" Da bent down to scratch a nearly recovered Viggo behind his ear.

"They're not. Qaachow promised me they wouldn't die."

Da came to an abrupt stop. "Not die? Don't you want revenge on them?" Something dark moved in his eyes. There was the slightest trembling in his set jaw.

"They won't die," she told him through compressed lips. "But they'll wish they had."

"Ah." Da tightened his hold on her hand. "How many days?"

334

She panicked. She attempted to free herself from his grip, but when he wouldn't let go, she collapsed to sit on the ground, hiding her face from him.

"Sarah," Da said, and very laboriously lowered himself to her. "It's alright, lass. We will sort it. Whatever happens, we're with you, your mama and I."

Sarah clenched her fingers around his, the instinctive clutching of a drowning person round a floating spar. "Oh, Da," she whispered, and began to cry.

The Chisholms rode in a fortnight or so later, bristling with curiosity and news. After a couple of days of rain, the late June day was fresh and crisp, the grass a shade greener, and the air pungent with the scent of heavy, well-turned soil and growing crops. Robert inclined his head in the direction of Alex, clapped Matthew on his back, went a bright red when he realised what he'd just done, and spent the following minutes apologising repeatedly.

"It's almost healed." Matthew shifted his shoulders, and shook hands with the other two brothers and Carlos Muñoz, now openly wearing a cassock.

"Are you still here?" Alex asked. "I would've thought by now you'd be long gone to safer places."

Carlos flashed her a triumphant smile. "England has a Catholic king again, the Lord be praised. Long live James, the second of that name."

"Charles is dead?" Matthew looked from Carlos to the Chisholms.

In response, Robert extracted a worn royal proclamation and handed it to him.

"In February?" Alex peeked over Matthew's shoulder. "That's almost five months ago." She studied the badly executed sketch of a man with very much hair and as prominent a nose as his brother, even if this one was more elegant, and sighed. "Not king for long," she muttered, and Matthew frowned at her. Alex frowned back. "Common sense. Parliament doesn't want a Catholic king. And what's he to do? Take the Test Act oath? Abjure his religion?"

"Reactions were joyful to his ascension," Robert said rather stiffly. "The people rejoiced at having a peaceful succession."

Alex raised her brows. "And what about the Duke of Monmouth? Charles' eldest son? Won't he make a bid for the throne?"

Martin Chisholm made a dismissive sound. "He's bastard born. Protestant yes, but not born in wedlock. Who would follow him against a rightful king?"

"Men do stupid things all the time," Alex said, "and when it comes to England and religion – it's not even forty years ago since the first Charles had his head chopped off."

Matthew took a firm grip of her elbow and steered her in the direction of the house. "Refreshments for our guests, Alex."

She stuck her tongue out, making him smile and stoop to brush his lips over her brow.

Thomas Leslie came by some hours later with Nathan. By then, Matthew, his sons and the Chisholms had consumed a sizeable quantity of beer, all of them sprawled in the shade of the oak. Thomas smiled when he heard Matthew laugh, and gave Alex an affectionate hug.

"Back again?" Alex said, returning his hug. Thomas had been round repeatedly the last few weeks, to begin with to sit on a stool for hours by Matthew's bedside, talking to him about anything and everything, lately to broach the subject of Jacob with Alex, listening patiently as she went on and on about the injustice of it all.

"He seems much better today," Thomas said, gesturing in the direction of where Matthew was sitting on one of the benches with Lettie on his knee and Adam leaning against him.

"He is. Did you know," she went on, changing the subject, "that King Charles is dead?"

"Yes, I heard it down in Providence in May. Not that it will affect things here much; too far away for the king to make much of a difference."

"Why didn't you tell us?"

"Would you have cared?" Thomas looked at her from calm grey eyes.

"No, I suppose we wouldn't have given a shit."

"Alex!" Thomas said, sounding somewhere between amused and disapproving.

She propelled him over to join the men. "Boys only, I fear, so I'll retire to do some mending or some other adequately feminine pastime."

In the end, Alex decided that the adequate pastime was to work in her kitchen garden where her daughters were. It was hot, even this late in the afternoon, and even more so up among her neat squares of kitchen produce. So much food: beets, carrots, turnips, cabbages, beans, beans, beans, squash, maize, more beans. Cucumbers for pickling, dill that looked wilted and meagre in the sun, parsley, garlic, and sitting in the middle of the potato rows was Sarah, her legs drawn up to her chin and a wild look in her eyes. Ruth was kneeling before her, and Alex knew that Sarah had somehow received final confirmation that she was with child. When she got closer, she could smell the reek of vomit and pulled Sarah into a hug.

Sarah moaned, hiding her face against Alex's chest. "I'll never get away from them now. For the rest of my life, they've marked me."

"We'll cope," Alex said shakily. "Somehow, we'll fix this, okay?"

"How?" Sarah tore herself free. "Can this be undone?" She whacked at her belly.

"Sarah, come here." Ruth held out her arms to her sister, but all Sarah did was shake her head and get to her feet.

"You know what they'll say," she sobbed. "And it's true, it's true! I'm a whore – they made me a whore – and this…" She hit herself again. "…this is a bastard." She wheeled and ran. Like a wild thing, she ran for the safety of the woods.

She was sitting by the river, throwing stone after stone into the water, when she heard the distinctive sound of a wooden peg tapping its way down the path. Sarah hunched together, wanting nothing so much as to disappear.

Carlos lowered himself to sit beside her. He made no move to touch her, he didn't speak, he just sat beside her, and in his hands were his beads, fingers caressing their way over one at the time.

She slid him a look, met two lustrous dark eyes.

"Shall we walk?"

"Aye," she said, and when he held out his hand, she took it.

"Have you told anyone what they did to you?"

Sarah shook her head. "No, I can't."

"But every night you relive it, is that not so?"

Sarah nodded. The first invasive thrust, the hard hands on her forcing her to do just what they wanted. She tried to tell herself she didn't remember, but she did, every violation stark and detailed in her head. She began to shake with fear. What if they had gotten away from the Indians? They'd come here, and Walter would whisper in her ear, and she'd do anything he wanted as long as they didn't hurt her.

"I don't think you need to worry about that," Carlos said when she voiced this fear out loud.

"I should have asked him to kill them. Instead, I wanted them to live in pain and humiliation, and now I will never know if they are truly dead or not."

"They won't come back," Carlos said. "They are surely very far from here right now."

Sarah gave him a wobbly smile. Samuel would know, she reassured herself, and he'd be back before autumn to tell her the Burleys were effectively destroyed.

She dug her toe into the ground. "I'm with child."

Carlos just nodded, commenting that many women ended up raped and pregnant.

"I hate it!" She spat to the side. "I hate it, I hate it, I hate it."

"The child is innocent. It can't help its father."

"Its fathers," she replied, and suddenly it all bubbled out of her – a long, detailed description of her ordeal that left Carlos pale and stunned.

"Oh, child," he murmured afterwards, and that made her laugh. This young, cosseted priest man call her a child?

What did he know of the pains of life?

"We all have different crosses to carry," he said.

"Aye, you lost half a leg while I've lost my honour and my dignity, and now my body is invaded by them as well. I wouldn't mind switching."

"God has given you this burden to carry, and carry it you will. You must pray for divine help."

"Divine help? I want God to rid me of it, not have me carry it!"

"But He won't." Carlos put his hand on her stomach; she gasped and shrank back. "Here is life, and He won't extinguish innocent life."

"But what about me? What about my innocence? How could He let that happen to me?"

"I don't know. God has ordained. Unfathomable as it may seem right now, there is a purpose, a good purpose behind it all."

"Why me?" she moaned. "Why did it have to be me?"

Carlos took both her hands in his and turned her so that they faced each other. Of almost a height they were, this slight priest and her.

"Because you're strong enough to shoulder it, and God will be with you all the way." He fumbled his hand through the side slit of his cassock to the pouch he kept within and brought forth a rosary in dark stained wood. "Here." He placed it in her hands. "You remember the prayers I taught you?"

"Aye, but I'm not a Catholic." The beads lay like a warm comfort in the palm of her hand.

"I don't think God will mind, and for you to pray to the Holy Virgin may not be a bad idea, given your condition."

"No." She ran a thumb over the first bead. "*Hail Mary, full of grace,*" she recited, "*the Lord is with thee.*"

It was a substantially calmer Sarah that came back to the house after her walk with Carlos. Resigned, but calm, the wild despair that had shone through her eyes for the last few weeks replaced by a shimmer of sadness and determination.

Across the table, she looked at Carlos and a smile fluttered over her face, reciprocated by a smile so bright it was difficult to miss.

Alex saw the exchange between them and wasn't entirely sure if she liked it. Even if Carlos was unaware of it, and would in all certainty hotly deny it, he looked at Sarah as a man would, not as a priest. A strong hand closed on her own, and she shared a concerned glance with Matthew. He had seen it too.

Chapter 41

"It's one of those horrible circular references," Alex said to Matthew one early morning.

"Hmm?" he asked, more interested in exploiting the possibilities of his cock-stand and her warm, naked body. He was voracious in bed, had been so for the last few weeks, a constant appetite for her, an urgent need to confirm his virility. Not that she seemed to mind, every now and then wondering in a pleased voice just how many women her age got laid on a daily basis. Aye, she was getting laid most regularly, and this morning would be no exception.

"Carlos," she said, which didn't enlighten him at all. Alex sighed, her hand stroking his cock so that it hardened even further. "Somewhere in the future, I have a son fathered by a man that's the spitting image of that small priest – bar the wooden leg. Ángel is – will be – a right bastard, and yet, in the here and now, his ancestor may be the one who helps my daughter cope with her terrible ordeal."

"Hmm," he repeated, and kissed her into silence. He didn't much like thinking about the stranger aspects of her, and what she had just said made him break out in gooseflesh, in particular given the looks he had seen flash across the table the last few evenings.

He banished these thoughts, concentrating on the woman below him instead, on the curves of her body, the smoothness of her skin, and the alluring scent of almonds and lavender that clung to her. His tongue drifted down, and she made a series of small noises somewhere between saying *yes, please* and *no, I can't stand it.*

He chuckled and raised his head to look at her. "One

day, I aim to tie you to the bedstead and have my way with you for hours."

She laughed. "Talk, talk, talk. We never have time for stuff like that."

"No?" In a matter of seconds, he found one of her shawls and tied her into place. She was laughing so hard she was almost convulsing, but she didn't laugh quite as much when he went back to what he'd been doing before. Or when he took her, in slow, steady movements, and just when she was about to come, pulled out and hunted about for his shirt.

"Where are you going?" She tugged at her hands.

He looked down at her and grinned. "For my breakfast. I'll come back shortly and finish with you then."

"Matthew!"

In reply, he kissed each ankle before tying them to the bedposts, leaving her spreadeagled and naked on their bed.

"Very nice. Stay," he said, laughing at his own jest as he closed the door behind him.

"Let me go," she gasped an hour or so later.

"I'm not sure," he teased, kissing her sweat-slick chest, "I'm not done yet, am I?" His cock stood like a quivering ramrod, demanding that he give it release, but Matthew was enjoying this new game of his, pushing them both almost to the limit and then holding back, hearing her grunt and groan with disappointment.

He released her legs before flipping her over on her front. She pulled her knees up, her cleft a damp, secret place that begged for him to take it. So he did, and there he was on top, she on her knees, and in his head swam an image of himself as he had been that day, with Burley riding him as he was now loving his wife. It filled him with rage, it made his cock roar in desperation, and Matthew took her roughly, violently. She pushed back against him, asking for more, and he closed his eyes and gave it to her, collapsing in a panting heap on top of her afterwards.

She strained against her bindings. "I have to pee."

Matthew raised a hand to undo the knots, and flipped

over on his side to watch her cross the room to where they kept the chamber pot.

"I'll start looking for a husband for her," he said.

Alex froze mid-crouch. "A what?"

"She has to be wed. She can't birth a child as an unwed mother."

"Sarah isn't marrying anyone at present," Alex said with absolute finality. "She has enough to cope with as it is without having to face the duties expected of a wife." She stood and looked at him. "Like in bed." She came over to sit beside him. "If anyone must be in love with her husband, it must be her. How else is she to overcome the fear and revulsion their treatment of her must have left in its wake?"

"She can't go about bloated, and my daughter at that!"

"Yes, she can." A dangerous glint appeared in Alex's eyes. "I won't have her sacrificed on the altar of hypocritical morals and conventions. She's the victim here, remember?" She stared him down, and, finally, he lowered his eyes.

"I won't force her," he sighed, "of course not."

When Julian Allerton arrived a month or so later, he didn't agree. In his opinion, Sarah needed to be wed as soon as possible, preferably to an older, kindly man who would show her the forbearance and patience she deserved.

"No," Alex said.

To the minister's irritation, the priest agreed with her. "Not yet, she's far too distraught." Carlos smiled over to where Sarah was sitting with her sister and Temperance in the bower, a tangled mass of various shrubs.

Julian eyed Carlos from under creased brows. Proselytising among his flock – he didn't like it, not at all.

"She will begin to show shortly," Julian said. "Surely you don't want to expose her to the shame of rounding with child whilst unwed?"

"She was raped." Alex's brows pulled together in warning.

"Hmm." Julian stretched himself for the pitcher and served himself some more of the elderflower cordial. The evening air was heavy with the scent of roses from the

343

rosebush that clambered its way along the main door to the Graham home. A soft breeze came floating up from the river, and from somewhere behind the house drifted the enticing smells of barbecued meat – a feast in celebration of Mark's newborn child.

Julian gave Matthew a considering look, wondering if the moment was opportune to press his own case – he wanted Ruth to be given him as his wife as soon as possible, take her away from her shamed sister. A quick look over his shoulder, and there she was, dark red hair braided, white skin, and that soft, plump mouth. Instead, he cleared his throat and wondered if Matthew had heard the latest about the Ingram girl.

"Aye, they found her in a whorehouse down in Jamestown."

Julian shook his head in pity. No longer entirely sane, the poor girl had insisted she had no wish to leave, none at all. Covered in bruises, accustomed to spending her whole life in the room where she received the men the whoremaster sent her way, she had stared round in shock at being outside again.

"So now she stays at home, following her mam like a wee bairn around the farm, not saying a word." Matthew sighed. "Her, they will never find a husband for. What man would want to go where countless men have been before?"

Julian nodded, his eyes resting pointedly on Sarah, sitting some feet apart from Ruth and Temperance, a vacant look upon her face.

"Oh, for God's sake!" Alex rose to her feet. "It's different, okay?" She turned to her husband. "It is, isn't it?"

"I hope so," Matthew said, rearing back when Alex crashed the pitcher into shards in front of him. "Alex! What else do you expect me to say?"

"Eff off!" she snapped, running in the direction of the house. Eff off? Julian had never heard the expression before but, from the look on Matthew's face, it was not a kindly one.

Alex retreated to the kitchen, trying to work off all that anger that seemed to boil through her bloodstream. When Matthew popped his head in to see how she was faring, she felt her face crumple together, and in two swift steps, he'd crossed the floor to hold her to his chest.

"It's just…" She rubbed her cheek against his shirt.

"I know," he said, and she could hear it in his voice, just how devastated he was. They stood like that for a long time, so long in fact that Mrs Parson rapped Matthew on the shoulder and told him to make himself scarce – unless he planned on cooking, of course.

After supper, Julian shared his other news with them: news of unrest, of revolts in both Scotland and the South of England against the new king.

"The Duke of Monmouth intends to make himself king," he said, "and I dare say he's well supported in his ambitions by his Dutch cousin."

"Dutch cousin?" Alex sat down beside Ian. "Is that William the Third?" Ian coughed in warning while Thomas Leslie smiled indulgently at her.

"Yes, William of Orange." Thomas sucked deeply at his pipe. "His mother was King James' sister, and now he is wed to the king's eldest daughter."

"How incestuous." Alex wrinkled her nose.

"Cousins," Julian said. "Hope and I were cousins."

"Oh," Alex replied, peeking over to study his daughters for any signs of inbreeding. "I suppose it's different depending on where you come from. In Sweden, you must have a royal dispensation to wed your cousin."

"You must?" Julian sounded very interested. "And the king has time to look into such matters?"

"I suppose he has someone who does it for him."

"Who is king of Sweden?" Julian asked, his eyes intent.

Alex frantically gleaned her brain. Gustavus Adolphus was dead, that much she knew, and after him came Christina, but she was probably gone as well. So then, who? Oh yes, the big fat bloke who rode across the ice to invade Denmark from the south.

"Charles the Tenth."

Julian raised a brow. "I think not. He died in 1660."

"He did? Oh, how terrible! And me not even knowing!"

Alex was pretty impressed by her own performance, but very worried by the fact that Julian must have spent time informing himself about Sweden. Why had he done that? To her relief, Matthew cut the conversation short by suggesting they all taste Robert Chisholm's latest efforts at making dark ale.

"Will you manage?" Alex asked Matthew next morning, frowning down at his foot. It was still very tender, breaking up to bleed at any major strain, and after two weeks of harvest it looked decidedly the worse for wear.

"I have to," he snapped. He relented and leaned forward to touch her cheek with the back of his finger. "I'll come and find you if it hurts too much."

"Yeah, right." She wadded the space between his fifth and third toe with lint and applied a linen bandage round it, mainly to minimise chafing. She handed him his stocking, and rose from her knees to wash her hands at the basin.

"Julian has formally requested Ruth's hand in marriage," Matthew told her.

"Surprise, surprise," Alex mumbled, using her damp hands to smooth back a couple of escaped curls.

"As soon as possible," Matthew went on.

"As soon as..." Alex turned to face him. "We've said: they wait until she turns eighteen."

"Which is in four months."

"So they wait." Alex scraped some mud off her light brown summer skirts and stepped into them, efficiently tying them together at the back. She had to sew herself some new clothes, and Matthew as well. At present, he had but the breeches he was in and a pair of woollen winter breeches, and he was down to four shirts, excluding his best.

"He wants her to accompany them back to Providence, as his wife, so that they together can take Temperance up to Boston there to wed Daniel."

"In Boston? But..." They'd missed his ordination due to the whole Burley situation, and now they were apparently to miss his wedding. "We can go up there, can't we? And Ruth can go with us." She counted money in her head: yes, there

346

was enough to buy them passages back and forth.

"And Sarah?" Matthew asked.

"Sarah? Well, she can come too."

"No, that she can't," Matthew said, "and nor do I think she would want to expose herself to being looked over and gossiped about."

Alex sat down on her stool, deflated. "I suppose you'll have to go alone then. But Ruth remains unmarried – for now."

"Alex," Matthew groaned.

"No." She threw him an angry look and hurried down the stairs.

It didn't help to escape Matthew to avoid the subject of Ruth's wedding, because no sooner was Alex on hands and knees in her garden, but her eldest daughter joined her.

"Mama," Ruth begged, "you know I love him. Why should we be made to wait any longer?"

Alex didn't reply, concentrating on the cucumbers, squashing caterpillars and bugs as she went along.

"He wants me with him," Ruth said. "He says he lives my absence like a constant pain."

"Well, he would have a way with words. We've said December, and as far as I know, nothing has happened to change my mind on that."

"Aye, it has." Ruth nodded to where Sarah was crouched with Betty behind the raspberry bushes.

"Sarah?" Alex shaded her face. "What does she have to do with anything?"

Ruth squirmed. "It's…" She wet her lips. "It's not seemly, that a minister's future wife be living with an unwed and pregnant lass."

Alex took her time squishing the bug presently in her hand to death.

"And is this Julian's opinion or yours?"

"Ju…both." Ruth raised her chin.

"Ah. And of course you'll take it upon yourself to explain to your sister that you must wed on account of her shaming you by allowing herself to be raped – future wife of a minister that you are."

Ruth went a deep pink. "I don't mean it like that."

"And yet that is what you just said, isn't it?"

"Mama…"

"Get your work done," Alex said icily, "and then you can scurry off to read your Bible and meditate on the word compassion." She heard Ruth's hasty inhalation and knew she had hurt her to the quick, but at the moment she didn't care. And as for Julian…

A whole delegation of Graham men came to find Alex later that evening, walking slowly up the slope to where she was sitting beside Jacob's grave. She heard them talking amongst themselves, all three voices low and dark, and she felt a piercing grief for the voice that was missing, forever silenced.

She brushed with her hand over the new stone, traced the dates of his birth and death and mouthed his name: Jacob Alexander Graham, born on a cold December night in Scotland, a night that glimmered with stars, dead in a nondescript little clearing in the bright sun of a May day. She placed the wreath she had made of roses on his grave, and stood up, shaking her skirts free of dirt.

"It's a beautiful stone," she said to Matthew.

He flushed at her accolade, studying his handiwork critically. "I had the minister read something over him."

"Oh, really?" Alex adjusted her shawl to lie closer around her shoulders. "I don't think Jacob had need of any words from him." She emphasised the pronoun and went over to sit on the bench, crossing her legs.

"But I did," Matthew said, and Alex felt her cheeks heat.

She looked her men over one by one. "I take it this means I'm outvoted. The Graham men have come down on the side of the eager minister."

Ian winced at her tone, and came over to sit beside her, lowering himself slowly.

"Your back?" she asked, receiving an irritated look in return.

"None too bad," he replied.

"Ruth was very upset," Mark said.

"She bloody well should be," Alex snapped, recounting what Ruth had said.

"Aye," Ian agreed, "it came out a wee uncharitable, what she said."

"Putting it mildly," Alex muttered, folding her arms over her chest.

"But that doesn't take away the fact that she loves him," Matthew said, "and you've always said that we should let our bairns wed as they wished for love."

"Huh, right now I'm all for an arranged marriage – why not with Adam Leslie?" But she didn't mean that, and she knew that he knew that.

"And not only does she love him, but he loves her too," Mark put in.

"Great." Alex sighed and looked away. "We've already agreed to the marriage, but we also said they had to wait until she was eighteen. So what has changed?"

"Nothing," Matthew said.

"Good. So they wait." Alex got to her feet.

"I've said yes," Matthew told her from behind her. "I have agreed that they may wed now."

"Oh," Alex said. "And that was after talking things over with your sons, but not with your wife?"

"I already knew your opinion, and I don't agree. Ruth is well capable of wedding as she is now."

"Of course she is!" Alex wheeled to face him. "But we decided she had to wait!"

"She doesn't want to," Matthew answered, "and it should be her opinion that weighs the most."

"I don't think she'll be talking much to you tonight," Mark remarked as he watched Alex striding away.

"Nay, probably not." Matthew was slightly ashamed for having agreed things with Julian without speaking to Alex before, but this matter with Sarah had somehow made it very urgent for him to see his eldest daughter safely wed. "She'll come round," he said, wondering where she'd choose to spend the night. Not with him, not in their bed, of that he was sure.

Chapter 42

"I don't understand," Julian said. "Why are you so displeased? We are but moving the wedding forward somewhat."

"Let's just say I have a problem with hypocrites and leave it at that, okay?" Alex shoved by him.

"Hypocrites? And what, pray, do you mean by that?" Two bright red spots appeared on Julian's cheeks.

"You're a minister. You're supposed to be a good Christian, a man who leads by example. And have you? No. Somehow you insinuate Sarah is to blame for what has happened to her, you urge us to marry her off so as to avoid the public embarrassment of a pregnant daughter, and to top it all off, you have the temerity to suggest to Ruth that it might be inappropriate for her to live under the same roof as this fallen woman, her sister. I must say I thought more of you, Julian, but it turns out you're more like Minister Macpherson than I suspected – narrow-minded and tight-hearted – and I'm not particularly pleased in marrying Ruth off to you. But then, that isn't my decision anyway, is it? Oh no, that's a decision between men."

Julian's neck had gone as red as his cheeks during this angry speech, and he drew in breath to launch himself into a reply.

"Don't bother. Thank heavens there's at least one compassionate man of God amongst us." Alex waved her hand in the direction of Carlos who was sitting with Sarah and David, all three involved in a complicated chess game.

Julian glanced their way and looked back at her. "I am no hypocrite, and I have never suggested your Sarah brought what happened down upon herself. But I still insist you're inviting more danger into her life by not ensuring she is married, as soon as possible."

"Who would it help? Sarah? Are you saying you believe a raped girl should be coerced into marriage for the sake of her reputation? What do you think would happen to her when he took her to bed? What would she relive, night after night?"

Julian looked away, mumbling that he hadn't fully thought about that aspect.

"No, you wouldn't, would you? After all, you're a man." With that, Alex was off.

She saw Matthew come towards her, and took a sharp turn to the right. She had no desire to talk to him, so she swished her way through the long grass behind the barn, ducked between the slats of the fence round the meadow where they kept the cows, and increased her stride when she heard him behind her. A swim, she decided, making for the river. She needed a long, solitary swim, and then she'd be able to think more rationally about all this.

Ruth had apologised to Alex last night, repeating that of course she didn't mean it the way it had come out, and she truly loved her sister, and Mama knew that, didn't she? Which Alex did, hugging Ruth briefly. So why was she so angry? She sighed and stalked down the last yards to the water. Normally, when they had house guests, Alex was circumspect about where she undressed, but now she didn't care. If Julian had a heart attack because she flashed him, all the better, and as to what Matthew might think – well, he could stuff it.

She was a good swimmer, Matthew thought as he sat on the bank to watch her. Like an otter, she moved through the water, every now and then turning to float downstream and begin all over again. She'd seen him, even if she pretended that she hadn't, and he looked at her openly when she swam in towards the shallows where she kneeled while she scrubbed herself all over with silt from the river's bottom.

"Are you still angry with me?" he asked.

"I don't know. I'm just generally angry, I suppose."

"Ah." He nodded, and decided that as she was speaking

to him, he might just as well join her in the water. "Nice," he said, swimming back and forth out of reach from the current.

"I'm disappointed in Julian, I think, because what Ruth said, she'd heard from him, and I expected more of him. He *is* concerned about how it reflects on him if his future wife has a sister who gives birth out of wedlock."

"Hmm," Matthew said, paddling over to join her in the shallows. He privately thought she was right but unlike her, Matthew could understand Julian's concerns. He did some brisk scrubbing of his own, climbed out to sit on a sun-warmed rock, and helped her up to sit with him.

"And then of course, I'm really, really pissed with you that you'd agree to moving the wedding forward when I so clearly said I didn't want to."

"But how can it matter?" And such matters were his decisions anyway, but he wisely decided that was not a comment to make.

"I don't know. It's just that I think it will be very difficult for Sarah. There goes her sister, happily ever after, and what does the future hold for her? Motherhood she doesn't want, stigmatised forever, and how is she ever to dare let a man touch her again?" She rested back against him, his legs her armrests, and closed her eyes.

"I hadn't thought of that," Matthew said, stroking her wet hair off her forehead, "I just...I wanted to see Ruth safely wed. The sooner the better, after what happened to Sarah."

"One daughter in safe harbour?"

"Aye. Is that so wrong?"

"Of course not." She opened her eyes to look at him. "A small wedding, okay?"

"Okay." He smiled.

"Maybe Carlos can officiate."

Matthew laughed. "I don't think Julian would much appreciate being married under Catholic rites."

"As a matter of fact, there's no major difference. Both the Protestant and the Catholic Church make a big deal out of the obey part for the woman."

"As it should be," he teased. "Women are, after all, simple-minded creatures."

"Huh," she snorted.

The day before Ruth's wedding, Sarah threw a fit, upended two of Mrs Parson's pies, and stalked off into the woods. From where he sat in the shade, Carlos watched her go, and after some moments of irresolution, he stood and followed her, clutching his beads in his hand.

He had avoided being alone with her for some days, afraid of the way she made him feel with her swelling body and blue eyes. He prayed through the nights, he punished himself physically, he woke in panic to a member that stood hard and throbbing, and he knew – as did God – that he had been dreaming of her, of Sarah.

I'm a priest, he reminded himself. I have given myself over to serve God and the Holy Church, and once the promise is given, there is no way back. The moment he closed his eyes, she danced before him, and he found himself daydreaming of a life that included her, which made him sink even deeper into prayer as he begged that God give him guidance and strength to fight the temptation of a pregnant sixteen-year-old girl.

And still…like a lodestone she was, and when he saw her walk off weeping into the woods, what could he do but follow, telling himself that this was a lost soul in need of pastoral care.

"I want it gone," Sarah said when Carlos found her sitting on a fallen log several hundred yards into the forest. "I try to pray, to remind myself it isn't the baby's fault, but I wish it would die and slip out of me, leave me myself again." She rubbed her bloated face against the rough serge of her skirts. "Mama says it was the same for her, with Isaac. But she had a man to help her, a man she loved and trusted, while I…" She moaned into the cloth.

"Isaac?" Carlos had not really heard of this child, nor had he known Alex had been married twice.

"He's dead." Sarah frowned and gnawed at her lip. "She

says she hated him. Even when he was born, she hated him at first, and it was her man who cared for it because she couldn't bear to look at him. But I don't have a man, do I?"

"Maybe you should ask your father to find you one," Carlos said.

Sarah looked so stricken he took hold of her hands.

"Most men are good," he said gently. "Most men care for their wives."

"Even when they come damaged to the marriage bed?" She looked at him, despair shading her eyes. "How am I to stand a man's hands on me?"

Carlos cried inside for her, and moved close enough that she could lean against him, placing his arm around her. "I'm a man, and you seem to be able to stand my touch."

Sarah rubbed her cheek against the black of his cassock. "You're my friend, and your hands I trust and like."

¡Ay Dios! Carlos bent his face sufficiently that he could brush his nose over her gleaming hair.

On the anniversary of their very first meeting, on a heat infested August day twenty-seven years ago, Matthew surprised Alex by serving her breakfast in bed, waving away her protests that there was too much to do with the impending wedding.

"You can take your ease for some time," he said, shedding his breeches to slip back into bed beside her. He was content today. The harvest was in, and it had been a good year, enough to compensate for the lost crops of last year's burning. The fine litter of piglets that the sow had farrowed in the spring was growing into a herd of fat young pigs, and all that ham and meat would bring in a substantial amount at the autumn markets.

His back was fully healed, even if it was criss-crossed by ugly pink scars, his toe no longer throbbed quite as wildly as before, and the brand on his buttock bothered him but rarely. Physically, that is; mentally, it most certainly did, because every time Alex salved it, he remembered that other humiliation, seeing in his mind's eye how submissively he had stood on all fours when Walter took the place of his brother. No fight, no attempt to crawl away, just a silent praying that it would soon be over, that someone would place a gun to his head and shoot him.

He frowned in irritation at having his head taken over by these memories, and turned to his wife with something hidden in his fisted hand. "Here, happy anniversary, lass."

He watched her as she turned the little wooden sculpture round and round. In butternut, the wood a pale light yellow, he had carved an image of their son. Not as he had been at the moment of his death, because try as he might he couldn't capture the face of the young man, grief drowning out the details, but rather as he had been as a lad, a lad of sun-bleached hair and slanted hazel eyes, a strong and sturdy lad that regarded the world around him with open curiosity. A lad that dreamed of going places, of seeing Rome and Paris, mayhap even Jerusalem, and who now was rotting to soil in his far too early grave.

"Jacob," Alex said, her voice unsteady. "Just like he was." She managed a smile, her eyes wet and glinting in the morning light. "Thank you." She rested her head against his.

Later that same day, when the afternoon sun patterned the yard with shadows and dancing sunbeams, the whole Graham family stood outside, augmented by the Leslies who were, in Alex's opinion, more or less family anyway. Alex stood with her heart in her mouth, watched her Ruth exchange vows with Julian and smiled tearfully at the way the groom kissed his new wife reverentially on her brow.

A rustle behind her, and out of the corner of her eye, Alex saw Sarah break away, a swift silent shape that had her hand pressed to her mouth. She took a hesitant step, looked back at her husband, busy congratulating their daughter, took yet another step, and was arrested by a light touch on her sleeve.

"I'll go," Carlos said. "You must stay, for Ruth's sake."

"For Ruth's sake." Alex nodded, watching as this handsome young priest darted after her youngest daughter.

Chapter 43

"You're in love with her," Alex said, unstrapping the peg.

"I can't be in love with her. I'm a priest," Carlos snapped. He was in a foul mood, having quarrelled with the Chisholms before riding over, Robert pointing out that his flock was not at Graham's Garden, was it?

"Oh, and being ordained a priest emasculates you? Lie still!" Alex frowned down at his stump.

"I care for her," Carlos said.

"Of course, you do. That's why your eyes glue onto her the moment you see her."

"I'll leave," he said, struggling to sit against her hand.

"If you move again before I tell you to, I'll slap you," she threatened, spreading a thin layer of something green and fragrant on his skin. "And you can't leave, not now. You're the only person she turns to."

"I have to," he groaned. "I can't put my immortal soul at risk."

"So you admit it then: you love her."

"¡Sí!" he exploded, glaring at her. "Yes, I do, and God help me, because I have no idea what to do!"

"And running away seems a good, proactive solution to your little dilemma."

"I have nothing to offer her. I'm a priest, wedded to my Church. I can never undo those vows." It was his father's blood, contaminated and weak, that led him to even consider an alternative to remaining in Holy Orders. Blood will tell, as Uncle Raúl at times would say.

"But you weren't exactly given a choice in life, were you?" Alex tied the poultice into place. She motioned for him to lie down. "I'll be back in an hour to take it off." With his wooden peg under her arm, she left the room, ignoring his loud protests.

Alex was still holding Carlos' peg when a commotion broke out outside. Whoops of joy, repeated calls for Samuel, and she was out like a flash, running towards her son. By a scant yard, she beat Matthew to their son, and then Samuel was in her arms, and she was hugging him close, breathing in his scent, feeling how his long hair tickled her nose.

"Mama," Samuel protested. She sat back on her heels to look him over in detail, releasing him so that he could greet his father and the rest of the family.

"He's whole," Qaachow's voice assured her.

"I can see that," Alex replied, taking in this stranger that was her son. Gone was anything that had been soft, replaced by long, sinewy muscles, expanses of skin that glowed with health and sun. Beside him, David looked almost puny, despite being half a head taller, and the younger Graham boys stared at Samuel with a mixture of awe and fear.

Her son was clearly uncomfortable being the centre of all this attention. He fingered the knife that hung at his side, said something in a low voice to Little Bear, and took a step towards him. Little Bear raised his fingers to him, and Samuel set his own fingertips to meet those of his foster brother. Little Bear tilted his head, said something, and Samuel nodded, eyes flashing for an instant in Alex's direction.

"Will you stay and eat with us?" Matthew asked.

Qaachow bowed his head, and led his men to sit below the oak, accepting food and drink. All the time, he kept a vigilant eye on Samuel, smiling whenever his foster son met his eyes for guidance, which was often. Each and every one of those fleeting glances Alex noted, and it was as if a metal hand had closed around her heart. She waved her premonitions away, set pies and cake on the table, touched Samuel at every possible moment, but all the time there was a pressure in her chest. When she met Matthew's eyes, she saw her worry mirrored there, and that made it all so much worse.

"The Burleys?" Matthew asked Qaachow once the trestle tables were cleared away.

"Ah." Qaachow glanced at Sarah, eyes lingering for an

instant on her waist. "With child?"

Matthew's jaw tightened, just like it always did when someone reminded him of his daughter's condition.

Alex placed a comforting hand on his shoulder, gave it a little squeeze. "Are they dead?" she asked, requiring some kind of confirmation that neither Philip nor Walter would be coming back any time soon.

"She didn't want them dead," Qaachow said, "and so they are not."

"They're not?" She plunked down to sit, staring at him. "But they must be! How else are we to sleep safe?"

Qaachow's lips thinned into a cold smile. "They will not be coming back. I doubt they'll survive the winter. Besides, I've sold them well to the west of here."

"What...?" Alex cleared her throat but however gruesome, she needed to hear this. "What did you do to them?"

Qaachow hitched a shoulder: no tongues, no balls, the odd missing toe, and reduced to walking about in nothing but their own skin – just like Sarah had wanted it.

Alex ran her tongue over her teeth, pressed it against the roof of her mouth. "No tongues?" Was it at all possible to speak without a tongue?

"They deserved it," Matthew said viciously.

Well yes, maybe they did, but still...

"They paid," Qaachow said, "for what they did to your daughter, to your man, to countless other innocents, many of whom were women of my tribe." He nodded in the direction of Samuel. "He was there all the time."

"He's a boy." Alex looked at her son. "He shouldn't have to witness things like that."

"To us, he is nearly a man," Qaachow said.

As they were making their farewells, Qaachow drew Samuel aside.

"In one moon," he said.

"One moon," Samuel echoed, swallowing deeply.

"It is your choice, White Bear."

Samuel swallowed, torn in two. Was he Samuel or was

358

he White Bear? He looked over to where Little Bear was standing.

"I know, Father," he replied, "but that does not make it easier."

Qaachow rested a hand his shoulder. "Men make choices all the time," he said before slipping into the dusk.

Mama was overjoyed to have him back. Those first few days, she was like a leech, always touching, hugging. Samuel was made uncomfortable by her behaviour, so at odds with how he recalled her, and he was even more disconcerted by how she ate him with her eyes – blue, blue eyes that assessed his every gesture, his every facial expression.

It was getting to the point where he began to avoid her, but then, one day, he came into the house halfway through the morning and heard a muffled sound from the parlour. He tiptoed over to the door, and there was Mama, rocking back and forth in her chair with Jacob's herbal clutched to her chest. She was weeping, and he had no notion what to do, so he slipped away on silent bare feet and went to find his brother.

"She does that a lot lately," David said with a little shrug. "Da says it is terrible for any parent to lose a child, but perhaps most for the mother."

"Mmm." Samuel kicked at the ground, inundated by the image of his weeping mother, grieving for her son. They made their way up to the little graveyard and stood for some moments by Jacob's grave. Samuel caressed the stone, wondering what it felt like to be dead. David moved over to sit on the bench, and Samuel followed.

"I saw him dead." Samuel suppressed a shiver when a gust of wind rushed through the trees. Despite Mama's nagging, Samuel had refused to put on any more clothes than what he came in some days ago, and so he sat half-naked by his brother.

"So did I," David said. "Mama says he died bravely, rushing at those evil men to try to save our sister."

Samuel didn't reply. His Indian father said that it was a fool that charged armed men alone, brave but foolish, not at all a warrior. Qaachow had stood looking down at Jacob's still white face for a long time before pulling the blanket back to cover him.

"Life is something you only get once," he had said to his two sons. "It is not something to be squandered on futile gestures. To die while in battle is honourable and at times unavoidable, and all men must face their death with courage, no matter in which shape it comes, but to throw it away, no, that is wrong."

Samuel had flown in heated defence of his dead brother, and Qaachow had listened to him before placing a hand on his head. "He lies dead, and what did he achieve by it? Nothing."

When they had found Da next morning, Samuel was prone to agree. Had Jacob bided his time and held his temper in check, none of what had been done to Da would have happened.

"Does it feel the same?" David asked, breaking through Samuel's memories.

"What?"

"Being back home."

Samuel hitched his shoulders, and pulled up his legs beneath him, scratching at a scab on his knee.

"I don't know. I no longer know what is home."

He tried. Pathetically, Samuel tried to find his place among his family again, but something indefinable had changed in him, and he had the sensation of standing outside himself and watching as the lad that was Samuel tried to find his way back to the surface.

He was shy around his brothers, preferring the company of the younger children who were content to just sit beside him in silence, their legs swinging in rhythm with his own. He called out that this time it was he that should be d'Artagnan, tussling with David over the wooden sword, but his heart wasn't in this game of make-believe, not now that he was nearly a man.

He did his share of the hard threshing work, and didn't notice until it was too late that, while the other lads were flagging, he was keeping up with the men, submerged in his own internal beat. David gave him a long look, took off his shirt and tightened his grip on his flail, and suddenly it was a serious competition that Samuel allowed his older brother to win.

He sat in the midst of his large, boisterous family over meals, and one part of him was happy to be there, reaching for bread warm from the oven, butter and cheese, while the other wished himself back to gourds of spiced squash stews, to Thistledown's low voice as she told her sons of the mysteries of the wilderness that surrounded them. He'd go to bed with David and Adam, but somewhere through the night, he'd slide out of bed to lie on the floor, close enough to the window that he could see the skies. And, all the time, he was aware of Mama's eyes, a silent, imploring gaze that was averted the moment he turned towards it.

"You can't go around like that anymore," David told Samuel a few weeks into September. The days were still agreeably warm, but mornings and evenings were tinged with the promise of autumn, raising goose pimples on Samuel's uncovered skin. "You're no Indian, you're a white man."

Samuel regarded his scant clothes and looked back at his brother. "I am as much Indian as white."

"Nay, you're not!" David snorted. "You're white, like me, and soon you will be coming with me and Malcolm to Providence and attend school there. In breeches and shirt, mind."

"No, I won't be going to Providence. I won't live away from the woods." Samuel's eyes flew in panic to the surrounding wilderness.

"Aye, you will," David said. "It's what Da wants."

"No!" Samuel swivelled on his toes and ignoring David's calls, rushed headlong into the wooded slopes that embraced the Graham home.

He was sitting in the clearing that had once housed an Indian village, but that now was a place of utter destruction and desolation, when Da found him. Samuel sneaked him a look: Da was limping, face set as he approached him.

"What happened here?" Samuel asked.

"I did that," Matthew said, "after Qaachow took you away, last year."

Samuel looked at him with astonishment.

"I nearly died, I got trapped beneath yon tree."

"For me? You did all this because of me?" Samuel took in the demolished barrows, the uprooted saplings.

"Aye, for the loss of you. It tore at me, to see you carried away from me, and I raged that I couldn't stop it from happening, that I didn't do something to keep you safe from that promise I gave so many years ago." He gave Samuel a perceptive look and sighed profoundly. "I gave you to him for a year, but he has stolen you from me, hasn't he?"

Samuel's tongue lay heavy and useless in his mouth. He didn't know how to explain, not without hurting them both, and yet he had to. Men make choices all the time, he reminded himself, and he was eleven, halfway to being a man. In less than two years, his hair would be shorn into a crest, his body decorated with tattoos to show he was a man, an Indian man. A hunter, a warrior, a man who roamed free in the woods, not a man tied to one place by fields and beasts.

"I'm one of them," he finally said, "and I'm one of you too." He tore at the moss beneath his bare soles. "At first, I wept for you. Every night, I wept for you, and I was forbidden to think of you or utter your names or even say my prayers. And when I did, I was punished, and my Indian father spoke for hours about the new me, White Bear. I was led to spend nights all alone in the dark, without a fire or a blanket or anything to eat. I was told not to sleep but to listen for the sounds in the dark, to allow the spirit of He That Creates Everything to descend on me."

"You must have been very frightened," Da said.

Samuel shrugged. "Aye, I was. And then, one day, Qaachow told me to follow him, and we walked for several hours, and it was very cold, and there was snow in the air, and my fath...Qaachow told me how I was to stay three nights by myself, and that then I had to find my way back on my own. I began to cry, but he said how men don't weep. Children do and women, but men they don't weep, and was I not more of a man than a child?" He hunched together at the memory of those horrible winter nights, a slight shiver flying up his spine. "And then he left me. And I was forbidden to leave until three nights had passed, so I didn't." He smiled fleetingly at Da.

"Little Bear told me afterwards how our mother berated our father for leaving me out in weather such as that, but that our father had said that either I came back or I didn't. And I did, and he was so proud of me."

"The priest was still there at the time, and he was in a poorly way. They didn't much like it when he spoke to them of God, and even less they liked it when he spoke to me in English, seeing as I was forbidden to talk that tongue. Not that it helped much. Every evening, before I fell asleep, I would lie and tell you all about my day, in English. I was that scared I'd forget it otherwise." He fell silent, his hand fingering the knotted string of twine around his neck: 365 knots, one for each day away from them.

"Qaachow was worried the priest would die, so we brought him back, and Mama saw me, and I thought she would die in the swollen, icy river, so I disobeyed my father and threw myself in the water, and he was very angry with me afterwards. She was quite something," he continued, turning to look at Da. "Mama, throwing herself in the waters for my sake."

"Aye, she was. A fool, mostly," Da said, but Samuel could hear the pride in his voice.

They shared a common smile, and Samuel reclined against him, liking the way Da's arm came round him to hold him close.

"It began to change sometime after that." Samuel retook his story. "There would be days when I didn't think once of you, and at times I struggled remembering the words of the Lord's Prayer. But I never forgot to tie the knot, nor did I forget your names. But I was more White Bear than Samuel, brother of Little Bear, son of Qaachow and Thistledown, brother to the newborn baby who still is nameless. At least once a month, we were taken out into the woods, all of us lads, to spend one or more nights on our own, and I would sit and hear the Only One talk to me, filling me with his spirit and strength."

He bent his head to fiddle with his amulet pouch, very aware of how green Da's eyes were, and of the moisture that shone in them.

"I am one of them now, Da. My blood runs with them. I don't feel comfortable in my own skin here." He looked pleadingly at Da. "I can't live behind doors and walls. I can't stay with you, nor go to school in Providence with David. It would make me die inside. I want to go back out there, to the forests that are my people's home."

The silence went on and on. Da stared straight ahead, his throat working repeatedly, and it came to Samuel that Da was working hard not to weep. Da's free hand trembled where it lay on his thigh, and Samuel had no idea where to look or what to say.

At last, Da cleared his throat. "You know that I can say no and you must obey. I can send you off as an apprentice to Providence or Jamestown, and you must go, for you are my son, not his."

Samuel nodded, biting down on his wobbling lower lip. Men don't weep, he reminded himself.

"And you will bide by my decision, you hear? If I say no, then you stay here."

Samuel nodded again.

"I told you." Mrs Parson sighed, setting down a brimming mug of ale in front of Matthew before joining him and Alex at the kitchen table. "A lad that young to be given into the keepings of the Indians..." She shook her head.

Alex had her face hidden in her hands, watching with distraction as slow tears plopped down on the table surface.

"Bloody *annus horribilis* this is turning out to be. One son dead, one son deciding he wants to go native, and our daughter..." Alex had known the moment she saw him so changed – hell, she'd known already back in May – and these last few weeks had only served to underline that her Samuel was in fact permanently lost, submerged into White Bear, no longer hers. She wanted to hit someone, to kick and shriek, but what would it help? Curse you, Qaachow, she thought. Damn you for wriggling your way into my son's heart and stealing him away from me forever.

"My son, my wee lad lost to me, and all because of that rash promise…" Matthew looked shell-shocked. Alex took his hand, and it lay limp and unresponsive in hers. She wiggled her fingers to braid them with his and squeezed. He turned unseeing eyes her way, eyes that were uncommonly dark.

"So when is he leaving?" Mrs Parson asked.

Matthew's brows pulled together into an impressive scowl. "He isn't leaving. Not unless I let him. I decide, and he obeys."

"And inside he will shrivel and die, and the moment he is old enough, he'll disappear anyway," Alex said.

Mrs Parson muttered an agreement. Her white head of hair glimmered eerily in the weak light of the single tallow candle, and she fiddled with her old-fashioned square lace collar, smoothing it down to lay straight and unwrinkled against her bodice.

"You can compromise, no?" she said. "See it as an apprenticeship. The lad must be home for harvest, mayhap at spring planting or Hogmanay as well. That way, he will still retain his ties with you, with all of us."

"And for how long do you think he'd live by that?" Alex asked.

"A long time, I reckon. The lad loves you both very much, of course he does. But if you force him to choose…" Mrs Parson left it hanging in the air, but Alex could see Samuel streaking off into the woods, never to return.

"And his spiritual well-being?" Matthew's voice was sharp. "What of living like a heathen, far from the word of God?"

"Send along a Bible," Mrs Parson said, "and you can catechise him every time you see him."

Alex laughed despite everything at the sudden, ludicrous

image of an adult Samuel in Indian garb sitting patiently on a stool while his father sternly took him through the Bible.

"And that way he keeps his reading skills, no?" Mrs Parson added in a very practical voice.

Samuel stood in silence and listened to the conditions laid down by his parents: Bible to be read regularly; at least twice a year, he was to come home to Graham's Garden, once for harvest and once for New Year; he was to pray every night in English and remember them all in his prayers.

"And if you don't know your Bible, I'll be mightily upset with you," Da said. "I might in fact have you shipped off to school to learn it, aye?"

Samuel smiled up at him, recognising his words as an idle threat.

"I assume Qaachow will bide by this as well."

"Aye," Samuel nodded, "he will."

Four weeks after he had come home, Samuel shed his white identity. White Bear – that was who he was, no longer a divided being hanging in between two worlds, but an Indian like his father and his brother. But in his hands he clutched the bundle that contained his Bible, and his eyes were misty with unshed tears as he studied Mama and Da, both of them standing shrunk and silent on the opposite shore.

"I have run a knife into their hearts," he said.

Qaachow placed a comforting hand on his back. "They will live, White Bear. They have many sons and daughters, grandchildren that fill their lives with sound and laughter."

"But they had only one Samuel Isaac, and him they will mourn as long as they live."

"Do you regret your choice then?" Qaachow asked him.

White Bear wiped at his eyes. "No, Father, I do not. But that doesn't mean it doesn't hurt."

"No," Qaachow said, "and that is yet another lesson learnt. All the important choices in life come at a price."

White Bear looked again at the two white people on the other side of the river, saw Da raise his hand in a wave while Mama hid her face against Da's chest. She had not been capable of bidding him farewell, eyes swollen slits in a face so bloated by weeping that it had made his stomach contract with shame. All she'd done was hold him, fingers sinking so hard into his back White Bear suspected there were bruises decorating his skin.

"I love you," he whispered in their direction. "I will always love you." And then he turned to pad silently behind his father.

Chapter 44

The days immediately after Samuel's leaving were taken up by the last of the harvest work and the hectic preparations before sending Mark, Ian, Betty and John down to Providence for the Michaelmas markets. Even worse, David was to go as well, and this time Matthew refused to listen to Alex's pleas that he be kept at home, telling her the boy needed his schooling.

So Alex shoved all thoughts aside, submerging herself in pickles and packing and writing horribly long lists that made Ian groan, saying they would need to buy more mules to bring all this back home. Alex huffed, described in detail to Betty just what buttons she wanted for Matthew's new breeches, before instructing Sarah how to fold the embroidered linens that were to be sold. She spent hours with David, bored him to tears with all her rules about vegetables and teeth cleaning, and embarrassed him more than once by hugging him far too publicly. The last night, she didn't sleep at all, standing in the kitchen swearing over the big stone jars she was attempting to close.

"If I see another jellied trotter, I think I'll throw up." Alex relinquished the obstructive lids to Matthew.

"You've never liked them," he said, smiling at her.

She sat down at the table, pulling the plate of half-eaten cake towards her.

"God, I'm tired." She pillowed her head in her arms and looked at him. "Spices," she murmured, "I have to add that to the list. That and vinegar and oils and..." She yawned and closed her eyes against the first rays of eastern sun. "Once they're on their way, I think I'll have a bath. I bloody well deserve one."

*

"I thought you were leaving," Sarah said to Carlos when they took their customary walk down to the river and back.

"I'm supposed to, but I find myself struck down by a most serious affliction, making it impossible to travel."

"Oh?" She laughed. "And what illness is this? Is it contagious?"

He looked at her and smiled. It's called love, he thought. An illicit love I shouldn't be feeling.

"Severe fungus in my stump," he said instead, and at her disgusted expression laughed. "No, *hija*, I have no mushrooms growing out of my leg, but who is to know that but me? And your mother," he added, grimacing in recollection of her last inspection. She had been very angry with him, going on about hygiene while she rather roughly cleaned his leg. "Do you want me to go?" he asked, breaking a comfortable silence between them.

"What?" Sarah looked startled. "No, of course I don't. I'm glad you're staying. Very glad." She looked at him from beneath lowered lashes, and Carlos felt himself beginning to flush. "As a good friend, of course," she hastened to add. "My best friend, actually."

He was very pleased, and impulsively took her hand.

"Does he know, do you think, that he's in love with her?" Matthew asked Alex, watching their daughter let go of the priest's hand as if it were red-hot when they stepped into sight.

"He does, and it plagues him. Poor man, he doesn't stand a chance in hell the moment she decides to set her sights on him."

"She could do worse," Mrs Parson piped up.

Alex threw her an irritated look. "You're supposed to be half-deaf with age. Instead, you have the hearing of a watchdog."

"If I didn't, I wouldn't find out half of what is going on, would I?" Mrs Parson replied, unperturbed.

"Hmph," Alex said, before reverting to the original subject. "He's a Catholic priest. His ordination is a sacrament that can never be reversed, he can never marry her, at least not under Catholic rites, and how is he to support them should he leave the Church?"

"He can't very well remain a priest and have carnal knowledge of Sarah on the side, can he?" Mrs Parson asked.

"Nay," Matthew said, "not unless he wishes to lose yet another part of his anatomy."

Mrs Parson studied her knitting and nodded in satisfaction at the perfect rows of knits and purls. "You don't need to worry. The wee man is honourable, aye? And your lass is not about to let a man fondle her intimately, is she?"

"Unfortunately," Alex said in a sad undertone.

After days of intense work came a strange couple of weeks, days filled with mushroom picking and berrying, evenings long stretches of silence between her and Matthew as they sat numbed by this their latest loss. The absence of her boys was a permanent ache in Alex's heart, and while one she could openly grieve, sitting often by his grave, the other was still alive but lost nonetheless. Where David had begun carving in Samuel's name a year ago in the nearby tree, Alex now added his middle name and his birth date.

"He isn't dead," Matthew remonstrated when he saw what she had done.

"He might as well be. We should have kept him here, with us."

"That isn't what you said at the time," Matthew said with something of an edge.

"I know, and I'm not blaming you. If anything, I'm blaming myself for giving up too soon. But it was so awful to watch, wasn't it? How he rose each day and squared himself, made this huge effort to try and be like he used to be. But it was all pretence, his heart wasn't in it, and it was as if there was no light in him. And when you told him he could go, he began to glow again." She dragged her hand across her eyes. "He's happy now, I think, and maybe that should be enough. After all, that's what any mother wants – that her child be happy." She caught his eyes with her own and gave him a wobbly smile. "But it isn't, Matthew, and I just hurt."

"So do I, lass," he said, helping her to stand. Golden

green, his eyes were in the low autumn sun, eyes shadowed by far too much loss and pain in far too short a time. She wondered if the same dark lived in the bottom of her own eyes, if it stood as easily to read. From the way his fingers came up to graze her cheek, her brows, she suspected it did.

She stood on tiptoe to brush his hair off his brow. "We'll just have to cope," she said.

"Aye," he sighed, sliding his arms round her waist. She rested her head on his chest, just above his heart, and they stood like that for some time, oblivious to the rising wind.

"Sarah?" Alex found her sitting slumped by the parlour fire, the mending in her lap forgotten. In her hand was a rosary, and from the way she flicked her fingers over the beads, this was something she'd been doing for quite some time. Alex suppressed a sigh. Matthew wouldn't be pleased by this overt papist praying.

Sarah started at the sound of her name, turning wary eyes in her direction.

"Are you alright?" Alex did a quick, instinctive inspection. Apart from the by now obvious swell, Sarah looked very well.

"I was thinking of Carlos." Sarah tucked the rosary out of sight.

"Oh." Alex sat down to do some needlework of her own. She didn't push, assuming Sarah would tell her in her own good time.

"He loves me," Sarah blurted.

"I know, and that puts him in something of a quandary, doesn't it? Caught between his heart and his religious obligations." Alex squinted to thread her needle, cursed when she missed the first few times, and looked up at Sarah. "Has he told you that he loves you?"

Sarah shook her head, her lower lip curving into a smile. "But I know."

"And you? Do you love him?" Alex thought this must be the most surreal conversation she had ever had, discussing with her pregnant daughter if she loved a Catholic priest.

She heard the rustle of cloth as Sarah moved on her stool, but kept her eyes on the fabric in her hands.

"I'm not sure." Sarah made a small sound at the back of her throat and went back to her sewing. "I think I need him now, but I don't know if I will need him afterwards."

"He's a man struggling with his vows," Alex said, "and, if you're not sure, you'd better back away – for his sake. It's a life-altering crisis for him to fall in love, and he's twisting with guilt."

"But how am I to know if I don't…"

"If you don't what?" Alex asked.

"Try," Sarah said.

Alex dropped Matthew's half-finished shirt into her lap. "You can't try, for his sake, you can't. Either you decide that he is the man you want, and whatever the complications – and by the way, they are enormous – we will try to help you, or you decide he isn't, and he can still be your friend. A friend you talk to, share secrets with, but don't hold hands with."

Sarah flushed at this. "But how do I know?"

Alex shrugged. "I can't help you with that, honey. You just do – or you don't." She returned her attention to the shirt, and as Sarah apparently had nothing more to say, they spent the coming hour in companionable silence.

"…and in my opinion, she isn't really in love with him. It's just that he's safe, a man she trusts because he's held in check by vows." Alex rubbed her hands with her latest concoction, a quite pleasing salve that smelled of roses and lemon, and as she was anyway at it, continued with her elbows and her knees. She bit back a smile at the way Matthew's shoulders slumped in relief. "So it's better that she's unwed and pregnant than that she marries a disgraced Catholic priest?"

He gave her a black look. "Out of two ills, it's the lesser."

Alex nodded in agreement. "It would mean spiritual chaos for him, and, even worse, he'd be repeating the transgression of his father." She frowned slightly. "But I suppose he'll have to do that, someday. Otherwise, how will that future Ángel Muñoz ever be?"

"He has cousins," Matthew said.

Alex wasn't entirely convinced. The physical similarities between Carlos and that future man were far too many. "Anyway, if she really loves him, we have a major conundrum on our hands. He can never marry her as a Catholic, and I doubt he'll want to convert, so I suppose that means they'll have to live in sin." From behind her, she heard a strangled sound, two eyes nailed into hers through the looking glass.

"That they will not," Matthew hissed, and when Alex burst out laughing, he heaved himself with surprising ease out of the bed and chased her into a corner before carrying her squealing back to bed.

Thomas Leslie had fallen into the habit of riding over on a regular basis for some hours of conversation and a chess game or two with Matthew.

"I don't understand why I persevere," he sighed, regarding the devastation that was his side of the chess board. "He can beat me blindfolded."

"Probably," Alex agreed, sharing an amused smile with Matthew. "Maybe you should try something else instead?"

Thomas gave her a resigned look. "He wins at that as well." He stretched himself for the pewter mug of brandy and sipped, patting the front of his coat for his pipe. The conversation turned to other things, mainly the news from England regarding the fate of the Duke of Monmouth.

"…the poor man, however much a royal bastard he might be, was dragged out for execution on Tower Hill," Thomas said. "It took five blows with the axe before they got his head off."

"Eeuuw!" Alex wrinkled her nose. "How terrible."

"He could have been hung, drawn and quartered, so just having his head chopped off was something of a reprieve." Matthew shook her head. "And the Dutchman sat on his hands."

"This being William?" Alex asked.

Thomas nodded. "Waiting in the wings, he is. Wed to James' eldest daughter, it's but a matter of time before England falls to him."

"Yon James might still have a son, no?" Mrs Parson said. "His wife is young, isn't she?"

"He might," Matthew said, "but I fear that wouldn't endear him to the English parliament. No, Alex is right in her earlier assessment: one Catholic king they can tolerate, a Catholic dynasty…no, I fear not." He looked away. "Not that it will help all those young deluded wretches presently held in gaol all over England, all of them guilty of treason on account of following the duke into the battlefield. They can expect no mercy, no leniency. It will be a bloodbath, I fear."

Halfway through December, Alex woke to a world of silent white. Using the sleeve of her chemise, she cleared a spyhole in the windowpane and looked out on a transformed world. Trees sparkled like jewels in the sun, the conifers standing like a dark background to better display the frost that decorated the latticed branches of the maples and the oaks, the plane trees and the odd birch. A few feet over the ground hovered veils of snow mist, tendrils of white that floated and undulated before dissipating with the rising sun.

"Oh!" She had never seen this much snow here before. Windblown drifts lay against the grey of the buildings, and when a couple of minutes later she opened the kitchen door, a small avalanche of dislodged snow flowed in to cover her floor.

"Holy Matilda!" she said, ignoring Carlos' displeased frown. "This is two, almost three feet of snow." She turned to the priest. "*Mala suerte*, too bad, it seems you'll have to stay on some more days."

Carlos came to look outside. "I can't walk in that."

"You generally ride, don't you?" Alex said. "But even your mule would find this hard going."

Adults as well as children spent most of the morning outdoors, building snow lanterns, competing in making the best snow angels, and, of course, taking part in a ferocious snowball fight where it was suddenly women against men, and Betty, Naomi, Sarah and Alex retreated behind one of the sheds to rearm and discuss strategy.

"Agnes is no bloody use," Alex grumbled. "She has the aim of a drunken chicken." She was expertly moulding snowballs, filling her apron with as many projectiles as possible.

"They're behind the stables," Sarah hissed. "They plan on coming at us from the side." She was big with child by now, but this was a fact Sarah preferred to ignore, her eyes narrowing dangerously whenever someone suggested she should take into consideration her delicate state. In fact, sometimes Alex worried that Sarah very much on purpose exerted herself well beyond what she should, hoping no doubt to rid herself of the baby. Not that Alex intended raising the subject with her, at least not now, when her youngest daughter was flushed and bright-eyed, looking young and carefree.

"So we go the other way," Alex said, and led her whole team into an elegant ambush that resulted in her running like a hare with Matthew bounding after her.

"Let me go!" She laughed as he brought her down in the snow. "You weigh a ton, you do!"

He grinned down at her, crumbled a snowball into her face and, once she had given up and kissed the victor on the mouth at least ten times, helped her up.

"I have snow all the way up my legs," Alex complained. "It's freezing my arse off." She yelped when his cold hand came exploring up her skirts. "What are you doing?"

"Brushing the snow off you," he said, wriggling his cold fingers in between her clenched thighs. "And warming my hand."

Later, they all sat crammed around the kitchen table, drinking rose hip soup with bread fresh from the oven. The room smelled of damp wool, clouts that needed changing, warm bodies, and, over it all, the fragrant and promising smell of meat pies in the making.

"Isn't it about time you give me your secret recipe?" Alex asked Mrs Parson.

"Why?" Mrs Parson said. "Are you worried I may topple over dead at any moment?"

Alex gave her a considering look. "Actually, it wouldn't surprise me if you live to over a hundred."

"Me neither," Mrs Parson replied comfortably. "Don't forget to remember me in your will, aye?"

"Oh, I won't." Alex grinned.

The children begged to be let out again, and once the women had finished the laborious process of wrapping them in shawls, putting on extra stockings and tying straw-filled boots and shoes to fit, the kitchen relaxed into almost silence, the adults sitting content in the bright shards of sunlight that cut in through the windows. Naomi and Mark were the first to break up, and then Ian and Betty stood, with Betty muttering something about seeing to Ian's back. Sarah asked Carlos if he wanted to play chess, they ducked off into the parlour, and Mrs Parson rolled her eyes wickedly at Alex.

"I reckon it isn't much of a challenge for the lass." She grinned. "Him making cow's eyes at her, incapable of even remembering how the pieces move."

"Hmm," Alex said. After her conversation with Sarah some weeks back, it was obvious to Alex that her daughter had taken several steps back from what had been on the verge of becoming a romantic relationship, but there were moments when she'd catch Sarah regarding Carlos with an avid interest well beyond the limits of casual friendship. He was good-looking, Alex admitted to herself, in fact very good-looking, peg and all... "I think it's good that he hasn't been here quite as frequently lately."

Mrs Parson made a very amused sound. "Oh aye? And have you never heard of distance making the heart grow fonder? The poor man is besotted with her, however much he struggles against it." She liked the wee papist, she added, for all that he was soft around the edges and given to self-pity. So much did she like him that she hoped he would see Sarah for what she was: a possible way to salvation in that he could convert to their faith and wed her, thereby performing a good deed by sparing her the shame of birthing a bastard. Not that Mrs Parson supposed Carlos had much chance of achieving a state of grace anyway, given his Catholic past, but at least he wouldn't be automatically damned to hell as he was right now, poor man.

Matthew listened to all of this and grunted, conveying just how disturbing he found this whole conversation.

"He'll never convert," Alex said. "His faith is as important to him as yours is to you."

"And the lass?" Mrs Parson asked. "Is she not important to him?"

"Unfortunately for him, yes," Alex sighed.

"Mayhap it would be best if I forbade him to come," Matthew said.

"Forget it. She needs him, okay? When none of us could reach her, he could."

He gave Alex a defeated look, but nodded. She omitted to tell him she also suspected Carlos was slowly but safely acquiring a convert of his own, thinking this was something that would keep – for now.

The warm, sunlit kitchen buzzed with peace. Matthew sat back and gathered Alex to him. Mrs Parson retired for a nap, and it was only them, the crackling of the fire, and the muted sounds of the children playing in the snow. So many children… If she closed her eyes, she could imagine she was hearing her own brood: the high, childish whoops of Mark and Jacob, Daniel as he angrily charged after Sarah, Ruth, David and Samuel, Adam, a laughing adolescent Ian…and Rachel, her peals of laughter ringing in the air. She rubbed her cheek against Matthew's chest, and his hand came up to knead her softly behind her ear. She almost purred, arching herself against his touch.

"I wish we'd been there for Daniel's wedding," she said drowsily.

"Mmm," he agreed, extending his legs before him.

Ruth had penned a very detailed description, not only of the wedding but of Boston as such, and Daniel had written as well, a letter that began stiff with the new found formality of husband and minister, but ended in genuine concern for their well-being. Sarah had clutched her own letter from him hard to her chest, and whatever he had written it had made her smile and cry at the same time.

"The pastor tending his flock," Alex had murmured at the time, thinking that at present, Sarah had quite a few interested pastors, with both Julian and Ruth writing long, encouraging epistles along the lines that God burdened as he saw fit, but helped the faithful carry. Very supportive…

"The brother comforting his sister," Matthew had reprimanded. None of them knew, as that particular letter was never shared with them.

The kitchen was suddenly full of shades: of long dead Rachel, darting from one corner to the other; of Jacob, his slow smile lighting his eyes, his precious herbal heavy on his knees; and of Samuel, standing to the side in buckskins and feathers. But Samuel wasn't dead, Alex reminded herself, he was safe and happy – somewhere else. And nor was Sarah. She was still alive, still here.

"What a terrible year this has been," Alex said. "Please God that we never have to experience something like this again."

Matthew kissed her hair. "Amen to that." His arm lay heavy round her shoulders, and he reclined against the wall.

Alex snuggled closer and yawned. Vaguely, she heard Sarah laugh, and smiled in response. "As long as there's life, there's hope," she murmured, pillowing her head over his beating heart.

"Mmm?" Matthew said.

"Nothing." She kissed his throat. "Love you," she said.

He glanced down at her and smiled, that long mouth of his softening. "Do you, now?"

She nodded, her eyes trapped by his.

"Show me." He cupped her chin to raise her face towards his. "Show me just how much you love me."

Alex rose to her feet, took him by the hand, and led him upstairs.

The Graham Saga continues in:

Wither Thou Goest

Uncharacteristically for Maryland, this winter had seen more snow than Alex Graham had ever experienced before. Huge, heavy snowfalls melted into a muddy sludge over a couple of days, and then there was a new blanket of snow, yet more mud.

Today was one of the muddy days. Alex had to tread carefully as she made her way across the yard to the laundry shed with a small bundle of linens under her arm. There could be no major wash until the weather improved, but a couple of shirts, some shifts and her single flannel petticoat she could hang to dry inside the shed, and, while she was at it, she was planning on submerging herself in a hot tub of water as well.

It was the second week of February 1686. The shrubs were beginning to show buds, here and there startling greens adorned the wintry ground. Alex lifted her face to the sky and drew in a deep breath. She could feel it shifting. Winter was waning, and soon it would be brisk winds, leaves on the trees, and weeks and weeks of toiling in the fields or the vegetable garden.

"About time," she muttered, slipped in the mud, took a hasty step forward, and had her clog sink with a squelch into a particularly soft spot. She stood like a one-legged stork, bending down to yank it loose.

"Bloody hell!" she said when she overbalanced and fell forward.

"Aren't you a wee bit too old to play in the mud?" Matthew grinned at her from some feet away.

Alex scooped up some mud and sent it to land like a starburst on his worn everyday coat. "Oops." She smiled, feeling a childlike urge to engage in a full-scale mud fight.

"Clean that off," Matthew mock-threatened, taking a few steps towards her.

"Make me." She managed to get her clog free, and sprinted like a hare on ice skates towards the laundry shed. Matthew came after, which made her run faster and laugh harder, so that, by the time she'd broken the world record on the fifty-yard mud dash, she was gasping for air, her hair had come undone, and her cheeks were very warm.

"Got you." Matthew pinned her against the wall.

"..." Alex replied, struggling to get some air back down into her lungs. And the stays weren't exactly helping.

Matthew released his hold. "Hoyden," he said, rubbing at a streak of mud on her face. "All of fifty-three, and still incapable of keeping yourself neat and clean."

"You, mister, you're pushing fifty-six, and look at you! Mud all over the place!" She wiped her hands on his breeches.

Ian walked past leading Aaron, the big bay stallion, and shook his head at them. "You're old," he said, his lip twitching. "Very old, aye? Grandparents should act with more dignity."

"Huh, as a matter of fact, I was sedately crossing the yard to do some washing when your father here attacked me."

"Nay, he didn't. You fell flat on your face all on your own, Mama. Go and wash," Ian added before going on his way, clucking to Aaron to come along.

"Go wash, he said. What does he think we are? In our dotage and in need of a father figure?" Alex stuck her tongue out in the general direction of her stepson and pushed the door to the shed open, smiling when she entered this her almost favourite place.

Over the years, what had been a hastily constructed lean-to, meant mainly to house the huge kettle, the rinsing trough and all other paraphernalia associated with the tedious and heavy work of ensuring the laundry got done, had developed into a solidly built little house with soaped floors, broad wall benches and, standing in place of pride, the wooden tub – big enough to seat two. The small space was at present agreeably warm thanks to the fire Alex had lit earlier, the air suffused with the scents of lavender and crisp mints.

Along the back wall, drying herbs hung in bunches. On a small shelf stood stone jars of oils and salves, pots of soap, and an assortment of lanterns. The only thing that was missing, in Alex's opinion, was a tap from which to turn on running water and huge terrycloth towels. Neither of those had even been invented yet, as she was prone to reminding herself, just as cars and washing machines and phones were still centuries away from materialising.

"Are you just going to slouch against the wall and look decorative or are you going to help?" she asked Matthew who had followed her inside.

"Oh, I don't mind looking decorative," he said, but came over to help her with the heavy cauldron. She set the few garments to soak with lye in a bucket, forcefully brushed the mud stains off his woollen breeches and coat, and then he helped her do the same with her skirts, stretching the fabric for her.

"I'll never get this off," she grumbled, inspecting the broad kneecaps of mud. "And look at my bodice!" The sleeves were encrusted with mud to halfway up the elbow, and once she had taken that garment off, the chemise beneath was just as dirty. Alex peeled it all off, hung her stays to sway on a hook, dunked the shift and petticoat in with all the other stuff, and found a bristle brush with which to attack the bodice. Matthew sat down on one of the benches and regarded her as she moved around, covered in her shawl and nothing else.

"It's impolite to gawk," Alex said sternly.

"Aye, but 'tis my right. You're my wife and I can gawk at you as much as I like."

"Glad you like it." Alex arched her back and winked, making him laugh.

They talked about this and that while she did her washing, Matthew coming over to help her fill buckets with water when she needed it.

"It does him good, these long winters," Alex said.

"Who?"

"Ian. No limping, no shuffling." She smiled, thinking that Ian at present moved with the fluidity and ease one could expect of a man just over thirty. Not that it would last, she sighed, because with the advent of spring and summer, his damaged back, in combination with all the work, would at times leave him white-faced with pain, reduced to hobbling round the yard.

"Ah." Matthew sounded tense – but then he always did when they discussed Ian's injured back, the consequence of a failed ambush by those accursed Burley brothers. Understandably, her man sounded tense whenever the Burleys were mentioned. He bore scars of his own on account of them, as did their youngest daughter, while one of their sons was dead – all because of Philip and Walter Burley.

Alex concentrated on her scrubbing. They're gone, she reminded herself, they're dead by now – or if not dead, almost dead.

Matthew poured a couple of buckets of ice-cold water over her scrubbed clothes, helped her wring them and hang them to dry.

"Look at my hands," she complained, holding them out to him: bright red, itching all over from the lye.

"Mmm," Matthew said, eyes glued to one of her breasts, quite visible now that the shawl had slipped. She let the shawl drop entirely, standing very still when his fingers grazed her flesh.

It shouldn't be this way, not when she was over fifty and had lived with him for almost thirty years, but it was, it still was. A current that surged between them, a heavy warmth spreading through her, breath that became shallow and rapid, knees that somehow lost in stability, and all because of him, the man who stood fully dressed before her and ate her with his eyes. She fluffed at her hair, met his hazel eyes, and smiled.

"Da?" Ian's voice had an edge to it. "Da, are you there?"

"Aye," Matthew said, the attention he had been focusing on her wavering.

"You'd best come out."

Matthew threw a rueful look in the direction of Alex. "Stay here," he suggested, buttoned up his coat, and stepped outside.

"Stay here," Alex muttered, shivering in the ice-cold wind that he had let in. From outside came male voices, and from the agitated tone, they weren't exactly here for a natter and a biscuit. She threw the half-filled tub a longing look and with a grimace slid into stays, skirt and the dirty bodice, wrapping the shawl tight before going to join her husband.

Their visitors were still in the yard. Alex smiled a greeting at Thomas Leslie, their closest neighbour, before nodding at the Chisholm brothers, also neighbours – a rather strange word to use for people that lived more than an hour's ride away.

"Scalped, I'm telling you! Not more than some hundred yards from my home!" Martin Chisholm was visibly upset, his normally placid exterior contorted into a hatchet face, small blue eyes staring like flints at his audience. "The poor bastards must have shrieked their heads off, and we didn't even hear them."

"Oh," Matthew said, sharing a worried look with Alex.

"Not Mohawk," Thomas Leslie hastened to assure them, and Alex's shoulders dropped an inch or two. Not her son, not his adopted Indian family. Grief rushed through her at the thought of her Samuel. He should be here, with her, not out in the forest with Qaachow and his tribe.

"Bloody nuisance is what they are," Martin went on, with Robert, his brother, nodding in agreement. "It would be best to enslave them all, put them to work on a plantation where they could be controlled."

"Maybe they don't want to." Alex picked some straw out of Adam's hair, cuddling her youngest son for an instant against her chest. All legs and arms, her not quite ten-year-old scrubbed his head affectionately against her shawl, listening avidly.

"Want to? What do we care what they want? Heathen is what they are, and to kill... Oh, my God! My poor nephew!"

"Your nephew! They scalped a child?" In her ear, Adam's tame raven, Hugin, cawed, seemingly as upset as she was.

"No, but he found them." Martin shifted from foot to foot, sniffing longingly in the direction of the Graham house, and with an internal sigh, Alex asked them all to come inside. On their way across the yard, Thomas leaned towards Matthew and whispered something, and her gut did a slow flip at the expression of shock that flew across Matthew's face.

"What?" She grabbed Thomas' arm.

"What? Oh, that. A matter between men. Nothing to concern you, my dear."

Alex pursed her mouth, unconvinced by Thomas' strained smile. "Never mind, I'll ask Matthew, and he'll tell me the truth if he knows what's best for him," she said, before wobbling off on her mud-caked clogs to ensure the guests were adequately fed.

"Yon men eat like horses," Mrs Parson said when Alex entered the kitchen. Alex gave the old woman an affectionate look. Mrs Parson was her best friend, an excellent midwife but first and foremost, the closest thing Alex had to a mother, a constant source of comfort and strength when Alex needed it.

"Lucky we have plenty of soup, then," Naomi said from where she was stirring the pot. Bean soup, from what Alex could make out. Not her favourite, but her daughter-in-law was partial to it, and it did have the benefit of being quite filling.

"I hate bean soup," Mark muttered from behind her.

Alex turned to flash her eldest son a grin. "Best tell your wife that, not me. She's the one who keeps on making it."

"I heard that," Naomi said, brandishing the wooden spoon in their direction. "And I'll have you know my father loves it."

"Great, Thomas can have my share as well," Alex said, laughing at Naomi's pretend scowl.

The Chisholms were solid men that took up a lot of room but after some minutes, the household and their guests were settled round the large table, albeit with less elbow room than usual. As always, Matthew sat at the head of the table while Alex had her chair at the other end, within easy reach of the hearth and the workbenches. Whitewashed walls, constant scrubbing of the floor and surfaces, ensured that the kitchen was clean and relatively light, the February sun streaming in through the two windows, both of them with horribly expensive glass panes.

"I had no idea that something so simple could be this good." Robert Chisholm stretched to spear yet another salt-baked beet on his knife, lathered the beet generously with butter, and bit into it.

"And it's good for you, full of vitamins and other stuff," Alex said, busy slicing bread.

"Vitamins?" Martin looked at her.

"That's what my father used to say," she temporised, which wasn't a lie, even if he'd said it in the late 1900s. "Maybe it's a Swedish expression."

Mrs Parson coughed loudly and placed the large pot of soup on the table before sitting down in the armchair reserved for her out of deference for her advanced age. She fiddled with her starched linen cap, and turned her black eyes on the little Spanish priest who had ridden in with the Chisholms. "Are you planning on staying to officiate at the funerals as well?" she asked, and Robert choked on his ale.

Carlos Muñoz blinked, an elegant hand coming up to smooth at his collar. "What funerals?"

"Well, you've wed most of the younger Chisholms almost two years back, you've baptised all the new weans, and so you can't have much cause to linger much longer, can you? Unless you're counting on them needing you for last rites and such nonsense before they pass on."

"Mrs Parson!" Alex said, glaring at Ian and Mark who seemed to be on the verge of exploding with laughter.

"It is no nonsense, and I'll not have you disparage the Holy Church," Carlos replied stiffly. "As to why I am still here, at present I find myself trapped due to inclement weather." He slid a look up the table to where Sarah usually sat, but now, in her last month of a most unwelcome pregnancy, their youngest daughter shunned the table when there were visitors. Alex stifled a sigh. The young priest had developed quite the crush on Sarah.

"You shouldn't tease him like that," Alex remonstrated with Mrs Parson once the men had gone outside, leaving them alone in the kitchen. "We both know why he's still here." She inclined her head in the general direction of Sarah's room. "If it hadn't been for him…" Alex left the rest unsaid. They both knew it was Carlos who had helped Sarah cope with her situation, chosen by Sarah as her sole confidant. Most unorthodox, given that Carlos was a Catholic priest.

Mrs Parson looked somewhat shamefaced. "He's a good lad, for all that he's a papist. But it's time he leaves, aye? For his sake, Alex. Yon lassie of yours won't want much to do with him once this is over."

"You think?" Alex was surprised by this assessment. In her opinion, Sarah was too fond of the priest, and at one point, Alex could have sworn Sarah was in love with him as well. She threw a distracted look out of the window, eyes lingering on Carlos, who was already mounted on his mule.

"She'll want to forget, all of this last year she'll want to bury, and wee Carlos is very much a part of it, no?"

"She can't forget," Alex reminded her. "There will be a child." She watched the Chisholms and Carlos out of sight up the lane before turning to face Mrs Parson.

"She doesn't want it. She has said so for the last few months."

"She might change her mind once she sees it." Alex was in two minds about this: one part of her hoped Sarah would change her mind, the other couldn't quite see how a child with Burley blood would fit into the Graham household.

"I think not," Mrs Parson said. "You must start thinking about finding it a home elsewhere."

Alex was so busy mulling over her discussion with Mrs Parson, it took her some time to notice her entrance into the little parlour had effectively muted whatever conversation

Thomas and Matthew had been having.

She set the tray down, handed them a mug of tea, took her own, and went to sit by the fire. First, she studied Thomas. Under her inspection, he fidgeted but by busying himself with his pipe, managed to avoid her eyes. Then, she turned her attention to Matthew, and he calmly looked back, but she knew him too well, saw how his little finger twitched, how still he held his head, and the hair along her back began to rise.

"Something's wrong." It wasn't a question. It was a statement, directed at them both.

"We don't know," Matthew said.

Thomas gave him a sidelong glance, and sucked on the carved stem of his pipe, holding his tongue.

"What is it you don't know?" Alex asked, but there was a hollow feeling in her chest at the look that now flared in her husband's eyes.

The men exchanged a look. Matthew sighed, beckoning that she should come over. She knew it was bad when he sat her on his lap, despite being in company, one strong arm encircling her waist.

"Philip Burley," he said.

"Oh, Jesus." The mug she was holding in her hands slid through numbed and ice-cold fingers to hit the floor.

For a historical note and more information about
Matthew and Alex, please visit Anna Belfrage's
website at www.annabelfrage.com